Von De Vorg:
The Mandate Of The Crown

Susan Drews

Von De Vorg:

The Mandate Of The Crown

Susan Drews

"When we do the best that we can, we never know what miracle is wrought in our life, or in the life of another."

Helen Keller

Gone

KATE WAS HALF WAY through a session at the group meeting she ran for young mothers when an uneasy feeling suddenly overwhelmed her. An unbearably sharp pain in her stomach overcame her, causing her to stop talking mid sentence. The day had started so well. Kate had talked to Sam on the phone; he was waiting at the airport to fly back home after being away for two days at one of the presentations he hated. It had all gone well and Sam had even been awarded a few new contracts. Happy to know that Sam would be home soon, Kate had focused on her meeting. She enjoyed them very much because they were usually filled with many joyful stories of the women's infants, and often they finished with laughter. That was most likely the reason for the good turnout – their group seemed to grow each time they met. And it was very convenient for Kate, as the meetings were held at lunchtime in her office building.

But today the fun was suddenly halted by a feeling of dread in Kate's stomach, a feeling more like fists than butterflies, a feeling of fear, terror, dread and anxiety, all mixed with alarm. Something bad had happened, or was in the process of happening, and if she had not been sitting already her legs would have given out on her.

"Ladies, all of a sudden I am not feeling so good, please excuse me ..." She must have looked green in the face, because the group stopped and looked at her with concern, but before anyone could say anything Kate dashed out of the room and ran to the bathroom to have a closer look at the toilet. Soon after she made it back to her office, where she stood bent over, holding onto her desk and trying to calm her breathing and talk herself down. She tried all the relaxation techniques she could think of, but nothing really helped.

Filled with the conviction that something was terribly wrong, she went through the list of people she needed to check on. Sam was on his way home. He had spoken with her before he boarded the airplane and everything was all right there, so she went to her computer and emailed her son Michael, who was finally on board one of those research ships he had always dreamed of, and at the same time she phoned Sam's son, Daniel.

Daniel answered right away. "Mom, are you all right?" were his first words to his stepmother. No hello or good to hear from you, but she could tell he was worried as well.

"Honey, you are all right, aren't you? Of course you are, you answered the phone, but Daniel, you can feel it too, can't you? Something is wrong ..." were the first words out of Kate's mouth, and she kept rattling on, afraid that if she stopped she would find out what it was.

"I am fine, how is Dad?"

"I spoke to him just before he boarded the plane, he was happy to be on his way home, and while I'm talking to you I'm checking the airport, and so far there seems to be nothing wrong with any of their flights, so all is well there too. Have you heard from Michael?"

"Nope, but give me a few minutes and I'll pull a few strings here and get back to you about Michael, Mom. And Mom, before you hang up, don't worry, all will be well."

She knew that he added the last for her benefit, but it was not working. "Yeah, right ... love you." And with that she hung up and went to send another email to Michael. What was so dreadfully wrong that she could barely breathe? The uneasiness in her stomach kept on growing, but since she had already emptied her stomach she did not have to flee to the bathroom again. Her stomach was twisting into a tight knot and then all of a sudden she felt a stabbing pain and with that the twisting stopped and she grew gravely silent. Sam! Her heart screamed out loud for him but there was no answer. But how could it be? She called the airport to check on his flight and they confirmed all was well, the flight would arrive on time, if not earlier, and they said that there was nothing unusual to report, so there must be another explanation.

She was still deep in thought when Daniel called and told her that his buddy had spoken to Michael on a satellite phone and that Michael was having a great time and was well, but before Daniel was finished telling her about their conversation she started to cry, and so Daniel stopped and inquired why.

"Daniel, it's Sam ... I know it, it's Sam ..." she said, and then could not say more.

"But Mom, I also checked his flight and everything is fine." Daniel tried to reason with her, even though he could sense that everything was not fine at all. "I have it in front of me. His flight is landing in just over an hour."

Kate's eyes just kept welling up as she tried to listen to Daniel's reasonable assurances. Everything must be fine, she must be wrong, she just had to be, there was no other option. Period.

She said a brief goodbye and slipped on her coat, closing her office and telling the front desk she would be out for the rest of the afternoon. As she passed by she told them that she was planning to go to the airport, and then to go home and get into bed to get over whatever had made her so ill.

The drive to the airport was a short one, but it felt endless. Kate looked at the arrivals board and sure enough, Sam's flight was expected to arrive not only on time but early. Good, then the agony would end sooner. She went to the airport's tiny Tim Horton's to get herself a coffee and sat close to the gate through which arriving passengers entered. She felt as if she aged years while the minutes crawled by, until finally the board showed that Sam's flight had landed. Several passengers came flooding into the hall to get their luggage from the carousel, but she could not see Sam anywhere. After the stream of passengers started to slow Kate could not stand it anymore, so she addressed a woman who seemed to have come in with the rest of the passengers on Sam's flight, and asked her if she had been on board.

"Yes, I was. We had a rather comfortable flight. Who are you looking for?"

"Did you see someone very tall sitting in the airplane?"

"They are all tall here, dear," said the woman and went on her way.

Kate grew increasingly impatient, so she went to the airline's service counter and inquired whether Sam had been on the flight, and after a few moments of verifying who she was, they told her that Sam was not on the passenger list.

"Is there any other flight with a similar number?" Kate whispered. The stewardess just shook her head, and that was when Kate slipped to the floor and passed out.

"Ma'am, are you all right?" she heard shortly afterwards. She opened her eyes to see a worried stewardess patting her cheeks.

"Give me a moment would you?" Kate groaned. And with the help of a concerned male passenger they sat her on one of the waiting room chairs.

"Do you need a doctor?" she asked.

"Yes, I will call my son, he's a doctor," was all Kate could say and then started to fumble for her phone. The stewardess passed it to her.

"It fell out of your pocket when you fell to the floor," she said as she passed the phone to her. After sitting with her for a moment the stewardess and the passenger decided that Kate was all right to sit by herself, so the gentleman left the airport and the stewardess returned to her duties, all the while keeping a trained eye on Kate from the counter.

After a few deep breaths Kate pressed redial and Daniel answered promptly.

"Told you Mom, he is all right," said Daniel relieved.

"He was not on board, please ... come home ... if you can ... Daniel, I need you ... here ... right now," said Kate, fighting through her tears to get out all the words she needed to say.

"I'm on the next flight," said Daniel, and hung up.

Kate had no idea how long she sat in the chair. The stewardess eventually came back to her with a cup of coffee and a cookie, but Kate declined both.

She closed her eyes and remembered something that they did when they were just married on the cruise ship, a long time ago. She rubbed her hands together and then put them against each other so that the light went from one hand to the other, creating a full circuit. That usually gave them heightened ability to reach each other, regardless of where they were. At the time it had been fun, almost like having a walkie-talkie, but now she hoped it would not fail her. 'Sam, answer me, where are you? Are you well? I am afraid. Please don't leave me. I don't know how to continue without you. Please give me a sign, I beg of you.'

But there was nothing. Maybe she was too far away? Maybe he could not hear her. 'Oh Lord, let that be it. Please Lord, don't take him away from me, whatever I did, whatever I can do, please, please, keep him safe for me, that's all I want and ever want. Please Lord let this cup pass me by, I will do whatever you want of me, but please don't take him away from me.' Her thoughts rambled on, pleading and negotiating in the way all people do when in crisis.

She dropped her hands and started to sob. The stewardess was worried about her, so she kept watching her, wondering what she should do. Eventually, the airport cleared of most passengers freeing her from most duties, so she came back to check on her.

"Can I call you a cab? Can I do anything for you?" she wondered.

"No, please let me sit here a bit longer and don't worry about me," Kate replied, but even to her own ears she sounded hollow and unconvincing. After a few more minutes the stewardess left her reluctantly, and with some words of caution to the other stewardesses behind the counter she left.

Kate sat there for hours and did not want to leave the airport, for she hoped that she had been mistaken about the flight number and that Sam would arrive on the next plane, but every plane that landed had no Von de Vorg on the passenger list. Eventually she must have fallen asleep, because the next thing she knew she was feeling a strong squeeze around her shoulders. When she opened her eyes she looked into Daniel's worried eyes. He had grown to almost the height of his father, with the same blue eyes, but his facial features were softer than those of his father.

"Daniel!" was all she could say, and then she fell into his arms, sobbing.

"Mom, aren't you worrying a bit too soon, I mean he could be delayed or whatever ..." Rationalizing it all away was difficult even for him, for he knew his father. If he were running late he would have called from the plane or from the airport. This was all so very unlike him. On the other hand, there was nothing that could confirm their worries about his whereabouts. So he preferred to wait and live a bit longer in ignorance, before he would allow himself to go to where Kate was and face the unthinkable.

"Let's go and get some stuff from home and then do our own research, OK Mom?"

Thinking proactively was exactly what she needed right now; the idea sounded very appealing, so she agreed to walk to the truck with Daniel. There he took the keys from her and drove them both home.

Kate went into the master bedroom right away, pulled out her hand luggage and was ready before Daniel could finish heating some food he found in the fridge. Before he could sit down to eat some of it she was already packed and ready at the door.

"Did you check all the flights?" Daniel inquired as he quickly stuffed a large mound of spaghetti into his mouth.

"No, only the one Sam said he would be on," she said as she came back into the kitchen, placed her bag on the island counter and sat on one of the bar stools.

"Why don't you turn on the laptop so we can check what flights have left Toronto today?" Daniel suggested, putting another loaded fork into his mouth.

So Kate went to her desk and turned on her laptop and brought it back to the kitchen. They both bent over the screen to find the departing flights from Pearson Airport. But all the searching was too slow for Kate, so she found the phone number of Pearson airport and called them, to find out if anybody with her husband's name had flown out.

After she had been passed around like a hot potato from person to person, she finally found the right person, who confirmed that Sam was on one of the smaller planes that had left several hours earlier, but it had dropped off the radar and they were investigating. They could give no more information about it, so the man took her cell number and promised to contact her when they knew more. Kate got up while he was speaking. Both she and Daniel listened to him on the speakerphone and as he was saying the last few words she backed up into the corner of the kitchen. After the man had hung up Daniel looked in her direction, worried. She was pressing into the corner of the kitchen, her whole body trembling.

"Daniel, I am alone in here," she said, crying as she patted her chest. "He is not there. He is not answering ... I am alone ... in here ..." She could feel herself crossing over the fine line between worrying and becoming hysterical. She slid down the wall to the ground, collapsing in a pile of misery and continued to cry.

Daniel knew how close his parents were. In some ways it was almost unhealthy. They truly completed each other, but they were so dependent on each other that they would battle to survive without each other. Daniel had always thought that it was beautiful to have such a harmonious relationship, but now in this time of crisis he thought that such closeness could also be detrimental. Their bond was so strong that if Kate said something was not right, then something was not right. On the other hand he had to be optimistic for both of them right now, so he pushed away his own feelings and slipped into the role of the physician. He had practiced for two years, and was able to distance himself emotionally from the situation.

"Mom, let's go. I'm not waiting to hear the news second hand. I want to see what is going on myself. Let's go and find Dad, what do you think? A bit of activity will do both of us good right now, what do you say?" He tried to focus her on something positive; anything would do.

But Kate did not move. Nothing Daniel said would persuade her, so Daniel was torn between wanting to find his father and not wanting to leave his mother in the condition she was in. Eventually the whole thing got to him as well, and in tears he picked her up like his father would have done, carried her to the sofa, and rocked her like she used to do when he did not feel well.

"Mom what do you want me to do?" he wanted to know through his tears.

They sat there for a few more minutes and then he heard his mother say: "We wait."

Exhausted, she leaned against her son and after some time she fell asleep and he carried her to her bed and gently tucked her in.

In her dreams she was searching for Sam. She was looking all over the airport and in all the airplanes and could not find him. She called for him over and over again but there was no answer. She saw in her dreams the fear that was within her. The smashed up airplane and Sam's lifeless body in a pile of twisted metal. She gave a piercing scream, which woke her up, and she sat upright in her bed. Why was she not waking fully from this nightmare? Waking beside her husband, cradled and comforted, why was she so alone within and physically now as well?

The dark was all around her, and she could hear Sam's faint voice in her mind. 'Kate ...'

'Where are you Sam? Come home to me, or take me with you wherever you are going.' But the only thing she could hear in her mind was 'Kate ...' as if he had not heard her. Her heart hammered in her chest, and she threw the cover aside and called out for Daniel.

He must have fallen asleep in his clothes, for he came rushing to his mother's side wearing the same clothes he had on when he arrived.

"Are you all right?"

"Daniel, I heard him!" she said with big eyes, but as she spoke it out loud she could hear how ridiculous it sounded.

"Mom, that kind of thing can happen, you know that yourself, being in psychiatry and all, the mind plays tricks ..."

He was right, the mind could play tricks when wishful thinking controlled it.

"I thought I heard him, Daniel, it sounded so ... him ..." she said quietly, her tears falling again.

"Do you think you could get some rest now? We'll do what we can in the morning, OK mom?" There he was again, the doctor. Kate patted the spot beside her on the bed.

"Do you mind sleeping beside your old mother? I don't want to be alone right now," Kate looked pleadingly at him, so Daniel slipped off his shoes and laid down on the bed, holding his mother and whispering comforting words until she relaxed and fell asleep again. But he could not fall asleep again. He was filled with worries about the future. His thoughts were racing. What would happen to her if Dad truly did not come back to them? They were so closely connected, one would not be able to live without the other. How would she cope? He would have to move up here, that was for sure. He had planned to help out Jackson anyhow, but not this soon. In Vancouver there were plenty of opportunities to learn interesting procedures, but now he was needed here. He had promised Jackson he would come up here at some point, but he had hoped to get more surgical hours and experience under his belt first ... but now his hand was forced. There was no way that she could manage without him, she would go crazy or she would run. Neither sounded appealing to him. He should call Michael pronto. He would have to get hold of him first thing tomorrow. He needed Michael as badly as Kate needed him right now, without a doubt they needed to get together as a family and support each other. He also needed to call Grandpa and Grandmother, hopefully they would come too, if they were not on their sailboat again. His list grew longer and longer until he woke to sunshine. His arms were hurting, for he had not moved since he took his mother in his arms and his back was killing him. He carefully laid her on her side and slid out of the bed to go downstairs.

He needed to talk to Mary, she was so wise, and she was the one Dad used to go to when all else failed. He would start with her, in fact he would go there in person. Besides, if he made any calls from the kitchen he might wake Kate, and he did not want that just yet. She needed sleep badly, and he would try to make sure she got it. Besides, Mary's was not far and a good jog would do his back and mind some good right now.

He slipped on a woolen sweater and grabbed his runners, opened the front door to the fresh, cold air he had missed in Vancouver, and closed the door behind him very carefully and quietly. Outside he broke into a fast sprint and was at Mary's in no time. It seemed she had been expecting him, for he had barely touched the door when it opened.

"Daniel my boy, how you have grown, good to have you home son, good to have you home," she said with sorrow but a smile.

"You know?" Daniel could never get over the foresight Mary had. "All right then, what do you know, Mary?"

"I can't make it out, something awful has happened but I cannot see it clearly, it is very disconcerting," Mary said.

"Well now, welcome to the way we see things," Daniel said with a grin to keep things on a lighter note, but it was hard for both of them to remain cheerful.

"How is Kate?"

"All I can say at this point is that she's not well," said Daniel, falling into one of the red easy chairs in Mary's sitting room. "She cried all night and had nightmares; quite frankly I don't know how to get her through this. You know Mary, if anyone could hear us they would think we're crazy. We're already mourning Dad, without any confirmation of anything," Daniel said, leaning his head against the soft headrest, his eyes closed.

"We are not like other people, you know that, things work differently here, even though I wish they didn't. Not knowing would be easier than being 90% sure that something is very wrong."

"Yeah, but there is the remaining 10% of hope, Mary and I for one, will not let go of even 1%. I have a feeling Kate would say the same ..."

"My heart is heavy Daniel. I am an old woman and I am not sure if I can handle this kind of hardship anymore."

Daniel watched Mary wheeling herself to the tea kettle, thinking that she did look much older today than she ever had.

"Mary, how are you holding up?" Daniel enquired, tired but beginning to worry about her as well. This had been hard for them all, but it must be especially difficult for Mary with her weak heart. If something were to happen to her now, when they needed her most, that would be the proverbial last straw that broke the camel's back.

"Don't even think about it Mary," he said in a warning tone.

"What Daniel?"

"You know I love you, I care for you, but you need to be as strong as I need to be right now, OK?" Daniel said firmly, but with a pleading smile.

Mary had to grin. "Don't make this old lady blush!"

Daniel was so much like his father it was uncanny. Those were the exact words Sam used, when he had protected Kate from them when they had come over to visit. She had just had that run in with her ex-husband, and she hid her pretty bruised face behind him so as not to shock them all. He even used the same tone: a trace of humor laced with seriousness.

'Sam my boy, you would be so proud of your son. Come back to us,' she thought – no, screamed – into the silence of her thoughts, but she heard nothing but silence.

"Where is Kate right now?"

"Finally sleeping, why?"

"Don't leave her alone for the next little while. God only knows what she is up to now, knowing her," Mary said, passing a cup of tea to Daniel. He took the cup, but then immediately put it back down beside her and got up to go out into the cold, wanting to race back home. At the door he turned and looked back at her.

"Next time ... Next time I come here I will need some advice, Mary, have some ready for me, will you?" and the door shut behind him.

Well then again, Mary thought, that was all Daniel, impatient and demanding, not at all like his father. But this time she had no advice to give. Her heart was hurting and her mind was screaming and there was no relief in sight. Kate had the only connection with Sam that was strong enough to show where he was, so if what Daniel said was true, then Sam was lost to them. Her heart hurt and she fetched a nitroglycerine tablet and placed it under her tongue to relieve the pain in her heart.

When Daniel got home the house was just as he had left it. Kate was sleeping. He checked on her first, then went downstairs to the kitchen, closed the door and did what he had been itching to do the whole night: he called his Dad's phone. It rang and rang and finally went to voice mail. Hearing his Dad's message almost killed him right on the spot, so he had to hang up, besides he thought that it might be possible to find him via his phone, so it would be better not to waste the battery. So he dialed Michael on the satellite phone, which he had promised to use only in emergencies. He immediately got the captain on the line. Daniel decided to identify himself formally as Doctor Von de Vorg, so as not to get Michael into trouble, and then shortly after spoke with Michael himself.

After hearing the bad news, Michael said he would be on his way as soon as they hit shore, and also promised to do anything he could do to pull some strings to trace Sam's phone, should the telephone company not be willing to do so. The next call Daniel made was to his grandparents. Grandfather had connections who could help with the search. After Daniel told his grandparents what had happened, they assured him that they would help with whatever was needed. Grandfather promised him he would get back to him as soon as he had anything. This time the men of the family were on the case, and the ladies were in the back seat. Daniel and his Grandfather both liked that a lot, although Daniel wished it had happened under more pleasant circumstances.

Before Daniel called his grandparents he got a phone call from the airport telling him what they already knew. The plane had disappeared over the mountains and they were searching for it, and would inform them as soon as they knew more. It was a small charter airplane; as Daniel had suspected, his Dad had wanted to beat the normal flight to be home sooner and surprise his mom. They only knew that they had to look for it because of the enquiries from Kate and Daniel.

Daniel was astounded that Kate was not woken by all the calls, but eventually he realized that it was not a matter of sound but of will. Late in the afternoon she still had not gotten up. Work had called and he had told them that they needed to cancel her shift and that she needed sick leave due to circumstances. He had checked on her, wanting to know if he should tell them anything before he hung up with her clinic, but Kate did not answer, nor did she want to leave her bed. She had fallen straight from grief into a depression and was wanting to shut down.

Pia came over with Jackson to check on them as well, after hearing the bad news, but Kate responded in the same way, and refused to see them, even though they had been very close friends for so long. Daniel could not get her to eat and the little water she drank was only because she felt discomfort in her throat. Eventually, after the third day, Daniel, Jackson and Pia decided that if she was not drinking enough or eating by the next day they would insist she get an IV, so that she could get through this without losing the function of her organs.

Daniel had to make a tough call as he sat in the kitchen that night. If Kate continued to refuse to drink, then he would put in an IV, whether she wanted it or not. He did not give a hoot about the ethical aspect, after all she was his mother, and he did not want to lose her as well. There had been no word from the team carrying out the rescue effort, apart from the reports they followed on the news regarding a missing plane. Sam's phone had died before they could trace it, and there was nothing else to go on. And judging by Kate's behavior there was little hope. She of all people would know, and that was the problem. Daniel was tired. He was waiting for reinforcements from his grandparents and his brother Michael, but they would not be here for another two days, and until then he had to hold on. His head sank onto his arms and he fell asleep leaning on the kitchen counter.

Suddenly he was woken by a noise in the living room and he listened to see if he had imagined it. Quietly he got up and walked on tiptoes towards the living room. Kate was standing on a chair in front of the fireplace, with both her hands on the family crest, deep in thought. Daniel closed his eyes to get in touch with a strange sensation. He could feel his mother's hands on his heart. Yes undoubtedly, there was no way he could ever explain this scientifically, but they were both closely connected to the family crest, which seemed to be the center of the family. The crest had powers, which it released in them and through them. Daniel could even feel the warmth of Kate's hands flowing through him and sense the waves that came from her. He could not hear what she was saying but when he opened his eyes he could see her glow intensifying. There was a connection between her and the crest, either it was feeding off of her or she was feeding from it. There was also one other possibility, which sounded just as crazy – that she was using the crest to magnify her senses.

Jackson was right. If he were ever to tell anyone about what he experienced up here, he would lose his license to practice and end up on one of those psych wards that Kate worked on. Nobody would ever believe what he saw or experienced, especially not right now.

Daniel watched Kate for several minutes which turned out, when he looked at his watch, to be almost half an hour, but when she appeared to be getting weaker, he began to worry she would fall, so he walked over to her, grasped her waist and helped her down.

"Daniel, did I wake you?" she said weakly with glazed eyes.

"Mom tell me, what were you doing?" he said very softly so as not to startle her.

"If he did not hear that, he will not hear anything at all anymore," she said weakly.

"I could feel you, Mom, you did good, but tomorrow I'm putting in an IV, I don't care what you say, unless you start eating and drinking. Either an IV or a nasogastric tube, you can choose, I don't care one way or another. So what do you want?" He spoke with the firm voice he knew his father used when there was to be no discussion about a subject. He looked down at her while he carried her back upstairs. She was so frightfully light, which made him wonder whether he should wait until tomorrow and not do it tonight.

"I have no say about that? Is that ethical, Dr. Von de Vorg?" Kate fought for a smile for him.

"Don't care, don't give a crap, I will not lose you too," he said, pouting like he had done when he was twelve years old.

"Daniel, what about the oath you took?" she said playfully.

"I won't be doing any harm, just protecting the insane," he said smiling back.

"Great, my son thinks I'm insane. Is there anything else you would like to add to that, while you are at it?"

"Yeah, start eating and drinking already, damn it." This earned him a weak punch, but he did not mind. He had distracted her thoughts, if only for a moment, and for a moment she had been the woman she always used to be, the woman who could put everybody at ease and get a smile out of anyone.

"Mom, Michael is coming in the next few days, maybe you will eat for him? And so are Grandpa and Grandma, we need them here, you are OK with that, right?" They were almost at the master bedroom door when he felt her stiffening in his arms. He looked down at her to see what was wrong and got an angry look that could have killed him right on the spot.

"What?" he looked concerned.

"What did you mean by 'eat for him'?! You think it has anything to do with you?? How dare you, you should know me better than that! How could you say something like that to me?"

"Sorry Mom, it will never happen again. Forgiven?" he looked pleadingly at her, but kept walking towards the bed before she could angrily jump out of his arms.

Kate looked at first angry, then disappointed, then she started to cry again, hugging him closely.

"Gee Mom, I am so sorry. Please, I did not mean to upset you so. Let's just forget it. I wanted to pressure you into eating more, and it came out wrong. Mom sorry, stop crying please ..."

"You just ... looked like your father there ... for a moment ..." she said between sobs.

"Mom, if it helps, if what you did downstairs worked, he would have heard you around the world and back again, maybe beyond even that. But we all need each other right now. We need to grieve together and help each other through it, we need to, I need you to. Could you do that for all of us, for me?"

He sat down with her. How odd. He could remember a time when he had been trying to impress his Dad and he had hit his thumb with a hammer instead, and then he had sat on his Mom's lap being rocked to soothe his pain, and now he was holding her to soothe her pain. How things go in circles, like everything in life. They sat like that for some time. The moon shone into the window and he looked up at it. 'The same goes for you Dad. If you are still out there, you owe it to us to keep fighting, to get back to us. Grandpa said we are not quitters, so get a hold of yourself and fight!'

He grew tired, not only physically but also emotionally. Just then, a burned out and tired calm came over him. It was only them: him, Kate and the moon, yet in the silence they grew stronger.

"OK," he heard his Mom say.

"Sorry?"

"OK. We will keep on fighting, we are not quitters."

"Was I speaking out loud?"

"No, I don't think so, but it seems when you aim something at your dad, some of it comes to me as well. And please don't ask me how this is possible. I gave up trying to explain anything that goes on around here long ago!" She looked at him warningly, poking his chest with her index finger.

"Well, that's kind of handy, don't you think? Saves a lot of talking and explaining, doesn't it?" he said, grinning.

"In a simplified version, yeah it does, but for now ... Let's get some rest. Tomorrow Dr. Von de Vorg, oats for breakfast and coffee, if you don't mind playing cook for the day?" she said yawning, and shortly after he had tucked her into bed she rolled onto her side like she always did beside Sam, as if he was there, and fell deeply asleep.

Within the next few days the house became busy. Many people came to voice their worries and sorrows for Sam. Nobody said what they wanted to say, what they all felt, and they were all extremely careful not to mention his name around Kate. Mary came over a few times, Kate's parents were also there, and when the call finally came, to let them know that they had given up any hope for survivors and had called off the search, the grief was felt collectively.

A black veil was swathed over the crown of the crest to show the loss to the house of Von de Vorg, and many came to pay their respects. Kate hid in the bedroom most of the time, but tried to be strong for her family and friends. She was asked to continue for Sam, for after all she would have to wear the crown until Daniel was ready to take on the calling. At this point he did not show any interest in it, and it would not be forced on him either. The crest seemed to make no push either, so they left that matter for now. The thing that puzzled Kate though, and she spoke with Mary about it when they had a brief private moment, was that her crest was still the same. She had assumed that it would fade away when the bond was broken. It had faded a little, but not much. The only explanations Mary could come up with were that it remained because she chose to hold on to it, and because Kate had high standing.

She must have inherited the crown from her own line as well as from his line.

It was beyond Kate's capacity to think that far. She felt like running until she came to the end of the earth, just to be able to jump into the void, to find relief from all the pain she felt. Even though her crest did not fade, her body did. All the stress and grieving, the lack of good rest and lack of appetite made her lose weight rapidly. The grief of the loss of Sam was unspeakable for the community, but now they feared that they would also lose the Lady of the house of Von de Vorg, and they decided that this must not happen. They owed it to Sam to keep her safe, even though it seemed that they would not be able to do this. The house filled with so many gifts of baked goods and dishes, that Kate's mother Mel could not find enough space for it all in the fridge and freezer.

THREE WEEKS LATER AT NIGHT, around the time when Michael thought it was time to return to work, he saw Kate's silhouette in the moonlight through her nightgown. She must have lost at least 30 pounds and looked awfully skinny. Even though she tried to appear strong during the day she could not fool him that easily. He had observed her almost every night when everybody was sleeping, walking slowly down the stairs with great difficulty, climbing onto the chair and placing her hands on the crest.

"Don't let me down", was something Michael heard his Mom say almost every night and at first he thought she was talking to Sam, hoping to call him back, but soon he came to realize that she was speaking to the crest, demanding that it show its power. There was something very weird going on, but it was also something cool, he thought.

In the weeks he had taken off, he had learned to know a few more people from the community. He learned about some of the strange customs and ways of the people who lived up here. There was something mystical going on and it started to affect him in a good way as well. He felt he finally belonged somewhere and was wanted and accepted for who he was, without needing to prove anything. It was also kind of neat that he felt special thanks to his connection to Sam and his Mom, and there was so much more that he wanted to learn.

Michael was glad he had taken some long overdue shore leave to spend more time with Sam's people, who were now also his people. Yet now he wished he had done it sooner, so he could have enjoyed Sam more, but those revelations always came too late. When Daniel told him that his mother was not eating anymore he suddenly realized that the chance of losing her as well was not as remote as he had always thought. Losing Sam, who had been in the prime of his life, was the first loud wake-up call that hit him in the depths of his being, for he cared for this man more than he would ever admit, but when he heard about his mother, the fear of also losing her drove him home at twice the speed. It was home to her and somehow also to him. There was something special about this place, he could tell, and somehow he began to connect with it. He would always love his job, but home to him would be right here in this place.

Also he and Daniel had never been closer than the last few weeks. They had been for long walks behind the house. Daniel told him that this was the route Sam and Kate used to take, when they needed to talk things through, so both of them could connect to Sam and Kate by walking the same path. Both brothers shared their feelings of loss and hurt, and shed tears of regret and sorrow, forging a bond that would never be broken.

One night when Daniel could not stand being at home surrounded by mourning people, Michael took him for a walk. It felt like they walked for hours until they came to a memorial Michael had never seen before. Daniel had been there only once or twice in his life, but he remembered enough of what his father had told him about it. Finding relief by connecting to his father via their past, Daniel told Michael about the family background, their heritage, what the crest stood for and what the crown meant. Michael was floored at first, then he thought Daniel was kidding, and when he realized that it was all real he stood there with his mouth open, taking it all in.

After Daniel was finished sharing with Michael they both looked up at the symbol of the past. The stone monument was a cross with a circle through it, and with strange writing on it that apparently some of the town folks could still read. It was knowledge passed down from generation to generation, going all the way back to the Vikings.

"I feel so alone these days, Michael, with whom could I share all of this? Mom is buried in grief and it is still questionable if she will pull through this, and if I tell any of my peers about this, they will have me committed."

They looked at the horizon, where the sun was starting to rise slowly over the edge to announce a new day, a new beginning and the start of something new.

"Daniel, as long as you need me, I am your wing man, you know that, right?"

"Thanks – believe it or not, knowing is one thing, but hearing it is another."

"You know, standing here on this place of the past, looking at the sun of the future, let's write this moment into our own history, so we will not forget, what do you say?"

"What do you have in mind, for it sounds great to me too? Michael the tough guy turns into a poet ... wow ... never thought I would see the day!" he said, smiling at Michael who was still looking mesmerized at the beauty of the rising sun.

"It might not sound so great for long, for what I have to suggest sounds more like something we would do among the navy guys, not with the PhD's."

"You sure get a kick out of building suspense, don't you? Or have you found a flair for dramatics?" Daniel grinned at Michael.

"All right, if you laugh I'll kick your ass to kingdom come, and we'll never speak of it again."

"Gee, and followed with brutal threats and force, this must be either serious or nuts."

Michael pulled out the army knife that he always had on him, ever since he could remember. He cut his hand along the inside of his palm.

"You've got to be kidding. You guys still do that?"

Michael just looked at him and with a sigh Daniel did the same. But then he stopped. He looked at Michael for a moment.

"Are you sure you want to do this? My line comes with a few hiccups, as you must know by now," but Michael just stretched out his hand to him and with a smile Daniel shook hands and the blood crossed lines.

"Damn, nobody tells you how much this hurts," Daniel complained and Michael just laughed out loud. "This coming from a doctor who can slice people from navel to chin ... rich ... now don't tell me you get dizzy at the sight of blood too, for then I will need to find someone else to look after me should I need medical help in the future!" Michael gave Daniel an amused look, shaking his head and rolling his eyes, but then Michael got very serious.

"You know you can always count on me, right? Just in case you forget, this is now sealed, I hope. I trust you understand why I did this. But don't think now you need to give me a lecture explaining what happens in your blood stream when it hits mine, and what happens when two different blood types cross, for I do not want to know. Just simply know that from now on, we are not only family but also blood-bonded. It sounds juvenile, I know, but it is a custom of the old times, the past with the promise of the future." He pointed to the monument and then to the sun.

"Yup a poet on top of it ... who knew?" said Daniel grinning but followed the direction in which Michael looked, straight into the sun, willing to face what was coming, embracing the past – together.

On the way home Michael wondered though. "Why did you ask me if I was sure about bonding with you via a bloody handshake? Sincere worries or just simply a lack of faith or trust in me?"

"Neither, you know enough to know that you need to carry my burden with you."

"With a huge difference though. Your grandfather was alone in it. Sam was alone in it, but you and I, we are in it together. So I say, bring it on, whatever the sun will shine on, bring it on, for it is a new day, and a pact has been forged. From now on this pact is forged not only though marriage, via my mother, but also in blood, through us. Now how cool is that!!!?" Michael slapped Daniel on his shoulders and they both walked confidently home.

At home both were tired and Michael started feeling a little unwell, probably due to being overtired, so they went to bed quickly, before anyone could hear that they had come home.

Hours later Michael woke, still feeling a bit hotter than usual.

"Daniel", he hollered up the stairs so Daniel could hear him, "Get your sorry ass down here and bring your PhD with you, you got me sick. Thanks a lot!"

Daniel came out of his room, still in his clothes from the day before. These days he seemed to make a habit of sleeping in his day clothes. He was not motivated much these days to take the time to undress, either being too tired or having to get up in the middle of the night all the time.

"What are you complaining about?"

Kate and her parents, as well as several guests who had come to bring more food, became quiet, for it was interesting to see the half-brothers interact. To Kate it appeared that the two of them had bonded much more closely. She could not quite figure out how it happened and was definitely not clear what the quarrel was all about. She got up from the kitchen table where she was drinking coffee with her mother and went to see why Michael was complaining. She was about to wish them both good morning when she froze in the middle of the hallway. Michael's back was to her.

"Daniel, Michael, both of you in my bedroom at once," she demanded, and passed Michael who swung around and watched her with a stunned face as she walked up the stairs, where she also passed Daniel who looked just as puzzled.

Both men looked at one another with bewilderment, wondering how they could possibly be in trouble with their mother so early in the day. As they both arrived in the master bedroom and Michael closed the door behind him, Kate looked from one son to the other.

"I love you both and even though you are two heads taller, several pounds stronger and heavier than me, believe me I will put you over my knee, if I do not hear at once what you guys were up to last night, if it was last night when it happened."

"Mom, we have no idea what you are talking about," was all that Michael could say and then he looked at Daniel and whispered to him, "Is she all right?"

"Don't you talk over my head Mister, for I am right here and can hear you perfectly well. I also can SEE everything I need to see!"

"Mom, you have lost us both, could you back up, so that we can say sorry for whatever it is you think we did?" Daniel suggested, feeling like a little boy again.

"All right. You are both grown men, you can do as you please, you are old enough. You are also and will always be my boys, and I am extremely proud of you, but explain to me how the lines got blurred?" The two men still had no idea what Kate was talking about, so she got up and turned Michael around so that Daniel could see what she meant.

"Holy crap!" was all that Daniel could splutter. "Say man, do you feel all right?"

"Apart from the fact that you gave me the flu or something like it, and a bit of a temperature, yeah perfectly fine, why?" Michael wondered and looked from Kate to Daniel, "What?!"

"I think you should see this for yourself," said Daniel and pulled Michael in front of Kate's bathroom mirror so that he could see his back in the other mirror.

"Well I've been drunk in my days, but I am pretty sure that I did not get a tattoo on my back of that size, I would have known or remembered."

"You did not get a tattoo, Michael," Daniel said and took his shirt off as well and turned to stand beside his brother, so that they could see each other's backs at the same time, "You got our family crest, only with one dragon and some other stuff I cannot recognize."

"Yeah, yours looks more messy than mine," said Michael grinning, "It's cool, I like it. Always wanted a tattoo, but this is better." Pleased with himself he flexed his muscles to see the tattoo move.

"Are you finished with 'mine is bigger than yours'?" Kate demanded, but both brothers looked at her, shocked and embarrassed. "MOM, please!"

But Kate was unwavering. She leaned on the doorpost and just pouted: "I am aging here!"

"You know what I told you regarding sharing and if you were sure?" Daniel said to Michael, looking soberly at him.

"Yeah and ...? ... OH ... I see ... still ... I like it, and I stand behind what I said too ..." Michael said and looked back into the mirror. "What's with the heat?"

"You get used to it, kind of part of it also," said Daniel, looking at the crest on his brother's back.

"Will I also be turning into a werewolf at full moon?"

"Nope."

"Too bad. Vampire?"

"Nope."

"No perks?"

"Not yet," Kate interjected into the conversation from which she felt excluded, so that both brothers looked at her. "Not yet?" they said together, then grinned at each other.

"Not yet, now backing up, let's sit on the bed and you both fill me in on what happened to cause this." Kate walked back to the bed and patted the place beside her to make sure they could not get away again so easily.

Both preferred to pace while talking, so Kate leaned back, made herself comfortable and tried to follow the rather fast conversation, with both of them explaining what had occurred during the night at the monument.

After both had finished, they fell into the chairs in the sitting area, exhausted.

"That's a rather sweet story. Yes, you are right, for generations the crown has been carried by one alone and still will be, but with the support of another it will be an easier burden, I am sure. I am not sure what the community will think of it, but I can see they have little to say when it comes to the ruling of the one that is chosen and chooses to do so."

"Ruling? Mom you are losing me again ... dumb it down for the simple folks, like me," Michael grinned at her.

"Michael, you are no longer simple folk, not according to your back, and Daniel, you just made your first ruling. You could not have done this without embracing the past, which you both did, that's how it works. I am still officially here to support you until you take your place, and Michael will be beside you for as long as he lives. The crest cannot be passed down from just anybody. It is a conscious choice by giver and receiver; this is how it worked between your father and me." Kate started to choke up again and her tears started rolling, but she wiped them off so she could continue to say what needed to be said.

"Daniel, you will have to take your place sooner or later, when the time is right and the crest chooses you. Take your time, there is no rush and no pressure, never was and never will."

"What does this all mean for us?" Michael wanted to know.

"No change in lifestyle. You still do your job, pay your bills, be nice to your mother and grandparents, but you will need to go to more official functions, and you will have a different standing in the community. Sadly, you will also lose your privacy, for people protect their ruler-ship or whatever it is, your father never said. Daniel, your crest still looks like your Dad's before he embraced his calling. Your tattoo will change to look like our crest in the living room, until then it will remain a woven ring, through which the dragons wave."

"Hey Mom, isn't this all a bit weird?" Michael wondered as he looked at her.

"A bit?" she started laughing. "You should know that you have both made me even more proud today than ever before. To be willing to be there and to support each other the way you do; and your desire to share the burden; this is ever so precious and could not make me happier as a mother. Your Dad would have been so proud of you both." And Kate's tears started to roll again.

"Gee, Mom you are really trying to make us blush, aren't you?" Michael tried hard to lighten the atmosphere.

"Is it working?" she smiled through her tears.

"Yeah, so I am leaving, got to protect my reputation. I need breakfast, anyways. See you downstairs." Michael stomped off shirtless, trying to get accustomed to the heat he felt. He was sure he would not feel cold anytime soon.

"Are you OK, Mom?" Daniel was still a bit worried about Kate's fragility.

"Go have breakfast. I will be down shortly." And she waved him out of the room.

Getting used to the constant flow of people, Michael and Daniel made their way through the crowded living room to the kitchen. Half way there, they could hear gasps from the people who had been standing in the living room.

"Well, it is our house too, we are hot and we are hungry, so I hope you don't mind if we grab some food too!" said Michael, a bit annoyed at the reaction, and nodded to Daniel who followed him to the kitchen.

With both having the crest visible for all to see, the word got around quickly that the House of Von de Vorg not only had a ruler but also had the support it needed to survive another storm. The grief, even though fresh and deep for all, was lightened by a fresh revelation about the new generation for the future.

Upstairs, after her sons had left and she was finally alone again, Kate rolled on Sam's pillow and drank in his scent, which was starting to fade away. "Sam, you have sons you would be so proud of, there is no reason and purpose for me to linger here. It's time for me to make space for the younger generation."

"Kate, come down at once," Mary called from the living room. The woman still had an eerie sixth sense.

Michael and Daniel looked at each other and then walked back out into the living room, each holding several strips of bacon.

23

Mary spoke to them firmly: "Gentlemen, I know it takes some time to get used to it, but get dressed, we need to talk. Before that, make sure your mom gets out of that bedroom, she worries me greatly."

Michael flew up the stairs, with Daniel right behind him.

"Mom, is there anything you would like to tell us?" both said as they burst into the bedroom.

"I am tired. I need your father, and you are well and on your way. I so badly want to go to him: I can't stay here anymore, it's going to kill me."

"How about some time away?" That was Pia behind them.

"Guys, a shower and some clothes? And please leave us!" and Pia ushered the two big guys out, closed the door on them, and walked over to Kate.

"What a long stretch that was, wasn't it?"

"Pia please, I want no more, why does nobody understand? I can't do without Sam; as little as he could do without me. Why is there no relief from all this? Make it stop!" and Kate buried herself in Sam's pillow again and sobbed.

"Life does not go like that. You still have a purpose; we just don't know what it is yet."

"Could you live without Jackson?" Kate looked up at her with red, puffy eyes.

"It would be very difficult, I can't even imagine it, but I would need to find a way to make it work. What does your heart tell you?"

"It will not let go," Kate said, after a moment of checking.

"Then hold on to hope, there is always hope, even for lost causes there is hope."

"I know what I need now, I need to see it for myself, I need to look for myself and I need to find closure."

"All right, there's a plan. But first you need strength, so eat. Let's go together. What needs to be found will be found," Pia said smiling, and Kate went to have a shower, and got dressed for the first time in three weeks.

Within a few days Kate improved dramatically. She went jogging to gain strength and endurance and soon was deemed fit to do whatever she wanted to do. Her parents agreed to stay longer. So Michael, Daniel, Kate and Pia took a plane to get close to the presumed crash site. They were helped by the new connections Kate had due to her status, and by the good salary that Pia earned as an MD. The two women rented several helicopter rides to explore the area further. But besides pieces of aircraft, there was nothing to be found.

Every day Kate felt more convinced that it was time to move on. She could feel that Sam was nowhere near, and after two weeks they decided to head back. Pia and the boys went straight home, but Kate decided to make a little detour and stay on the Sunshine Coast for a short while. It was somewhat therapeutic for her to be away from the place that connected her to memories, and the ocean seemed to wash her tears away whenever they wanted to surface.

Life had to continue one way or another – or completely stop, that was the other choice.

Invitation from Old Friends

BAD NEWS TRAVELS FAST, so while Kate was near Vancouver her friends sought her out. On several evenings a few friends from her old class got together to share stories from the past and catch up. All agreed that Kate needed to be reminded of the other things that defined her, apart from being the widow of a wonderful man.

When Kate came back from a long walk on the beach to the place she had rented for the month, she found a letter in her post office box. It was from her friends in North Vancouver, friends she had not seen for some time. She had missed them for they had always had a wonderful time together, with lots of laughter and fun. So she opened the letter before she even entered the house, anxious to see what they had to say.

Hello Kate,

We just have found out about Sam. Kate, we are so sorry to hear about it all. We hope you are well otherwise, well as good as we can hope and pray for.

Listen we thought about it for some time and decided you need some time off ... so what do you think ... some time on the water? Good idea? We are going to go up Indian Arm by boat again, wanna join us? Let us know.

Sincerely
your bestest of all friends :)
Zhara and Yvonne

PS: Yvonne asked me to add to the letter that you should call us, as soon as you read this - please. I added the please, she was more demanding! Well you know her, when she gets something in her head ... Anyhow, do call, we need to hear your voice. Remember, we care about you and for the sake of my peace please call, otherwise I will never hear the end of it from Yvonne ...

Yes, Kate did know Yvonne. Lovable but stubborn. She seemed to run the household, but to be fair, Zhara enjoyed not having to make any of the decisions that Yvonne was always ready to make. Together they made a good team: Yvonne the headstrong go-getter and Zhara the laid-back, calm character who balanced Yvonne out in a really good way. Not to mention the sense of humor they both had. Well, thinking about it ... yes, going on a boat trip would be kind of nice and was a good idea. She always found it so relaxing when she spent time with them ... Besides, the long weekend was coming up and both her sons were busy with their life and work. There was no need to rush back, so going on a boat trip for a few days sounded more and more attractive to her.

She went straight into the living room, still holding the letter as she dialed the number.

"Hello?"

"Hey Zhara, it's me, Kate, I just got your letter," said Kate, while making herself comfortable on the sofa.

"YVONNE!" screamed Zhara to Yvonne, who must have been

out of the room, and Kate pulled the phone away from her ear, which was buzzing from the unexpected scream.

"Yvonne, for heaven's sake come here, it's Kate, I told you she would call," Zhara hollered.

"Yeah, and I am still on the line," said Kate laughing. "Half deaf though, after that," she added, smiling.

"Sorry Kate, I was just so excited. How have you been? Where are you now? What's happening with you? We are so sorry to hear about Sam ... YVONNE!" Zhara screamed again, this time not straight into the phone. "She is going to kill me if she comes back and has missed your call! Where the heck is she?" Zhara was obviously irritated.

Kate had to laugh. "Zhara, I can call back later if you like," she said, laughing.

"NO ... no, absolutely not, tell me Kate, tell me ..." and after a pause she added softly, "How are you, I mean really?" The warmth in her voice made Kate's heart swell and brought tears to her eyes. They were close, despite the fact that they had not seen each other for a long time. They connected as if no time had passed at all and that felt ... good.

"Really ... Hmmm, not so hot, but that is the unofficial version, otherwise fine," Kate said, angrily wiping away her tears.

"We don't care about the political crap, you know that." Kate heard Yvonne on the other line.

"Oh hi Yvonne, good to hear your voice," Kate said, surprised.

"Not much choice, with all that racket! These days one can't even get a quiet moment in the bathroom, but now I'm here ... I have the other phone, Zhara is still on the phone in the kitchen."

"I got your letter. Thank you both. The idea about the boat ..." Kate stopped and thought.

"Is fantastic, I know! It was my idea, therefore it's a good idea," Yvonne said happily. "Plan is, well we hope you will be able to meet us by late Thursday afternoon, so we can get out on the channel before nightfall. Everything is packed; well almost everything ..." she said in an insinuating tone, mocking Zhara, who responded right away, with a "Yeah yeah ..." and something else that Kate could not understand, but still she had to smile. Those two were still the same; it was good that some things did not change.

"Well ..." Kate was thinking about whether she could make it down there that fast.

"What do you mean by WELL? I am picking you up from wherever you are, and that is that. I have to go now. Zhara will tell me all that you had to say later. I have to get ready for work. See you soon, Kate. We'll catch up then. Bye." And that was that. Yvonne, in the flesh. Or on the phone, at least.

"You heard the boss," Zhara said laughing, "And don't blame me, you called," she added. "So when do you think you could let us know when you could be ready for pickup?"

Kate was glad that there was no longer any way to get out of this. She needed something to look forward to, and this was exactly what she needed.

"All right then ... let us know by tomorrow – Oh, and Kate," Zhara said quietly, "I am so looking forward to seeing you again," and then she hung up as well.

"I am too," Kate whispered back to the empty line and hung up as well.

That Thursday she met the two women at Vancouver Airport. Yvonne had to get something from Delta, and thought it was easiest to pick her up from the airport. Kate grabbed a quick coffee from Tim Horton's and went to stand by the totem poles in the entrance hall, so as not to miss Yvonne, who arrived shortly thereafter.

After a big hello and plenty of hugs, Zhara and Yvonne got all her stuff into the back of their truck, and they all headed to the harbor. Packing the boat was slow because they chatted away, talking about old friends and past and new occurrences on both sides of their lives, while avoiding the painful subject of Sam's death.

It seemed they all agreed that that subject would have to wait – for now, none of them wanted to add heaviness to their reunion.

"Still Psyching, Kate?" said Yvonne over the loud noise of the motor as she steered it out of its parking spot and headed towards the open sea.

"Yeah, still a Psych nurse, why?"

"Who do you talk to when you need a psych nurse?"

"A psychiatrist, like everyone else, or a counselor, why?"

"Just wondering ... in fact I always wondered ... who heals the doctor when the doctor is sick?"

"The poor nurse?" said Kate, and they both started laughing.

"Indeed, physicians must make crappy patients ..." she added loudly over the sound of the motor, which became even louder as their speed increased.

"We'll talk later," said Kate and went downstairs to join Zhara, who was still trying to find a place for everything in the cabin.

"It always surprises me how spacious it is inside here, considering how small it looks from the outside," Kate said, while finding a seat in the sitting area so as to be out of the way of Zhara's busy organizing.

"Yeah it is. Lots of hidden compartments do the trick in here," Zhara agreed.

Outside the world passed by. Houses that had been built on the shoreline, tankers at anchor. There was a lighthouse on the right on a small island, which looked enchanting. Seagulls and bald eagles circled the evening sky for a last minute catch before the night took hold over the landscape. Kate loved the journey up Indian Arm, and once again enjoyed the beautiful scenery that seemed to change around every bend they took. Evergreens leaned over the steep edges of the ocean shore. Here and there was the odd house, and the yacht clubs already had several boats in their harbors: a definite sign of the weekend that everybody wanted to take advantage of.

Apart from the ripples that the boat created, the water was calm and quite. It was a mirror to the sky above reflecting the clouds, sky and land perfectly. The world here seemed to be still in order and in harmony. Nothing much had changed since the last time she had been here. All was still just as she remembered from the last time she was up here.

"I packed some yummy stuff for our meals. You just relax now, will you, and enjoy the time," Zhara said, watching Kate looking out of the window, taking in the scenery unfolding in front of them.

"Thanks for thinking of me and taking me with you, Zhara, I needed this," Kate said gratefully to Zhara, who now joined her at the window.

"Everything will work out fine, Kate, you will see. It always will and always does," Zhara added, and then she busied herself again with getting the kitchen organized.

How could it, Kate wondered. When someone is faced with the ultimate and definite end of something she had counted on to last to the end of her life? If someone could give Sam back to her then yeah, she would believe that everything would work out fine, but that was not possible, now was it?

They passed a few other boats and it even started to rain a little, but not for long. Weather did not matter much up here. People made the best of it, and they did whatever they wanted to, regardless of whether it was rain or shine. That was the difference, she thought, people up here lived independent of weather conditions; besides, considering the steady flow of rain on the West Coast, one would never leave the house if one waited for a sunny day. After all, it was the rain coast with rainforests, so what else could one expect? It was therefore not unusual to see people diving in February when it was still freezing cold; or to see boats going upstream to find camping grounds even when the weather did not promise to be sunny. On the other hand, one never knew when the weather would surprisingly change and become sunny.

Today was just such a day, and forecast for the weekend as well. The forecast had called for rain, but eventually the sun won and it was still shining warmly through the glass on Kate's face, even though the sun was setting already. She closed her eyes and let the warm rays penetrate her eyelids. It was so relaxing and soothing.

Oh, how I wish Sam could have seen this too, she thought, but he was now in a better place and she had to make the best of what she had left. He would not want her to give up, but it was oh, so tempting.

"Of course we will put you to work, you know, when we get to our place. There is always stuff to clear and clean," Zhara said over her shoulder, which made Kate start to smile.

Zhara and Yvonne had cleared a little parcel of land on the side of one of the steep slopes of Indian Arm and had built a cabin all by themselves. It was a beautiful spot, but summer houses require some maintenance.

"Of course, that is why I am here in the first place, cheap labor, right?"

"Of course," Zhara laughed back. They told her that joke every time she went to their cabin. An hour passed fast and they docked on the floating dock close to the shoreline, just as the dark claimed the land. From what she could still see, the place had not changed much either. Plenty of improvements had been made since she had last been there, but it still screamed relax, put your feet up, and enjoy nature. It was just that kind of a place.

Yvonne was busy with the boat and Zhara got the dinner started. They had decided to spend the night on the boat, and then claim their place for the weekend in the morning. It was just not much fun to unpack in the dark, they told her. Yvonne got the generator on the deck running and in no time the BBQ was going full blast, which aided Zhara's food preparation.

Shortly after they sat and enjoyed a nice steak dinner. Fresh air exhausted Kate, so Zhara sent her off to bed, while she and Yvonne stayed up to get a few more things done before they also turned in.

Dreaming of Sam

ZHARA AND YVONNE stayed up a bit longer to get everything ready for the night. Yvonne checked the fuel level of the generator for the heater in the boat, and Zhara cleaned the BBQ and covered the rest up to protect it from the wind and rain. By the time they had everything ready Kate was already deeply asleep inside the boat.

"Poor girl," Yvonne whispered to Zhara. "Has she said anything to you about Sam, Michael or Daniel?"

"Nope, and I did not think it would be good to bring it up so soon," Zhara said, looking at Kate through the window of the boat. "I don't know what I would do if I were her, so dying on me is not an option, do you hear me, Yvonne?" she said rather threateningly, which made Yvonne giggle.

"I would not dare to, for you would haunt me even if I was in a better place ..." Yvonne said, grinning at her as they both quietly slipped into the boat, past Kate to their bed in the back of the boat.

In no time the heater was running, and with the comfortable

heat all three of the women quickly fell asleep. However, Kate woke a few times in the night from the movement of the boat. She looked outside at the full moon. It lit up the bay so she could see the waves and the boats at the yacht club nearby. The tide must be coming in, she thought, considering the restless water, and then she turned around in her sleeping bag, trying to get more shuteye.

The boat's swaying back and forth in the night brought back memories and Kate began dreaming. She could remember sleeping with Sam next to her, she could swear she could feel his hands around her, and the movement of the waves felt a lot like the movement of his breathing. "Sam," she said, groaning. "I miss you so much," she said in her dreams, expressing the deep need and sorrow which her mind was still working through, even though she thought her body was done grieving. "I miss you too sweetie," she heard him say.

"Do you remember when we went hiking in the mountains with Yvonne and Zhara? Remember them? They wrote, and I am with them right now on the boat. It is so nice to get away but I miss you, miss you so much."

"I do remember love, I remember you sliding down the hill with one hand on the rope straight back into my arms," he said with a smiling voice.

"I do remember that as well, you said that you missed holding me as well, but you did not think that I would remedy it so quickly," she said, smiling back. She could hear him chuckling.

"Do you remember what you said?" he asked, still chuckling.

"I think I said I would keep the speed limit in mind next time," she said smiling.

"Yeah, I laughed so hard that I almost let go of the rope," he said, grinning.

"Sam?"

"Humm?"

"Please don't leave me," she said soberly.

"I am always next to your heart love, you never have to look far," he said, but the rest started to fade away.

"Sam where are you going?" she said in panic.

"I am tired. Later sweetie? ..."

"When? ... When?!" she said anxiously, but he did not answer her anymore.

"Kate, wake up!" Yvonne shook her awake. "You are dreaming, wake up!"

Kate looked around, totally disoriented and confused, and saw Yvonne's worried face above hers.

"Sorry Yvonne, did I wake you, what did I do or say? Was I that loud?" Kate said sleepily, looking up at Yvonne, and at Zhara who had joined them.

"You hollered 'When!' Several times," Zhara said sleepily and sat down, right beside Kate's feet.

"Wanna tell us what that was all about?" said Yvonne, and went to the stove to turn on the water to make tea.

"Oh, I was dreaming, I could have sworn, that I was talking to ... never mind ..."

"You can say it, you have been dreaming about Sam, is that right?" said Zhara, ignoring the scowling look Yvonne gave her.

"Kate, I know that you might not want to talk about it right now, but it might be good to speak your fears and sorrows out loud and share them with us, you might feel better," Zhara said quietly beside her.

"Don't rush her, Zhara," Yvonne said impatiently over her shoulder.

"Sounds like you have been talking already," said Kate and sat up. "Well then, what would you like to know?" She wiped her eyes and then gladly took the cup of tea Yvonne passed to her.

"What happened with Sam?" Zhara blurted out, which gained her more sharp looks from Yvonne.

"You do not need to answer that Kate, if you feel you don't want to," said Yvonne, looking accusingly at Zhara, who just shrugged her shoulders and then looked pleadingly at Kate.

"They say he crashed in the mountains, but they do not know where. I found the crash site. The plane was in pieces; I cannot see how anyone could have survived it, even though lately I can feel him like I used to. I know this sounds stupid and crazy ... but lately..." she said, thoughtfully.

"You miss him; that is natural," said Yvonne, and Zhara only nodded her head.

"Yeah I do, but we talked in my dream about something I had forgotten and he reminded me of it ... Do you remember the time we went hiking on the mountain, Zhara? We came down on that mountain

35

side and I slipped and slid right back into Sam's arms, who was below me, do you remember that?"

"Yeah I do remember. I was so horrified, but the way he caught you ... you guys just made it look cozy and romantic in some way, I remember that very well ... Good heavens, I had almost forgotten about that!"

"So had I, Zhara, so tell me, how it is possible that my memory is reminding me of something I had almost forgotten? How is that possible?" Kate demanded, looking at them both, puzzled.

"Well, the mind does strange things, you of all people should know that, being in the kind of nursing field you are in, and all ... Hallucinations, or whatever they call it ..." said Yvonne, but even Zhara was not quite sold on that explanation.

"Well ... all right ... it is unusual, but I also know that you two were very close, so I would not be surprised if your mind is playing tricks on you, or is telling you whatever you need and want to hear, Kate, to find peace. Well ... enough of the heavy stuff ... Let's get to bed and we'll chat some more tomorrow, or should I say today? What do you guys think?" Yvonne got up and took the empty cups from Zhara and Kate, and put them into the sink. For her the day had long passed and it was time to go back to sleep. This was fine with Kate. Deep within she was hoping to find a way to talk to Sam some more. She was at the point at which she could care less how the information and conversation came to her, as long as they came to her. Everybody found their way back to bed and the lights went off. Only the light of the full moon above and the reflection of it on the water lit the inside of the cabin.

The sky was clear and the stars were brilliant, glittering in the sky. Kate looked out of the window and found herself again wishing to share this calming beauty with Sam. There was such tranquility here, which both of them had always enjoyed when they were here. A few times they had come with Yvonne and Zhara, and then decided to follow them in a separate boat which Sam had rented. Getting away from all the stresses and demands of daily life was always a relief for both of them. With the extra boat they could get away if they felt like being alone, or if they felt Yvonne and Zhara could use some alone time, but it also allowed them to leave and explore the Arm further and then return a few hours later.

They often went into one of the quiet coves and had a glass of red wine on the boat, or had a bit of fun, which was something they both always enjoyed. But that was in the past now. It is good to have good memories, but it was really time for her to put them where they belonged, in the past, so that she could move forward into the future. But that was where the whole problem lay. She was not sure if she wanted to move into a future without him; instead, joining him where he was sounded more and more appealing as time went on.

Because of her line of work she recognized that she was having suicidal ideations, and that if she mentioned it to any of her friends and colleagues she could quite possibly be admitted to a mental hospital involuntarily. But just snapping out of it was also not working, and she knew from her own experience and that of her patients that the thought was not superficial. It was deep within her and seemed to spread further and further into her feeling and living. But she felt that Sam would have been disappointed in her if she had given up that quickly. So she would hang on as long as she could and after that ... after that she would do what she felt she needed to do – and that was that. With her plan set in place, peace overcame her and she fell back into a deep and dreamless sleep.

The two days on Indian Arm were fun. They worked on the hill, clearing out debris that had collected there during the storm the week before. In the evening they sat on the dock, telling stories and grilling steaks. Eventually Kate was able to open up and answer some of their questions. She told them what Daniel had been up to, and how Michael was doing. She told them a bit about the journey she had taken with Pia to find the crash site and how she had to come to terms with it all. She spoke in a matter of fact way, and then smiled and changed the subject. Zhara just looked at Yvonne, shaking her head, and later Yvonne told Zhara not to say anything until she was ready to.

It was time to return before they had a chance to really talk. Kate said good-bye to her friends, with a promise to return for another trip with them, and watched them as they drove off, waving. She felt more alone than ever. Well, back to work and home she thought, and busied herself with preparations for the next few days.

Awakening

AWAKENING TO THE SOUND of heart monitor machines is never pleasant. For Sam though, it was an awaking into one of his worst nightmares. His memories took him back to the time when he was standing in the OR, surrounded by beeping monitors. The pain he remembered was that of almost losing everything he held dear. Vividly his memories brought him back to that terrible moment when he held his dead, premature daughter in his hands, and Kate, his sole reason to live, was on the OR table, with Jackson and Pia and lots of nurses fighting to save her life. The beeping of the machines had been so loud and so slow, and was often interrupted by warning beeps when Kate's blood pressure and heart rate dropped to dangerously low levels. The horrors of that day had written themselves into his memory and soul as if carved in stone, and now they resurfaced mercilessly.

Yet something was different this time. The beeping of the machine was way too fast, much faster than in his memories, the pain was not only in his heart but all over his body, and he did not recognize any of the voices around him. None of them were Pia's or that of his best friend and chief surgeon, Jackson. Lying motionless on the bed, he became more and more aware of his body and of his real surroundings. The beeping was not Kate's monitor but someone else's – possibly his own. Besides that, he could feel that everything hurt, no not hurt, rather burned in the worst way. He could not recall ever being in such pain before. He felt like screaming, yet there was no sound. Unable to move to find help and relieve the pain, he was reduced to just listening to all the rushing and commotion of a busy hospital day. Besides all the voices there were the endless beeping and clicking sounds of IV pumps, vitals machines and bed alarms. Why was nobody aware that he was awake? Why did nobody realize that he was in such pain? Then his hope grew as he felt someone approach his bedside.

Someone touched his wrist to adjust something that was attached to him, and then he could hear her reading numbers off the screen that must have been above him. She read them out loud to someone else who was charting it down, but nobody was talking to him. How was that possible? He concentrated on his fingers to move them, but they did not obey his commands; neither did his feet.

By the time he thought of trying to elevate his heart rate to get her attention she was gone. Sam could not remember when he had ever felt so helpless and hopeless in his life. All right then, he was alive, but where was Kate? Did she know he was here? What had happened? Who had brought him here? And most important of all, wherever is here? He tried to calm himself, to focus on not feeling the burning pain all over, and to focus on the things he could remember to distract himself. What was the last he could remember? He had spoken to Kate from the cockpit of a private plane, to let her know that he was on his way home. He had hoped to surprise her with his early arrival, by hiring a small private plane. Truth be told, he did want to surprise her, but an even more compelling reason was that he was so anxious to see and hold her again. Then he remembered what had happened next, and that was something that should not have been possible. The pilot had been even more shocked than him. Something had exploded, then they had been plummeting towards the ground with terrifying speed, and the next thing they both knew was that they had crash-landed somewhere and the plane was on fire.

Sam had made it out before the plane exploded, but not before he had reached over to the pilot to tell him to get out, only to find that he had not survived the impact. After tumbling out of the smashed plane onto the snow, Sam welcomed the cooling of the snow and ice on his burning skin. He had landed on his stomach, but quickly rolled over to cool his burning back, and when that was cool enough to tolerate he had turned back over to his stomach, and by so doing had lost his grip on the slope. He started to slide down the hill on his stomach and did not stop until he was at least a hundred feet downhill from the crash site. At first he was angry that he had slid so far, for he knew it would be easier for rescuers to find him if he was near the plane. But when he heard the plane explode, shredding into small pieces, as he could see from the flying debris that came down around him, he thanked his lucky stars that he had been as far away as he was. It most likely had saved his life. He was thinking that planes don't just explode like this, and that there was just something off about the whole thing, but he could not contemplate that thought for long as the big bang echoing in the snow-covered mountain set off several avalanches. He could hear and feel the rumbling and tremors all round him, and then he felt the ground under him shift and he was pushed further down the mountain. With all the tumbling and shifting he lost consciousness and then finally fell into an endless darkness. And now he had awakened in this place. He had no clue how long he had been out and how long he had been there.

The pain started to claim his mind again. Trying to reconstruct his memory was not enough to keep his mind off the pain, so he would have to figure something else out. He remembered Kate telling him a long time ago about some research she was excited about, in which they had people with chronic medium to severe pain imagine pain as a flame. Then when the pain intensified, they had to focus on the flame and concentrate on making the flame smaller. She said that in this way people had been able to control their pain better. Well here goes nothing; he had to give it a try. He started to concentrate, but somehow it did not work. Well then, what about going to the happy place that people say can make one feel better? He had to try that, but the thought of Kate made his insides long for her and his mind started to groan ... how he missed her. Suddenly he heard a firm woman's voice:

"Margaret, is this patient yours?" he heard her say.

"Yes," another woman's voice answered.

"What can you tell me about this patient, Margaret?"

"Well, we don't have a name yet. He was in a coma for quite some time, and was taken off life support several weeks ago, but he remained stable, without any changes. Severe burns keep him on this unit. I check his vitals every fifteen minutes, as you asked me to," said the obviously younger woman.

Sam stopped following her report when he heard the words "in a coma for quite some time". How could he have been in a coma for so long and still be alive? Didn't people who went through stuff like that become vegetables? What were his chances for recovery? Would he be able to get up again and live without pain, to see Kate again and the boys? His heart grew heavy and even though the conversation continued for quite a bit longer, he had heard enough. What a lousy deal and on top of that hellish pain, which was almost unbearable ... it was time to go back to his happy place.

He tried to hide in the depths of his heart, close to her who had his heart and was far away from this living hell he was in. He stretched his mind and then he heard her within his head.

"Sam ... I miss you so ..."

"Kate," he groaned.

"Have you not noticed the fluctuations on this monitor?" But then she stopped mid sentence.

"Fluctuations?" the young nurse was stunned.

"Sir, can you hear me? Squeeze your eyes shut if you can!" the older nurse urged him and started to pinch his shoulder to evoke a reaction from him. In normal circumstances he would have given her a piece of his mind for pinching him like that. The woman was supposed to be a healer, not an inflictor of pain, but she certainly knew how to inflict pain. When he heard what she asked the only thing he could think was: you have got to be kidding me! Now that he really did not want to do anything but hear Kate, they finally noticed that he was awake? He squeezed his eyes as hard as he could and heard a gasp.

"Thank you, I can see it," she said, relieved. Then she urged him further. "Do you have pain? One squeeze for yes, two for no."

Sam squeezed once.

"Increase the drip and call the physician," she fired at the other nurse, whom he could hear running away from his bed. "Sir, it might be better to put you back under again, because we cannot increase the dose much more, and I can only imagine what kind of pain you must be in."

The increase of hydro-morphine did help a little, but the idea of sleeping for a while without pain sounded much better.

But first he went down to find Kate again. She needed to know he was hearing her as well. Her heart was very heavy, he could make this much out ... still, he was amazed that he could hear her in the first place.

'I miss you too sweetie' he said in his heart. Then he listened, hoping and praying he could hear her voice once again. His mind was obviously playing tricks on him, but he did not mind. He obviously was desperate to hold onto something, or the morphine was giving him hallucinations, but hey, who cares? He listened patiently and when he could hear her again, his heart started racing for joy. She was telling him about something she remembered.

'Do you remember when we went hiking in the mountains with Yvonne and Zhara? Remember them?' she asked.

Of course he did. He wrote those days into his soul in the hope that he would never forget them. Those were the good, fun times when he had her close, which he liked best, in the company of those interesting, funny and enjoyable friends of hers.

Kate continued. 'They wrote me and I am with them right now on the boat. It is a nice get away but I miss you, I miss you so much!' She was fighting to keep her composure he could tell, even though she seemed not to be fully aware of where and how they spoke. He was afraid that she would stop telling him more or that the connection would break, so he tried to encourage her to keep talking by trying to remember the time she was reflecting on.

'I do remember love, I remember you sliding down the hill with one hand on the rope straight back into my arms.' He had to smile for he could remember her body against his, her hair ruffled from the movement and the wind, cheeks glowing red from the sun exposure and exertion, looking delicious. If the concerned gazes of her friends had not been on them, who knows what he would have done next.

'I do remember that too, you said that you missed holding me as well, but you did not think that I would remedy it in such a hurry.' Her tone was lighter now. He had eased her worries, at least temporarily, and when he thought of that moment back then, he had to chuckle for it had been a funny moment.

'Do you remember what you said?' he asked when there was a momentary pause, which worried him, but he still had to chuckle thinking about it for he remembered every word she had said that day.

'I think I said ... next time I would keep the speed limit in mind,' she said, smiling; he could hear that in her voice. How good it was to talk to her, if that was what they were doing, but whatever they were doing, he loved it.

'Yeah,' he was still grinning when he thought about it, 'I laughed so hard, that I almost let go of the rope.' It was a fun and oh-so-good memory.

'Sam?' He could hear the worry that had found its way back into her heart.

'Humm?' He had a hard time concentrating for he could hear the doctor discussing with the nurse that it might be best to put Sam under for a bit longer, until they had him through the worst. It sounded good to him. On the one hand he was relieved to get a break from the pain, on the other hand he was afraid he would lose touch with Kate as well.

"Can you hear me?" the doctor asked Sam, his mouth close to Sam's ear.

Sam squeezed his eyes once.

The nurse explained: "This is how we have been communicating, by squeezing eyes, for he seems to be unable to communicate in any other way. He must have lain here in pain for some time, because the new nurse did not notice the fluctuations in his vital signs and realize that he had come out of the coma."

"I think it would be best if we put you into an artificial coma for just a bit longer, so as to limit the suffering and give you more time to heal, is that all right with you? It will not be too long and we will keep you under close observation, isn't that right?" he said in an accusing tone to the nurse beside him.

"Yes, of course," she said and then she fiddled with something on Sam's hand.

Well, that was all Sam needed to hear. He squeezed his eyes once more to acknowledge and agree with the doctor's decision. Then he became impatient for he wanted to get back to his conversation with Kate. He could hear her pleading with him, which almost broke his heart.

'Please don't leave me,' she said, worried. He needed to say something that she could take with her until they could speak again.

'I am always next to your heart love, you never have to look far.' No matter how hard he was trying he could still feel himself slipping away. The medication they were giving him was starting to work.

'Sam where are you going?' She could hear that he was fading away and was beginning to panic.

Quickly, think of something that will not worry her and sounds normal ...

'I am tired.' He was hoping he could think of something better, but this was all he had for the moment and time was running out. 'Later sweetie?' and then the dark took over and he felt himself relaxing and dropping into a deeper sleep. Far away in his mind he could hear her calling for him, but he could not answer anymore.

"Until some of the worst skin grafts have healed we will keep him under, nurse. Inform me of any changes, but his body, as damaged as it was, is healing surprisingly well. I think this is the best way to keep him comfortable. We also need to find out as soon as possible who he is, so that we can contact and inform relatives and family. There has been no information about him yet, has there?"

The physician and the nurse continued their conversation on the way to the nursing station and Sam was left to rest under the supervision of machines, hoping for better days to come.

SEVERAL WEEKS LATER Sam woke up. The pain had decreased, but it was still bad. They had just done new skin grafts that were not healing as easily as the other ones had, but they felt they needed to bring him out of the artificial coma they had been keeping him in.

Many miles away Kate woke up that very same night bathed in sweat. The pain she experienced was unexpected and intense. She actually woke up from her own screaming. What was this all about? What had she dreamt that was so painful, and since she was awake now, why was the pain continuing? Tomorrow I will go and have this checked out, she thought, I don't get enough sleep as it is, I certainly don't need to be woken by this kind of pain as well. She tried to narrow down where the pain came from. It was not as much internal as external. Her skin was on fire. She got up and pulled up the sleeve of her shirt, but there was no sign of irritation, no redness or swelling, and no bumps. She had not eaten anything out of the norm, had not been out or been exposed to any chemical she could think of, so what could it be?

She went to the bathroom, thinking that maybe a shower would do the trick, and on the way there she left a trail of clothing behind her, stripping off every piece that was bothering her skin. Yet even the long shower seemed to bring no relief; on the other hand, the emptiness in her heart had gone.

Great, she thought, I finally feel emotionally better with the price of feeling physically like crap – excellent trade off ... not!

She was about to climb back into bed with the hope of relaxing and making the burning go away when the phone rang, but she did not feel like answering it. Go away, I am not feeling well, and with the way I am feeling right now I am not good company, anyway.

She tried to concentrate more on making the pain go away, but nothing really seemed to help. She just could see this one coming. She would go to her doctor's office and he would find nothing wrong with her and write her off as psychosomatic.

Concentrate on the pain and then lower it to a level that is tolerable, so concentrate darn it, she thought.

The answering machine came on, it was Mary.

"Sorry for calling you this late, but I was wakened from ... well anyway ... I was awake and thought of checking in to see if you are all right. I truly hope I did not wake you though. Well, in the morning call me, will you Kate? Thanks, and give my love to Michael and Daniel when you see them. Bye."

Kate had fallen asleep but Mary on the other end of the line was in a blissful frenzy. How was it possible, she thought over and over again, but however it was, thank you Lord Jesus!!!

Not caring about the time, Mary called Micha and demanded that he be at her house within the next half hour. It took Micha a moment to really wake up and realize that he was talking to Mary in an official way not as a friend, so he briskly got up and made a few calls as well. When Mary called in this way he knew that he was reactivated as security for the crest, but who was there to protect? The boys had not stepped up yet, Kate was all right judging by the conversation he had had with her on the phone the day before, and there was nobody else. But when Mary called for duty, one came without questioning. It was a bit weird that she had called so early in the morning, however.

When they arrived at Mary's house she was already at the door, expecting them. She was the same as ever. Perhaps a bit skinnier due to all the worries they had gone through, but she had the same old spark in her eyes that he had been longing to see again.

"Well Mary, what was so urgent that you had to get me and the guys up at two in the morning?" Micha demanded as Mary drove ahead of them to the sitting room in her wheel chair. She asked them to sit in the chairs, warning them that what she had to say would most likely knock their socks off. So they sat and looked expectantly at her while she took her time pouring herself some tea.

"Micha, you and your guys are up again," she said. Although she was excited she spoke quietly, but she could have been speaking Chinese, for they did not understand a single word she said.

"Come again, Mary?" Micha was not in the mood for guessing. He would have preferred to still be sleeping in his bed, so he hoped that she had a good reason for getting him out of his warm bed.

"I need you to find Sam," she said again clearly and the room became so quite that one could have heard a pin drop.

"Sam?" Micha shifted uncomfortably in his seat, trying to find the right words so as not to hurt her feelings. "Mary ... uhhh ... you do remember that we buried Sam last fall? Remember the funeral?" He was hoping that the grief had not caused her to drift into some kind of dementia. She was still so needed by them all. But Mary just giggled like a schoolgirl.

"Yeah, we buried an empty coffin because we could not find any of Sam's remains, and we needed to get closure, but you know ... tonight I realized he is still alive ... Now do your job, and find him!" she said, looking around the room as if wondering why they were still sitting there.

Meeting in the Dark

DANIEL HAD BEEN RIGHT. Keeping herself busy was the best thing to do. So Kate had decided to go down to Vancouver to do a course she had signed up for. Several other things needed to be taken care of as well, such as refreshing her First Aid and CPR; and she wanted to expand her knowledge and possibly work towards her Masters if she had enough energy. There were plenty of options and thanks to frugal living and the savings she had accumulated, she had enough money to do pretty much anything she wanted to do. So she checked out what classes were running that would make her re-entry into school life a little bit easier. Thank the Lord though; the extra effort would keep her preoccupied enough to keep her thinking of other things apart from Sam, who was more and more on her mind these days. Why she did not know, but it could not possibly be a good sign.

Kate was counting on the intensity of the courses to give her no time to dwell on her thoughts of gloom and doom, and maybe the exposure to new people and duties would give her the strength to start over again. This would be her third new beginning, and certainly her last one. The first round had been with Dale; the second one with Sam; and now she had to try once more for herself, simply to survive. To her surprise, Mary had fully agreed with her decision. Kate assumed that it was most likely because she had been fading away. Kate tried hard to keep weight on, but it came off faster then she could think of eating, so she had lost so much weight that it worried them all. Since Sam's funeral she had lost over 60 pounds. Even the nasogastric tube that Jackson had inserted to get some nutrients into her had not helped much. Her whole body was reacting against the psychological onslaught of the loss and the emptiness she felt. All the support she received did not make a difference.

Neither did her sons change the way she felt. Of course she was infinitely proud of them both, but they were grown and had no more need for their mother in a real sense, so Kate just could not find purpose in her life. Her body felt weak and exhausted all the time, and if she had it her way she would be sleeping most of the day. Out of desperation Daniel, Michael and Jackson had spoken with Mary and they had all agreed that a change in scenery would do Kate some good. Both sons could hold the fort until it was decided what was to happen with the seat of Von de Vorg and the transfer of the crown.

Mary was a bit reserved about it all. She mumbled something about wanting to do a bit of research herself, which would help her to keep her mind off things. She had for some time now been asking certain people to come to her house, and they had left puzzled, but had carried out her requests. Micha had been one of them. After the meeting with her he had left, booked a flight without saying a word to anyone, and they had not heard from him for some time. The same had happened with a few of the other men who were known to be in the circle of security for the crest. When Mary was asked what she was up to, she just said that something was not right and that it was her duty to find out what it was. Mary also maintained that something was off with the time line for the crest, but when she started to talk about it, people started to fade out of the conversation, for it was too complicated for the best of men to follow her.

Daniel had the same feeling, for he took care of his father's affairs, yet the crest on his back remained unchanged. Then there was the fact that Kate's crest was still as clear and brilliant as before, including the crown, which did not make sense to anybody in town. It should have faded like Mary's, even if she had chosen to keep it as Mary had chosen to keep her late husband's, but that was not the case. Somehow the crest kept on acknowledging Kate as carrier, even though Kate herself was withering away under the strain of it all. Jackson, highly trained in science and very educated, was stretched to his maximum to tolerate strange facts and ways of living. Everything he had experienced and observed was long past weird, and now there was the Hocus Pocus of magic and of a choosing crest and all that. Now he was asked to accept that the crest was like a living thing, making choices about who it wanted or who it wanted to pass itself down to; it was just simply too much. He was wondering when the point would come when he would either snap or admit himself to Kate's wing. The only one that could keep him sane and who he could talk to was his wife and colleague, who like him just shook her head sometimes as she did her rounds. Yes, that was exactly how he felt as well.

What made things worse was that they had all been very close, and now to send Kate away to get a break from it all was the hardest thing they all had to do. It felt to Jackson as if he was losing yet another friend, but it made sense to him that if he did not send her away she would possibly never return to them anyway. Missing her badly was to be expected. She was a vital link in the community, and her absence would be felt badly. But sitting there together they all knew that they had no choice. Kate had a few more pounds to go before her body would shut down due to lack of energy and nutrition, so drastic measures needed to be taken.

Jackson called one of his old classmates in Vancouver who specialized in eating disorders. Although that was not the case with Kate, Frank had agreed to keep an eye on her while she was down there. Jackson was pleased that Frank had taken his request so seriously that his office had set up an appointment for Kate to see him shortly after her arrival.

Daniel and Michael had convinced Kate to go ahead with her idea of expanding her knowledge base. She had agreed to sign up for some courses, but it was really hard for her to leave their house and home. For her it was her last connection to Sam. While she was there it felt like he might walk through the front door and back into her life at any moment. His scent had now faded from his pillow and his shirts. She had refused to put them away, for she needed to feel that he was still present, even if it was only through his clothing. Now, leaving the house felt a lot like giving up on her crazy hope, but reason eventually won and she caved under the pressure and signed up for some courses sooner than she had planned. Besides, it seemed that Jackson was set on her seeing his colleague in Vancouver, who might be able to help with what was going on with her physically.

Resigned, she had packed a couple of things and was on her way. Michael had arranged for her to stay with some old friends who had a house near campus and rented out their basement suite. They had gladly agreed to have a mature woman living with them, and had been even more pleased to know that they would be helping out a good, old friend. Michael was pleased at how everything had worked out, and also that there was someone who could help his mother should she need help, and who could keep an eye on her. She would not be totally alone, and the greatest bonus was that he had spies who could tell him at any time how his mother was doing.

Kate settled in fast. There was not much to settle in, in the first place. The basement was fully furnished and most of what she needed was supplied. On the second day she bought the textbooks for the courses that she would start in a few days. And after Jackson had left several text messages for her, she had confirmed her appointment with the doctor's office, just to get him off her back. But in the evenings she just curled up in a ball, trying to keep warm with endless hot water bottles, and eventually deciding to get a heating blanket to keep herself warm at night.

Being back at school had advantages. She was so wrapped up in her studies that she could hardly think of anything else. If there was a moment when she had a break, she had to be at the doctor's office and thanks to him she had stopped losing weight, and had even gained one pound in the last two weeks. They had not been pleased, but considering she was no longer losing weight Kate was happy. She had always wanted to be thinner, but being so very thin provoked even strangers to tell her to take better care of herself. It was a nuisance to say the least, but she would probably have done the same. Her classmates had been kind about it, but she could tell they were also itching to teach her about proper nutrition, as if she did not know about it herself.

One morning she had just about had it. She got up and turned to the class.

"All right, let's get it out in the open. I am not anorexic, nor do I suffer from bulimia. I went through hell and back losing my husband in a tragic accident, and I did not do so well with that. We don't know why, but my body just does not want to absorb nutrition, the food I eat gets rejected – so I throw up. So you can see there is nothing that you or I can do, unless my doctor can find a way to sooth the nerves of my colon, or can fix whatever it is that is preventing my body from taking in nutrition. Will this do, or do you have any more questions?"

"I do," said a woman in the back row, "How long has it been that you cannot eat anything?"

"Too long, as you can tell," Kate said tiredly. "But I am seeing a specialist, so don't worry about it anymore, OK?" And magically, that did the trick. Their focus shifted to other matters and finally she could sink back into her chair and enjoy not being noticed anymore.

For Kate things were on the mend and progress could be reported to the family back home weeks later. Kate was able to eat only a little, but she kept it down. She was on a special diet that helped to keep her energy level up.

Back home, Michael worked on his research, mainly working from home, and Daniel got used to the small hospital life, working alongside Jackson. Mary on the other hand seemed very withdrawn. She seemed to be preoccupied and busy with something she did not want others to know about yet. Some thought that it was her way of dealing with her grief over Sam, and others worried that having Kate gone as well had caused her to become unglued.

Kate talked regularly with her sons. Losing Sam had brought them much closer, closer than they had ever been. Michael had called her the night before from his research station, telling her that most of the leg work had been done and that he would do now all the rest on the computer back home, so he would soon be moving up there permanently. Daniel had some interesting cases he was working on with Jackson and Pia, and he was comfortable as well. He asked her how she was doing, and after talking a bit about her classes they agreed that she would come back up to spend time with them for the holidays.

Two months into her classes they just had finished the last midterm when Kate started to take a turn for the worse again. Her body again began to reject everything she ate, baffling even her specialists. At first they thought it might have been stress-related due to her midterms, but it soon became evident that there was more to it, for she did not improve after all the midterms were done.

Kate felt especially bad this morning. Her body and mind seemed not to be on the same page, which was frustrating. All the progress she had made had been destroyed in one week. In her second class she could not remain seated anymore, so she excused herself and left the class. She could feel a pull that her body seemed to be drawn to, a pull that was more important than anything else, so she followed it. It was impossible to find the words to make others understand this feeling, so she did not even attempt to explain herself to her friends, who came to check on her.

"I am just going to sit here in the lobby for a moment to calm this nutty body of mine down, and then I will be back in class. Take notes for me will you?" was the only thing her classmates could get out of her, before they returned to their classroom.

"I was hoping you would come," said a man who had been sitting in a chair far off to her right, and who had now walked over to her.

Kate looked around to see if he was talking to someone else, but since she was the only one sitting there she looked up at the man. He was tall, nice looking with a friendly expression; he was smiling at her, but his green eyes were assessing and almost probing her at the same time. His light blond, slightly curly hair was tamed by a nice haircut. He was dressed casually but smartly, with slacks, and a fine knitted pullover over a white shirt and a tie. He wore a black leather jacket and did not look at all like a student.

"Sorry, do I know you?" Kate asked carefully, glad she was in a public place. But somehow this man looked like someone she had seen briefly before somewhere.

"No need for alarm," he said, raising his arms to show his good intentions. "I was not sure if it works, but, never mind ... don't ask, it would sound nuts," he said with a winning grin, so that she leaned back into her seat.

"Nuts? Well, I have had my share of weird and unexplained over the last few years, believe me. Actually, 'nuts' doesn't come close to what I have seen and experienced ... umm, what's your name?" Kate looked at him. Having him talk to her made her even surer that she had seen him somewhere, but where?

"Oh, sorry. Micha, nice to meet you, and yeah we have met before, very, very briefly."

Kate just shook her head. They had spoken but she was none the wiser. The man enjoyed talking in riddles and if that made him happy, she was the last to challenge him. After all she was just simply too exhausted to care, even if the queen came through the front door.

"Who was that?" he wanted to know, pointing back to where her classmates had gone.

"Concerned fellow students, why?" Kate wanted to know, but really she had no interest in continuing the conversation. Go away, she thought, leave me alone, I am tired and need some downtime so that I can get my stomach in order and get my body to relax. This is what the specialist had told her to do. Easier said than done, but she had to try harder.

"Can I interest you in a cup of coffee?" Micha wanted to know.

"Can't say I wouldn't love one, but I am not allowed to have it, sorry!" Kate wanted to let him down easy, but let him know that she wanted to be alone, but somehow the man was not so easily discouraged.

"Tea?" he asked with another winning smile.

"Thank you, I really don't want anything," Kate looked back at him. Some people have a hard time taking no for an answer, she thought.

"Peppermint?" He got up, waving his hand as if asking her to walk with him, as if she had agreed to something he had suggested.

"No thank you."

"Please? I just have a question for you and I will never bother you again, if you wish," he looked at her in a pleading way.

"ONE question, that is all?" Kate looked doubtfully at him.

"Promise. Scout's honor," he said hopefully.

"Oh, all right, for trying that hard ... and maybe tea will help," she got up and followed him to the next building where the cafeteria was.

"Shoot away with that ONE question ..." she said while trying to keep up with him. People who are very tall have long strides, so her shorter legs had to work doubly hard, tiring her out quickly, "... for I can't keep up anymore, you walk too fast for me." She bent over, trying to get her breath back.

"On second thought, get the tea, I will wait here," she said, resolved not to walk any further.

Micha could see that she was not willing to do more than that and so as not to lose the progress he had made, he agreed to get her tea and come right back.

Kate sat down on a bench and tried to focus on where she could have run into him, but she came up empty. Then all of a sudden she could feel her heart leaping and she got up to follow the pull she felt. She ended up back in the building in which her class was, except that she walked down the hallway to the left, instead of to the right where her classroom was.

Curious, she went down the hall, past a few more classrooms, and arrived at the back where the conference rooms were located. What was back here that drew her so strongly? She felt the need to open one of the doors to the conference rooms and walk inside. These rooms had no windows for they were built in the interior of the building, sandwiched between classrooms.

Trying to adjust to the dark her hands began to search for the light switch, gliding along the wall. But when she felt the edge of the hard plastic of the light switch she also felt a hand already cupped over the switch. Almost jumping out of her skin, she backed up deeper into the room. She was illuminated by the light that came in from the open door, but too blinded to be able to see who was standing in the dark.

"Who is there?" Her heart was pounding like crazy and she was feeling increasingly dizzy. Her heart was telling her body what her mind needed to hear, and then it crossed her lips.

"Sam?" she whispered hoarsely, almost choking on the name as it crossed her lips. "Not possible. How? ..." She was choking on her words, for her tears had started to flow, anxiety was setting in and she could not breathe. She braced herself on a chair, trying not to pass out so as not to miss him, telling herself to calm down and to control her breathing, but without any success.

The door slowly closed automatically as she stood there fighting for every breath. "I – can't – breathe ..." was the only thing she could get out, but her anxiety had a tight grip on her chest and her stomach did not like it either. With the click of the door she was now standing in a pitch black room listening to her own strained breathing. Her panic was rising and her tears started to flow as she began to cry, which made it even harder for her to breathe. It seemed as if air just did not want to enter her lungs anymore.

Suddenly she could feel a hand on her arched back, soothingly smoothing over her back with circular motions and the deep voice which she knew so well coaching her to breathe: "... deep in, and slowly out ..."

"Sam?" after a little while she slowed her breathing down and started to straighten out, stretching her hand out in front of her, trying to search in the dark for him. He had stepped away but she could feel he was still there. "You are still alive, we all thought ... we buried you ..." was all Kate was able to say before she started to cry again, unable to comprehend how it was possible that he was still alive.

"Oh Kate, what have you done to yourself, you are reduced to skin and bones ..." was the only thing she could hear in the dark, further away than she liked him to be.

"As if you would have done better without me ..." she said while walking toward his voice.

"Don't!" he warned her. "Don't come closer."

"Why?" She froze in the middle of the room, hurt replacing her happiness. "And why did you let us suffer for so long, believing that you were dead?"

"I was not aware of what was going on. They told me you were doing fine, so I took my time recovering. Recovering ... yeah right! Well ... All the king's horses couldn't put Humpty Dumpty back together again ..." he laughed cynically.

"Do the boys know?"

"NO! And you do not know either!"

"Why?"

"Safety reasons," was all she heard, and spoken in a tone that made it clear that the conversation was over for him. "You will not tell them – promise! This was not supposed to go this way. I just could not wait ... I wanted to see you, but I did not think that you would find me ..." She reached out to him again.

"NO Kate ... don't!" she heard him say in a warning voice, making it clear that he wanted her to take him seriously. "Besides, I am still not together and will need more skin grafts until I can be around ..."

"Around what? Around me? Don't you think I should have something to say about that too? Why do you shut me out? Do you think I would think less of you? Since when have looks had anything to do with how we feel about one another?"

And there it was again, the breathing became heavy again, this time out of anger and excitement and the force with which she delivered her words. It was simply too much for her to take in, and in the dark she developed a full-blown asthma attack. Asthma had not been an issue for her for a very long time, but this had been anything but normal times and the strain had been too much for too long. Now she was whistling with every breath, and Sam realized that Kate needed help fast. Before she sank to the floor and passed out she saw the door open, there was a scuffling and the door closed again. When she came to again she was surrounded by her classmates.

"Kate, are you all right? A guy told us you were in trouble here and to come and help you?" Kate had a hard time coming to her senses again and her breathing was still bad. The only thing she could utter was "Puffer ..."

"Gee, Marg, run to her bag, I think she needs her puffer. Asthma Kate, since when? Quick, get that darn thing. Hurry!" Kate recognized that voice. It was Joe who was firing out demands; he was the classmate who sat beside her in class. While Marg ran out, Joe and her other classmates helped her to sit on a chair so she could bend on the table to ease her breathing.

"Kate, breathe in deeply ... calm yourself, slow your heart beat, slow your breathing, calm, calm, peace ..." Joe coached her as Kate fought for every breath, in a cold sweat. Soon Marg came storming back into the room with Kate's bag in her hand, going through the pockets in front of her.

"Where do you keep the darn thing??" she said in frustration, and then she found it. Kate had not used her Ventolin for years, but she made sure that she had always a current prescription and puffer with her just in case of an emergency like today. Today was the first time in many years that she had needed it, and she was very happy that she had it.

After she had her breathing back under control she looked around to find Sam, but the only people beside her were her classmates and her instructor.

"Sam?"

"Kate, you were alone when we came in. A gentleman in the lobby told us he heard you and that you needed help and so we came running. What are you doing in here?" they wanted to know, looking at her in bewilderment.

"Did you see anybody leave?" she asked, starting to cry.

"Kate, you are scaring us. Go home now. Take it easy and if you feel better tomorrow I will see you then, otherwise you must stay in bed and rest. Someone can help you get home if you need assistance." That was her instructor. What wonderful vibes I am giving off, thought Kate. Half way through the semester and I am falling apart on them already.

"I will be fine in a minute. You go back to class and I will take my time and go home. Take notes for me, K?" and with that she hoped that they would leave her alone in her misery.

"Let's give her some space, guys. Kate, we will see you tomorrow – possibly, if not, call in and let us know, all right?" was the last thing she heard from her instructor and with that they filed out of the room, leaving Kate sitting and thinking about what on earth had just happened.

Sam was gone – again – but alive! That is all she wanted to know and all she needed to know: he was alive.

As Kate sat there in a trance the door opened again and Micha came in with the peppermint tea he had gone to fetch.

"Is it safe to come in, or should I wait until the next batch of nurses have gone away?" he wanted to know, grinning. "I never had such a hard time delivering peppermint tea to anybody – ever! It sure is hard not to take it personally!" And with that he sat beside her with the cup of tea and a coffee for himself.

"Where is Sam?" she whispered.

"Sorry?" the man looked at her, stunned.

"Micha was your name, right? I do remember you … now… from home … the tavern … troubles with the wife, right? Where is Sam?" she whispered, more to herself than to him.

He just looked at her and said nothing.

"I see. Thank you for the tea, but I think I will go home and your question will have to wait."

"Take the tea with you, for you have already answered my question," he said helping her up and passing her bag to her. "Need a lift?" But as soon as she stood up she got dizzy and had to sit down again. That was the downside of those wonderful puffers.

"Micha, why are you here? And how is it that you show up at the same time as Sam?" she asked weakly.

"To make sure you are all right," he said matter-of-factly.

"You are my security detail?" she said jokingly, nudging him playfully with her elbow.

"No, I am Sam's," he said seriously and matter-of-factly.

"I was kidding!"

"I was not," he said and then he helped her up and offered her his arm, so she could support herself on him. "The driver will give you a lift home and you make sure you rest, can we agree on that?"

"IF you tell me where Sam is I will do anything you ask me to," she said, giving him the most winning smile she could manage.

"I fear you have got this all wrong ..." he said formally and led her out of the room, down the stairs and into the parking lot. He whispered something into his phone and shortly afterwards a car pulled up in front of them.

Micha opened the door and helped her into the back of the car.

"Stay safe, please." He closed the door and they drove off. It did not take long before the car stopped in front of her house.

"How did you know where to bring me; I have not given you my address yet?" she asked the driver, but he just smiled at her and came around to open the door for her.

"You knew where I live? For how long?" she wanted to know, but the driver just smiled and walked around the car again and drove off.

"Fine then, don't answer!" she hollered after the car that was disappearing in the distance, "... but this is far from over. So take that!" she added angrily.

She searched for her keys and walked to the door of the basement suit. After she had shut it she went straight to the telephone and dialed her specialist's office.

"Yes, hello, this is Kate Von de Vorg, say ... no, the appointment is still fine, say, if I needed to get skin grafts done and I wanted the best in town, where would I go?" she asked and then listened to the secretary's reply. "Thank you," was the only thing she answered and hung up without any explanations.

After a few more phone calls she had the information she needed and after a short nap to rally more strength, she phoned for a taxi and waited for it to come to pick her up.

"Two can play at this game," she said and set out, determined to find the answers to her questions.

Down in the lobby of the clinic she had decided to try first, she asked at the reception for her husband's room and promptly got the answer. Bingo! she thought as she walked to the elevators to get to the floor his room was on.

She could have found it with ease, for there were two men sitting next to the door. One was Micha and the other she did not recognize.

When she walked towards them Micha recognized her right away.

"Don't bother!" she hissed at him, and with a look that could make any tough guy freeze she opened the door.

"Micha, you come with me, and you ..." she looked at the other stunned man, who had no idea what was going on, "You make sure that nobody enters this room until we have left!" she hissed at the other man, who shrank back as he noticed her crest, and also because of the tone of her voice. Yes, she was ready to kill should anyone dare to try to stop her.

Micha just nodded at the other man and then held the door for her so she could enter it quietly. Kate had to grab Micha's arm to get her bearings back, for a sense of intense pain hit her – pain which she now knew was Sam's. After a moment of breathing and pushing the feeling down into her gut, she walked into the room.

The curtains were drawn around the bed and she could hear Sam groan in pain. He could hear steps and had assumed that a nurse was coming to give him more medication.

"The last stuff did not work so well, do you have something stronger?" he wanted to know before she could open the curtains.

Kate looked at Micha, suggesting that he answer.

"It's me Sam, do you need anything?"

"Something for pain would be good for starters," he said. "And the other thing you can't get me anyhow."

Kate opened the curtains and was shocked to see that Sam's face and upper torso were covered in gauze.

She looked questioningly at Micha, who seemed to understand what she wanted to know.

"Sam, your surgery was just a little while ago, shouldn't you still be out? Should I ask someone for more meds?"

"More!" groaned Sam, but Kate took Micha's arm, signaling him not to leave, but also not to follow her further. Micha was curious as to what Kate wanted to do, so to ease his curiosity and concern, Kate opened the curtain so that he could see from where he was standing what she was doing. She looked at him with raised eyebrows, almost asking if it was all right with him and Micha just grinned politely and apologetically back at her.

Kate walked closer to Sam's bed. How badly she wanted to touch him now, but she could also see that that might cause him more pain than he was already in. She rubbed her hands together as she had done the other night, focused her whole being into her hands, closed them into fists and then opened them with her palms down against his body, where she thought his main discomfort must be coming from.

"Thanks nurse," Sam said, feeling some relief from his pain; in fact, he could feel his body healing. "Whatever this is, it is good."

Micha came over and watched her with curiosity, encouraging her to continue. She stopped, exhausted, and caught Micha's arm just in time before she lost her balance, and he walked her back out of the room.

"That was awesome," he said looking down at her, astounded.

"It was ancient," she said as he guided her outside to a chair. He quickly fetched her some cookies and tea.

"Well, whatever it was, you need to get your strength back." Micha waited until she started to eat a little and even though she had a hard time eating, it stayed down. Half an hour later she got up and looked at Micha.

"Micha, we need to work with your strength. You hold me and my arms and I will supply the rest, you think we could do that?"

"Should you not rest some more?" he suggested, worried.

"Will you help, or do I need to do this by myself?" she asked with authority. So Micha went into the room with Kate again. Sam was sleeping. The break in the pain had given him the rest he needed. Carefully so as not to wake him, Kate stood with Micha beside her, and rubbed her hands together again. Her hands hovered over Sam's upper body, then down his arms and down his legs. Then she started on his feet and worked her way up his torso, over his arms and then over his face. Sam felt the healing of his body in a rush of comforting warmth, and when he became aware of the bright light around him through his eyelids, he opened his eyes and found himself looking into Kate's face.

Lost and Found, but Lost Again

"KATE?"

"Hey handsome ..." she said, tired but smiling down at him.

"How does a good dose of ancient light from home feel to you?" she said grinning.

"What did you do?" he said wonderingly.

"I found out a few weeks ago that my hands had some kind of strength and light coming from them. It's the same thing we saw in that family chamber. Do you remember, the light that went from the writing on the walls, to the center stone and into us, remember that? Well, one night one of my friends was suffering from a headache; I massaged her neck and she said her headache went away immediately after I touched her neck. So it came to me that this might be another thing that we needed to discover. Cool ehh? Do your hands do that too?" she wondered.

But instead of answering her he pulled away from her.

"Micha! Take Kate out of here. Kate leaves now! Please do not return." He spoke coldly and firmly, demanding that his wishes be obeyed as if nothing had happened.

"What? What did I do? – Sam! Answer me!" But Sam turned away from her and Micha came to take her arm and to pull her away from the bed to the door.

"Micha, did my husband just dismiss me? Did I hear this right? Did I hear what I heard?" she asked in shock.

Micha did not know what to say. He was stunned. He looked at the woman who had most likely given all she had for her husband, and as he looked down at her not knowing what to say, he watched her face fall as her heart broke into many pieces, and he saw the glitter that had reappeared in her eyes begin to fade. He did not understand why Sam was pushing Kate out of his life now that she knew. There was no point in concealing him from her anymore. It was now obvious to him that those two came as a package deal, and that to keep them apart for safety reasons did not make any sense.

As they stood there Kate's feet gave out. Micha was not surprised. She had been weak already, after she had done such a strenuous thing for Sam, and now her heart that had been keeping her together was shattered. She seemed reduced to a pile of sorrow. He swung his arm under her knees and carried her out of the room as she started to cry.

It felt like hours that he held Kate crying in his arms in the lobby, but then she seemed to collect herself and looked at him with swollen, red, questioning eyes.

"I do not know why," Micha said, knowing what she wanted to know. "I was born into the service and circle of securing the safety of those who carry the crown, but I do not always understand your decisions. That is beyond me, I am so sorry, but I cannot help you there."

Kate looked down at her folded hands for some time, and then took off her wedding band and placed it in Micha's hand.

"Don't Kate, please give him time to come to his senses. It is his pain or the meds speaking. You know that stuff better than me!" Micha pleaded with her, but she just closed his fingers over her ring and held his hand in hers for a moment.

"Do what you do best, Micha. Keep him safe for me. Now I will tell you with whatever authority I have, that you will not come and find me ever again, I need to go and find my place in MY world. Give my boys my love, will you? And Mary ... give Mary a hug from me. Now it is time to find my own way." She got up, took a deep breath and walked to the elevators.

She waved at him, and then the doors closed, leaving a stunned Micha standing in the hallway. He had no idea what to do now, but he picked up the phone and talked to someone in a very quiet voice. Then he hung up and walked back to his post, where he got questioning looks from the other man standing there.

"I'll be damned, but I think we just made the worst mistake by letting her go ... that is what my gut is telling me right now," he said to the other man, who raised his eyebrows, and replied, "Funny you should say that, I was thinking the same thing. What was all that light coming out of the room?"

"Now that was something I will never forget," said Micha and closed his eyes from the strain he felt. When he opened them again he knew what he had to do.

"I'll be right back," he said and walked into the room beside Sam's room, and pulled out his phone while closing the door, then dialed a number he knew by heart.

"Listen, I need to talk ... do you have a moment?" Micha said into the phone, and after listening for a while to someone on the line he continued.

The windows in both rooms were open and Micha and Sam welcomed the fresh air. Sam was having a hard time breathing, but told himself, it was all for the best. It would keep her safe and that was worth all that hardship. Standing at the window he marvelled at how well he felt. Moments ago there was such a burning pain, but now ... he loosened his bandages to inspect his skin, when he heard Micha in the other room and stopped to listen.

"I want out. I have had it. This is all wrong, you hear me? All wrong!" Micha had grown louder and angrier, and after another pause he replied, even more angrily. "What do you mean I can't, hell I can! I cannot protect one life by destroying another. This is just not right. Crown is crown, don't give me that crap. And I don't give a damn about history and honor and all that fancy stuff. I have seen with my own eyes the shining and I tell you there is something important we are missing here, and it is not all about Sam either ... yeah, yeah, he is the biggest part, but he is not the sum of all!"

Micha was pacing up and down the room, holding onto his phone as if he was concerned about losing the connection.

"What are you talking about? I am not getting a thing here? Who can't do what?" he said, growing more and more impatient and loud, and then he listened again to the person on the other end of the line.

"No she has not, but she gave me ... oh shit, you should have seen her, there was no hope in her eyes, and I just let her walk out. I cannot be everywhere ... but I tell you, the crest was glowing like it does at home, and the crown was very visible on the crest, as if it wanted to tell me that it had chosen to stay with her, regardless of how badly we treat her, so there! Your precious history walked into the elevator and left, saying she did not want to be found again ... So now what?"

"Don't snap at me ... of course I am not angry with you, I just ... Oh, I don't know! Either I get some help here or I am relieving myself of my duty and going after her ... choose!" he said threateningly. "I don't know half as much as you about this history crap, but I can tell you this much, that every fiber in my being tells me that men in our past never deserted our women. Never, period! And even more so when they had been chosen and sealed, and for sure not when they had sacrificed so much for people to whom they had no prior connection. This I know, as much as my crest reminds me daily of my duty."

There was silence and then Sam heard one of the beds squeak as Micha sat on it.

"Maybe I need a break, or a translation of this madness," he said, sounding resigned, and then listened again. "Yeah, yeah, I will do my best, whatever ... sure, sure ... How are things at home?" Micha had had enough of the subject and diverted the conversation.

"Why are you not? Where then?" and then there was silence again, and Sam turned away from the window. He had heard enough. Micha was his right hand, top gun in his security squad, but now he was not doing so well with the decisions he had just made, but how to explain to him that it was better she was gone and alive than here and in grave danger? Yet he had to agree. This decision did not feel right to him either. Absentminded and deep in thought Sam kept on unwrapping his bandages and as the gauze came off he could not believe what he saw. He was almost in shock when he hollered for Micha to come in, forgetting that he was on the phone next door.

Micha hung up quickly and rushed back to Sam's room on high alert.

"What's wrong?" he wanted to know, scanning the room but seeing nobody there beside Sam.

"Look!" Sam said to Micha as he continued taking the bandages off his hands and arms and face. "Oh Lord, look!"

Micha could not believe his eyes either. Sam's skin was certainly not perfect, but it was healed. The grafts that had been done hours ago had healed seamlessly, there were scars only where the sutures had been, but the rest was all healed.

"The only thing that did not heal is my back, it's still burning like hell," said Sam to Micha.

"They did not touch your back, and I am not a nurse, but let me have a look," Micha said after marveling and gliding his index finger over one of the scars that had been open earlier. Sam turned his back to him and pulled his hospital gown so as to expose his back to Micha.

"Nope, nothing there, but your back is full of scars and ... ha, and justice ... my friend!" Micha said, and bit his tongue after it was out. He had gone too far and he knew it. On the other hand, being dismissed from Sam's detail would free him to do what he was itching to do anyhow.

Sam went to the dresser to pull out his undershirt and dress shirt.

"What are you doing?" Micha wondered.

"Getting dressed, what does it look like?"

"You have not been cleared by the doctor, and the nurses have not seen you yet. What will you tell them?"

Sam stopped briefly, thought for a moment and then continued dressing.

"It's a miracle, I will shout," Sam said, grinning, as he grabbed his slacks. "Time to leave this place, I hate hospitals." It had been so long since he could dress himself without pain, which made doing so even more enjoyable now.

"Whatever," Micha mumbled as Sam sat down on the chair to tie his shoes. But when Sam heard Micha's comment he stopped, looked up, then finished the tying and sat back in the chair. This was also something he had not done without pain for a long time, but to fully enjoy it, he had to clear the air first.

"All right Micha, what is bothering you?" Sam asked, pretending he had not overheard the conversation earlier.

"Nothing, this is your business and your choices we have to live with," said Micha and hurried to the door to get out of the room before he lost his cool again.

"Sit!" came from Sam, and it clearly was not a request, so Micha turned around reluctantly and cautiously sat on the other chair beside Sam, but not before moving it away from him a bit.

"Talk!"

"About what?"

"Talk! Off the record," Sam said forcefully but he decreased the tension by slowly lowering his hands that he had stretched out before him. "Tell me what is bothering you so much."

"You need to ask?" Micha looked at him, surprised. Sam could not be so forgetful or so callous as to forget what had occurred just an hour ago. He had his hand in his pocket playing with Kate's ring, but it seemed to burn his fingers so he stopped that and pulled his hand out of his pocket again.

"You disapprove that I had to send Kate away, am I right?"

Micha just made a face, showing Sam he was on the right track.

"All right, let me explain. She is not safe around me, as YOU pointed out before, and I have to agree now. We still don't know what is going on and who is after me, so if they get to me, they get to her. She is better off without us, Micha believe me ..."

"Yeah right, that's why you call out her name at night all the time, and that's why she looks like the walking dead. Yeah, I can see the logic ... sure!"

"Don't you see ...?" But Sam did not get to finish, for Micha got up and looked at him angrily.

"Off the record??? Well, let me tell you something. What you did was shitty, low and below anybody's standards, so low that even your crest is giving you hell for it. We can all feel it." He pulled up his sleeve to show Sam the crest that was on his inner lower arm. It had the ring with the crown in the background, but a sword and a dragon on the handle.

"This thing is hurting all of us right now, not only you. Why? I'll tell you why; it's because the decisions you make still have to be approved by the crest. Your choices have to be for your people and not just for you, and if you don't do that, that's when it makes itself known to you and to all of us ... From what I saw in that elevator, the crown was more strongly visible than ever on your wife, dismissed or not!" he added angrily and then he sat down again, deflated. "How could you? After all she did for you and for us?"

"Safety first, is what she always said," Sam said quietly, sounding determined.

"Yeah, that's the other thing. When you do something like that, you are telling the rest of us that we are not doing our jobs right, so that you feel you have to pull a stunt like that. How do you think me and my guys are feeling right now? Reduced to incompetence? Why don't you say it straight to our faces?"

"That was not my intent, Micha, believe me ..."

"Listen, since we are at it, let me finish!" Micha cut him off again, he was past etiquette and politeness. "McGregor did not know Kate from before, so when you sent him to check if she was doing well he had no reference point to compare to, so it is not his fault that he reported to you that she was doing well. Maybe he should have just said, she is alive, but that was all. We are here to serve the crown, all right, to keep you safe, but we cannot keep you safe from yourself, that is beyond our abilities. And the way this is going I can say we are losing the battle, never mind who is after us or who is not. The enemy that is causing the most harm right now lies within, and it most definitely has to do with you refusing to see things as they are. Based on my experience, I can tell you, that a rock alone can be kicked around like it's nothing, but cement that rock into a wall and it can withstand any enemy. But even in that your enemies are winning, for they have succeeded in getting you to believe that you are better off alone. You fool, do I have to spell it out to you, that you are better off in the wall, surrounded by those who can make you stronger, not by yourself? Don't you know better? No, this is worse. You KNEW better. I did not realize this, until today, something that you must have known all along, being together with her for years. Something that became clear to me just a few hours ago ... I had it all wrong ..."

Micha was at a loss for words. He had to reconcile what he knew with what he now learned and witnessed, which changed most, if not all, of his prior opinions. He continued on in a whisper, "I have never, ever seen anything like it before, nor did I think of it as possible." Then he looked up and said strongly, "Do you have any idea what strength lies hidden behind the solidarity of the both of you, or do you choose to ignore it for us who did not know better? The crest has never given rise to as many security details before, at least as far as I know. This tells me, that either you are important, or that both of you are important, or that there is something larger going on than ever before between the two of you, or just simply that there is much in store for you ... You act as if you have not the slightest idea, and maybe you don't, but we do, maybe it is part of our job to know, but the moves you are making these days sabotage all our efforts. Hell ... I am done ... I cannot help you, go ... do ... as you will. I will pack my things tonight."

Sam listened and his emotions went from anger to surprise to thoughtfulness and back to anger, just like the long, colorful rant from Micha. But when Micha was finished Sam was quiet for a moment as he reflected on what Micha had said.

"No, I don't think so Micha," he said calmly. "I used to have Jackson around to set me straight from time to time, but I can't let him know that I am still alive. But you are honest enough to say what you think without holding back, and I like honesty. You are 'IT'," he said grinning. "But next time, Micha, don't wait until you are boiling over; come and talk to me and with your help, I will have a council. Maybe that is why we have such a different security detail. They are all more than that, smarter, thoughtful and observant. Let's start working together. In my company at home it worked wonders. We all started to work as a team and things picked up faster than one could ever have hoped. No more unilateral acts on my part; of course I will still have the last word, but only after I have a bit of input. Now what do you say Micha, are you on board?"

Micha had not seen that coming. He was hoping he would be able to either go home or go on a search tonight, after being released from Sam's service, but now he was being pulled in even closer than before, as he was to function as part of Sam's council as well. He was not sure what to make of it. Either Sam was extremely smart to increase his team, or extremely insecure, so that he had to hide behind others. The latter just did not fit.

"Say again?" he finally said.

"You heard me. Get the doctor, I need to get out of here, then we need to get to the hotel and get together as a group and talk about the next step, what do you say?" Sam put his hand on Micha's shoulder, looking expectantly at him as Micha battled to get his bearings.

"I guess so," was all that he could say for the moment and walked out of the room to fetch the doctor.

To the Jameson family,

Thank you so much for letting me stay with you. The time here has been wonderful, but I need to leave and do not know when I will be back. So not wanting to let you wait indefinitely I am leaving you a month's rent as a 30 day notice, a bit extra for the cleaning, and add again a big, big Thanks and gratitude.

When you hear from Michael, with whom you are in contact for sure, tell him that I had to go away for a little while, but will let him know where I am - when I get where I need to be.

My thoughts will be with you all and ... my thanks will follow you wherever you go and never catch up with you ... ha ha ...

Anyhow, thanks again

Yours truly
Kate Von de Vorg

After writing the letter she felt better. She put it in the envelope, along with the money, grabbed her suitcase and walked out of the door, locked it and pushed the key and the envelope through the mail slot of the door upstairs. She hoped they would understand and felt sorry she could not explain it in person. She took a taxi, and as they travelled she called her school and cancelled the rest of her semester due to illness. Along the way she also stopped at the bank to withdraw a healthy amount of cash, and finally she got to the airport.

Hours later she was on a plane to Paris, France, which she thought was as good a place as any other to begin her journey. In Paris she found a store where she bought good camping gear and transferred all her belongings from her suitcase into her new backpack, rolled her new sleeping bag up, got herself some comfortable clothing and runners, and felt equipped to take on Europe, starting by touring through Paris in a taxi.

When she had had her fill of Paris, she took a taxi to the train station, where she bought a Trans Europe ticket and boarded the next train. The train took her north to the Netherlands but since the train ride had not felt long enough she continued on. Denmark, she thought, would be a good place to rest up a little. The country was mainly flat. A persistent wind blew everywhere. She took a short bus ride to the coast. She ended up renting a room in a small fisherman's village on the west coast of Denmark close to Agerrac. The walks through the small town were the distraction she was looking for, especially the harbor auction hall. New fresh fish of all kinds arrived constantly from the boats, in flat plastic boxes, covered with lots of ice. The men in the back stood around and an auctioneer guided the auction in an unfathomable mumble, which only the men around him seemed to understand. Kate marvelled at how each person participating in the auction had a specific sign to let him know that they were bidding, even though there was hardly any movement. One man winked, another just nodded ever so slightly, and the next tipped his hat. It was like a well-choreographed play, very amusing to watch.

After the auction finished she went off to discover the beach. The dunes, covered with sparse, thick grass seemed to go on forever. She walked on the beach that seemed to have extra sand hills piled up to preserve the dunes. Holding her shoes and socks, she stepped into the water that was cold, even though it was late summer. The waves washed almost angrily around her feet, making the sand below her feet move and causing her feet to tingle. After standing there for a moment she decided to walk down the beach to see what the shoreline would be like further down. Finally her stomach made her realize how long she had been walking. She turned back and it took her several hours to get back to the town she had started off from. Tired, she went to get a bit to eat. Her hair was all messed up from the wind and the salt air and she was physically drained, which felt great considering that she had felt more emotionally than physically exhausted for the longest time. This type of tired felt good and healthy. In her room she drew a bath and soaked in it for as long as the water was comfortably warm. Just don't think was her motto, just don't think. After she had tucked herself into bed and watched a bit of TV, of which she understood little, she turned off her light and slept soundly. She kept up this routine for almost a week, discovering the coastline by foot, sometimes taking the bus inland but always returning to her room. After that week she decided to see Copenhagen, which looked not too far away on the map, and after that she planned to go to Ireland – another place on her bucket list.

Meeting Tina

EVEN THOUGH COPENHAGEN was a beautiful city with a unique character, Kate soon grew restless and felt like moving on, so she was soon on her way to Ireland, but even there she did not stay long. The old country roads winding through the long stretches of green meadows, the old pubs and the towns rich with historic flair all had their charms, but she still did not find what she was looking for – whatever that was. It did not help that the late fall was not the best time to go traveling in northern Europe. One evening while sitting in front of an enchanting fireplace in one of the older cottages that offered room and board, she went through some magazines that had been lying around in her room and came across pictures of Greece and Spain. As she was having a hard time staying warm, the pictures' promise of warm weather, blue skies and warm water quickly made her plan to go to those lovely warm places. She had been here long enough and it was time to give the countries of southern Europe a try.

The next day she packed and headed for the next city to find a train station. Traveling by train was definitely the way to go here. One could see so much on the trips and if one chose to sleep until one got there, that was also an option.

She was in the line-up for a ticket, when she noticed a woman with curly, red hair standing in the same line. She was reading a travel guide, but like Kate she was traveling with a backpack and a sleeping bag, which she held tucked between her feet. She only moved and looked up from her book when the line moved, otherwise she was totally concentrated on what she was reading. It was obvious to Kate that she was not from here, not only because she had American flags on her backpack but also because she seemed more North American than European. That gave Kate some food for thought. What made people from North America so different compared to people from Europe? Well for one thing, she noticed that most North Americans love to talk to strangers if the opportunity arises in a line-up, while most Europeans seem to be much too reserved for that. If they talked to each other it was either professional or because they knew each other from somewhere. Besides that, one just simply did not talk to strangers. Perhaps it was because European countries were over populated, causing people to be rather protective of their privacy.

"Where would you like to go, Miss?" The woman in the booth had started to get annoyed with her. Wrapped up in her thoughts, Kate had not realized that she was in front of the line, and the woman had already inquired once.

"Do you still want a ticket, Miss?" Kate looked at her apologetically and then purchased her ticket and walked to her gate. Day dreaming, she thought, was a new thing she had apparently started to do. Then she remembered the woman with the red hair and turned, but she was gone and Kate felt she had missed talking to someone from closer to home. Home ... well she was not sure where that was any more. She did not feel good about calling it home, for it was after all Sam's house and he no longer wanted to have anything to do with her, so the house, as much as she loved it, was out. But the boys, well the boys who were now grown men but in her eyes were still her boys, they made home to her wherever they were staying. Home is truly where the heart is. She was wondering how they were doing and was longing to get some bear hugs from them, but she was a naturally bad liar, so she was afraid that if she went home they would all be able to read the news of Sam's survival on her face. So in order not to blow his cover, she had to stay far away from the support system she really wanted to be closest to right now:

her boys, Mary and Pia and Jackson. If one wants to be alone that is one thing, but knowing she could not return to see the kids because she could not lie, felt to her like being cut off, and as such so very lonely. Many times she had the phone in her hands just to call them to let them know she was all right, but then she feared they would ask where she was and what would she say? By now Michael had probably been informed of her sudden departure from Vancouver and most likely had set everything in motion to find her, but since Kate did everything with cash it would be hard for him to do so. She was sure the boys and Mary and her friends would most likely be the only ones missing her. She had told Micha not to bother to look for her, not that he would. Micha was a kind soul and was torn when they said good-bye, she could tell. His allegiance was with the crest not only with Sam, but his responsibility was mostly to Sam, the one who wore the crown, so he was bound by this calling, but she could tell he wanted to extend the courtesy to her as well, for she also wore it. She hoped that she had made the blurry lines clear to him again, so that he had a way to continue functioning without feeling torn between Sam and her.

"Is this seat taken?" Someone pulled her out of her thoughts again. While Kate was pondering and missing her boys she had boarded the train, found a seat and was sitting staring out of the window.

Kate looked up, startled and somewhat annoyed with herself for the bad habit she had started to develop, that of being oblivious to her surroundings. She looked straight into a friendly face surrounded by curly, red hair; it was the woman she had seen earlier reading the travel guide in the line up.

"No, please do sit down," was Kate's reply, and she was glad that the day seemed to be taking a good turn after all. She wanted to talk to the woman so badly and had been disappointed when she had missed her opportunity, but now it seemed that fate had other plans.

"I am so excited to be going to warmer places. The damp weather up here reminds me a bit too much of home," the woman said while taking off layers of clothing, stuffing them into her backpack, and pushing it into the upper compartment. Then she sat down across from Kate, still holding her travel guide, and looking so enthusiastic that it infected Kate and she started to look forward with the same anticipation.

"I think you are not from around here either, but from somewhere in North America like me, am I right?" Kate wanted to know to satisfy her nagging curiosity. The other woman just started to laugh and then said in an upbeat way, "How did you guess? Yes, all the way from the other side of the pond. Now in search of warm weather, handsome men and colorful flowers and uhhhh so much more ..." she said, so excited that she had a hard time containing herself and remaining on her seat. Kate just started to laugh as well.

"Nice to meet you ... my name is Kate."

"Pleased to meet you, I'm Tina," she said, stretching out a hand, which Kate gladly took. Tina had such a hearty shake that Kate laughed and said, "I'm not as robust as you are Tina, so take it easy with the hand shake."

Tina let her hand go immediately. "I am so sorry. First of all I am so excited to get there, then second I wanted to meet someone just like you to travel with and third ... well, I have forgotten what's third ... Oh look, we're moving! Several meters closer to our destination!" she proclaimed, while looking excitedly outside. The train had started to roll and Tina's positive flair changed the atmosphere in the cabin from sad to excited, embracing life not burying it. This was exactly what Kate so desperately needed.

"Well Tina, I am glad I ran into you as well," she said, while watching her new companion pointing out things that were flying past their window.

For hours Tina told her excitedly of the things she had learned from her travel guide, things she said they would have to see and where they could be found. She truly had studied the guide from cover to cover, Kate could tell, so she listened with interest to all the things Tina told her. By the time they felt hungry and wanted to go to get a bit to eat at the bistro, Kate thought that there was no point in going to Spain anymore, for she felt she now knew almost everything that there was to know. When she mentioned this to Tina, Tina just looked at her, shocked: "Hearing things is one thing Kate, but seeing and ohh tasting it, now that is another thing altogether." She pronounced the end of her statement heavily.

"Oh all right then, we will go with educated but fresh eyes and conquer Spain. Have mercy on their souls! Harrrgh," she said imitating a pirate, so that Tina started to laugh. "Oh this is good ... you are good! Are you an actress or something?" Tina wondered as they worked their way along the narrow hallway of the train.

"Yeah right, no way ... " said Kate, looking further ahead. She had started to feel dizzy again and was hoping they would get there quickly.

"You feeling all right?" Tina stopped her, holding her elbow and turning a surprised Kate around so she could look at her. "I can see green in your face. I am no doctor, but the color does not suit you," she said with big eyes, so that Kate had to laugh again.

"Tina, I think it's you who is the actress! I haven't laughed so much for a long time. So yeah, I am a bit dizzy, but I think I can see the bistro already, so let's get going," she said, glad that Tina was such a clown, otherwise having her turn and touch her might have seemed a bit weird.

"Kate, you let me know if I can help with anything, OK? I know we have not known each other for long, but it feels to me like I have known you forever. I enjoy this very much, so pooping out on me is not really an option ... soooo ... let me be a good friend. If you would like me to get you something while you wait in the cabin, I would be honored to do so ... but speak up quickly, for I might change my mind and rescind my offer," she said with a big smile.

"All right. A nice sandwich and a Coke would be great. I will keep the light in the window waiting for your return, oh Romeo," Kate said, at first a bit deflated but then with a strong tone of humor.

"Well Juliet, I will do as you command. Sandwich and Coke coming up and then into the resting position with you. Doctor's orders," Tina said.

"You said you are no Doctor!" Kate complained, so Tina put her hand in front of her mouth, looked suspiciously to the right and left and whispered to her, "That does not mean that anybody needs to know." Expecting something serious and then receiving this funny statement made Kate laugh out loud.

"All right Dr. Tina, off with you and I will head back to the cabin," and with that she turned and was glad when she found their booth and could sit and rest. Her weight had improved, well all right, only a bit. She had not lost any more weight, and had gained a few pounds over the last few weeks, but still it was not enough to keep up with the demands of all the traveling she was doing.

Before Tina could return Kate was fast asleep. When she woke it was dark in their compartment. Tina was sitting in her seat looking out of the window. On the seat beside her was Kate's food. Tina had patiently waited for her to wake.

"How long was I out?"

"Oh, don't worry about it. A few hours or so, you obviously needed rest more than food." Tina looked at her with concern, and pulled out the table in front of Kate and placed her sandwich and Coke on it.

"Say Kate, I have a proposal to make, and I hope you find it appealing."

Kate looked up from her sandwich and waited for what was to come.

"It looks to me as if someone should look out for you a little, and you seem to me a person who could keep me out of trouble, so why don't we keep on traveling together from this point on?" Tina looked pleadingly at her, so that Kate just had to grin, and then she took a big bite out of her sandwich, chewed for a minute and looked at Tina, who was becoming uncomfortable with the prolonged silence.

"I mean if you would prefer to be alone and all ..." Tina slid in before Kate had her mouth empty enough to answer.

"That will be just fine with me Tina, no worries. But I might change my mind if you keep me from eating my sandwich," she said, grinning as she took another large bite out of her bun.

"I am so glad, we will have fun, you will see, and I will be quiet now ... and let you eat," Tina said, and sat so straight in her seat that Kate had to laugh again.

"Why don't you read me more out of your book, while I am eating ... what do you say?" Kate said after a moment and Tina gladly obliged.

Their journey was pleasant. They left the train in Köln, spent several days there to see a bit of the city, and continued onto Frankfurt where they also explored the surrounding towns, and then boarded a train to Madrid, which would cut straight through France.

"You think we will get to see a bit of those beautiful lavender fields in Provence?" Tina wondered.

"Oh that would be good, wouldn't it? I would enjoy that a lot as well. I so love lavender, don't you?" Kate said, forgetting her problems thanks to the wonderful distraction of Tina. And as luck would have it, they saw several lavender fields on the way, close to the border of Spain. Life could be so wonderful if people did not make it so hard for each other. It did not make much sense why people did it, but the fact remained that if there were no Tina, she did not know where she would be right now. "Thank you Lord for Tina, my saving grace," Kate prayed and fell asleep, listening to Tina reading a page out of her book about lavender production.

Arriving in Madrid, Kate could see why Tina was counting on her to keep her out of trouble. She was like a butterfly, wanting to go in a million directions at once. She wanted to see this and that, all at the same time, so that Kate had to prioritize what was possible in one day.

Because they could share a room they did not need to go to cheap hotels, but were able to afford nicer hotels and still save money. Some people looked questioningly at them, wondering if there was more to them than just friends, but Kate could not care less what others thought of them, she was having fun and so was Tina, and nothing would be allowed to stand in the way of that. Kate started to enjoy living again, laughing and eating. She looked much healthier and the sun tanned her skin and bleached her hair lighter. She looked positively healthy in no time. Not only the presence of a refreshing, life-loving person like Tina had done that to her, but also the weather, the colors, the people and the country itself. She felt like ... she had come home somehow, even though it was ridiculous, as she had never been to Madrid before.

During the day they were always on the go, sightseeing, shopping and going for coffee, and at night they fell into their beds, exhausted. Soon there was nothing new to see as they had speedily visited everything in the city, so Kate suggested one night that they keep on traveling along the coast. Something had caught her interest and something was drawing her. She wanted and needed to know what it was. Having been in Madrid for long enough to visit everything at least twice, Tina was all ears when she heard of Kate's plans.

"We could start at the northern end of Spain and go full circle all the way around along the coast, what do you think?" Kate said, waiting for objections that did not come.

"Cool, do you think we should rent a car, or go by bus or train?"

"I have asked around and I think we will get the most out of it if we go by bus. Would that be all right with you? We could travel only short distances, visit the areas along the way, and do that over again for as long as we need."

"When do we leave?" Tina wanted to know, getting out her suitcase.

"Not tonight, Tina, I am beat," said Kate with a big grin, "How about in the next few days?"

Arriving in Spain

"HOLA MARCUS," Duke de la Rosa de Maya sat beside Marcus and waved to the waitress for a cup of espresso as he spoke in Spanish to his nephew. "Marcus, I will have to go down to Madrid in the next few days. You will need to take care of things for me here."

"No problem, do you know when you will be going and when you will be back?"

"No, not yet, but I have a feeling I will know soon," said the Duke, looking out to sea. Leave it to Marcus to know where one could relax with the best view on the coast, he thought. This was an especially beautiful spot. Today they could see all the way to the islands. The sun was warm but the breeze from the ocean kept the temperature comfortable. Looking out to the water they could see the starchy, white sails of sail boats against the bright blue sky, and as the Atlantic was especially calm today the reflections of the boat were as clear as the boats themselves.

The waitress came with the espresso and the Duke looked at her appreciatively and took a sip from his little cup. "Gracias," he said as she smiled at him and walked off.

"How is business, Marcus?" He looked with interest at his nephew.

"Good. Busy at the moment," Marcus replied. "We are building apartments on the coast and there is much to do. Crazy right now to be precise, so I thought I had to escape for a moment, so as not to go totally insane with it," Marcus said, smiling at him while turning his index finger on the side of his ear and making a crazy face with it.

"You are born to lead, you will do fine," the Duke said seriously to him and then looked back to the sea. "The waters are too calm. Trouble is coming," he said.

"Don't tell me that you believe in those old wives' tales!" Marcus grinned at him. But the Duke remained serious, looking back out to the Atlantic as if he was looking for something. "You young people need to listen to your history and surroundings better, it would help you a lot. But what can I say besides, son, that soon you will see it. I feel these things in my bones," he said, deep in thought.

They sat there for some time discussing business and family matters, until they observed from the right over the tree line, two white triangles gliding towards the mouth of the port. His uncle was on his feet in seconds, watching the sails in shock, but Marcus took it as enjoyment. A beautiful two-mast sailboat came around the tip of the shoreline, turning and approaching their harbor. It had two flags. The hull of the boat was unusual and original. The beautiful shape of the boat told every sailor that its owner had taken great pride in details and that this was a custom design.

"We have to get the boat out one of these days," Marcus said, getting up as well, marveling at the beauty that had turned towards them. Its flags were Canadian, plus another that looked a bit more complicated and had an obvious crown on it, declaring that nobility was on board.

"Por la chupaja!" said the Duke and grew pale underneath his tan. Marcus looked at his uncle in stunned amazement, as he rarely ever heard him swore, and looked in the direction he was looking to see what was bothering him so much. "I told you the water was too calm, trouble has found us," the Duke said, scowling at Marcus and then walked off, abandoning his coffee. Marcus slapped some money on the table and rushed after him.

"What is the matter?" he wanted to know, having a hard time catching up with him.

"They have finally returned to claim what is theirs, after all these generations," the Duke said, "I knew this day would come, but I was hoping it would be after I was gone."

"What and who have come? What are you talking about?" Marcus had a hard time keeping up with him.

"Did you not see the flag on the second mast?" the Duke said, looking annoyed. "He has returned to claim what is his," said the Duke while flying up the stairs to his car. "I will have to greet them, even though I should sound the alarm and start running," he said, out of breath, "But I will have to do my duty."

Marcus stood there totally confused, watching his uncle drive off towards the street that led to the marina and just shook his head. 'Is the old man losing it?' he wondered, but then he looked at his watch and realized that it was time to get back to his job site, so even though he wanted to see what all the commotion was about, duty called and he walked towards his car.

Arriving down at the marina the Duke turned off his motor and walked out to where the sailboat was trying to drop anchor. He watched a man and a woman who were talking loudly in English with each other and shortly after started laughing, as their attempt to pull the boat closer seemed to be a bit harder than they had bargained for. The woman looked familiar somehow, somewhat like one of his relatives, but he did not recognize the man. After a moment of trying to pull the boat to the dock another man came on deck. He was very tall and big, yet slender; he also spoke English and helped the other man to pull the boat closer to the floating dock, which he did with ease. After the Duke looked at them he knew who the larger man was without a doubt, but he was puzzled about the woman.

After the boat had finally come to rest, the sails had been taken down and all the ropes had been fastened, the Duke carefully approached the side of the boat.

"Hola? Bienvenidos a España," he said with a bow. The two men looked at each other but the woman snapped up to look at the Duke.

"Frederico?!" she said a bit louder than necessary. The Duke looked at her, puzzled and confused to be addressed in such an informal way and also by his name. How did she know his name? He decided to overlook the impoliteness and just answered with "Si?".

The woman started to laugh and then spoke Spanish to him.

"Frederico, it is me, Melanie, have you already forgotten me?" That was when realization dawned on the concerned Duke.

"Melanie? Dona Melanie de la Rosa?" he said, happily surprised and still wondering what she was doing on a boat with the flag of the enemy. "Poor Melanie, you had to fulfill the deed? But having what we owed him, why has he returned?"

"What?" Melanie jumped over the edge of the boat onto the dock and stood in front of the Duke, looking stunned, but then decided to hug him anyway.

"What are you talking about? Are the years getting to you?" she said still in Spanish, grinning at him. "Let me introduce you to my husband, Mike." She pointed toward the shorter man on the boat and said in English: "Mike, this is the patriarch of my family, Duke Frederico de la Rosa de Maya. I have no clue how we are related, but here in Spain that is not an issue. You must have met him many years ago, do you remember? We are related somehow through the sister of my mother's cousin, but he remains as always the head of the family de la Rosa. And Mike remember, he is a Duke, so you had better be on your best behavior," she scowled at her husband. The Duke gave Mike a nod, but his interest lay with Sam.

"Sea bienvenido don Von de Voergenson de Islandia," said the Duke and bowed again to Sam, who was just as stunned as the rest of them, having understood only the little Melanie spoke to Mike.

"He said, you are greeted, Von de Voergenson of Island, I think," Melanie translated, puzzled. Sam was surprised that the man knew him, even though he was a bit off with the name. He walked over to him and stretched out his hand. "Sam Von de Vorg, and I am also from Canada. But please call me Sam," he said, waiting for the Duke to take his hand.

Melanie quickly translated what Sam had said to the Duke into Spanish, whereupon the Duke looked in amazement at Sam's friendly gesture, and then hesitantly took his hand. "Duque Frederico de la Rosa de Maya, su servidor," he said, bowing while shaking his hand.

"He said Duke Frederico de la Rosa de Maya, at your service," Melanie said with a questioning look at Sam.

"Melanie, the man knows something we obviously do not, could you fill us in?" Mike said to Melanie, after exchanging a confused look with Sam.

"I have no idea what is going on Mike, but for now let's just enjoy the hospitality and then we can ask him if he has seen Kate anywhere. If anyone will know, he will. Sam, he is the Spanish version of your Mary at home, and like you he is important as the head of the family and ruler of this region and has the say around here, if you get my drift. So I do not understand why he orders himself under you though, Sam," Melanie said and then looked at the Duke expectantly.

"You must have anticipated our arrival, how is that?" Melanie said in Spanish to the Duke.

"First my dear, your Spanish, even though with a bit of an accent, is still very good, and secondly, no, this has been a surprise to me as well. Why did you not let us know that you would be coming home to visit? We could have gotten the whole family together. They would all love to see you. But I am not so sure about Lord Von de Voergen," he said to her, the last part so quiet that only she could hear it.

"Frederico, he is our son-in-law and we love him like our own son, what is your problem with him? We have not been here long enough to get into trouble or cause any issues, so what's with all the concerns?" Melanie said to him in Spanish, and climbed back over the edge of the boat to Sam and hooked her arm around his.

"Mel, is there a problem?" Sam wondered while looking down at her.

"I have no idea," she said, "But I will find out, believe me Sam, nobody picks on my son and lives out the day unharmed," she said while she looked inquisitively at the Duke.

"Well, I will be expecting you for dinner at 6 o'clock Melanie, you know the way, and bring your company, I see you have found a way to make friends with those we never could." The Duke spoke quickly in Spanish to her and was about to turn to leave.

"Ask him how he knew I was on board," Sam whispered to Mel and she nodded and then asked the Duke quickly before he could leave. The Duke merely pointed to the top of the boat, at the flag on the mast. Then he walked off, shaking his head all the way to his parked car. This would be difficult to explain to his family, especially the older generation, who knew their history well.

Evening came and Sam did not feel very well. He was looking forward to meeting Mel's and therefore Kate's family, but he was just not up to it. So he excused himself and stayed behind, but not without having Mel promise him that she would do everything she could to find out more about Kate's whereabouts, if it should turn out that her family knew something.

The evening was wonderful, even though there was little time to be alone with the Duke. He had been busy, and had got almost the whole family together; they sat together out on the veranda overlooking the vineyards, with the Atlantic and the harbor clearly in view, as well as the yacht on which they had come. Even though Mike spoke not a word of Spanish, he had no trouble in communicating with Mel's family, using his hands and facial expressions and gestures to communicate what he wanted and to answer their questions. After that evening he thought he should be undefeatable at charades, when he got back home.

Journey to Spain

S AM FELT BAD, he did not want to be unsociable but he really felt
weak and a bit sick to his stomach, and after Mel had made sure
that he was all right she had decided to leave him behind with
some Gravol and a hot tea on a lounge chair on the deck. She had
noticed that he seemed to handle the cold of the evening unusually
well, and appeared to be rather happy to be left behind. She had asked
him if he felt unwelcome due to the behavior of the Duke earlier, but
he had reassured her many times that it had nothing to do with that, so
reluctantly they had left him on the boat.

Sam enjoyed the time alone. Ever since he had started to represent
the crown, there had been always security details and people to meet.
He so longed for some private time, time with Kate at his side with just
them alone, down time. He had to find her soon, but for now rest was
on the program. Micha was to meet them soon on land if they chose to
remain here, but if it was possible he hoped to travel longer with Mike
and Mel. Confiding in them was the best thing he ever did. They had
been so shocked when he stood in front of them at their front door.
Mel had started to cry and Mike who was fighting tears just took him

in his arms.

After he had given them a moment or two to regain their composure, of course they wanted to know how Kate had reacted when she had found out he was alive. He had no idea how to tell them that he had actually sent her away. So he had been at a loss for words, until Mike demanded, "What has she done now?"

"No, this time she went beyond the call of duty, but I messed up," said Sam miserably. They went into the living room and after Mike had poured them all a glass of his best wine they waited patiently to hear the whole story. He told them about the time in Vancouver and what he had felt, that she would be safer if he sent her away, at which Mel gasped.

"Please Sam, tell me you are joking?" she said. He just shook his head and kept on talking, telling them that after they felt it was safe again, they had started to search for her. He was wondering if they knew where she would go, for they had lost the trail months ago and had no idea where she might be now. They could not trace her through her credit cards because she was traveling with cash. She had told Micha that she did not want to be found, and just how serious she was about that was now very clear to them.

"Sam, when she does something, she does it right. I am afraid if she has decided she does not want to be found, you will have a hard time finding her ...she gets that from me ... the same determination," Mike said and then he looked at Mel. "Say Sam, your blood hounds... What have they found out so far?" he said, which made Sam smile.

"Not sure how Micha would feel about being called a blood hound, Mike, but I like the comparison," Sam said, putting his head back onto the cushion of the sofa and closing his eyes.

"Well as long as it's just us, I can call them whatever I like. When did they say they would come back to babysit you again? Do they even know you are here?" Mike asked with a grin, but then he saw his wife's scowling look and thought better of it.

"When was the last time you slept? I mean slept well, Sam?" she wondered, watching him.

"I don't sleep well without her, you know that already, so you can imagine how long. My hope was you would know where to look next." His disappointment was written all over his face.

"Well, maybe we can come up with something for you," Mel said, worrying about Kate as well. "Do you have any clue at all?"

"I believe she went to Europe, for there was a booking in our name on a flight to Paris, but that was over a month ago. She could be back already by now, but we cannot find any trace so far."

"Mel? She wouldn't go and see your family by any chance, would she?" Mike wanted to know.

"She does not know them. Besides that, she does not know about her roots and family history, so why would she go there?" Mel said dismissively, but Sam was desperate for any possible solution, so he perked up.

"Why did you never tell her about her extended family and your family history? Mine was always very important to me," Sam asked curiously.

"Oh, it's nothing like as interesting as yours, Sam, ruler of tribes," she said, pretending to bow to him, which got them all to laugh. "My family is part of the Spanish court, but my mother asked me to go overseas and take Kate with me and to never come back, due to a curse or something like that, which was placed on the girls and women of our family. Well, as a well-educated person, this did not sit very well with me, as you can imagine."

"Yeah, I can remember that, Mel," said Mike, "We visited them briefly and you went into labor prematurely, so Kate was born in Spain." Mike leaned back and tried to remember more about that time. "We thought she would be a boy, but she was such a cute little girl that all my hopes for having a boy just went out of the window as soon as she looked at me with those big eyes and smiled at me. I loved that kid from the first moment I laid my eyes on her. But your mother and pretty much all of your relatives were so concerned for her safety, right after they saw that she was a girl. They said something about … goodness, what did they say, Mel, I forgot … anyhow, they asked us to go back to Canada and to keep her away from Spain."

Mike was straining to remember all the details and even Mel had a hard time remembering it all. However, she said that she had stayed in touch with her mother and the rest of the family via Skype and phone, but Kate had never known much about that part of her family. She never really missed it, for Mike's family was so big, so there was no lack of cousins and aunts and uncles and she never really missed the other side of the family.

"Well, by now I have learned that often history calls upon us to fulfill itself in us, that is how it was for me, as you most likely know, from what Kate must have told you. Maybe we should look there and see if we find some indication of her whereabouts," Sam said through almost closed eyes.

"Yes, yes – yes … we will do that … now rest Sam, you are safe here … rest," said Mel really quietly, waving Mike out of the living room, and minutes later Sam fell asleep.

Mel and Mike went into the kitchen so as not to disturb Sam while they discussed the matter further. "I think it's possible that she might have followed her instincts to find a home somewhere else, where she would not be reminded of him, what do you think?" Mel looked at Mike.

"I am not flying girl, if that is what you are getting at, and that boy out there has no energy left for a trip like that," Mike said pouting, but then he started to grin so mischievously that Mel was nervous of what was to come next. "So … what do you think … should we put the big lady to the test? She is made for high seas, perfect for the task, and it would be relaxing for Sam as well. We would not need much security around, besides we will keep them busy on the boat in other ways, and it would be great for some highly overdue one-on-one time with him, what do you think? Pretty please, oh come on honey, say YES!?" Mike pleaded, yet Mel did not look convinced. "Mel, it would be fun for all of us and we would have the whole Spanish coast to ourselves to find her, say yes, Mel, honey, please? How about I do the dishes for the whole journey …"

"Oh all right, you do the dishes all the way there and back and we have a deal," and Mike took his wife and swirled her around in excitement. "Put me down this instant or I will change my mind," she threatened him, which he did with the biggest grin one could imagine.

"I will go tomorrow and check her out and have her lowered into the water. You need to convince Sam it's a good idea, could you do that and we could be off in a week, tops? You think he would stick around that long?"

"Stick around for what?" Sam stood at the doorway with heavy eyes and looked at them, puzzled. "I apologize, I must have fallen asleep. Sorry about that. What are you up to Mike? I can see from your face that you are having a hard time containing it." Sam looked sleepy but he grinned at Mike, who tried to make his face as serious as possible. "Well son, we thought we could take the big lady and check Spain out with you, via boat. By the looks of it you could use some down time. What do you say, are you on board with this plan?"

"To Europe via sail boat? How long would that take?" Sam wondered, yawning. "Sorry – again," he said apologetically to Mel, who just waved it away with a hand motion in mid air, letting him know that there was nothing to apologize for. "Who cares? Are you in a hurry to get somewhere?"

"Yeah kind of," he smiled, insinuating that he was looking forward to getting the search over with and was in a hurry to come to rest again.

"Well, I'll tell you what," Mel came over to Sam and put her arm around his waist, "You get some rest first, then we will go shopping and look for the stuff we will need for the next few weeks, and the rest Mike will take care of. Is – that – right?" she looked at her rather pleased husband, who just nodded in full agreement.

"We will let your blood hounds know where we are going, and they can meet us there, how about that?" Mike's wheels were turning at an incredible speed. "To please Micha, we can take a couple of your blood hounds on board, but they will do anything but security, for there is much work on a big sail boat like my big lady. We will of course not tell them that most of the work could be done electronically." Mike was visibly pleased with the plan and kept on going. "It might also give your men some shore leave when we leave with the boat, they must be homesick by now, are they not?"

That was a point on which Sam had to agree with him. Giving Micha and his men some time off would do them good. They deserved to go home and see their families and from there, they could fly to meet him later. He would promise not to leave the ship unless they had arrived, that should convince Micha.

"All right, it's a plan," Sam agreed, giving in to the pleading look of Mike, who now clapped his hands and was half way to the door. "Got to check the boat and get her into the water … much to do, see ya later," and with a slap on Sam's shoulder and a peck on his wife's mouth he left in a hurry.

"There goes the boy I fell in love with; some things never change. With Mike it's always the water and the boats," Mel said.

"Yeah, and do not forget yourself. He would not do it without you," Sam said, grinning down at her.

"He better not," she smiled back up at him, which made him remember Kate so much that it hurt, and Mel seemed to guess what he was thinking.

"You miss her badly, eh?" she said when she saw the pain in his face as he walked back to the living room and sat in one of the chairs and closed his eyes. Even if it cost him everything he had, he would find her and win her back, he swore that on everything he held dear. He must have fallen asleep until an hour later when he heard, "Sam, I am going out to run some errands, all right? Will you be fine?"

"Yup."

Mel left, closing the door behind her and locking it. She looked around but the neighborhood seemed to be the same as ever. After hearing of the threats that Sam had to deal with these days, she wanted to make sure that he was safe in their house.

Sam got up and looked around. He found a bookshelf of photo albums and found the ones of Kate's childhood, and went back to the sofa with three large photo albums and began to look through them. He came to one picture that looked a lot like she looked today and he held his hand on it and just called her through it, but she did not answer. This is how Mike found him an hour later, returning before Mel could get back from the grocery store. Mel's truck was gone and he had assumed Sam was with her, but when he got into the living room he found him sitting with his head back again, sleeping with his hand on the picture of Kate, when she graduated from her second degree. This man really did love his precious girl and it was endearing to see him so hurt. Mike went into the kitchen to make some noise, so that Sam could get his bearings back.

"Gee, I seem to drift off a lot in your house, do you have laughing gas somewhere around here that does that to me, or what is it?" Sam said, walking into the kitchen where Mike was making coffee.

"Sorry for waking you, I thought you would be with Mel. Don't blame you, she will be flying around the grocery store trying to get everything yummy she can think of to spoil you as much as she can, for she is back in mother mode," Mike said, grinning. "She does spoiling well, and I enjoy having you here too, son, so don't mess it up."

That's when the doorbell rang. "End of the peace," Sam said and walked to the door. "Hey Micha, come in and get to know my in-laws,"

Sam said to Micha, who scowled at him.

"I had to have your truck tracked to find you, you know that?" he said angrily, so Sam looked outside at his truck and hollered, "Traitor!" then he pushed Micha through the door into the kitchen.

"How about picking up the phone to let me know where you are or where you are going?" Micha said furiously, but stopped when he saw Mike.

"Mike," he said and got the same back: "Micha," but he had to grin.

"Could you knock some sense into that royal skull of his!?" he pleaded with Mike.

"Nope, that is your job. Here he gets spoiled. Coffee?"

"Ah, yes that would be nice, thank you," Micha said and then looked at Sam again. "How long are we here, so that I can tell the guys to spread out?"

"Why don't you tell him about our plans, Sam?" said Mike, as he placed a couple of cups in front of Sam and Micha.

"Oh, please do," said Micha mockingly, so that even Sam had to fight a laugh.

"Looks like you guys will have some time off in the next little while," Sam said, taking a sip of coffee. Micha's mouth fell open as Sam turned and said with a grin to Mike, "Good coffee."

"Care to elaborate?" said Micha, disregarding his coffee.

"Well, by the end of week I will be on the sail boat with Mike on the way to Spain. Before we go ashore I will contact you and you can meet me there. You guys can go home meanwhile and then fly to Spain. You don't have to worry: I will stay on board until you guys have arrived, now how is that for a plan?"

Micha had remembered his coffee and taken a sip but now he almost choked on it. "Sail boat? Spain? What am I missing?"

"Micha, you guys are overdue for some leave. When I am on a sail boat you will not be able to do much, so take the time off and go home, leave me with some guys if you have to, but they need to be willing to work on the boat as well. So, go home my friend, see your wife and your children and take most of the guys with you."

"I will see your route and you will check in with me regularly. You swear that you will let me know before you go ashore, and that you will wait until we arrive, yes?"

"Swear," Sam said and then he remembered Kate, how she did that with him and he with her, the scout's honor thing. How he missed her, but he had to think of something else now.

Micha and Mike looked at each other and Mike just gave him an insinuating glance, they both knew where Sam went in his thoughts.

"We leave in a week at the latest Micha. You can see us off if you like, does that work for you?" Mike looked at Micha who nodded. "You know that nobody can know about Sam's survival, until we have the people who are behind it all, right?"

"Yes, I got that. What suspects do you have so far?" Mike was familiar with military actions; he had been in the navy all his life and had worked his way up to the top ranks, so he was keen to hear the details.

"Don't worry, we will find them, that IS my job, as you pointed out already," was all that Micha would say.

Sam remained stuck at home for the rest of the week with either Mel or Mike but he did not mind, for both told him things about Kate that he had always wanted to hear.

The night before the planned departure Mike came home with a present for Sam, which he was to open right away, for Mike could not wait to see his reaction. Micha and the guys had been invited for coffee and they all watched Sam open it. It was a flag with his royal crest on it.

Micha was not so excited for he was concerned that it would attract unwelcome attention by showing that Sam was on board, but all agreed that if they only raised it on the mast once they were out at sea it should be fine.

All went well; even the send-off was picture perfect. Much on the boat was automatic, but Mike did not reveal this to the three men who joined them on the journey. With the extra help Mike could save the power the electronics would use. In the evenings the men usually kept to themselves below deck, which made it possible for Mike and Sam to be alone. They had a great time bonding and shared much with each other. Mike was very much like his own dad, Sam thought, and that was most likely the reason they got along so well.

When Sam opened his eyes on deck he noticed that it had grown dark and the solar lamp had started to glow. Further down the dock he also noticed a figure approaching. It was neither Mike nor Mel. That much he could make out.

Sam was on full alert, when he noticed a second man approaching a bit faster and catching up with the first. For a moment he considered, if sending his skeleton security detail of three men to scout out the town, might have been not such a good idea, but then he thought differently, as he recognized one of the two men who came close to the side of the boat, and heard the Duke speak to him in Spanish. Sam did not understand what he said, so the other man translated for him.

"Don Von de Voergenson, buenas noches, please be not alarmed, my name is Marcus and you have met Duke Frederic, my uncle, already, I believe?"

"Yeah, but you did worry me. My full security detail has not yet arrived, and if something had happened, Micha would never let me out of his sight again – and I do enjoy a bit of privacy and personal space ... at times," Sam said, grinning.

"You did not come to dinner, because of the lack of security?" he said, astounded.

"No, I am not feeling well tonight, I guess after the constant motion my stomach needs to get used to solid ground again," Sam said and waved them on board, offering them the chairs in front of him.

The Duke took one seat and then he pointed to Marcus. He spoke with very fast Spanish to Marcus, who now found a seat as well. Sam sat as well, and Marcus addressed him. "Don Von de Voergenson, we ..."

But now it was Sam who held up his hands, which made both men look at him in surprise. "Let's try that again. My name is Sam," he said and stretched his hand out to the Duke. Marcus translated, and the Duke looked at Sam for a moment and then smiled and took his hand and said, "Para it yo soy Frederico," and then followed up with a flood of Spanish, which made Sam look pleadingly at Marcus.

"He said that he is pleased to meet on friendly terms, even though it was more than he was hoping for and deserved. So he said you may call him Frederico, which I must tell you is highly unusual for him; he is extending a great honor to you."

"Marcus, tell me, why would he do that?" Sam wondered, but then the Duke unleashed another flood of Spanish and Marcus translated again.

"He said that this would be a subject for another day. But first let me catch up with what he wanted me to ask you earlier. He was wondering since he heard from Melanie that you did not feel well … well … he wanted to know if there was anything he could do to help. We brought a strong – ahh, alcohol, I think you would call it. We use it for upset stomachs. If you would be interested and trust us enough to try it, it will help, but I warn you, it tastes … well, awful, you will feel like dying for 30 seconds it tastes that bad, but then you will feel well, I promise."

"You seem concerned about my trust in your intentions. Is there any reason why I should not trust you, after all, you are family, are you not?" Sam found this all a bit strange, but then again this was another country with different customs, maybe this was the norm.

"Marcus, please translate," Sam said as the man just stared at him. He turned and translated to the Duke, who looked at Marcus with something close to shock, and then he looked at Sam again and appeared to have tears in his eyes. "Si la familia, si!" he said with a broken voice.

Now that was something Sam could understand even without translation. The Duke agreed.

"Believe me, we did not expect this from you," said Marcus, which was obviously not a translation from the Duke, but his own thought. "We will talk more, but for now let's tend to your stomach." He pulled a bottle out of the bag he had brought along, and then unpacked white bread, large slices of cheese and some grapes from a basket, placing it all on the table in front of them.

Sam took the offered glass and drained it with one swallow. He felt sicker after the drink than he had before.

"All right Marcus, are you trying to kill me?" he said, coughing and holding his stomach and growing greener as the moments passed.

"No, no, it will get better, just wait a moment, count to thirty and you will see," Marcus said as both of them looked at him, concerned.

With Marcus translating, the Duke told Sam that if this did not make him feel better, they would take him to the local doctor. But as Marcus had said, Sam's stomach started to sort itself out after a minute or so. He could breathe again and he looked at the bottle. "Dam, what is in that stuff?" and Marcus translated so that the Duke started to laugh. "He was wondering if you felt better?" Marcus said to Sam.

"Yes, thank you. Tell him I owe him one," Sam said, but the Duke just became serious again. "No …" he said shaking his head. Marcus added, "He said that the debt will never be paid unless …"

"Unless what?" Sam wanted to know for he had a feeling he was missing something important.

"He does not mean to be disrespectful, but he wanted to know why you have come, since you obviously did not come with ill will," Marcus asked him.

"Good that you asked, because that makes it easier for me ask you. I am looking for my wife Kate, Melanie's daughter, has he seen or heard anything about a Canadian woman traveling through the region? Mel told me if anyone would know, then it would be him," Sam said, looking expectantly at Frederico.

"No por favor, no lo dejas suceder denuevo," the Duke said, looking shocked.

"Marcus?"

"He said please don't let it happen again," Marcus said.

"Again?"

The Duke got up and bowed to Sam and waved at Marcus to follow him.

"Was it something I said?" Sam looked at Marcus.

"Let us do some research. We will let you know if we find out anything. Thank you for your hospitality, see you soon, Don …" but Sam cut him off, "I'm Sam to you too …"

"Thank you Sam, we will keep you posted. Rest your stomach and keep the bottle for later use, if you need it, buenas noches."

"Buenas noches Marcus. Frederico," said Sam. Marcus grinned at him. "Pretty good. Just stay for a little bit longer and you will speak great Spanish."

"You think so? Now what did I do to offend Frederico so badly, that he runs off like that?"

"History Sam, but I need to catch up with him. See you again soon."

"I guess so …" said Sam, puzzled, watching them walking off quickly. He was disappointed that they had not been able to tell him anything about Kate.

First Trip in Spain

S AM JUST HAD RETURNED with Mel and Mike from the plaza. His stomach had settled after the treatment with that rather awful tasting yet highly effective liquor he had received from Frederico and Marcus. He wanted to send them a note and hoped that Mel could translate it into Spanish so they would understand without Marcus having to translate. Mel thought it was a wonderful idea and was fully committed to sit down right after they arrived at the yacht.

Mike and Sam had had some laughs that day at the plaza, when Sam had told him about his first impression of Spain.

"You know I thought you accidentally shifted the map and got us to Ireland, Mike when I came up on deck looking at the Spanish coast," Sam said.

"Yeah, you sure sleep a lot for someone who comes from a direct line of some important Vikings. If your ancestors had done so, they would have ended up in Canada long before they actually did, missing Spain altogether, drifting right past it and all the way to the Canadian coast. Maybe then they would have woken." Mike was holding his sides from laughing, imagining snoring, fierce-looking Vikings in drifting boats. His laughter was so contagious that they all had to laugh.

"Well I was imagining white beaches, but most of the time I saw high cliff sides along the coast, which is what I would expect from Ireland," Sam added, to recover a little of his dignity. "I did enjoy reading your family book, Mel, in fact I was reading it till late that night, before I set eyes on your homeland. It is so interesting, come to think of it, that must have been the reason why it is noted in our books as the land of the people living on the rocks. It makes sense now. But we should head back to the boat. Micha will arrive shortly with the guys and I had promised not to go ashore before he got here."

"You did not leave the boat for days," Mel answered surprised, "Not your fault if the flights were all booked up, now was it? And we needed to have some nice native cuisine for a change. You would not let me go to dinner alone, now would you?" she looked at him playfully with big eyes.

"Puppy eyes ... And Kate always accused me of having those. You are worse, Mel," Sam said laughing, then looked at Mike. "What do you do when she does that?"

"Pray for mercy, what else can I do?" Mike said and kissed Mel on the forehead and pulled her along. "Let's get the boy back to the boat, before we get an earful from his people, Mel," he said grinning.

They walked back to the dock and found a note taped to a chair on the deck. Sam picked it up and read it out loud so that Mel and Mike could hear what was written on it as well.

Hola Sam,

I could not find you, so I thought I would leave this note.

My uncle wanted me to let you know right away, that Kate has been seen at one of the local markets, we believe. Our family is big, as you know by now, and he called around after he had spoken to you, to have eyes everywhere. If she has the same crest and mark as you do, then he believes it is her.

I have been asked to meet him tomorrow, if you would like to join me, it is a nice drive, and you are welcome. I will have to stop at our main estate first though. If you would like to come, then meet me at the cafe at the pier tomorrow at 7a.m. We have a 2-hour drive ahead and you could see a bit of

our country along the way...
Marcus

"Well that settles that. I know where I am going tomorrow. It will be interesting to see how Micha will react to that excursion," Sam said, passing the note to Mel who read it over again.

"What will you do, I mean, when you find Kate? What do you plan to tell her so she will listen?" Mel wondered out loud.

"It will come to me," said Sam disappearing through the door, and then added not so confidently, " ... I hope." But before she could add anything she heard footsteps on the dock, which announced the arrival of Sam's security detail.

"Sam," Mel hollered after him, "Take a deep breath, it will be your last one as a free man – for the cavalry has arrived." And with that she turned and waved to Micha.

Micha's Arrival in Spain

SAM AND MICHA IMMEDIATELY BEGAN to make strategic plans about how to find Kate. Thanks to Mel's relatives this should not be quite as difficult as first expected. Extended relatives in Spain, Sam still had to wrap his head around that idea. Who would have thought they would end up here, and what else was in store for them to discover on this journey, he wondered.

Micha on the other hand was not so pleased, suffering jet-lag from the flight and only having half of his crew present did not put him in the most pleasant of moods. Just a week earlier he had found out about the shooting at home and had delegated half of his resources to that. He was battling the war on too many fronts. Trying to keep the boys safe in Canada, now Sam in Spain and Kate, well who knew where she was, it was daunting. Somehow he had to get them closer together to be able to ensure better security. Sam was all upbeat and positive but he had a hard time remaining positive these days. The failed attempt to kill Daniel in front of the hospital had been too close a call for him. Of course they had concealed from Daniel and Michael what was really going on. Both had believed the story that the bullet was meant for the woman who was actually hit. He knew better and so did the council members. There was a real threat to the Von de Vorg family and what made it most difficult was that nobody knew who was behind it and why. His suspicion was that it must have something to do with the revelation of Sam's status. They were still researching who could possibly be opposing Sam, but besides old tales and long past historic events nothing seemed to pop up that could remotely make sense.

Whoever it was, they were always a step ahead of him and it had started to get to him. What was he missing? On top of it all there had to be so much secrecy about the whereabouts of all the family members, and then there was the constant obliviousness that the Von de Vorgs seemed to enjoy that drove him crazy. Well, that was with the exception of Michael. Micha thought about him for a moment. Yes, surely he was starting to clue in more and more to what was really going on. It must be due to his connection with the Navy, which made him more aware of true dangers, so he had to be extra cautious around him until he could finally tell him the truth. He hoped that this would be sooner rather than later, for Michael would be a valuable asset to the efforts to keep the family safe.

Mary, who kept them all connected, seemed to believe that Michael and Daniel would be safer if they did not know, but he had a feeling that she was starting to second guess her decision. She was also the only one at home who knew about Sam's survival. It was just amazing how she knew everything before he could tell her. She had known that Sam was alive long before she had sent Sam's main security person to search for Sam. First he had thought she would not survive Sam's funeral. She had withdrawn and fallen into silence, grieving the death of yet another monarch of Von de Vorg. She had seen too many deaths over her lifetime and this blow seemed to be the hardest of all. For weeks they barely heard or saw her, she had withdrawn into her house and requested to be left alone, refusing any visitors. They all worried about both Kate and Mary, for Kate also seemed to be having great difficulties dealing with the loss. In these times they realized how they had depended on the strong characters that were the glue that held the community together. Without them they had to fend for themselves and they did so with great difficulty.

Weeks after the funeral it had become obvious that Kate would be better off away from the places that reminded her of Sam, and they had all agreed to encourage her to go south for a little while, either to do some courses, or to do some extended visiting either in Vancouver or with her parents. After Kate had left they had focused on getting Mary through the worst, which was a bit more difficult at first, but after a few months of having both boys in town she had started to step up again to assist Michael and Daniel in the possibly pending shift of authority.

Yet it seemed to never be the right time. The crest did not shift allegiance, which puzzled not only Mary but many others as well, including him. After a year of trying to figure it out they just left it to be dealt with when the time was right. Mary was deep in her books and it was around the time of the first anniversary of Sam's death when she suddenly demanded that he and some others from the security detail meet at her home in secret one night.

She was her old self, only a bit older and worn from the strain of the past year. The sparkle was back in her eyes and she fired commands when they all arrived at her place. Somehow she knew that Sam was alive and they had to find him. Why she did not know sooner no one knew, but her worries were now a thing of the past. Even she was not sure how she knew, but she wanted to have him check on Kate without telling her what they suspected, and she wanted the men to work in teams to search the crash site again and follow up on any clues they could possibly dig up after such a long time.

Micha remembered that heavy moment well. He remembered having very little hope they would find anything new, but he also knew that Mary was never wrong when it came to the crest and its descendants. He had learned long before that when it came to Mary, relying on faith was the only way to go. But as he had suspected, all the people who they had talked to a year before could not tell them anything more; rather they remembered even less than they had remembered then, so he had decided that this time he would conduct the search differently, not trying to find a body but rather trying to find a survivor. They had extended the search to hospitals, rescue and rehab centers and an endless list of private clinics in the area of the crash site and beyond. They received a list of people whose names had not yet been positively identified, either due to injury or because nobody had reported them as missing. He was surprised how many there had been, and so they split up to cover as many as possible over the large area they had decided to search.

That was how they had finally found Sam. It turned out that he had come in with severe burns on his back, under arms and legs, and had been in a coma due to blood loss and shock. Apparently, he had been in a coma for several months but the hospital had not taken him off life support, as there was no one to make that decision. How Sam had got to the hospital remained a mystery. The front desk had heard someone scream for help and they had all run to see what was going on, and by the time all was sorted out nobody had seen who had delivered Sam.

He had arrived with no identification on him, except for an elaborate ring. Of course they could not find him in the database of missing persons, for Sam was presumed dead. After several months the director of the hospital decided to take responsibility and turn off the life support machines, to give Sam the peace he deserved. Their trauma and burn teams had done their best, but healing had to come from the person himself, and that was going at a very slow rate. After the machines had stopped they had all waited for him to die but he had not. They still called it a miracle, but he started breathing on his own while remaining comatose.

Several months and skin transplants later Sam had wakened. It was not clear for how long he had been awake, for the nurse had not noticed the changes in his vital signs at first, and he was unable to speak. After that, due to the high level of pain, he was kept in an artificial coma and then when the worst had passed they had decided to let him slowly regain consciousness. By then they had still not completed all the transplants Sam needed, so he was put under several times more for pain control.

That had been the state in which his men had found Sam. Yes, that was a moment he would never forget, he thought. It was that moment when he got the call from Leo he almost passed out himself, but then he had passed on the news to his men, and when they arrived he made the executive decision that needed to be made on Sam's behalf. It was amusing and he still had to grin when he thought of the shocked faces of the healthcare team when they found out whom they had nursed for so long. He had assured himself first that it was really Sam. He was allowed into Sam's room only after he submitted to the nurse's demands to put on a hospital gown, mask, gloves and shoe protectors as a precaution against infection. At first he thought this was slightly over the top, but when he saw Sam he understood perfectly. In fact he could have started to cry right on the spot. Here was his friend and head of the house of Von de Vorg, with tons of gauze wrapped over the still healing and angry looking skin of his back and legs. It took all his strength not to start crying, and he could only pray that it looked worse than it was. After that shocking experience he went into the lobby, gave some instructions to his team, took out his phone and dialed Mary's number. With great care he constructed in his mind what he would tell her. She was fragile these days as it was and he needed to be really careful about what he told her. Enough to give her hope but not so much as to give her a heart attack. Mary answered on the first ring.

"Yes Micha I know, you found him," she said happily, "But nobody can know, you hear? As long as he is presumed dead, he is safe. We have to find out what is going on and who is behind all this first, do you hear me boy?"

'Boy?' he thought, he was almost as tall as Sam and could take on several men at once if he had too, so he was hardly a 'boy', but the way she said it was more endearing than belittling, so he let it go.

"Well then, what else would I have to say? You seem to know it all. Who told you?" he wondered.

"Nobody needs to tell me, Micha, you know that, I could ... feel it ... somehow, and when you called I knew it was to confirm what I already knew, but nobody can know, you hear, not even Kate. We need to make sure that the living are safe first before we look after the safety of the considered dead, do you understand what I am trying to say here? Oh I could dance on the roof if these old legs would let me. What a happy day it is, is it not?" she said happily through the phone.

"Mary ..." Now how could he tell her what a terrible state Sam was in, after she just told him how happy she was?

"Don't worry Micha, he will be fine, I know it, believe me I KNOW ..." Then she began to sing, "Oh happy day..." and he could not bring himself to tell her what he had seen and shortly after they ended the conversation.

"All will be fine," he repeated, "All will be fine ..."

Then he had to deal with the hospital administration, so his gloomy thoughts and feelings had to wait for another time.

In the meeting with the hospital administrators they had agreed to keep Sam nameless and had allowed him to take care of the security detail, as long as he and his men did not interfere with hospital routines and dressed according to hospital policies and infection protocol. Later in the week a substantial sum of money had been transferred to the hospital by Mary. She had spoken directly with the hospital director himself about what she wanted done, and he had been very accommodating after her convincing communications and considerable 'donation'.

From that moment on everything had gone well. Sam had improved considerably faster once he had him, his old friend and his personal security, by his side, as he could understand him better and convey his needs to the nurses. Yes, everything went well, until Sam asked him where Kate was, and that was when things started to deteriorate. At first Sam was infuriated that they had not told Kate of his whereabouts, but then he had understood the reason behind it and had agreed that it would be for the best if she remained in the dark a bit longer. For her safety, nothing was too hard for Sam.

As soon as Sam was able to do some exercise and walk a few steps again, his reason went out of the window and it did not take long until they decided that he and Sam would personally check on her, just to make sure she was all right. The reassurances from the two men he had sent out to report back to him about how she was, just were not good enough for him anymore. He had to see it for himself, and so he had arranged to have Sam transferred to the special unit in Vancouver General Hospital for some more skin grafts, and prior to that he would arrange for them to be somewhere where they would see Kate without her knowing it.

The plan was flawless until Kate almost recognized him in the lobby where he was shadowing her. He could have ripped off the head of one of his men, for Kate looked anything but well. She had lost more weight and looked like a walking skeleton. The two had never really met for there was no need for security at home; only once when she was new in town, he had wanted to introduce himself and she had suggested that he come to a counseling appointment at her office. It must have been something Sam had done to set him up, he was sure. It was so like him, but otherwise he could not remember ever speaking to Kate directly, except to congratulate her at their wedding on the cruise ship, but there had been so many people she most likely had not even noticed him, and that was exactly how it needed to be. Security needed to be unseen until needed, and in those times all was well, there had been no need for them to step up. Oh yes, those good old quiet and innocent days.

Well Kate had not quite placed him when she had seen him in the lobby in Vancouver. After what had happened, he would never underestimate the bond between those two ever again. Kate had not seen Sam on that occasion, but somehow she had known he was there. Following her instincts had led her straight to the room which he had suggested to Sam they use as Plan B, should something go wrong. The room had no windows and the plan was that he would find a way to get Sam out of there, or keep him concealed until she was out of sight. Yeah the plan had been good, except Sam was still in the room when she made it there.

Micha could still remember that awful day like yesterday. He remembered the ride to the hospital after Kate had collapsed when she had recognized Sam. It had taken three of his men to hurriedly get Sam to the waiting car. He had stayed behind to ensure that Kate was taken care of.

After he found her surrounded by people who were taking care of her and made certain she was all right, he quickly caught up with the car that was taking Sam to the hospital. He had traded places with one of the men in the car, but found that Sam was not saying much, which was usually a bad sign, for that was when Sam was fighting for control.

He thought he had pushed their friendship to the max, for he had come between Sam and the woman who he treasured more than life itself, and that was a most dangerous place to be. Sam had been so angry with him; one could have cut the air with a knife it was so thick with negative energy. When Sam finally spoke he threatened him, saying that if he ever again abused his trust, he should leave quickly before he could catch him, and he knew that Sam meant business. He shook his head sadly as he remembered.

Sam had said harshly that he could even feel the bones on her back, she had been in such a state of 'well being'. He thought that the only thing that kept Sam together that day most likely had been those bandages and the pain that was created by the exertion of trying to contain and control himself. He thought that if Sam had not been in such good shape, he would most likely not have survived the ride to the hospital. He was so beside himself. Sam expressed his complete disappointment in him, and he could not blame him. He explained to him that the men he had sent to keep an eye on Kate had not known her before, so they had no reference point as to how she had looked before. For them she was alive, going to school, and being with other people, which to them added up to being well. Yet he had to shiver to himself. Kate had looked awful, no question about it. If she had lost just a few more pounds, they would have had to admit her to an eating disorder clinic involuntarily.

The phone had finally rung and he had answered it gladly. Every chance to get a bit of distance from Sam was a welcome distraction right now. It had been Mary, who sensed that something was awfully wrong and wanted to check with him. Before he could say much Sam took the phone out of his hand and for the first time in his life said harsh words to Mary. He could remember them as if it was yesterday. Sam had made his position clear to her. He told her that this time she had overstepped her rights and gone above his authority, which was noted and not appreciated. He had said that if she ever again made decisions over his head regarding his wife she would have to bear the consequences. Sam had said that so sharply that he had held his breath. Mary had apologized, telling him that it had been for Kate's safety, and urging Sam not to be angry with him for he had simply followed her orders while Sam was unconscious.

It was the first time he had heard Sam speaking with the full authority of a leader and letting his subjects know he was in control. He had hung up on the poor woman and given him an angry look but said nothing, which was almost worse than if he had given him hell. He hated silent treatments more than anything else. Finally at the hospital, Sam opened the door before the car even came to a complete stop, got out and went straight to the door of the waiting director, who had been notified that his hospital was receiving a rather important patient. Sam was not in the mood for any pleasantries but he put on a good face for the excited man, and followed him as he took care of his needs and arranged teams for his care. He and his men just followed like puppies. Nobody wanted to make any fuss regarding security so as not to rock the boat. They also did not want to make themselves conspicuous, because that might attract the attention of the people they were trying to hide from.

When Sam finally went for surgery, he could breathe again. Sleeping, he looked so at peace. How deceiving looks could be. He vowed at that moment that he would make it up to him if it cost him everything he had. Relaxed and relieved he sank on to a stool and dialed Mary's number fully expecting to hear a sobbing voice, but on the contrary she sounded angry.

"Micha," he remembered she had said to him, "How directly do I need to tell you my wishes for you to know that I mean what I say? Did I or did I not tell you that Kate had to stay in the dark for a bit longer, until Sam was past the worst and we knew what we are dealing with here? And please elaborate on why Sam was so infuriated. I do believe I have never ever heard him so angry and upset. What on earth happened down there?"

"I know Mary, but you also know Sam, if he gets something in his head ... and his demands and wishes supersede yours, forgive me, but they do, and he wanted to see her. I just did not realize how connected they are. Man, they don't even need to be in visual distance, they know where the other is just by feeling it ..."

"That does not explain his emotional state, Micha. What are you not telling me?" Mary demanded.

"It is Kate, Mary. She is a walking skeleton, a shadow of herself, she looks awful. I don't know what's keeping her on her feet, but if there is no change soon, there will be nothing left of her. Sam saw that, he was beside himself when he noticed he could feel the bones of her back when she started to get an asthmatic attack from the excitement of seeing him. When she collapsed in shock, it took all of us to get him away from her."

"You said the guys said she was doing well ... I do not understand!" Mary was speechless. They both knew that Sam's reaction was called for and they had dropped the ball somewhere, but there was just so much that had happened that nobody knew how it had happened.

"Mary I should have checked on her myself. The guys just did not know what to compare her to and thought of her just as a skinny lady and did not see anything wrong with that. They did not know that Kate is not normally like that. It is my fault, I should have checked myself, but I also did not want to leave Sam's side ..."

"No, this one is on me Micha, I am sorry for leaving you hanging like this with so many loose ends to take care of, we should have been more aware. Kate is not part of your care, not directly, the lady has her own security detail, and I totally forgot to activate their service. I am getting old and forgetful."

"What do you mean she has her own? I am head of the security detail: is there something I should know?" he said, puzzled.

"You know Micha, the crest had her detail activated but I did not clue in. Now that you tell me what is going on, I understand and realize that I have missed some important things that I must remedy pronto. Keep your detail on her a bit longer, but I am sending her security detail down immediately. I will let you know when you can focus just on Sam again. There is much to do now. But before I go, do I dare ask how Sam is doing?" Mary asked sheepishly.

That had brought a smile to his face. He almost could see her through the phone. Relieved that he would get some help for Kate and that the air was less tense between them he had informed her that he was back in surgery. Some of his scars had broken open due to his exertion in the car, but besides being in a bad state emotionally, he was in pretty good shape physically, so the doctors told him. Since they had taken him into the operating room he could finally get a breather. She had assured him he was not alone in all this and that she would do her best to get things going to ease his burden and to hang in there.

He had then hung up with the request that she should give his wife a hug and a kiss and tell her he loved and missed her. Mary had giggled like a young school girl and said that she would go as far as a hug but that kissing was up to him when he came up to see her again, and then hung up. He had thought then that things could not get worse, but he had been wrong.

Kate was resourceful and it had only taken her a day to find them. She was not even angry at him even though he felt he deserved it, but she came to do the most incredible thing he had ever seen. She used the ancient light to heal Sam. She went at it relentlessly, resting in between and then with his help she did it over and over again, mending him with a light that was so bright that he had to avert his eyes, not wanting to close them and miss what was going on. Then he had hoped that when Sam came out of it, all would be better and they would pick up where they had left off two years ago, but Sam had sent her away.

Sam had chosen the worst possible time to accept the necessity of staying away from Kate for her own safety. For Kate it was the last straw. She had now lost the one thing that had kept her together and that broke her. After she had given him her wedding ring and had left the hospital that day, he could have beaten Sam up, or at least left him to his own fate. He so wanted to straighten him up, but who could do that with someone who was struggling with so much pain and agony?

The only thing that kept him there was a talk with his wife. He had talked to her wanting to leave Sam's side, loyalty and royalty had its place but he could no longer find his place in it. She had a way of calming him down even though to this day he could not fully understand why Sam had done what he did. Yes safety was important, but surely they could have managed better with them both together? And then the reversal had come. Kate was lost and he and Sam were searching for her, only this time she was determined not to ever be found again, and she had succeeded up to this point. Finally having caught up with her here in Spain gave him hope that there would finally be an end to a long saga of grief and sorrow. He was more than ready to bring it to an end; a happy end if he had anything to say about it.

"What do you think, Micha?" he heard Sam say, when he opened his eyes and realized that he had fallen asleep while reminiscing about the past.

"What? About what?" Micha said sleepily and looked at Sam with half open eyes. The sun here was way too bright for him and he really could use some shuteye right about now.

"Well I was suggesting we split up and go up and down the coast but I can see that will have to wait until tomorrow. You guys are a bit too tired to get to work right away so we will take it easy for a few more days. It will not make much difference ... I think ..." he said, not sounding very convinced.

"While you sleep and relax I will talk to Marcus a bit more," Sam said to reassure Micha that he was being taken care of, so Micha could truly rest and get back on his feet again in his own time.

"Who is Marcus?" Micha wanted to know, a bit alarmed that Sam was around someone he had not yet checked out.

"You will never believe me," Sam said smiling.

"Well try me, by now I can see that I will soon see pigs fly," Micha said, tired and worn out.

"Marcus is a relative of Kate, I think a cousin or something like that, and he is a duke, I believe. They still have those here," Sam said grinning and feeling smug as he finally knew more than Micha did.

"Dukes ... Kings ... chambermaids ... I need my bed. So if you can manage to stay out of harm's way for a few days that would be appreciated. You think you can pull that off?" Micha got up and looked at Sam expectantly with a critical eye.

"Party pooper," was all that Sam could say, but he was grinning from ear to ear.

"I don't like what I am seeing, so I better stay up..." said Micha and sat back down, disappointed.

"Oh all right, I will do my best. Mike will keep an eye on things and Mel will translate should the need arise. You have checked their criminal records out already, right?" Sam said, fighting really hard not to laugh.

"Very funny, but I can see you have enough people around you for a little while, so yes, I will go and rest now. See you in the morning, maybe ... if I ever wake up again from this bloody nightmare, that is ..." and he got up again and left to find his room.

"When was the last time you were with your wife, Micha?" Sam hollered after him.

"Thanks to you it has been so long, that I think I will need an introduction when I finally see her again," he hollered back down to him, but he had to smile as well. Sam's mood was contagious. Well, maybe it was the beautiful weather down here or the hope that came with every day. Who knows, he enjoyed Sam this way more than when he was all downcast and depressed ... but for him now, bed was exactly what he needed and he would claim it without any further delay.

Painful Memories

"OOH, I SO LIKE A LITTLE INTRIGUE. Tell me more, Sam," Marcus said over a good cup of coffee that was almost too strong for Sam. The two men had met for an early breakfast on the balcony from which the Duke and Marcus had seen Mike's boat with Sam's flag the first time.

"Well, I thought, after you had finished what you needed to do today, you could show me around a bit. We could get to know each other a bit better, which would be good from a family point of view as well as diplomatically. What do you think? I thought a ride through the country or along the coast line with the top down ... kind of having some well-deserved fun, with the purpose of looking for Kate, how does that sound to you?"

"This sounds good to me, but go back to the beginning, you had me there already," Marcus said looking over his cup to Sam. He was a large man, Marcus thought, and if his eyes were not so friendly and mischievously sparkling he could come across as rather intimidating. What he had learned about Sam so far was all good. The man had a good sense of humor, enjoyed a laugh, took life in his stride, although that might be expected having had a near death experience recently, but he was also well educated and interesting to talk to. His cousin did choose well, he thought; if he ever got to know her, that would be the icing on the cake.

"So how do you think we could flush her out?" Marcus wondered, reaching for a bun and some cheese.

"First of all we need to check the hotels; everybody needs a place to sleep. Secondly Kate loves to dance. Being on a holiday, I cannot see why she would deprive herself of going out to dance if she had a chance. Therefore we might need to do a bit of bar hopping," Sam mumbled with his mouth half full of bread and delicious homemade jam.

"Bar, what?" Marcus looked up at him wondering if Sam was pulling his leg.

"You know, going to a few bars and dance clubs, to ask around a bit if someone has seen her. There can't be too many Canadian women traveling on their own here, now can there?" Sam wondered and looked expectantly at Marcus, who thought about what Sam was proposing.

"You would be surprised, but it is worth a shot. Well, when do you want to hop the bars?" Marcus wanted to know, for he needed to plan ahead as well. The thought of getting back to his sites had now been buried, for he would never get an opportunity like this to get to know someone like Sam, never mind what their history was like. Sam knew much about business and economics and there was much they could learn from each other, so he had put his site manager in charge and decided to enjoy the time with Sam and his uncle.

"Nope, we hop no bars, we go bar hopping, big difference," Sam said, amused. "In the daytime you can show me around and in the evening we can check out the dance clubs, what do you think? We could ask Mike to join us, in fact why don't we do this along the coast, moving up via the sailboat and checking out all the nice places in Spain, are you in?" Sam said leaning over to Marcus expectantly.

"Who can say no to such a face?" said Marcus mimicking his mother so both men started to laugh.

"What do we do with the guys that came yesterday?"

"Well considering how beat they are, Mike and I thought of making them a permanent quarters below deck on the boat. There is plenty of space and we figured out we could get some supplies this morning to get them set up. When we start our 'Hopping thing'," Sam said that while making quotation marks in the air, "They can rest while we have fun, oops, search for leads – of course," Sam said leaning back, rather pleased with himself.

"That could actually work," Marcus said, thinking about where they could get all the material they needed for the boat that Sam wanted fast, in one stop.

"There is a place near where my uncle met me this morning. I will drop you off, you collect what you need and have it sent to the boat, while I will show you the coastline from up there. While you are building what you need to build in the boat I figure you have plenty of help to get it done fast, so I will go back up to our family estate. We can meet up down here to hop tonight."

The rest of the breakfast was combined with making plans and lists of what Sam needed. Sam had already made the plan the night before and shared it with Mike, how he would suggest changing the belly of the beast so as to maximize comfort below deck. Mike had been impressed. Now it was only a matter of putting it all into action. Before they knew it an hour had passed and so they left in a hurry to make up for lost time, and by the evening the bottom of the boat was set up for six men to sleep comfortably in cots, with some storage for belongings. Sam was rather proud of his craftsman skills, never mind that working with wood was something he loved to do and found therapeutic anyway. The design came rather fast, since his architect training kicked into full gear, especially when they needed to shape cots to the shape of the boat, so that it was practical and also aesthetically pleasing.

When the first cots were completed Mel and Mike took a cab into town. When they returned Mike carried a load of bags with bedding, foamies, cushions and pillows. Finally arriving at the boat, Mike fell into the second best chair, exhausted.

"This woman is going to be the death of me one day," he complained to Sam, who just grinned and looked at a pleased Mel, who started to put the bedding over the pillows and to stuff the light blankets which she carried into the duvet covers, wanting to be ready to take over the site as soon as construction and cleaning was finished.

Micha was also pleased with the result. He could get more rest, which was a big plus, while he was able to keep an eye on Sam, which made it perfect. A match made in heaven from where he stood. Yet the idea of Sam driving around the countryside with Marcus did make him feel uneasy. It took some articulate persusasion from Marcus to convince Micha that with all the tourists around, they would not attract any attention at all, so Micha decided to temporarily agree to it and see how things developed.

After Mel took over the finished cots, Sam and Marcus went for a ride around town to see if by any chance Kate had been there, but there had been no trace of a single Canadian woman, according to the shop and restaurant owners. They soon gave up, since the town was not that big and Sam was exhausted from the hard labor they had done on the boat. After saying goodbye to Marcus on the dock, and after agreeing to start their plan to travel around the Spanish coast the next day, Sam checked on the men who were finally able to go to sleep, knowing he was on board. The area below deck was cozy. Mel's woman's touch made it look comfortable and elegant at the same time. What a difference a woman's touch can make he thought, even the pillows looked like they had been custom ordered and were color coordinated with the bedding of the cots. Mel and Mike had been waiting for him for a nightcap and soon all the lights went out.

The next day driving with Marcus was more than fun. Marcus seemed to be carved out of the same wood as he was. Business oriented, with good taste in women, judging by the picture of his wife and children who were still in school in northern Spain. He lived with a similar life philosophy to Sam's, taking every day as a gift and making the best of it. They laughed about the same things and enjoyed the occasional disagreement when trying to convince the other of their point of view. In short, they hit it off right from the start. The only difference was their physical appearance, for Sam was at least two heads taller than Marcus, and their complexions were very different: Sam was blond and blue eyed, while Marcus was much darker with black hair, dark brown eyes and a deep tan. Otherwise they could have passed as brothers due to the way they interacted with each other.

"Ah, what a shame you came from those Vikings," Marcus said slapping him laughingly on the shoulders.

"Yeah, quite a shame and what a shame you come from those softy 'High and Mighties' from Spain," Sam laughed back, "You have potential to be more, man," he said, holding his sides because he was laughing so hard, but then he sobered right up.

"Marcus, where are we?" he wanted to know urgently.

"I don't know. Haven't been paying attention. In Spain?" Marcus said, laughing. "Well, we are close to the boat, look over there, it is coming around the bend. They are not far behind."

Sam pulled out his phone and called Mike.

"Hey Mike could you hang back a bit?" and then he listened to what the other person said on the phone and added soberly to something the other person said on the phone, "Yeah, would not give us away too quick, element of surprise, you know," and he hung up. Marcus looked at him, then stated with a shrug: "Oh never mind telling the stupid 'High and Mighties' what is going on. I just take orders these days of where I have to go," Marcus said looking at Sam expectantly.

"Well this one I cannot explain to you, but you see Kate and I have ... a connection ... we know and sense each other's presence. Now since I was less distracted, just sitting here and enjoying your beautiful country side, I sensed her right away when we came around the bend up there. If we are lucky she is busy and has not clued in yet. It helps that she does not know that I have caught up with her and am looking for her." Sam looked apologetically at Marcus, hoping he would understand what he was talking about, and not think he was crazy.

"Nah man, I do understand. I can be in a crowded room of thousands, but I know if my wife is looking at me from the other side of the room, so yeah I have an idea," he said and then he cautiously continued, "Now I do not want to interfere or stick my nose into something where I should not stick my rather nice nose, if I may say so ..." with that he looked into the side mirror to admire his nose, which made Sam laugh again.

"Oh you're so vain," he started to sing.

"Shhh, don't scare the wild life, we have a law about that," Marcus said, "and I have to say... there is nothing as perfect ... as my nose," he added laughing.

"Is Pinocchio a Spanish story, or did they get the inspiration from you, I wonder?" Sam roared, hitting his knees, which stuck up a little due to the low seats in the sports car.

"But honestly Marcus, Kate would suggest by now you should have your estrogen levels checked, for something is off here," he wiped the tears from his face that came from laughing so hard, "Yeah, yeah, you look perfect," he said laughing, "... to your wife," and then winced.

"You OK?" Marcus stopped joking and looked at Sam with concern.

"Yeah, well you know they put Humpty Dumpty back together again, but it left a lot of scars and they act up at times. Kate did wonders but there are a few she did not catch. So they still bother me a bit when I exert myself. Nothing to worry about though," he said when he saw Marcus's concerned face.

"All right," said Marcus and pulled the car to the side. "Listen, we are family, no? You can trust me, no? So first, who is after you that you had to be stitched together in the first place? Then next I would like to know, whatever happened between you and Kate that sent her running this hard? And ... NO ... my friend, I am not continuing the ride until I am satisfied with the answers." With that he turned off the motor, took out the keys, put on his sunglasses, pressed one of the buttons to recline his seat, leaned back and relaxed.

"Wow, is that the stubborn Spanish way to interrogate unsuspecting tourists?"

"Start Sam, I am aging here!"

Well there was no escaping and he was being asked to speak out loud what he had not even dared to think through in his mind, but there was obviously no escape.

"We still don't know what or who is after ALL of us, not only me, Marcus. The boys escaped a bullet last week, and Kate is a target too, but thanks to her travels, it must be hard for them to keep up with her, which possibly has been keeping her safe. Happy?" Sam asked, but Marcus put up two fingers to point out the second question.

"Oh man, you drive a hard bargain, Marcus. My patchwork is thanks to whoever caught up with me. I was the first to be targeted, so we did not see it coming. There was no reason to worry before. Well ... I crash landed in the mountains, I remember seeing the pilot lying dead beside me and that I slid on the snow for some time after getting out of the plane, before it totally combusted into small pieces. The rest I do not remember, only waking up in an intensive care unit with unspeakable pain; you have no idea. So now can we go?" Sam looked expectantly at Marcus.

"Kate?" Marcus said.

"Don't want to talk about that," Sam said and crossed his arms and sat back.

He heard exaggerated snoring sounds from Marcus.

"Why do you want to know?" Sam said, irritated.

"She is my cousin. I need to find out if I should protect her from you, and I hope not, for I would need to beat you up so you know where we stand … OR is it that … that I protect her by helping you, that simple," he said indifferently.

"You beat me up? Good one," Sam said grinning.

"Well if you were well, then I would not even attempt it, believe me, but since you are Humpty Dumpty, well I can see chances right there," said Marcus grinning with still closed eyes.

"I like your sunglasses, where did you get them from?"

"Madrid, and don't bother changing the subject, I have two sisters: they tried that all my life and they failed – every time," he said, yawning.

There was silence for a moment. Sam tried to sort out his thoughts and struggled to find a way to get out of the spot he found himself in.

"You do not play fair, friend," Sam said, looking at him, "I am totally at your mercy here, with you having the keys to the car and you being the only one who knows where we are."

"Yeah, I am rather enjoying this, I have to admit that … Sam, get back to Kate, I am waiting …"

Sam looked at him and then out to the sea. Well he might as well face his demons and so he made himself go back to that dreadful afternoon in the Vancouver General Hospital. First Marcus thought that he would not answer but soon he realized that Sam was sorting things through, so he gave him a few more silent minutes. When Sam began to talk, Marcus was so startled he almost shrank into his seat, having gotten used to the silence in the car.

"I could see and understood Micha's point," Sam began. "If Kate was nowhere near me, she would be safe. It was not right of me to seek her out and bring the danger to her, we did not know if we were being followed; well, we still do not know," Sam said quietly.

"That's why you have those guys here?" Marcus added encouragingly.

"Yeah, but I do not know how useful they will be when things hail down. Not knowing where the next blow will come from makes protection or precautions a bit difficult and useless, you know?"

He thought some more and after another five more minutes of silence, he groaned and blew out the rest of his breath. "When I woke from the anesthesia I found her standing over me. She … well you will not understand what she did, but the point is she found me and I was angry with myself knowing that if she could find me so could those who were after her or me. I sent her away. I said some awful stuff so she would leave me."

He turned to Marcus and said defensively, "I had to, she would never have left my side otherwise," then he sunk into his seat in a heap of despair and added, "I had to keep her safe, she is my life, and I know I am hers, but if one of us died the other would follow quickly. Those bastards have found out about that one. Nice, a two for one, if you will. You should have seen Kate. Thinking I was dead, she was reduced to a walking skeleton. When I saw her after lying in the hospital in an artificial coma for so long … I was so shocked. She looked so awful it turned my insides out when I saw her. I think those bastards did not have to do anything to her, for she did a good job herself. But – I was wrong about it all, we are stronger together not apart … and … I need to fix it – even if it costs me everything, I have to fix it. Mike and Mel are here for the same reason. The guys are more for damage control … to keep the casualties down, so to speak …"

Sam could not stand the confinement any longer so he opened the door and walked away from the car. He had to get some air. A little down the road there was an olive tree and he sat under it, looking out to sea. Mike's yacht had made a turn and went back to find shore a bit further along where they had been hours before, until they heard from Sam again. Micha most likely would have a heart attack, when he found out that he was stuck on the boat and Sam was here on land.

It took only a minute until his phone rang. Sam knew who it was; he did not even have to look at the call display.

"Yeah Micha," he said tired and depressed. Micha was about to let him have it, but the tone of Sam's voice took the wind out of his sails and he stopped dead in his tracks. "What happened?" he wanted to know.

"Nothing, memories are catching up with me," Sam said quietly.

"Now don't beat yourself up over something you cannot change, but right now I am here and you are there, and I am pissed off to say the least." Micha had found his anger again.

"I will be good. Please come to shore and drop anchor in the dark and lower the flag. I do not want anybody to know we are here. I will wait for you on the dock. Happy?" said Sam resigned.

"Well I guess so. You are sure you are all right?" Micha felt a bit guilty at having been so stern at first.

"I will be ... soon ..." and he hung up the phone.

He heard Marcus close by waving at him to get back to the car. "If you want to burn your pretty head out here, then this is the way to go. Come back to the car, the air conditioning feels great." And with that he turned and walked back to the car fully expecting Sam to follow. Yes Marcus had much in common with him. Both were men of power and they expected their orders to be followed.

Well fine, cooling down in the car sounded good right about now, so he followed Marcus who was standing leaning against the car looking at the shoreline. Sam went to stand beside him looking for the thing that was attracting Marcus's attention.

"Marcus," he said and took a big breath and continued, "I am sorry I have brought trouble into your country," he said, frustrated. It seemed these days, that whoever was around him was threatened by the same danger that threatened him. Marcus walked over to the driver's side and opened the door.

"You did not, Sam, Kate did, and you followed. Her instincts brought her back home for shelter, most likely without her knowing it, she is running on autopilot. When humans are in danger, all of a sudden home has a different meaning and our instinct guides us to find our way there." Then he looked up at Sam and spoke sternly. "She will get the protection and safety of her people. Family is important to us, Sam, the most important thing to us," and with that he sat in the car, closed the door and started the motor.

Sam got back in the car and grinned at Marcus: "Are you satisfied with my answers, or will I be interrogated some more?"

"It will do," Marcus said, grinning back as he pulled out on the street, "... for now. I realize that this was hard for you, but this is not the time for hidden intentions and thoughts. Oh, and Sam, forgive me, but I do need to share some of the things you said with my uncle, he needs to know as well. I will leave the details out, just tell him the important things. We would never forgive ourselves should anything happen to you both ... here in Spain. All right ... and yes, if you would like to accuse the softy lofty Spanish royalty of being proud, then just go right ahead. We are rather proud of our pride as well," Marcus grinned and elbowed Sam in his side and then they kept on going, winding back to the harbor of the town that was tucked into the stony coast line.

"Now that we have established that we are on the same side, tell me what is your gut feeling telling you? Is she here?" Marcus asked.

Before Sam could answer Marcus's phone rang. He answered in Spanish and continued on in Spanish so Sam did not understand a word.

At first he could hear that Marcus's voice sounded matter-of-fact, then it became excited. He seemed to ask for people and at the end he sounded apologetic. When he hung up his driving style became more aggressive and he said nothing for a few minutes.

"Can you tell me what that was all about before you turn us into road kill? I would like to know why I died ..." Sam wanted to lighten the atmosphere that had suddenly become negatively charged.

"Oh, sorry Sam," Marcus said and slowed down considerably.

"Well? You wanted to know everything from me, how about returning the favor?" Sam continued.

"That's only fair," Marcus said after a moment.

"Yeah, only fair," Sam looked expectantly at Marcus.

"Well you need to know anyhow, since it was about you," Marcus said and Sam grew restless. Why was Marcus so uptight when they spoke about him?

"So now I am not your friend anymore, because of some reason I do not know of?" Sam suggested carefully.

"Why would you think that?"

"Let's see ... the tone of your voice for starters," Sam stated, matter-of-factly.

"Oh, that was more about me than about you," said Marcus casually. "You?"

"That was my uncle. At first I shared some of the concerns I have for your safety and only the essentials of what you told me to help us to protect you and Kate, when and if we find her. Then he told me that the Dons wanted to meet with you at the Grand Hotel. They have heard of your arrival and were disappointed at not receiving an invitation, as is customary here in Spain. They were surprised that we did not have a party for you and thought that this was the reason why no invitation was sent. So they took it upon themselves to invite you formally. I was just interested to know whether a specific Don would be there as well, for he owes me money. Lost in poker you know, and I saw my opportunity to collect, well that did not go over well with my uncle so he became a bit personal, let's leave it at that. He does not approve of a few harmless games, you see?" he smiled apologetically at Sam and then paid attention to the winding road again. "We are invited to a formal meeting as I said, tomorrow noon, sorry Sam."

"So much for staying under cover," Sam said quietly and then dialed a number to speak with Micha.

"Oh, finally you call, I was starting to feel like a doormat," Micha said accusingly. "For crying out loud let me do my job and stop interfering, would you? For starters ... get me off this ship!" he said quickly before Sam could say anything.

"All right, the playing field is yours again. My cover is blown somehow, but maybe for the better, who knows?" Sam said, resigned because he had been enjoying the freedom he had up to this point.

"What's happened now?" Micha wanted to know, frustrated.

"Well, Marcus and I just have received an invitation to an audience with the Spanish court, whoever is important enough and was available to meet tomorrow noon at the Grand Hotel, so you know what to do, I leave this up to you. Just tell me where you want me to be and what I am to do."

"Hey Sam, am I really such an ass?" Micha wanted to know.

"I'd like to be me again for a change Micha, just me, how would you feel if you were me?"

"Hey you are the crown boy not me, and I am rather happy with that, so we'll leave it that way, but Sam ... let's make the best of it and don't sound so gloomy. We'll chat later, K?"

"OK," said Sam and hung up.

"I am sorry Sam, but this means nothing really, only we have possibly more eyes and more shields, both important for our task, no?"

"Yeah, I guess ... yes, yes I know you are right, but this was so nice while it lasted."

"I thought you were looking for Kate – or were you running away from your responsibilities as well?" Marcus wondered.

"Oh shut up and drive," said Sam grinning, "Don't you want to run sometimes too?"

"I do at times, and sometimes I am successful, but not like you. I do it with my family. We go overseas to Disneyland or Europa Park for the kids. Nobody WANTS to follow me into that hellhole of amusement parks, so we spend most of the time in the zoo. The kids love it and we have peace for a little while," Marcus said while pulling into a parking spot near the harbor. "Let's meet up with your guys, without a flag for now. But tomorrow you will not be that lucky. It needs to be up for the meeting. Let's hope Kate is not here and your cover is not blown in regards to her."

It did not take long for the sailboat to arrive, which caused many heads to turn. She was a beauty of a boat, there was no doubt and Mike clearly was very proud of her.

Micha met them half way up the dock and Sam waved him over to Marcus. He wanted to rest and Marcus could fill Micha in better than he could.

"Sam?" Mel wondered when she saw him jump over the rail onto the boat. But he did not respond; instead he went to his cot and closed the door. Back to being the puppet, he thought, with Kate it was at least fun, but this felt like a charade to him.

Sam did not sleep well that night. Somehow he could not get Kate out of his mind. His thoughts were wheeling in circles and it took almost until the morning hours before he found rest.

Micha knocked on his door a few times, but because Sam did not answer, he assumed he was asleep and left what he wanted to tell him until the morning.

Sam was standing on deck with a steaming cup of coffee in his hand, looking over the waters at the rising sun, long before anybody else was up. Well then he thought, he had to get into his dreadful formal suit. He usually loved to wear it, but not in this heat, but it was the only thing that was suitable for this kind of meeting. His heart was excited and he had no idea why he was so worked up over meeting some officials. It was not the first time after all, but this felt so different, why he had no idea.

"Good morning Sam," came from behind him with a yawn. Micha of course. "You must have slept like a log, for I needed to talk to you last night and you did not hear me knocking," Micha said and poured himself a cup of coffee and stood beside him to take in the fresh morning air.

"I heard you," Sam said quietly.

"Well ... you should have answered then. I have good news, do you want to hear it or not?" Micha said, pleased with himself. But somehow

Sam was not impressed.

"How do you feel?" Micha wanted to know.

"A little unnerved or restless, for the meeting I guess, yet I have no clue why," Sam said without any interest.

"Unnerved? Restless? For the meeting?" and to Sam's surprise, Micha laughed out loud, clapping his knees hard, forgetting the coffee in his hand.

"Goodness Sam, you trust your feelings so often and when you should, then you don't," he kept on laughing and turned back to fill his cup again, for he had spilled his coffee.

Audience

PASSING BY THE FRONT DESK of their hotel Kate and Tina were interrupted in the middle of a heated argument about who could hold their breath longer under water. They just had come back from the beach and were looking forward to a shower to relieve the sticky feeling that the salt water had left on their skin.

"Excuse me Mrs. Von de Vorg, I have a message here that my colleague took earlier today, it says that someone is requesting you to be at the meeting hall at 5 p.m. I am sorry for the short notice. We have tried to contact you a few times," the man at the front desk stated with an apologetic face.

Tina froze beside her, so that Kate looked first at the front desk and then at her friend.

"Oh relax, Tina. Nobody knows me here, so I think it is a mistake. They think they have someone else here, remember I am new to this place and the conversation will quickly become one sided because ..." and she began to laugh at the thought, "I don't speak Spanish!" and she kept on laughing. "Can you imagine how well this will go?" Now Kate was holding her sides as she thought of the puzzled faces and the hand language that would be necessary to exchange even a few sentences.

She walked over to the front desk and leaned over the counter to look at the name tag of the front desk clerk.

"Stephano? Am I saying that right?"

"Yes, Mrs. Von de Vorg," was his polite and formal response.

"Stephano, that someone knows us here is impossible ... unless ..." Still leaning on the front desk, Kate looked back at Tina who was standing where she had left her in the middle of the hall. "Unless ... our 'shy' Tina over there gave that attractive fellow at the beach the name of our hotel. Which leaves me only one question, and that is, why did you tell him you were me, Tina?" Kate looked at her friend with her eyebrows raised mischievously.

"Nope, it was not me," was all Tina said, with a serious look that took away the fun of it all.

"Oh, I am not upset, girl, what are friends for, but it would be fun, if I would show up instead of you!" she said, laughing again. "Sorry Stephano, when did you say I needed to be at the audience?" she looked back at the front desk clerk.

"5 p.m., Miss," he said shyly.

"And now I am getting younger on top of it all, this is a great afternoon. First a name change and now I am a Miss. Thank you people, you've made my day," she said, waving her arms around in appreciation, while she walked back to where Tina stood. "And I did hold my breath longer under water than you did, Tina," she said gleefully and walked over to the elevators.

"We better hussle, 'Kate'," Kate said to Tina, "If you want to make it to that meeting we have to rush."

"Oh dear ... Hold it ... hold it ..." Kate walked back to the front desk and leaned towards the clerk as if she wanted to tell him a secret. "You said someone, but not if it was a female or male," she said intrigued. "Tell me, good looking? Available? Tina, over there, really needs a man, you know ... " But then when he just looked puzzled, Kate laughed again and walked back to the elevator.

"Never mind Stephano, we will let it be a surprise for us all. Coming Tina? Or should I say 'Kate'?" she said as the door of the elevator opened.

"I never said I was with you and I did not tell anyone we are here!" Tina protested.

"Sure, sure, so what do you think you want to wear? Want to borrow something from me?"

"I am not going without you, that is a fact and all right, you seem to be getting a kick out of it all, so let's go all the way and dress like we want to go to a formal beach party. If you wear that new white beach dress with the wide waist band then I will wear ..."

"Oh you know what ... you borrow the red one that looks like Arabian nights on you, the one that you tried on the other night ... please, please, I love how you look in it and I can only wear one dress at a time!" Kate folded her hands in a pleading way and put on her puppy face, employing all the persuasive skills she had. Eventually her conservative friend agreed to go out on a limb in fancy wardrobe.

"I will even say you held your breath longer under water if you say yes ... yes?" Kate looked at her, excited and expectant, and for a moment there was silence. Then Tina groaned: "All right! But I'm not going to pretend I like it!" she said pouting, and as pleased as can be Kate almost jumped up and down like a little girl, having a hard time containing her excitement, causing the elevator to shake.

"Oops ..." she said and calmed herself. Then she bent over to Tina and said, "We'll braid our hair too, OK?" trying to push her luck just a bit more.

"No more than that ... or I'll change my mind!" Tina looked at her scowling and as the elevator finally arrived at their floor, Kate was out before the door was completely open.

Tina's phone buzzed and she said apologetically, "Got to take this ... you know ... just go ahead and take a shower, I'll be right there."

"Don't tell your parents that you're going to see a guy now, otherwise they will change your mind ... We can't have that now, can we? No need to worry them ... trust me, I'm a mother. What they don't know will not hurt them." And Kate opened the door and went in, leaving Tina in the hallway.

"Yeah. No! I do NOT think that it is a good idea. Why? And for heaven's sake why now?" Tina said on the phone.

The other person on the phone answered in a frustrated way: "My thought exactly. I said the same, but stubborn as he is, he did not want to wait any longer. He is very persuasive. So please do your job, it will be over soon. We miss you so much, but you know that, don't you?"

"Me too, I am not happy though, this is just not fair to her. She never did anything wrong and she has had it so bad, it's just not right! Besides, she just recovered to a point of positive ..."

"Do your job is all I can say at this point, grin and bear it. Nobody said that you should get personally involved, say girl, where is your training? On the other hand I know her. It is hard not to like her, even though I met her so briefly."

With a click the person was gone and Tina leaned against the wall. She hated to lose the friend she had grown so fond of. She started to hate her job and for the first time she thought how good it would be if she could just quit, but that was not possible. She was in it for life. So she took a deep breath and opened the door. The water was running in the shower and Kate was singing. How easy it was to make her happy and how short lived their time would be from here on. Kate had laid out the two dresses she hoped they would wear, so Tina walked over and picked up the red dress. It was pretty. They had found the dresses at the market and the lady who sold them to them had given them a good deal. The dress she held had loose transparent material on the sleeves, with a solid, red fabric string dress below. Both dresses were floor length.

"You will look stunning!" Kate had come into the room and was watching her swaying the dress in front of her while standing in front of the mirror. Embarrassed, Tina dropped the dress and looked into the mirror at Kate, who came to stand behind her.

"In that towel you will not impress anyone," she said to Kate, who laughed again.

"Tina, Tina, if I did not know better, then I would think you just made a joke! Now it is your turn to hit the shower. I am drying my hair and when it is dry then I will braid yours. It will be easier to tame it when it's wet ..." Resigned, Tina went to do as Kate suggested, closing the bathroom door and turning on the shower.

She could hear Kate singing as she got dressed and then decided to enjoy the time with her as long as they had it. Let things fall as they may, she thought.

With ten minutes to spare the two women looked into the full-length mirror and inspected the sight. Like the night before, Tina did look like a person from Arabian nights and Kate looked a bit like a Greek goddess.

She had on a white tunic with white, laced, short-sleeved arms.

The lace followed the shape of the dress, coming down to a lower décolleté overcrossing and disappearing in the wide embroidered band that hugged her slender but no longer too thin waist tightly in dark burgundy material. The same pattern was repeated on the back. Like the long skirt, the band fell in straight lines to the floor and again ended up with full embroidered lace, which made her look even more beautiful and innocent. She had a long, see-through scarf wrapped around her neck to mask the crest that these days was a bit too prominent for her liking. It helped to have help with her hair, which Tina braided so that she had curls peeping through the French braid. Tina let her braid her hair to the side, which made them both look ready for a red carpet occasion.

"Have mercy on his soul. The sirens are on their way. This poor sucker has no chance. He will have no choice but to want to take us out! Free dinner here we come ... and ..." she said with a raised finger, when Tina wanted to interject, "... and if it doesn't work out we will go out anyway, on me! Nah Tina ... Can you say no to that?"

"Kate you shouldn't do that!"

"I want to, don't spoil it for me!" she said absentmindedly, trying unsuccessfully to pull up her top so it would hide a bit more. "Let's go, we do not want to make whoever it is wait."

"Let's stay here and watch a movie," Tina begged, for she had decided not to go along with what was planned anymore.

"Dressed up like this? Don't be ridiculous!" and Kate was already out of the door with her clutch in her hand.

"Dam, cheerful Antoinette – on the way to the guillotine," Tina muttered under her breath and followed her.

Downstairs, Kate went back to the front desk. "Well Stephano, what do you think?" and she turned in front of him showing off her dress, "Do you think we are overdressed for an under qualified conversation in a language Tina and I don't speak?" she said beaming at him.

"You look beautiful, both of you Mrs. Von de Vorg. Fit for a king."

"Nah, Stephano, I don't need a king any more. A nice man who could take care of my friend Tina would be good enough. If he is a good man, he can even be a beggar! But a handsome one!" And she whispered to him again, "He better be, otherwise I will not know what to do with her," nodding her head towards Tina, who was fidgeting.

"All Spanish men are handsome, Senora," Stephano said, grinning at her and giving Tina an encouraging look.

"Now where is the 'meeting hall' where we are supposed to be in five minutes?" she looked at him.

"Follow me, por favor," he said as he showed them the way down the elegant hall towards very tall doors. "In here Senoras," and he left them standing in front of the closed doors.

"Now what?" Kate whispered.

"You are the one who is running the show here, why ask me?" Tina whispered back.

"Let's go back to Stephano and tell him that he can tell the guy, whoever he is, that we will meet him on our own terms. My heart is desperately trying to tell me something, but I am not really sure what it is ... So let's chicken out," Kate said and hooked her arm under Tina's and started walking back to the front lobby. "There were posters all over the beach today about a beach party. Let's go there instead." She was about to turn around the corner in the direction of the front desk with the relieved Tina at her side, when Stephano came running towards them.

"Senoras, you need to open the doors. I have been called to check where you are."

"Never mind Stephano, we are leaving," said Tina rushing Kate down the hall, when they heard the doors behind them open. As if called, Tina stopped in mid-stride and turned. A gentleman with a concerned but friendly expression was looking down the hall at them. He was formally dressed, with the dark hair they all seemed to have around here, good looking, Kate thought, if that was the guy, Tina could do worse. Then he closed the door and walked over to where they were standing. He gave Kate a deep bow and formally said: "My lady, would you please follow me?" and then he looked at Tina with a questioning expression.

Kate looked at Tina with a puzzled frown when the gentlemen turned to lead the way and mouthed 'my lady?' but she did not say anything. "He speaks good English too, so communication between you two should not be an issue, on the other hand, you should tell him that Miss or Mrs. is sufficient these days," she whispered to Tina encouragingly, who did not look so happy anymore. As they approached the doors, she looked behind her and saw Stephano gesturing to keep on going. Well then, there seemed to be no escape route.

"If you would please wait," he said to Tina, stretching out his arm to the sitting area and she followed his suggestion and sat on a bench that had been elegantly arranged close to the doors. He looked at Kate, gesturing to her to wait where she stood and opened the doors and closed them behind him.

"If you leave me, I will kill you!" whispered Kate to Tina.

"Would not think of it!" she whispered back.

"Hey, he looked good, you have to admit that much?"

"Who looked good?"

"The 'my lady' guy," Kate explained, nodding towards the door through which he had disappeared. "But we need to trade places soon, you hear, say in about five minutes, then we will surprise him, what do you think?"

"Yeah ... Maybe ..." was Tina's reply, but it was not as convincing as Kate was hoping for. Something was up, every fiber in her being told her so, but she could not figure out what it was. Her stomach was full of butterflies, in a way she had not felt for a long time. Well then let's get it over with. Just then the gentleman returned.

"If you would follow me, my lady," he said and she went through the doors that closed behind her. The room was huge but elegant and so beautiful. Kate could see why Stephano called it a hall. Huge was not the right term, it was gigantic. You could easily fit a thousand dancing people with room to spare. It had very high ceilings, painted in traditional Spanish ways with clouds and angles, the left side of the room was an endless row of windows, the back wall had a gigantic elegant fireplace and the wall behind her and to her right had a lot of tall doors, and in the space between, on the walls, were endless, huge pictures of people from old Spanish times. The decor was rococo with many candles everywhere and a lot of gold on the walls, ceiling and furniture. The chairs and tables along the wall and along the windows could have been from a museum and in the center in the back of the room was an oversized, very long, polished table with high back chairs around it.

There were men in black formal suits sitting there, and they stood up when she entered the room and bowed to her as well. Some had official sashes over their suits and some had medals on their suit pockets, which seemed to be the only difference between them. Most of them were elderly men, all of them looked rather aristocratic, fit to be depicted on one of the walls. She felt flattered that these men, regardless of who they were, showed such respect to a woman. One had to give it to the Spanish, they knew how to treat a lady. It felt just as if she was in a Jane Austin novel again.

NO! This was the clue in her mind that pulled her to the reality that she was staring at this moment. No, no more of that Jane stuff anymore, she had sworn that to herself. It was connected to her core pain that she had carried for too long and which had almost consumed her, well ... if it had not been for divine intervention in the form of Tina. But the traces of the shattered heart and trust in others, that, she would carry with her for the rest of her days. She would not allow herself to ever be in such a vulnerable state again. She would and could not be hurt like that ever again. If that meant she had to die alone somewhere in a back alley, so be it.

But then she recalled why she was here and said, relieved, "I am sorry gentlemen; I seem to have been led into the wrong room. Please excuse me." She was about to turn when one of the men moved away from the group and walked slowly towards her.

Even if she were blind she would have recognized him. "Sam," she groaned very quietly, her heart screamed in agony so she held up her hand to make him stop. "NO! Not a single step this way. I believe what needed to be said, has already been said. This, whatever it is, is over."

She spoke angrily and loud enough to be heard on the other side of the door. Again she had a desire to run out of the room to safety. Who would have ever thought, that she would have felt safer running away from him than towards him? They were so close once and so much in unity with each other, sharing the same destiny. Her crest on the base of her neck reminded her of that, for it came alive in his presence and started to burn and to glow, so she pulled down her scarf to get relief from the burning heat she felt under it and threw the scarf on the ground in protest.

The men in the room saw the crest on her as well, and gasped in acknowledgement, but Sam turned and just said, "If you would excuse us?" and Kate heard someone translate his request into Spanish, and they all left through various doors of the room.

"Micha," Sam said and Micha walked towards her past Sam, and when he was almost where she was he looked at her pleadingly and apologetically.

"You look wonderful, Kate," he said in a whisper as he passed her and then went through the door she had come in by; closing it quietly behind him, he took up his position behind it.

Kate looked at Sam as the room slowly cleared. He had not changed much. A few scars on his face gave a small indication of the agony he had gone through. His hair showed a few grey hairs on the sides, which suited him well. He kept his hair shorter these days than she had seen it last. He wore a black, double-breasted, expensive-looking suit, a white shirt with a burgundy tie and a small golden pin on his collar, to identify his position. A bit overdressed she thought, considering this was a hotel where people went to chill, not to go to gala meetings. He was still handsome enough to make any woman's heart melt, and all right, hers as well, she had to admit that. His tall frame was huge even from half way across the room, and she was reminded of how she felt around him, sheltered and secure. But it was he who had hurt her most, who had stolen all she had held dear, and who had almost driven her to self-destruction, she reminded herself. Nice, she thought, this is all on his terms, his conditions, with no way out for her. He forced her to confront him now, while trapped in elegant surroundings. Well, even a gilded cage is a cage. Well then, he can have it, she thought. It is never smart to corner a wounded animal.

After the gentlemen had left and the doors had closed behind them she took a big breath and opened up the hell that was locked within her, ever since he turned her away at the hospital.

"How dare you!" she screamed. "How dare you ... be here? Was it not good enough to put me through hell, make me believe you are dead for over a year, no, you had to give me the final blow, you of all people gave me the final blow, when I was down and bleeding?" Her voice was so loaded with emotions that it started to break. Her tears began to flow in an endless river down her cheeks and she wiped them angrily away and stared resentfully at him.

"First you disappear, leaving everybody who cared about you to suffer the grief of having lost you. Then you show up and leave me lying on the ground to be helped by strangers, and then you turn away from me when I find you again, as if I was not worthy to be in your presence. How dare you try to repeat what you have done so well in the past, how dare you? Don't you think you've done enough damage already?" she said loudly and angrily, sobbing.

Sam wanted to interject as his hand came up to his chest, reminding her of the crest on her chest, but she did not allow him to say a word. Instead she gave him a bitter smile.

"Ah yeah, the crown, the crest ... that's the next thing I will hear, of course," she raised her hand. "Well ... you can have it back!" she stepped one step closer to him. "I have sacrificed enough for it, including my Michael. I think that should be more than enough as repayment for resentment and withdrawal, hurt and agony, wouldn't you think? My first husband stripped me of my pride, but you took my essence. There is nothing – nothing! – more I have to say to you, just go in peace and leave me alone! Forever would be preferable, and don't come back, for there is nothing I want anymore, but to be left alone in peace!" With every word she said she took a step back, ending up with her back to the wall next to the door, and when she was finished with all there was to be said, she slid down the wall into a heap of agony and cried uncontrollably. Her whole being began to convulse with a radiant glow of many colors, expressing the journey of intense emotions that ran through her, all connected with sorrow and pain.

Sam was at her side in less than a second. He helped her up but he could not hug her because she pounded her fists against his chest and through her tears he heard, "How could you? How could you do that to me? How could you?" followed by more agonized sobs. Soon she ran out of energy and just leaned against him and wept with her hands over her face. Drained, her knees started to give out, so Sam picked her up and walked back over to the table and sat her on it. He took his handkerchief out of his breast pocket and wiped the tears off her face. She might have thought of it as a sweet gesture, if she had not been so crushed by her hurt and anger.

"Why? What have I ever done to you?" she whispered, looking down at her hands that lay now folded and defeated in her lap.

Sam rubbed his hands together and slid his glowing hands over her as she once did to heal him. Her being became calmer and more peaceful, the colors stopped changing so radically and remained the same shade as his, but the hurt was still shooting through her soul, pulsing through the color they shared.

"Why?" she said almost inaudibly. Those whispering questions were even harder to stand than the accusations, screaming and sobbing he had just endured, that broke his heart as well.

"Kate," he took her chin in his hand and pulled it up to him so he could see her face. She was more beautiful than he remembered, even with her now swollen face and red eyes and the streaming mascara. The sun here in Spain had bleached her hair to a more golden tone and her tan made her look like a vision.

But he had no words to make her feel better. "Kate," so he lowered his face and kissed her carefully on her lips.

"I always loved you and always will," he said, loaded with emotions himself. Maybe the council was right. They were both still too raw to get back together, but he could not stand one more moment away from her and she needed to know that.

"If this is love ... I don't want it," Kate said looking at him, heartbroken.

"Kate, I needed you as far away from me as possible. My job is to keep you safe and I did." She was about to say something but he put his finger on her lips so she had to wait.

"My accident was suspicious and turned out to be more than an accident. We did not know who was trying to get to me, but if they could not remove me, they knew that they could get anything from me through you. You were in danger when you were close to me, and that was the last thing we needed throughout the investigation. I was not able to contact you because I was in coma for several months, then I was put in an induced coma because my injuries were so severe that they needed me to be lying totally still. I had endless skin grafts due to the severe burns and it took over a year to get this Humpty Dumpty back together again. My security detail and my council and advisors as well as my new found friends and family here suggested giving you more time to recover, to give us more time, so that when we met again both of us would be able to handle it better. At first we also wanted to wait until we knew who was behind it all. So I had no choice. I did right and I did wrong, there was no right way here, but I knew you were safe from others and that is all I needed to go on. When you showed up at the hospital it was a shock. But you healed me completely, even those scars that did not want to mend. Because of you we could continue the search for the answers much sooner, but you also needed to be removed from the danger as soon as possible. It was the hardest thing I ever did. Yet it was wrong. We are stronger together, and as soon as you knew, there was really no need to keep you away any more, Micha was right about that. Only we could not find you anymore."

"What?! Back up ... someone tried to kill you?" Kate's mouth dropped open.

"Yeah, and just to be sure they tried to do the same with you, but probably seeing you in the condition you were in, they decided to save themselves the trouble, for it seemed you were doing such a good job yourself. You did look frightening, even in the dark, it was unbearable, believe me."

Outside the door Tina could hear Kate's angry and hurt voice, and then her crying, and she was only able to stay away because Micha was there to hold and console her. She was crying in his arms for Kate's sorrow.

"It is not right, Micha ... to hurt her so!" she kept on saying to him.

"I know honey, but eventually they had to find each other. The strength that they create together is incomparably greater than when they are separate. I admit the timing is not so hot, but when will it ever be? As I said to you on the phone, he is also persuasive in his own way. Look how hard it was for us to be kept apart even though it is part of our destiny, but we at least had some phone conversations, they had nothing."

"I know, but she is such a beautiful person inside and out, she gives so much and considers others before herself, even when she runs on empty, she did not deserve any of this, any of our stuff."

"She is the lady of the house of Van de Vorg, it is her stuff as well, forever, and yes I agree, Sam did well to choose her. She is fit to fill the place beside him," Micha said, noticing her hair was in braids. "Well, well, Hello Honey. If it did not mean I would have to leave my post, then I would say let's go and celebrate whatever there is to celebrate. You look real good!" he said looking her up and down.

Then they noticed the silence in the room behind them.

"Either there is death or life. I don't think they do anything in between," Micha said, worried, but waited for the word from Sam.

"Where do we go from here?" Kate leaned her exhausted and pounding head against Sam's chest. "I don't know what to think or do or who and what to trust anymore. When I said I am done, I meant it. I am done with everything. I am tired of everything. I would like to lie down and close my eyes and find peace. I am tired of fighting, hurting, running and feeling. I am done, Sam. I have nothing left ... for myself – I'm done."

"Yeah, I can see that," his hand moved up and down her weak aura. "I am so sorry, but you see even in this it shows why we are so perfect for each other. Whenever we arrive at that spot the other is the supply. Let me refresh your memory. When I had given up on living you came into my life and rearranged it so that it seemed exciting again. When that louse attacked you in your office and when those idiots in the bar slipped you something, I was there for you. After seeing you so skinny and worn before I had to go through another skin graft and so much pain that day, I was at the same spot you are in right now, nothing left for myself, and who showed up? You ... against all odds you found me and I left the hospital – all the physicians were stunned that I was fully recovered and healed. I was wrong though to keep you away from me, for you see, there is something my grandfather never told me about. Wanna see?" he sounded a bit like a little boy who had found a new toy.

"It came to me one night when I saw my own hands in action and remembered yours that day in the hospital. Say you want to see it, come on ... say it!"

"All right, let me see," she said tired.

"That's all I get for excitement?" But when she looked up at him with a weak smile, tired and disillusioned, he nodded.

"I will take what I can get, all right, now watch. If it is what I think it is, then this is huge."

He rubbed his hands together and gestured to her to do the same. She did as she had been told, too tired to put up a fight, then he clenched his fist, waited for her to do the same, then he snapped his hands open and she did the same. Touching his glowing hands to hers, the bright blinding light that had filled the chamber in the hills at home now surrounded them both. Energy flew out of him to her and from her to him. He almost recoiled when he tasted her intense sorrow and grief, but he held her hands even closer, wanting to ride out this feeling. She drank in his healing optimism, relief, hope and happiness at having her so close again. It all looked so clear and resolved from his point of view. The light expanded throughout the room so that it was even visible below the doors.

"Told you ..." Micha said to Tina, when they noticed the bright light below the door.

"Unreal," was the only thing Tina could utter. "No wonder they are a threat to the other clan leaders. That is where we should look, I think. I would not want to mess with this kind of power. What do you know about it?"

"Not enough yet. But we are able to find out, since they are together now," Micha was all optimistic, "Our secret weapon ..."

"I don't know. This is a bit too fast and easy, don't you think? Did you not hear Kate? We women are not able to stuff that kind of deep hurt and sorrow away like it is nothing and carry on, you of all people should know better. Remember ...?"

"Oh I do remember, but perhaps they are able to deal with grief differently, thanks to that power within them," he pointed to the door, "And the energy of the light?" Micha whispered to her.

"I don't know, they are still human, aren't they? I just don't know, but I think the storm has not passed yet. We need to keep our eyes open now more than ever, that would be my best guess ... and that is coming from a woman with pretty good intuition ..."

"Oh man Tina, I want to go home ... this climate drives me nuts, it's too hot here all the time," Micha groaned. "What is your female intuition telling you about that? Will it be soon? – Besides, I want my wife beside me in my bed again, that's for starters ..." he looked sheepishly at her.

"Well for now," she looked and listened at the door, "It appears all is safe and ..." she stepped into a room that was filled with cleaning supplies, but was otherwise empty.

"I like the way you think, woman ..." Micha used his microphone to confirm there was someone to cover his post, and then he finally attended to the most pleasant part of business of the day, grinning and following her, closing the door behind him.

Sam and Kate broke free after a minute and he took her head into his hands and kissed her so passionately that she could have almost forgotten what she had been so angry about, but the pain was too deep. The sorrow he felt from her was so intense that his heart screamed to have healing himself. That healing they always had when they kissed and it was the same now, more than ever before. When he lifted his lips from hers he looked longingly into her eyes.

"No more tears, love, OK? Now, this light, as we found out, is something only you and I have and it has not occurred for many generations, thanks to the nifty ingredient of your high standing, which you brought along with you. That is the ultimate perk, as far as we can see. I can use it to communicate with my people without saying a word, just with my hands ... cool ehh? And we still need to figure out what else it can do. Only it seems someone else has figured it out as well, and that's why we became a target and everything went south as it did. But I could not do without you for another minute, Kate, you have to believe me."

"I want to ..." she said tiredly, but there was so much damage in her heart, she had no idea how to fix it and make the pain go away.

"What can I do?" Sam was starting to get desperate; she could hear it in his voice. He took her hands in his, kissed them, and then he put them back in her lap, rubbed his hands and laid them on her. But the tears kept on rolling down her cheeks and he could not remove the heaviness from her heart.

"It's not too late for us, Kate, not if I can help it," he whispered to her, and then took her face in his hands, kissed all the tears away and claimed her mouth again. When she relaxed he deepened his kiss, embraced her further, reached out with his hand and swept the room. The response was that the doors locked from the outside, having heard his command to have the room sealed off from any type of interruption.

His hands moved over her body and pulled her closer. Her body was reacting to him as he expected, but not her heart or soul, he could feel that. Well then, whatever I need to do, he thought.

'Kate I need you,' his mind screamed at her, 'Please find your way back to me ...' Kate was almost shocked to hear his thoughts as loud as she could hear his voice, but Sam kept her in his embrace, misunderstanding her retreat.

Just when the embrace began to become intimate he could hear her thoughts as well, very faintly but he could hear it. 'Take what you need,' she replied.

"NO!" it took all the strength he could gather to pull apart from her and away. Out of breath he just could utter "No, not like this," he said, feeling his eyes fill with tears as well. "Not for what I need, Kate ..."

"I did not say a word!" she looked shocked.

"You did not have to," said Sam bitterly.

"You can hear what I am thinking as well?" she said, shocked.

"Apparently, though I wish I had not." He pulled down her dress and lifted her sleeves back up to her shoulders, than he straightened his own clothing and walked away from her to stand by the window.

'Sam, can you hear me? If you can, give me time, this is going way too fast for me. My heart needs to do a lot of mending, and a lot is an understatement, it is shredded into a million pieces and even I do not know if it can ever be mended again.'

Sam hid his face in his hands, what had he done to her? He had destroyed her more than her previous husband Dale ever had.

'Sam?'

'Yes, I heard you. Please don't give up on me or on us ... If time is what you need, then time is what you'll get.'

Kate looked at him, shocked. She could hear what he was thinking?

"Did you say that out loud?"

"No, and yes I can hear your thoughts and it seems you can hear mine as well ... nice ... at least that ..." He was not looking at her but was holding onto the window frame, looking out of the window. Then he shielded himself from her. He hated the idea of more time. Had they not been apart long enough, he thought resentfully. He would kill anybody who had had anything to do with the hurt and grief they had suffered.

When he turned he could see she had not heard what he thought, for she would have been angry with him for thinking of revenge, she was that kind of a person. Instead she looked at him, waiting. So they could shield their thoughts from each other as well, in the same way as they could communicate if they wanted to, good to know too.

"Let's rest, the day was taxing enough for all of us, and tomorrow we leave to go back home. There we will sort everything out," he said with a set face. For him the subject was done.

He was about to walk to one of the doors when she called him back.

'Sam ...?' He turned to look at her.

'Still practicing the mind thing?' he wondered.

'No, I do not want to be heard by anyone. I need to talk to you privately and our minds are a very private place, are they not?' she looked at him questioningly. 'How long have you been here?'

She needed to begin from square one, connecting on an elementary level and he seemed to understand. Sam looked at her. Well at least she wanted to talk, better than nothing. So he walked back to the table on which she still sat and leaned against it beside her.

'We have been here for a day I think, we arrived yesterday. I have been resting most of the time since we arrived, but I still haven't regained my full strength, so the guys continued the search for you and found you where we expected.'

'How did you find me?'

'Top secret,' he grinned at her. 'Some things I will not tell so quickly ...'

'Torture?' She suggested back to him and he remembered that this used to be his way to get things out of her, torture her with kisses and whatever else came in handy at the time, and now she was using it on him in the same way.

"Maybe ..." he said out loud, but she just smiled at him and covered his hand with hers. It was now more scarred from the burns he had suffered. He could feel that she could tell the difference in his skin texture and wanted to pull away from her, but she just held it firmly in her hands.

'Sam, I am longingly ... searching desperately for my husband, not for the ruler ... He is the only one that can save me now.'

'But I am here, Kate, what am I doing differently?'

'I cannot tell you, I don't know myself.' She leaned her side against his shoulder.

"Don't say it or think it, let me guess. Time, right?" His hand turned and he took her hand, pulled it over to him and covered it with the other hand.

'I am sorry if that makes you sad, but ...' Kate thought, 'but ...'

'Kate, when we did that thing with our hands ... My scars healed with the exception of a bit of pulling here and there, but otherwise I am healed, but you Kate, your scars are inside, you have not even started to heal yet ... What can I do to help? I feel so helpless when it comes to you and I hate that feeling. Help me ... help you ...?'

"... And ..." he continued sharply out loud, "Don't you ever, EVER do or give me something for my sake, unless you want it too!"

"For starters ... could you just hold me," she said and he turned and picked her up, walked over to the overstuffed leather couch and sat down with her on his lap like in the old days. His arms came around her protectively and covered her almost completely.

'This will have to last now for some time,' she thought, and Sam looked down at her, alarmed and puzzled.

"Sorry?" he said worried about what she might say, but she changed the subject quickly and effectively.

"Have you been home yet? Do the boys know you are still alive?" she sincerely wanted to know.

"No, it was not safe. As long as it was believed I did not survive it gave us an advantage to continue our investigation uninterrupted. Boys? Both? And what did you mean earlier about sacrificing my Michael. Besides he has not been only yours for many years but ours, BOTH, have been for many years ... did that change too!?"

The glow that came back into Kate's face when she thought of the kids, the glow in her face was what Sam had hoped to see for himself, ever since they met, but he should have known better. The fastest way to a woman's heart is always through her children.

"No, I was just angry and needed extra ammunition," she said. After a moment of silence she added, "You would be so proud, Sam, so proud," Kate said turning towards him and opening up.

"Honey, tell me in there," he said pointing to her head.

'Sam, can you hear me?' He nodded, smiling that she was still doubting and insecure about it, but then she continued, 'This is so weird and something to get used to, the weird, I guess, is not finished with us yet.' She moved so that she had his full attention.

'Michael came up to support us through our grief.' She bumped him accusingly hard with her elbow and then continued. 'Anyhow, the next thing I knew was that both boys had the crest on their back, like you did once before everything went to hell in a basket.'

"Both? That is impossible Kate," he said to her, shocked. She tapped his forehead to remind him to use his thoughts and then continued.

'Since when is impossible an obstacle for our family? I have asked Daniel to tell me the story over and over again and he gladly did, for he was so grateful to Michael as well. You see, Daniel was so distraught and he did not want to let me see half of what he felt, having lost another parent, but he opened up to Michael one night. They went for a long walk. That's when Daniel told him that he felt so lost without you and with me being only half present, so Michael promised him to be always at his side whenever he needed him.'

'Still ... This is a blood line thing, Kate, it is not transferable, we are born with it ...'

'Hang on, my story is not finished. Anyhow, to make this permanent, Michael did the boy scout or navy thing or whatever you call it. He said it is a custom of the past to seal the future, he cut his hand and Daniel did the same and they shook hands to seal it in blood. This must have hurt badly but the bloodlines crossed and the next thing was that Michael woke up with the crest, slightly different and with other icons on it, also a simpler version, but quite obviously your crest on his back. I only saw it because he blamed Daniel for getting him sick and said that he thought he had a fever. At the time we had plenty of people in the house and they saw it as well, including Mary. You should have seen her face. Also, Michael is now extremely pleased that he finally grew a bit more, not quite to the height of Daniel, but he did shoot up over the past few weeks before I left.'

'Two ... there have never been two heirs, who knows about it?'

'Well as I said, everybody who was at the house that day, for we always had a lot of people over, bringing food for the grieving family. I can't look at another casserole for the next hundred years, I tell you, but the support was so sweet. They all gasped the same way as your guys did when I came in.'

'Wow ... You got any more bomb shells like that in store for me?' was all he could say.

"They are now much closer than they ever were before. Michael backs Daniel up whenever he can, except in the hospital, he said he hates hospitals, so there Daniel is on his own. Oh, did I tell you that Daniel gave up his position in Vancouver and is now working right beside Jackson? Michael took leave as well, so he could be with us for at least a year or so, and who knows what he will do then. That is all I know, for I have not been there since you showed up.'

'That was almost a year ago, why did you not go back home? Why did you not go and see your parents?'

'How could I? Lie to them when they were grieving over your loss? That would be cruel. So in a sense I was cut off from them all, you see?'

'I never thought about it that way, there is much I need to make up to you, it appears,' he said, and then he was all business again. 'Well, let me think this through. What happened with Michael was most likely possible since he has, through you, a positional right to rule, but via Daniel he received a new designation, so it will not be through your line but through my line. Would he be willing to take my name do you think? He is in his late twenties and will have to have a say about it.'

'Ask him, I am sure he is not fond of carrying his biological father's name, all things considered.'

'Well, I will straighten everything out when we get back home,' Sam thought, all business again, 'Michael needs to catch up on what we know, like on what the crest is about and what it means to carry it.'

Kate's face dropped. She had hoped to talk to the father of their children, but he was being the ruler again, so she wiggled out of his arms and walked towards the door.

"What did I say?" He looked at her, shocked.

'It is not only what you thought, but what you did not think. Do you mind?' she thought, pointing to the door and he waved his hand and the man behind the door opened it and Sam watched her leave, leaving him standing there puzzled and lost.

On the Run

"TINA?" KATE CALLED OUT LOUDLY; she was in a panic and needed to get away fast. "Tina!"

"I am here, what's up?" Tina asked innocently, catching her breath as she raced from the janitorial room out into the hallway, back to where she knew Kate would be.

"Where have you been?" Kate wanted to know, confused.

"I was desperately looking for the ladies' room. What went on behind those doors? Besides ... you look awful, what happened? They would not let me in, you know."

"Yes, I know. Let's go to our room; I need rest and I need some time to think."

Both took off back up to the room and Micha, who had been standing like a statue in the janitorial room, waited until they had left and then rushed to Sam's side.

"What happened? She ran away from the door as if a devil was following her," he asked Sam, who was still looking at the open door.

"I have no idea, but we are telepathically linked with each other, that much I found out."

144

"You found out? Sam! She is your wife; you needed to reconnect to each other, what was this to you ... an experiment?"

"No, of course not, but this might have been a bit too early for her after all, I think ..."

"You think? ... Are you kidding me? After you twisted our arms, and forced the issue? Sam, do you know what is at stake here? For once, could you try to think like a love sick puppy?"

Micha knew very well that he was overstepping his boundaries again, but he had had enough of the lofty thinking his friend displayed.

"Will you at least meet her for dinner?" Micha asked, quietly shaking his head as he looked at Sam's stunned face. "You've got to be kidding me ... NO follow up?"

"I told her we would work it out at home, whatever needed to be worked out," Sam said defensively and walked towards the window again.

"I would not say this unless you were one of my best friends Sam, but you did ask me to be part of your council and to straighten you out when you need it. I must wonder what you are thinking ... After chasing her for this long, you barge in and tell her she is coming back home with you, and you think she will just do so? Well hell, if she does, then I take it all back, but I tell you from what I have seen this far, she will put up a fight."

"She did not even want me to touch her," Sam said.

"Good Lord, don't tell me you tried? Have you any idea what she has been going through? Have I not told you what Tina told me? Good heavens, Sam!!! Shall I smack your royal head to try to knock some sense into it?"

"What would you have me do!?" Sam responded angrily.

"Court her, you idiot, sorry, you royal idiot, get her interested in coming back with us, not because you said so but because she wants to. Reconnect with her. Ah!" He flailed his hands in the air when his phone rang. "Hold on, my phone is ringing and I bet it will be Tina giving me an earful, my Lord ..." he said cynically and walked off, scowling at Sam.

"Yeah? I know ... you want what? NO ... honey ... I do not think that this is a good idea!"

"What is not a good idea? Give me the phone." Micha obediently gave him the phone.

"Tina, what is up?"

"I am infuriated with you all, after many generations of service, I am speechless … it has always been an honor until now!" Tina was beside herself. "What are you thinking, may I ask? Did Micha tell you that there was not one single night that this woman didn't wake up screaming, and cry herself to sleep again? Did she really deserve all that?"

"What did I do?" Sam was completely at a loss, so that Tina became a bit softer.

"Sam, Kate needs her husband, someone who shelters her, loves her, courts her, makes her feel better and helps her to get over the incredible trauma she's been through. Sam, with us you can be whatever you need to be, but with Kate, she is your wife and the mother of your children, and also a person of high standing on her own, she does not need a reminder, she needs a human being. We raced up to the room and now she is in shut down mode. She is not even talking to me, there's a wall there, and to tell you the truth, that could be bad news for us, for you and her. I am not a psychiatrist, but I think this just took a turn for the worse. She said something before she went behind that wall … that she believes she is not needed anymore, the kids are doing well she said, you are doing well, and 'the Moor has done the deed the Moor can leave', kind of thing. Are you reading me – SIR?"

Sam moved the phone away from his ear, for she had become very loud, and looked at it. Tina suddenly hung up on him, and Sam said to Micha, "I don't think I've ever heard Tina so beside herself."

"I have been married to her for over 15 years and believe me, this is a first for me as well. A lot has to happen for her to lose it like that and to forget your position. Mind you, I do not blame her one bit." And he stretched out to retrieve his phone.

They sat down for a few minutes. "Sam … do I need to give you pointers on how to woo a woman?" Micha asked, grinning.

"You know, if you were not such a good friend," Sam said repeating what Micha had said earlier, "… and I did not rely on your input as much as I do, I would give you a good kick in the behind."

Micha grinned back and looked into his folded hands for a while. "Now, how to fix this is the question." He remained sitting like that for a few more minutes deep in thought and Sam walked over to the bar to pour himself a drink. "I think I will go to my room as well. I am tired and frustrated," he said and swallowed the drink with one gulp.

The phone rang again. This time it was Micha who hesitated to answer, but then he thought differently.

"Hello honey, be nice will you, it's just me," he said looking sheepishly at Sam, but then his face changed from charming to serious. He got up so fast that it startled Sam.

"When last? Yeah I will check, leave it with me. Go, I will cover this end, stay in touch. Love you too, till next time?" and he hung up the phone and looked up at Sam.

"She is gone."

"Who is gone?" Sam looked bewildered.

"When Tina went back to their room, the shower was running and she thought Kate was taking a shower, but when it went on too long, she checked if she was all right, but there was nobody in it. She left you a note though; it is still in the room. Tina went after her; she is the best tracker I ever met. She will find her guaranteed, good security breeding for generations… she is the first female born with the sword; at least that I can remember. Destined to do something special and by now we know what it is."

Sam went completely white. "Where did she … where would she go? I thought she would go back home with us tomorrow …"

"My guess would be anywhere but there. Sam, are you listening to us or not? After all this, who could blame her? Only this time … Now she has come to terms with her belief that there is no purpose for herself anymore, which puts her at high risk. God only knows what she is up to now. You are aware, that you are reduced to only half of what you could do without her, if you think in these terms only. Tina will never forgive me that I agreed to all this."

Sam rushed out of the room with Micha at his side and in no time the whole building was secured.

"Sam, stop, where are we going in such a hurry? Let cool heads prevail, all right? First we will go to their room and get the letter she left for you, and then we will wait until Tina gets back to us. She is the best, believe me."

"She wrote a letter?" Sam came to a complete stop.

"Well more a note as I said earlier, have you been listening at all? It is for you and Tina said she left it for us to find, so she could go after Kate without delay."

Just as he finished talking the phone rang again.

"Yup. Slow down. OK. Yeah, keep me posted." After he hung up he called another number.

"Sepher, yeah good to hear your voice also. How is everything at home? Who has been shot? And? Related to the Von de Vorgs? ... Why? Well yeah, I see the lights have been going on for you as well, we need security up there now too, include Mary just in case. Can you handle that? How bold to come onto our own turf and threaten us in this way ... they will pay, I tell you. Here? Hell, to say the least, I keep on running but don't seem to get ahead."

Sam was waving at him so Micha looked up, "Hang on Sepher, just a minute," he looked at Sam questioningly.

"Give me the phone, now," Sam demanded, quickly catching on to what was going on, but Micha shook his head.

"You are dead, remember?" Micha warned him, but Sam gave him a look that demanded submission.

"Sepher, this is Sam ... yeah, yeah forget the formality, yeah I am glad to have survived also, but let's cut to the chase. You have a security detail on my sons, is that right?"

"Ah yes, we do, for there was a suspicious shooting up here again and a bystander was killed. But we have our suspicions about it all. But that you are alive – that will be great news for all the folks up here," said Sepher.

"Sepher, nobody can know yet, we have no idea who some of these guys are, we are throwing around some ideas, but we are not sure yet. Listen, for you guys up there ... not only Daniel has the crest, but Michael also," he said to Sepher and Micha's eyes widened.

"We know Sam, we've seen it. Man, it is so good to hear your voice."

"Keep your lips sealed for a little while longer, OK?" Sam asked in a kinder way than he had started the conversation.

"Anything for you."

"Later." And he hung up the phone.

"Now to you, why are you so on your toes? Why did you say you can't get ahead of things?" he looked at Micha.

"The first call was from Tina, she told me that when she went to the front desk to inquire about Kate's checkout the hotel clerk told her that it was kind of weird, for right after Kate had checked out two dark looking men also checked out right after and followed her. He said that he was about to notify her but could not catch her. He said he had worked in the hotel for a long time and knew people, and that those people were giving him vibes of being up to no good. Sam, I think we just led some of those shady guys to Kate, I am getting sloppy, but how did they ... well now we have an even larger problem."

Sam had to sit down to get his breath back.

"You feel OK, Sam? Don't give out on me now, we have to concentrate on getting Kate and you in one spot so we can better protect you both. We are spread too far and too thin to be effective. Let's get that letter first, and then we'll pack up. The hotel is not safe anymore."

He accompanied Sam to his room, then went to Kate and Tina's old room where he picked up the letter which he found exactly where Tina said it would be and brought it back to him.

"Sam stay, I called Marcus and he will be right over. He and some of his men will help us out. For the sake of us all, let us do our job; maybe rest up until it is safe for you to move back to the boat. Stop looking so distraught, watch us at work, you will be amazed at what we can do ..." he said with a grin and then closed the door.

Outside two security men were waiting. "Nobody in or out! Except Marcus," he threw at them and rushed down the hall. First he spoke with the man on the front desk and then with the hotel manager and clerk. The man was observant and gave him a good description of the two men who had followed Kate, so he could convey it to Tina.

Tina had caught up to Kate rather fast. Kate was standing on the edge of a bridge.

"Hey Kate, why did you take off without me?" Kate heard behind her. When Kate looked up she saw Tina leaning beside her against the bridge rail.

"Wanna jump now too? Heard that it has unhealthy consequences, but then again, who knows how reliable hearsay is these days ..." Tina said, grinning at Kate.

"I was not wanting to jump, but I was wondering what it would feel like standing here," Kate replied.

"Sure," and after a little she added, "Nice view, isn't it?" so that Kate had to laugh.

"Tina, you are my lifeline again. What would I do without you?"

"Travel around Europe bored, I suppose, trying to get your

adrenaline rush by jumping off bridges ... you know, to keep the excitement going ..." Tina said with a grin. "Where to now?"

"I like Spain, let's look at something quieter on the coast for a change, away from all the people, what do you think?"

"Thank the Lord, I was thinking the same ... snorkeling would be lovely ... and this time, you are not going to get competitive with me about holding breath ... because you see ..." Tina said with a smirk, "with snorkeling you don't need to hold your breath," so Kate started to laugh again.

"Good plan. Let's get a taxi to the train, or should we take the bus again?" Kate asked.

"I think we should do some fancy foot work first, for we need to shake someone off our trail, since that 'interesting' meeting earlier," Tina said, leaning over to Kate so that Kate looked around to see who it could be, thinking it was one of Sam's security men trying to convince her to return.

"What do you have in mind?" Kate asked her, whispering back as if the people were right behind them.

"Let's have some fun as payback, at their expense," Tina answered. She could not have set this up any better.

"It sounds to me," Kate said, while looking around like a spy, "Like you have some experience in this, or maybe it's just that you've watched too many movies, which one is it?"

"Does it matter?" Tina said playfully.

"Nope, lead the way, mysterious Tina," Kate said and followed her off the ledge. Like Tina she squared her shoulders and they crossed the bridge, flagged down a taxi in the wrong direction, then changed cabs and went the other direction, crisscrossing around town until Tina was satisfied and they found themselves in front of the train station.

"Now we will catch a bus," Tina exclaimed.

"A train station has plenty of trains, why not take the train?"

"Just as a precaution, what would you assume if you followed someone to the train station?"

"Uhh, smart, of course you would expect they had caught a train somewhere," Kate said smiling.

"But we won't," Tina said, satisfied. Her subject was much easier to redirect than Micha's and she was enjoying herself again. "We are not far from the coast, so what do you say we get the next bus and see where it takes us?"

After some confusion, they finally headed off on a bus going in the right direction. Kate took the travel guide from Tina to see for herself what would appeal to her the most from the pictures and descriptions of locations in it. Then she decided to look up coastal towns.

"There is a small town here … look, what do you think? But you know, Sarriera also sounds good. It is a small fishing village with a nice but short beach with a coral reef, what do you think Tina? This sounds perfect!"

"Sarriera, here we come," said Tina with her finger on her phone so Micha could hear her conversation. "But that is some way yet, how about this place for a stop in between?" and pointed to a place right in the middle of where they were and Sarriera. And Kate agreed.

The bus ride was a bit too hot, after they arrived in town they were glad to leave the bus, and very relieved that they had chosen to stop earlier than to travel all the way through. They stayed there for just one night, then pressed on to their desired destination, a place that promised to be everything they were looking forward to. After another long and hot bus ride, they arrived the following day in Sarriera. It was everything Kate was looking for. A small village with a little dock, but more beach for swimming. Everything the travel guide had promised was there. The houses were built of sandstone, in its various white shades, mostly with tiled floors and were pleasantly clean and well taken care of. They found a little hotel that suited them well and after paying for a week in advance they made themselves comfortable in their room.

Kate changed into one of her beach dresses and talked Tina into doing the same. This time they went to the market first, found a beautiful hat, which Kate had to get, so Tina haggled a bit about the price and soon they were both set up with large brimmed hats, cute shoes and some candied fruit to snack on. After piling on a lot of suntan lotion they decided to give the beach a closer look as well. Of course the water was enticing, so Kate was in the water faster than Tina could say 'wet' and after a nice swim they went back to the room to have a quick nap.

Later that evening they went to a street party with live music and dancers. The joy of life was so contagious that Kate forgot all her worries and started to enjoy life again. Too soon they were back in their comfortable room watching some Spanish TV, even though they did not understand a single word, and turned in late. Yet Kate just did not want to go to sleep and so Tina decided to ask her straight out.

"Hey Kate, you don't need to tell me if you don't want to, but I was wondering what happened the day before yesterday, in that room?" Tina held her breath and hoped she was not making a mistake.

"I don't mind at all. I was surprised you did not ask me sooner considering how curious you looked when I came back out," Kate said while playing with the fringes of her blanket. "They had not made a mistake. The meeting was for me. My husband ... oh, did I mention to you I am married? Well yeah, he had caught up with me and it was not such a good reunion," Kate said, staring up at the ceiling.

"You guys having problems?" Tina wanted to keep her talking.

"Well he was kind of gone for some time without me knowing where, and now he suddenly shows up, and ... he expects me to be happy ..." Kate was crying into her pillow.

"I am so sorry Kate, I did not want to make you so upset, we can talk about something else if you like," Tina was not happy that Kate was in such a state even after such a fun-filled day.

"Do you still love him, Kate?"

"That's the thing, love was never a problem for us, but everything else!" Kate said in a teary voice.

"Darn, so John Lennon lied when he sang 'all you need is love?'," Tina said, keeping the humor going.

"No Tina, all you need IS love, but if it gets undermined with other stuff, then '... love is all you need' gets undermined and the purpose of a relationship becomes secondary."

"Note to self: Find a guy that loves me and keeps that as his priority," Tina said, looking at the ceiling as well. "So your husband does not love you anymore, but something else?" Tina probed, pretending naivety.

"Well come to think of it, he does love me, and I know that he does, but I fear that his job is more important to him," Kate said more to herself.

"How do you know that he loves you? How does anyone know they are loved?"

"That is truly a good question. When someone loves you, you will know, I promise you, you will."

"But looking at you, it does not seem to be such a good thing, to be loved ..." Tina said.

"He is doing well and so are my children, I am just not needed anymore Tina, I have become just a means to a greater goal, but it seems that I am not worth considering just for myself anymore."

"If you ask me, that does not sound like love at all." Tina looked at her, "If you were him, what would you do differently, how would you treat you?"

"I would be more careful, more forthcoming, more ... I would not push him away when he needed to be close, I would not desert him when he needed me the most, I would take him and cover us up and let the world float past us! That is what I would do and never ever would I keep such big secrets away from him regarding any danger!! That is what I would do," the last part she said angrily. "Sorry Tina, not your fault," she looked apologetically at her.

"Nah, let it out girl, seems it has been there for way too long," said Tina.

After a while Tina started to sing one of Kate's favorite Enya songs.

"Who can say where the road goes, where the day flows, only time, and who can say if your love grows as your heart chose, only time ..." and Kate continued for her:

"Who can say why your heart sighs as your love flies, only time, and who can say why your heart cries when your love lies only time ..."

"Hey we are good at karaoke, do you think they have something like that here? We would do great duets, what do you think?"

"Maybe," Kate said after a while.

"Tired yet? How about... some shut eye?" Tina said, yawning.

"All right, let's give it a try," and not long after that both women were sound asleep.

As usual Kate woke in the middle of the night screaming and then hid in the bathroom so as not to wake Tina, and there she just cried until she was tired again. The dreams were usually the same: she dreamt she saw Sam crashing and dying in the alpine meadows of the Rockies. Now that she knew he was alive, she felt stupid having those dreams but they kept haunting her; she had no clue why.

On occasions when she did not have that particular dream, then she dreamed she was at Sam's side at his hospital bed, and he was ordering her to leave his room and never to return ever again, even though she knew that in reality, when she was there, he was in so much pain he would have never been able to utter a single word, but she kept on feeling the rejection over and over again until she was numb from heart ache.

The door opened and Tina looked in, sleepy-eyed.

"One of these days you will have to tell me what you dream about, for your dreams must be horrific to make you wake up screaming like that."

"I am so sorry Tina, should I get a different room?"

"Are you kidding, and miss all the action? Not a chance." She came in and sat on the toilet cover and pulled her feet up on the seat.

"Well, what is it you dream about? Skeletons? Spiders? Dragons?" Tina said, looking at her.

"None of the above," Kate replied.

"Oh, too bad there goes that theory. Then what frightens you so?" Tina looked so sincere that Kate could not help but tell her more than she had planned to tell.

"You will find this stupid, but I dream of airplane crashes and rejection," Kate said, "Just like any other person would." She tried to rationalize her dreams and behavior.

"No, not everybody dreams every night of airplane crashes and rejection, Kate, I am your friend ... well at least I like to think so ... so tell me, why do you dream of those things?"

"I don't know ... I guess I am still hurting and missing my husband a lot. You know how it goes: I can't live with him, but I also can't live without him, that kind of thing," Kate said, while splashing cold water on her face.

"Kate, forgive me for sticking my nose into things that are not my business AGAIN, but it sounds to me that the 'can't live without him' is more the case for you, rather than 'can't live with him'. Could that be the truth?"

"I don't know. Maybe."

"And just to play devil's advocate, maybe he is just as unsure about how to deal with the situation?" She paused and looked thoughtful. "If he was here right now, what do you think he would do?" Tina wondered how far she could push Kate until she either threw her out or got tired of her.

"He would just hug me and tell me it will all be fine," Kate said and started to cry again.

"Yeah I can see, that is definitely something we do not like and want. A really bad thing," and Kate had to smile about that and bumped her elbow into her side.

"Smarty pants," she said.

"Say Kate, if this is the worst he does, he would not have a brother for me now would he? I kind of like those awful things he does, such as hugging you and telling you everything will be just fine," Tina added, grinning.

"You think I was too hard on him?"

"We women are never too hard on the guys, usually they deserve every bit of it, but they also deserve a second chance, so what do you think about making a phone call tomorrow?" Tina said yawning again, "But now a bit more sleep, yes?" And she got up, washed her hands and went back to sleep, hoping Kate would follow her.

Maybe she was right, Kate thought. Maybe Sam was having a hard time adjusting to the situation, just like she was, and she had put a bit too much pressure on him. Maybe she should give him another chance. They needed to be a family with all the weird and scary stuff that was going on. But now sleep. And she slept well into the late morning and so did Tina.

"What do you think, breakfast and a swim?" Kate said from the bathroom cheerfully.

"Sounds great. How late is it?"

"Ten to eleven," said Kate from the bathroom.

"Gee, breakfast is only till eleven, let's hussle," and she jumped out of bed into her swimsuit and wrapped her sundress around her and proclaimed, "Ready, let's go!"

Kate came out of the bathroom looking at her in surprise, "Wow you are fast ... brush your teeth, and then let's get coffee before they run out."

The two women chased each other down the hall to the dining room. Luckily, they were not too late and were able to grab a last minute breakfast.

There were still other guests sitting around. An older couple who spoke French, so they must have been tourists as well, a gentlemen reading the paper and another at the bar looking for more buns.

Otherwise they were the last to enter the dining room.

When they picked up the milk with coffee Tina looked into her cup, disappointed.

"Where is my coffee? Are they out already?"

"No, no that is what they call cafe con leche or coffee ole," Kate said grinning, "When in Rome, do as the Romans do!"

"Yuck, I need coffee, Kate, black strong coffee that makes your hair curl, not whatever you call this," she complained.

"Try it first, you might like it."

Tina was not convinced enough to like the coffee ole but the rest of the breakfast was delicious. They went back upstairs and changed for the beach, that is… Kate changed, for Tina was already ready for some action on the beach.

"Hey, did you make that call yet?"

"What call?"

"Kate!"

"All right, I will call from the front desk, there is no phone in here, as long as you promise to back off," and Tina crossed her chest to show that she promised.

They grabbed their beach towels, lotions and snorkeling gear and headed to the front desk.

Kate asked for the phone and dialed Sam's cell number.

"I will make a call quickly too if you don't mind, be right back," Tina whispered to her and walked to the other side of the room and called Micha.

"Hey, tell Sam to turn on his cell, Kate is trying to call him," she whispered into the phone.

"How did you manage that?" he wanted to know, "Better yet, where are you?"

"In Sarriera, did you not get my phone call?"

"Yes I did, and we are also here. Sam drove us crazy so there you go, what can I say? Do you think this is good or bad?"

"Have you been followed?"

"No Tina, but you have. We took one of the guys out, but there is still another around here somewhere. We have been watching the area, but there was nobody suspicious that we could see."

"He is here?"

"Who? The bad or the good guy?" Micha wanted to know with a grin.

"Both, are you the bad guy?"

"Uuh very bad indeed, remember?" Tina laughed remembering the little private moment with him in the janitorial room, but she kept a trained eye on Kate who was waiting for an answer from Sam's phone. But then she hung the phone up and waved to Tina that she was finished.

"Why did Sam not answer his phone?"

"He is not here, I don't know but I will check and see, later girl, love you, oh wait, where did you say you are staying?" Tina quickly gave him the name of the hotel and then hung up on him. Kate was becoming restless.

"And?"

"Did not answer."

"Well, later then. Ready for a swim?"

"Yes, let's go."

Dance Club

THE EVENINGS WERE ALWAYS APPEALING to Kate in this place. The ground was still warm from the sunny day and the temperatures never dropped below comfortable levels. Walking in the evenings on the beach was a pleasure. The moon reflected on the water as the sun had earlier, and the lights became increasingly crystal clear as the night progressed. Tonight though, she did not really feel herself. Tina had noticed the change in her mood as well and after waiting for her to bring it up, which she did not, she decided to ask her directly.

"Soooo ... Kate, what's up?"

"The sky, and a lovely one we have tonight... don't we?" she said grinning.

"So, Kate, what's up?" she repeated again, making sure that Kate understood that she was not willing to let it go.

"Oh, I do not know, somehow the past is haunting me more than usual. These days I sometimes feel so close to Sam, and then get angry with him ... maybe I am PMS'ing. I know I need to move forward, leave the past in the past and move to a place that makes me happy again.

Spain is a wonderful location for that, don't you think?" Kate looked around and waved her hand at her surroundings as she spoke. "Let's do something different tonight, let's go dancing," Kate said, excitedly looking at Tina.

"Yeah, that would be something really 'different,' since we have been doing that every evening for the last few weeks," Tina started laughing at her, "But let's go anyhow, it seems to keep you in a happy mood. Any particular place in mind?" she said, grinning.

"You know that place that is not too far from here; I would really like to try that one, what do you think, could we go? Please, please, please?" Kate was fluttering her eyelashes playfully at Tina, who just started to laugh and then played along.

"Gosh, well gal if ya ask like that, who could resist ya ..." she said in a playful thick southern accent, which made Kate laugh, and she wound her arm into Tina's and they both went purposefully to their room to change for the night, which did not take too long. Soon they arrived at the dance bar, grabbed a drink and then went to find a table.

The music was good tonight and whenever something good came on, Kate went to dance by herself on the dance floor. Tonight she seemed to make exercise out of it, Tina thought, it appeared to her that she wanted to dance something out of her system and was not quite succeeding. After a while she came back to their table and looked at her breathlessly. "You – not – coming?" she was barely able to get out.

"You seem to be dancing enough for the both of us," Tina shouted so she could hear her over the music. But then she could see Kate tense up, and Tina began to worry. "What's wrong?"

"Nothing, I guess ... it's time to leave ..." but then she stopped and listened. Kate was not so sure herself, but she did not go back on the dance floor. She decided to rather remain watching and waiting for the feeling to pass, for her heart to stop beating so fast, not due to exertion but to expectation. Tina watched as Kate walked over to request another song. Well, maybe Kate wanted to dance one last dance before they went home, but this evening was somehow different, Tina thought.

When she returned she told Tina they would leave through the back door, without even waiting for her song to be played, and that was the end of the evening. Stunned, Tina followed her to the back and out into the alley, battling to keep up with her.

"What in the world has gotten into you?" she demanded. "Please, why are we running?"

"We are not running we are walking ... with purpose ... in a hurry ..." Kate said stubbornly. In the distance she could hear her song starting.

"Well stuff that," she said and then turned and kept on walking, fighting back tears.

"Stuff what?" Tina became impatient. "Darn it, Kate, answer me!" and she stopped in the middle of the street so that Kate had to turn around and drag her up the hill.

"He is here, I cannot believe it. How did he find me?"

"Who is here?" Tina said, beginning to worry, but then the light bulb came on, "Oh, YOUR guy ... well is that really so bad? Is he good looking? Well? Remember me asking for a brother of his? Did you not want to talk to him anyhow? Saves you money on phoning ..." Tina asked teasingly. "Why are we running away from him?" She looked at her puzzled.

"We are not RUNNING, we are walking with PURPOSE!"

"Oh yeah, right, big difference, my mistake. You must obviously be important to him if he keeps on following us, how did you know he was here in the first place?" Tina said in the most indifferent tone she could manage.

"He sent ME to hell, and I was there, and now HE can stay there, for all I care, at least... for a little bit LONGER!" she said rather loudly to Tina, who shrugged, not expecting that kind of response.

"Well then, to hell with him then, but it seems you are still there as well, are you not?" Tina said, looking at her questioningly.

"I have found a comfortable spot there, where I will wait things out," Kate said, but then when she envisioned it, she had to grin.

"I never heard of anybody finding a comfortable spot in hell, but hey if you did, more power to you!" said Tina in a light tone.

"Wanna join me there?" Kate said lightly, feeling bad that she had shouted at her, for it was not her fault.

"Nah, the place is taken," Tina said, and then she drew a sign with her fingers in the night sky and spoke slowly as she wrote, "It says: Kate's ... pity... party ... and ... nobody ... is ... invited." They both had to laugh, and then they arrived at the bus stop and the bus arrived immediately, so they got home faster than they expected.

Outside the club Micha was sure that the area was well covered and safe, so he watched Sam from a safe distance.

"Marcus, I think we are at the right place," Sam said excitedly.

"How do you know?" Marcus wanted to know, looking at the rather unimpressive exterior of the dance club. But Sam just looked at him and then Marcus caught on.

"OH ... yeah, that feeling ... now how do we make sure ... well, how do we flush her out of this, this ... mad house? I did not know that these places were so well attended, there are so many people here, how can we find her?"

"I have an idea."

When they got inside they had to scream at each other as the music was very loud. Sam told him about his plan. Marcus looked questioningly at him for a moment, but then he stopped Sam, who started to pull out a few bills and nodded in the direction of the DJ.

"Forgive me Sam, but this is my turf here, wait here while I take care of it. Tell me again, what do you want him to do?"

"Well if you insist, tell him to play Meatloaf, 'I will do anything for love' I think it is called, that should do the trick. We will watch the crowd and we will soon know where she is."

Marcus looked at him doubtfully but he did as suggested. Sam could see him fighting through the dancing crowd, working his way to a man in the back. He spoke briefly with the man who apparently arranged the music, and when a man with long hair finally looked up and recognized him, he was more than accommodating, even without the money.

After a long search around the club, Sam had to agree with Marcus. The place was way too dark, with the flashing lights it was hard to make people out. It was also a very fast moving crowd, so that it seemed impossible to find anybody in here, even though an intense feeling told him she was here. When Marcus had finally found his way back to him he made a face at Sam. Taking the hint they decided to go for a bit of fresh air outside, to give their ears a bit of a break. While standing beside some planters, they heard the DJ announce a special request and Sam's song came on. Waiting to see if something out of the ordinary would occur, they watched the crowd, but without success. The couples on the dance floor paired up and danced to the slower parts of the music, but no Kate.

Then a new song started and everyone began to dance as before. Marcus looked questioningly at Sam. "And?" But Sam just shrugged his shoulders. He was about to give up when another song started to play and the DJ stated that it was also a special request. He played Madonna's 'Hung up on you' and Sam started to laugh so hard, that he had to hold on to Marcus's shoulder so as not to lose his balance.

"I guess this is another one of those inside jokes? Care to share?" Marcus looked at Sam in confusion. The dance crowd was hopping up and down to the beat, but Sam just shook his head trying to catch his breath.

"She was here all right Marcus, and she is talking! This is good, very good ..." Marcus just looked at him, confused, and both men fought their way back to the front door.

"Sam I am a patient man, but ..."

"Listen ..." Sam said to Marcus, "The song is all about a woman who has grown tired of waiting, and has left ... she is expressing her anger through the music. I can work with anything, but not with silence."

"You mean she did the same thing you did, requested a song to let you know what she is thinking?" Sam just nodded. Marcus looked baffled. "I see ... Words and talking things out are highly overrated for you guys, are they?" Marcus looked confused again.

"Well, she's gone, so we can call it a night as well," Sam said. Micha just shrugged his shoulders, as he could not see her either. If Micha had known that this was going to be such a close call, he would have staked out the club from all sides, but who communicated with him about anything these days? Soon they were all back at the boat. Nobody had seen the women leave, so they had no idea where they could have gone or where they should look next.

Back at the hotel room after a long shower Tina was lying on the bed, singing and waiting for Kate.

"I would do anything for love and there will be no turning back, I would do anything for love, I would go through hell and back ... yup... that sounds like someone who does not love you anymore, Kate, oh hell, give the guy a break now would you!"

"Look Tina, here is my problem. I do love the guy ...still... I do, but I cannot live with the fear that he will dismiss me every time things go south. With that kind of fear, love can't grow. I think I might be better off not going there again. We are in a nice place here, are we not? We are doing well without that worry, are we not? And thank the Lord that the dance club was far enough away from here, for him not to know where we are right now, otherwise I would feel like leaving again. I like it here a lot. Sarriera is a place one could get lost in dreams again, don't you think?"

But Tina did not answer for she had fallen asleep already.

When Kate finally fell asleep she started to dream.

'Where are you running to?' she heard Sam asking her in her dream.

'I am not running … I am moving with purpose,' she replied.

'Really?'

'Why are you here?'

'I love you, Kate.'

'Now he tells me.'

'I miss you.'

'I cannot do this anymore. All this … it's not enough. Besides, I need to think of me now as well. I feel like I am losing my mind, and that after I thought I had finally recovered a little. So leave me be!'

'I can't Kate, you know why.' Then he faded away into the mist.

"Kate wake up!" Tina looked at her, concerned.

"What's wrong?" Kate wanted to know, yawning and wondering why she would dream such a silly dream.

"Well for starters, you thrash around like crazy when you dream. Goodness girl, what were you dreaming about, if you don't mind me asking?"

"A silly dream, sorry for waking you Tina," she said, turning onto her other side and closing her eyes.

'Sweet dreams, till soon …' she could hear him say, which made her open her eyes again, because she was not yet asleep, so she knew she could not be dreaming.

"Tina. I need to find a psychiatrist tomorrow, I am losing it, I need to talk to him about auditory hallucinations … maybe a psychotic break … stress related …" she whispered to Tina, who just mumbled back: "Could have told you that free of charge …" and with a smile she fell asleep again, and both had a restful night after that.

The next morning Tina had a very early call and after she hung up she walked over to Kate and woke her. "Say Kate, I would join you today on the run from the Huns, but I need to go and see someone regarding my papers, would you mind waiting until I have returned and then we can make plans for the next mad dash ... maybe see Madrid ... do some sightseeing?"

But Kate just groaned at the word 'sightseeing'. "Tell you what, Tina," she said sleepily, "You go, I stay, sleep longer ... I really like it here, so no worries, I will wait for you to get back. Then we can check out this town, the beach and the reef, and just generally relax, but I need a break from all the moving about. I am an old lady, you need to know," she said, smiling. She opened one of her eyes to look at Tina. "Deal?"

"Stay at the hotel though, I do hate missing out on things, and when you go exploring without me, then I miss out and I hate that! Well, I'm repeating myself here, did I mention I hate that?" After she saw Kate mumble something into her pillow she was satisfied, got dressed in a hurry, and by the time Kate could answer she was almost out of the door.

"Maybe ... no promises ... ain't jail, you know?" Kate said and turned over onto her other side.

The Past Catches Up

MORNINGS HAD NEVER been Kate's favorite time of day, but in Spain it was a different story. This morning she got dressed without Tina, knowing that Tina would be half way to Madrid by now. Poor girl, why did she need a visa she wondered, oh well, who knows, but knowing her, she would spend the rest of the day there seeing the city. Kate found the solitude rather pleasant. The peacefulness was conducive to finding peace within. She had secretly looked forward to a couple of calm and quiet moments alone for some time, when she was collecting shells on the beach, walking up to the market or having a long breakfast or a late coffee at a cafe. Of course she enjoyed Tina and the time and travels with her a lot, but she had to admit that a little down time sounded more enticing right now than seeing Madrid.

So she put on one of her summer dresses, wound her white silk scarf around her neck to mask her crest, which was annoyingly bright these days again, slipped on her favorite sandals and grabbed the new bag she had bought a couple of weeks before at a market. This morning she took her time with everything, she even applied a bit of make-up before she went down to breakfast. In the lobby a few people were still sitting at the tables next to the buffet, eating breakfast. She went to get her breakfast at the buffet and picked a table close to the veranda door to catch the warm breeze from the Mediterranean Sea. The coffee here was more milk than coffee, but it had a wonderful hazelnut flavor and was just as delicious as the fresh-from-the-baker buns with the jam the owner's wife must have made herself from scratch.

She leaned back in her chair while she ate her bun and looked around. This time there was an older couple sitting at the back, obviously finished with their breakfast, sipping their coffee and discussing something they had been reading in the guide in front of them. Two tables over sat an older man in shorts, reading his paper. On the other side of the room sat two well-dressed gentlemen, discussing something in Spanish. Both must have finished eating their breakfast for their table was clean and they only had a big, old book in front of them, which they seemed to be discussing heatedly. Judging by their appearance they must be wealthy, for their clothing spoke of wealth and style, and was obviously custom tailored, for each of them. The older gentleman looked like the father of the younger one, and the younger one was not much older than herself.

She took another bite out of her bun and looked at the buffet, where a young family who must have just arrived chose their breakfast. The little girl was set on a chocolate muffin and even though her mother wanted her to choose something healthier she was set on the muffin and she let it be known loudly. After a moment of struggle her mother gave up and agreed on her having it, with the stipulation of a bun first, which brought peace back to the room. Kate was reminded of Beth, Jackson's daughter, a little bit. She was the flower girl at Kate's wedding, and since that time, she was always close at Kate's heels. Having lost a baby girl herself due to a miscarriage, Kate enjoyed having Beth around her. Now, looking at the little girl, she realized that she had curly hair similar to Beth's, and that might have been the trigger for her to remember Beth. The older boy beside her seemed to be more interested in his music than in the many choices for breakfast. He took off his headphones reluctantly, when his father gave him a warning look. Then he quickly grabbed what was in front of him, filled his plate, walked over to an empty table, sat down and put his headphones back on again. Yeah the younger generation with their gadgets, which they seemed to be unable to live without, just like her boys at home, only she had to remind herself that they had not been boys for a long time. Daniel had finished his Ph.D. in medicine early and was now back home practicing at the hospital under Jackson, and Michael was even older than Daniel, so no, there was no way she could still refer to them as boys, even though that is what they always would be to her.

Thinking of them made her feel homesick, so she forced her attention back to her surroundings. Outside the balcony doors was a beautiful, sunny day. The architecture of the buildings and the colors all around were just as positive and inviting as the weather, light, warm and full of life. The main local building material was light cream sandstone. Most of the floors were tiled. In this town flowers were everywhere, their fragrance following her wherever she went. If she could choose a place that would be perfect to retire, then this would be it. On a few occasions the little harbor had enticed her to pick up her brush and start painting with her oil colors again, if only to hold fast in oil the wonderful views and memories, to capture forever the feeling of comfort and peace. The streets outside were of cobblestones like in the olden days; come to think of it, time seemed to stand still here, or at least to pass at a very slow pace. The occasional breeze that came in through the doors ruffled her hair. It was a warm breeze with the smell of spices and the sweet scent of orchids. She got up and went back to the buffet to get herself another cup of coffee ole and sat down again. Now that Tina was not here she could have breakfast for as long as she wanted and there was really no need to get up anytime soon. This was heavenly.

She was studying the little alley that led up the mountain when she heard a voice next to her, and it made her almost jump out of her skin. The older, well-dressed gentleman was standing beside her now. "Permiso Condesa, puedo disponer un momento de vuestro tiempo?"

"I am so sorry Sir, but I do not speak Spanish, at least not much, so I am not able to help you," she said apologetically and looked up at him.

"Puedo preguntarle de donde viene Usted y cuanto tiempo se va a quedar?" he said to her and she looked around for help, not knowing what to tell the poor man, who had obviously mistaken her for someone else. "Maybe you should find someone who can speak a bit of Spanish, for I speak none," Kate said, still looking to see who she could ask for help with translation. At the table where the older gentleman had been sitting, the younger man was watching them with amusement, and after another moment he took pity on her and said something to the older man in Spanish, which the older seemed to disagree with, and then the younger man came over to her table as well.

"Excuse me Signorina, but my uncle here seems to believe, that if he spoke a little longer to you in Spanish, you would understand him," he said with a winning smile.

"Well, could you tell him please, that if this was the way to learn a language, I would be multilingual by now? So I need to apologize, for I cannot help him. By the way, what does he want in the first place and what did he say?" Kate wanted to know, becoming curious herself.

"He was asking you if you had a moment for him and then he asked you where you came from and how long you are staying," he said, while he looked from the older gentlemen to her.

"A lot of personal questions to ask a stranger, don't you think? Or is it Spanish custom to have so many questions for visitors?" Kate said, looking at the man who was kindly translating.

"Let me introduce myself. I am Marcus and this is Duque Frederico de la Rosa de Maya," he pointed to the older man beside him, who bowed to her and took her hand and kissed it, "Es un honor de conocerla."

"What did he say?" Kate whispered to Marcus.

Marcus leaned over and translated, "He said that it is an honor to meet you. And I have to agree," then he smiled winningly at her.

Kate blushed, but she was still confused by it all. "You said he is a Duke. What do I do, considering he is a Duke? Do I get up? What is the polite thing to do?" Kate was totally at a loss.

But Marcus just started to laugh, which caused both Kate and the older man to give him curious looks. So Marcus turned to the old man and spoke in rapid Spanish, and then the older man looked at her, puzzled. "¿ Conoce usted sus antepasados?"

"I can see it would be best if I translate for both of you, for this has the potential to become confusing," Marcus chuckled. "I translated your reaction, and then he wanted to know if you knew who you were? Now secondly, would you mind if we join you at your table, there is much we have to catch up on, it appears," he said with a handsome and charming smile that made it impossible for her to say no, so she pointed at the chairs across from her. Marcus translated her invitation to the older gentleman and he reluctantly took the chair across from her, while Marcus went to get them both a cup of coffee. Uncomfortable, she got up, which made the older gentleman rise as well, and carried her plate back to the dirty dish tray, so that when she came back she also had only a cup of coffee standing in front of her. They waited for her and only sat down when she returned to the table. This was obviously an old country with old customs and traditions, she thought, so she tried not to make it obvious that she was surprised at their gentlemanly behavior. In fact she thought it was kind of nice to be treated like a lady.

The Duke seemed to feel as uncomfortable as she felt for he sat stiffly on his chair, not touching his coffee. "Say Marcus, your uncle seems to have a lot on his mind and yet he seems to be rather uncomfortable around me, so what is this all about?" Kate asked Marcus for she really wanted to break the ice now.

"Well you invited him to sit with you, which he could not decline, but he also feels it is not correct, being in the presence of a person who shows more dedication to her family than any person with a noble title ever did in our family, " Marcus said, while looking at the stiff looking Duke beside him. "This is my fault, I forgot how he must feel," he said apologetically to her.

"Dedication? Do we know each other? What do you know about me? And besides that … you lost me … if he is so uncomfortable, why doesn't he just go back to his table? Why make himself miserable being here at my table, when there are plenty of empty tables he can choose from?" Kate wondered, becoming a bit uneasy herself, with the eyes of the Duke on her.

"I am not sure, but it seems so important to him that he called me to be with him here. When he asks … one follows his wishes," Marcus said.

"You know Marcus, up to this point nothing you have said has made any sense to me, and if you do not explain quickly I will get up and give the Duke what he needs, that is this table to himself, so he feels comfortable again," Kate said warningly, but then she smiled. "You are talking in riddles and I am not enjoying it."

Marcus turned to the Duke and spoke to him in Spanish, then the Duke looked at her and with a firmly raised voice he spoke to her again directly.

"Tiene que escucharme. Despues puede hacer lo que quiera, pero tiene que poner atención a lo que digo."

Kate did not understand anything he said, but she could tell this was important and she shied away from his voice a bit, a reaction that concerned the Duke, but he was glad he had her full attention.

"Además, no podemos huir de nuestro pasado, como no podemos huir de nosotros mismos," he added more quietly.

"Marcus?" Kate looked at him with concern, waiting for the translation.

"I told him you are ready to bail and he got upset, for he wanted you to hear him out and then you can do whatever you please."

"Yeah and that was not all he said, was it? What did he add quietly?" Kate looked at Marcus, "... and please, do not edit this conversation, Marcus, I am curious about why this is so important to him."

"Sorry. He said that one cannot run from the past, nor can one run away from oneself or the future, if that makes sense to you and I translated correctly," he said and took a big sip of his coffee.

"The flavor of this conversation reminds me of something I am trying to forget. So could you get to the point, so that I can take my leave?" said Kate, while busying herself with her coffee cup and adding an extra cube of sugar.

That's when the gates swung wide open for the Duke for he started to speak in rapid Spanish at her for a minute, so that she barely dared to pick up her cup to drink her coffee. What made him stop was Marcus's hand on his shoulder, asking him to slow down so that he could catch up with the translation.

"My great uncle was in the area to buy olives, they grow here the best. He buys them himself for our estate for he believes it is the fruit and pride of Spain. Well anyway, he was at market at the same time you were there a week or so ago, in a town several hours from here ... you remember, Si? Well anyway, he saw you there and noticed the crest you are wearing," he said and as he mentioned it, her hand came up to cover the mark, subconsciously. "Well anyhow, he could not believe his eyes and he went back home right away to talk to ... ahhm ... well ... the family about it. We also looked it up in our family history books for I did not want to believe any of it, but we found it, and I have to admit I am now a believer," he said, smiling.

"He found what?" Kate looked at him, frustrated.

The Duke began to talk in Spanish again and Marcus listened, intent not to miss any information he needed to translate. Then the Duke stopped and looked at Marcus who only said to him: "Are you sure?, oops wrong person, ¿ esta´ Usted seguro?" then he turned and looked speechlessly at her and back to the Duke, so that she had to prompt Marcus to continue to translate.

"Ah, well, ah, he said that he looked it up to prove a point to me, but then he also found your crest in one of the oldest crests in our family history books. You see he is the one in our family who believes that traditions need to be kept alive and that the days of old are not past. We all disagreed with him, but now I am wondering if we were all wrong," he said, looking at her in shock and shaking his head. He turned his head back to the Duke and spoke Spanish to him again.

"Tio, por favor nos lo muestra de Nuevo?"

Then he turned back to Kate and said, "I asked him if he would please show it to us again." But the Duke just looked at her again and continued sending a flood of Spanish words her way. After a moment of silence, when he was looking expectantly at Marcus to translate, Marcus began to speak, again looking stunned.

"He said that in the early entries there was a story about the invasions of the people from the North. Trying to avoid being overrun or overtaken by those large barbaric men, the Duke of the Northern regions of Spain, our early ancestor, decided to offer his oldest daughter to the leader of those Nordic men. He was hoping to create a treaty or alliance for the exchange of the safety of his people from the pending doom. Now those Nordic 'people' were not known to make such treaties, especially if they could just as easily overrun everything, kill whatever was in their way and take what they wanted, but I guess the daughter must have been a beauty and the guy went for the treaty. It was agreed that she was to be sent to him by boat after he had returned home, escorted by two of his own ships, and she was to stay with him for 15 years. If she wanted to rejoin her family after that time, she could do so. Only the treaty was broken, for she went up there, but she returned after two years, apparently not being able to stand the rough life they lived up there. She must have been very refined or spoiled. After she had given birth to a son in Spain, the Nordic servants took the child, when he was only one year old and returned him back up north to the father who was infuriated that she had left. We have for generations tried to make up for the treaty, but no noble woman was willing to sacrifice herself, to do what the first one didn't want to do."

Kate interjected, stunned: "What happened to her?"

Marcus replied, "My uncle said that it is noted in the books, that after her son went missing she joined a convent, and remained there to the end of her days."

Kate started to quickly put two and two together, and turned paler by the minute. She looked at the Duke and asked him, "Nordic man, you mean Vikings, right? And the leader would have had the last name Von de Vorg, am I right? That's why you are telling me that, right?" But she was desperately hoping he would say no.

The Duke looked at her and leaned back, satisfied, and just said, "Si, no es Von de Vorg sino Von de VoergENSON. " He pronounced the ending a bit louder so she could hear the difference, then looked with satisfaction at Marcus and said, "Usted ve, ella entiende Español."

Marcus turned to her, smiling weakly, and translated, "You proved his point that you do understand Spanish."

"Yet he is wrong, for he said Voergenson, and my name is Vorg so it must be a case of mistaken identity, for sure."

Without even translating for his uncle Marcus just replied weakly, "Well, names change over generations, especially when they are transferred to new languages and new countries, but the big thing that did not change is the crest attached to the name." He could see how badly she wanted them to be wrong, but how futile her attempt was.

Kate decided to shut this conversation down. She had heard as much as she needed, enough was enough. If all else failed there was always good old-fashioned denial. "Look I am not open to this kind of nonsense. I have tried really hard to get away from the freaky stuff and I do not want to listen to this anymore," she said firmly, gathering up her stuff, ready to get up and walk out. Her reaction elicited an angry glare from Marcus.

"Listen, even though my uncle and I are Dukes that does not mean we sit around and have nothing else to do, than to talk nonsense about the olden times, as you call it. I have a large company that builds condos on the shore line of northern Spain and right now we are in peak season, meaning I am needed up there. So if you do not mind, take this seriously, since I have been dragged down here to share this with you. You better believe me that I would much prefer to be on one of the sites that is in need of my attention right now. He ..." pointing his finger at his uncle, "runs our large estate, single-handed, so he has much too much on his plate to be sitting here telling you fairy tales. So keep your resentment to yourself and stop treating him as if he was a senile old man. Believe me he is not, he is smart as a whip and can take you on any day, but he hesitates because according to his books you outrank him. However, because there has been no royal crossing for so long in your history, you do not carry the title any more, but in his books you do and ... apparently deserve it as well." He looked sternly at her.

"I am so sorry Marcus, there was no disrespect intended to either of you, and I can assure you both that I do not outrank either of you. I am just a woman from Canada hoping to get away from some crazy and sad stuff, but it appears it has followed me, even here where I hoped to be safe from it."

The Duke looked angrily at Marcus and then apologetically at Kate. Then he began to speak gently to her and Kate listened, looking to Marcus for translation.

"He said you are part of our family and took on the burden of the treaty, therefore we will be forever in your debt," Marcus said, just as quietly as the old man spoke, feeling a bit guilty for having spoken angrily. She was right about one thing, he thought. She was here to look for safety and her blood had brought her home to them. Now they were again exposing her to something she was trying to be sheltered from. Her reaction was understandable.

"Marcus, you need to let him know that I did not choose my husband, but that he chose me. In fact, at the time it was a marriage of convenience, which later turned into more. But we have separated and I do not think there is much chance for reconciliation at this point. So I am just as much a disappointment as the first lady in your story ... in your historic books was," Kate said through the tears that started to well up in her eyes again.

But the Duke did not wait for the translation, he just put the book that was on his lap on the table and opened the first few pages, which were most likely the first entries of his family history. He took her hand and kissed it apologetically, and then pulled her over to look at the book with him.

Kate got up and went around the table and stared at the crest that was drawn in it with faded ink. It was the same one that Sam had on his back and they had on the fire mantel.

"This is unreal," Kate gasped, and even Marcus was shocked to see the crest in the book just as his uncle had said. The crest he had seen high on the mast before. Marcus looked at her asking for permission, and with a finger he pulled down her silk scarf to see her crest and to compare it again.

The Duke got up, bowed again and said, "Es un gran honor conocerla, Condesa Katerina de la Rosa de Maya de la Von de Voergenson, nuestro escudo de armas nunca miente. La deuda de nuestra familia sera´ pagada totalmente y nuestra seguridad esta´ garantizada. Usted ha retornado al país de sus antepasados para informar a nostros que nuestra deuda esta' pagada. Mi…, nuestra infinita gratitud. Usted necesita conocer a sus antepasados."

Marcus looked at her miserably and translated, "He said that it is a great honor to meet you Countess Katerina de la Rosa de Maya de la Von de Voergenson. He says the crest never lies and that he is glad that the family debt is paid and the safety of your people is secured. He says he feels he is in endless gratitude for what you did and that you have returned to let us know. He wants you to meet your family … of old."

"I feel so awful now, but you need to let him know, that I will have to let him down as well," Kate said miserably.

"I know. I am worried what that will do to him. What do you think happened that made this so final?" Marcus wanted to know, but Kate just looked out towards the street. She needed time to think, but she was not sure if the Duke was ready to let her go yet.

Marcus bent over to the Duke and translated what he dreaded to tell him. Just like Kate he hated to disappoint him, but to his surprise the Duke just started to laugh. Then he spoke to Marcus and Marcus translated back to her.

"He said that this might have been a possibility before you had taken the crest, but this crest is permanent and cannot be removed by men. The treaty he spoke of in his family book was only for 15 years, but you Countess have taken it a step further and made it permanent, by taking on the crest of his ancestors. So no, you did not let him down, you did rather the opposite and he is rather proud of you. He says that things will work themselves out like so many other things that have worked themselves out for you. He says you need to trust in the unseen and believe in it, believe that you have been chosen. If I am translating this right, then I believe he said that not just anybody can be the carrier of the crest, but that it is a destiny kind of thing. You should feel honored. Besides, he has seen the love that binds you two together and he is sure that this matter will be resolved soon."

Kate looked at the Duke in confusion, and he smiled at her and pointed at his neck, reminding her that the crest had powers. Marcus hoped that she had been distracted enough by the Duke to not notice the last statement, for it kind of blew their cover, implying he must have met Sam, which she did not yet know. To his relief, she did not notice.

"Marcus, tell him my husband has more or less dismissed me, so I do not think there is anything I can do." As soon as Marcus had finished translating, the Duke turned to her and spoke with a smile on his face, while Marcus translated: "Countess, you need to read up on HIS ancestors' customs, if you would, then you would know that he does not have the power to do so."

Marcus looked at her, shrugging his shoulders at her confused look. "Don't look at me, this is all new stuff for me as well," he said lifting his hands in defeat. But then he had also had enough of it all and turned the conversation to more pleasant thoughts.

"Come, you must meet your extended and intermediate family. I am sure they are all anxious to meet you as well, Katerina," Marcus said. "My uncle wants to stay for another week for he says that there is nothing more important to him, than to be here for you. But I want him to rest now and I need to make a few calls to the job sites before it all goes to hell. We will see each other soon. Please feel free to contact us anytime if you have questions. I can imagine that this must all be a shock for you, so you might want time to think as well. Just know we are here and we are your support in it all. After all ...." he said, smiling at her, "You are family and we are close and rather protective of our own. You ARE safe here, even though the crest has caught up with you ... Come to think of it, our family has grown over the last few weeks in a most interesting way."

He said something in Spanish to the Duke, who got up, bowed at her and smiled warmly. "Hasta luego, Condesa Katerina." For that she needed no translation. She could tell he was a wonderful man who was happy to have found a lost sheep. Well maybe he had, and now things made sense to her. The ribbon of a crown she also carried made more sense to her now, the light she created in the room of the Von de Vorg ancestors ... All of it made sense now. One huge problem with all this was that she was still not sure if she wanted to be part of all that fuss anymore. Besides, did Sam not make his point clear in Vancouver? On the other hand, he wanted to take it back from what he had told her at the hotel, but this back and forth did not make sense to her anymore, and she was not ready to forgive and forget.

Barcelona

AFTER THE TWO SPANISH GENTLEMEN had left Kate felt a strong urge to leave the hotel. She needed to get some fresh air, since all the information she had been told over the last hour or so was a lot to take in. She hoped that it would somehow sort itself out in her head. But first she wanted some more information to satisfy her curiosity. After that she would go down to the water and take a stroll on the beach for relaxation.

She asked around and soon found out that she would have to go to the next town to find a library with a computer. So she took the next bus and off she went. Soon she found herself on an old computer with a dial-up Internet connection, which took so unbelievably long to load that she started to have a new appreciation for high-speed Internet access. There was an enormous amount about Viking history, many books had been published, but she found that there was much fiction and myths within the facts that blurred the lines of fact and fiction. In one of the books she read up on Viking history and social structures and dynamics. Contrary to her preconception of Vikings as being unrefined, unstructured and well, all right, bullies, she discovered that they had a rather well functioning society with similar family structures and customs. Certain things that were treasured and upheld in the western world of the time were not taken as seriously nor seen as important. But apart from that, there were gender roles, rights and liberties, duties and honor to the clan and many political alliances, as had been customary around the world.

Kate read up on the family structure, the dynamics between husband and wife, and was stunned by the notion on one website, referring to divorce and separation between husband and wife. Now that was certainly different from what she ever heard before, but she had to smile. Even though women had little say in the choice of their partner, they were in charge of the house and property while the men where away conquering, invading and killing, and it was also the women who had the right to divorce her husband, not the other way around. Now that was interesting and somehow funny, considering that these big men were somewhat at the mercy of their wives in that respect. Nice! This is what the Duke must have been referring to, but regardless of how one looked at it, she did not want to be around someone who had obviously decided that he would be better off without her, even though he had changed his mind rather often about that. On the other hand he also mentioned that this right was only possible without the crest, but she carried it on her, and she knew this was a permanent mark for them both. Darn.

Data saturation, she thought, enough. What she had learned did not really change how she felt very much, but it helped to pull all the pieces together. Now it drew her back to the romantic little village where time stood still, back to the beach. She took the next bus back and walked from the bus stop straight to the harbor. Feeling the warm water of the Mediterranean Sea between her toes was so comforting and relaxing that she felt she wanted to be surrounded by it. Without waiting she went back, changed into her bathing suit, added her beach skirt and walked back out to the beach after grabbing an apple from the lobby, which she finished while warming up in the sun. Enjoying the warmth of the sun she drank in the view of the shoreline, the vegetation and the way the town was situated. The houses hugged the shoreline and mountainside. Sarriera, so small on the map, had won a big spot in her heart. This place was so welcoming and peaceful, who would be able to resist its charm? After she felt warm enough she went into the water and soon found herself diving to see what was beneath it. She discovered a vast amount of sea life, which made her feel as if she was in an aquarium herself. There were fish swimming around her that she usually only saw in pet stores; brilliant blue Damselfish, red Groupers and Angelfish, yellow Surgeons, even Clownfish as well as Puffers were swimming around her, free from all the worries of the world. Not far off she discovered a coral reef and after swimming on the surface for a short while to get her breath back, she dived and found herself surrounded by wild life again. The whole reef seemed to be alive. Even the sea grass, moving with the current of the water, seemed to be in the rhythm of the anemones, sea stars and the fish that relentlessly looked for food between the rocks. There was such a harmony in it all, that it pained her to have to come to the surface for more air.

All right, she had to admit it, this was one of those moments which she would have loved to share with Sam, if ... but Tina would have to do, and oh, wouldn't she be mad if Kate confessed that she had seen things without her. To make it up to her, she would show her this spot as soon as she returned from Madrid. After diving a few more times, she felt out of breath and for safety reasons decided to head back to shore. Arriving at the spot where her bag was, she noticed that she was not alone. Marcus was standing there holding her towel out for her. He shook his head at her and smiled. "Go figure – another water rat. I was wondering if you had any plans at all to join the humans on land again, or had decided to become a mermaid instead, remaining on the reef."

Kate started to laugh. "Let me tell you, it was a close call. It was so beautiful out there that in truth, if I was not so out of breath and starting to get tired, I would have stayed out longer. Mermaid, ehh? Are there any more myths that I should know of?"

"Nah, no more than that what has already been spoken of, as if that was not too much already. After we spoke I had to get my footing as well, and I am not even as involved as you are. It must have been a shock to you to hear that you came home without knowing it, and then to realize all that about your past. I felt a bit sorry for you. So I came looking and did not find you. Where did you go?" Marcus wondered, while draping the towel around her.

"I took a bus to hunt down a computer ... and found a really slow dial-up computer, something that seemed to be from my grandmother's times," she said, grinning back as she dried her hair. "How do you live without high speed?"

"Oh it is very hard, but we do survive," he said laughing. "I have high speed in my pocket and at home; believe me, not everything is as laid back as it appears."

"Where did you learn to speak English so well, Marcus?" Kate was looking at him curiously.

"In the USA; I went there to study a few times, and I sayed in Toronto a few times as well. We believe we need to learn about our customers to know how better to cater to their needs ... so we can improve our customer service. Tourism is a big market here," Marcus added and then stared at her crest.

"Something to get used to, isn't it?" Kate said as she dried herself.

"Do you mind?" he asked. He wanted to touch it, so she stood still so he could see it better. "Did it hurt?"

"Yes, but in a different way than you think."

"Did you ever regret going that far?"

Kate had to think for a moment and then she said thoughtfully, "No, not for a minute. Well until today. Permanent sounds rather unending these days to me, you know."

"So, you love him still?"

"Marcus! Isn't that a bit of a personal question?"

"Think of me as a far removed cousin, which I am, family, remember? So, do you?"

"I did very much and then everything went to hell in a hand basket."

"What happened?"

"Sam's plane crashed and for almost two agonizing years we thought he was dead. Then I found out he had survived and instead of being happy to see me, he sent me away. That's the end of my sad story; and how was your day?"

"Why did he send you away?"

"He says for security reasons, so that is that. Hungry?"

"Katerina, that you are not happy is as obvious as my empty stomach. So yeah, let's go and get some food, but you do need to tell me more, for we are very protective of our family. If he hurt you in any way, he has no ground to stand on here – ever. I will see to it. He may be big, but I have moves of my own," he said, doing some karate moves that made them both laugh.

"Another Daniel. How sweet. But no. He did not hurt me, except that he let me believe that he was dead, then killed me with words, and isolated me from everybody who was important to me, including my boys, and for that he will not get any forgiveness."

"Do you want to work it out?"

"I do not know if that is possible. Are you married, Marcus?" she asked him as they walked back to the hotel.

"Yes. And I have two children. Girls. Mercy!" he said laughing.

"Well think, if you were me, how would you feel?"

"I don't think I want to go there, to be honest."

"You are making my point."

"Katerina, what would you do if you were him?"

"Howl at the moon," she said with a laugh.

"Come on, seriously," he said impatiently.

"Considering how much damage was done, start again from the beginning. Start to rebuild trust, for example ..."

"You don't trust him anymore?"

"Well if it comes to what he says, I would put my hand into a fire that you can trust his words. He is bound to what he says, it's part of his honor. Trust him with my life, I would do that also, he is the best man to have in your corner when the shit hits the fan, excuse my language, but it is so fitting. But trust him with my heart, no. I am afraid of being hurt again, no wait, I think I am more afraid of being left and deserted again, yes, I think that is what I fear the most. We were so close that the thought of being lonely has become rather awful. Can you follow what I mean?"

"I think so. So you were like I am with my wife, one starts the sentence the other finishes it, right?" he said, looking at her.

"Believe it or not, much more than even that," she said, putting her hand on her crest. "We do that even at the level of thoughts."

"Wow. Now I am wondering, how would one let go of something like that?"

"As I said, fear of abandonment. I do not have the capacity to take another blow, Marcus. Life has not been that easy and Sam was not my first husband either."

"Could there be threats from that ex-husband that we need to know of?"

"You need to know of? Marcus, we just met and you want to

become my protector?" She started to laugh but Marcus did not seem to find it so funny.

"Listen, you owe me nothing. If I accidentally did something good for my family, I am glad, but you do not owe me anything. So do not burden yourself with me," she said as she started to climb the steps up to the hotel.

"Too late, Countess," he said from behind her.

"Oh come on Marcus, not you too?!" she said looking behind her and bumping him on his shoulder with her hand in a friendly way.

"Oh," he said playfully, holding his shoulder. "Abuse! I will sue!"

Kate laughed out loud. "Marcus, you have been in the USA too long. Leave the excessive suing to them, it does not suit you."

"You don't think so?" and he straightened out again, and looked entreatingly at her, "Is there any way I could blackmail you into coming with us to our family estate, so I can get my wife off my back? She is after me to see you, ever since she found out you are here."

"You think you need blackmail for that?" Kate started to smile at him, but Marcus got uncomfortable and changed the subject. "Well, what do you feel like eating, Katerina?"

"Marcus, call me Kate like everybody else, I would love to meet with my family any day, and right now I feel like eating sushi. But there seems to be no place around here that offers it, so seafood would be good, any suggestions?"

Marcus shook his head, amused at her. "Seafood is really hard to come by in a fisherman's village like this one, Kate. Goodness, there is a seafood place on every corner, but I think I will ask my uncle what he would like to eat, that will narrow it down a bit. You would not mind, if we joined you for a late lunch/dinner, would you?"

"Of course not, but no more talk about wacky stuff. I need a break," Kate grinned up at him and excused herself, wanting to run up to her room to take a shower and get ready. They agreed to meet again in the lobby. But just when she was about to dash up the stairs and Marcus wanted to turn to get to his room they heard from the front desk: "Senorina, Katerina, Senorina, we have a message for you. There was a phone call for you earlier." Kate walked back and got the note. It was a print out from the computer, saying that Tina would like to meet her tomorrow in Barcelona. She had a surprise for her and she should come prepared for swimming on the beach, and also bring her beach dress for an evening out. She would meet her at the train station at eleven a.m.

"Well then, my tomorrow is planned already, Marcus. So you will have time off to relax or take time for business, for this headache will be gone for the day."

"No, you are no headache Kate, more … a growing concern for me, I think."

"And that is better?" she grinned and walked up the stairs.

"What is to happen tomorrow?"

"Barcelona, I meet my friend Tina at the train station at 11 a.m. and then we will have a fun day there. You can start praying for the city," she said giggling and was soon out of Marcus's sight.

After her shower and after she had a really good meal with her new found relatives, she felt much better. "Wow, Marcus this was the best calamari I ever had. If I eat any more I will explode. Death by calamari …" she said smiling at Marcus and he translated what she had said to the Duke. After a flood of Spanish, Marcus translated back, that she was welcome and that he was glad she enjoyed the meal as much as he did the company. He excused himself, said something about needing to make a phone call and left. Poor Marcus was constantly translating for the both of them, but he did not seem to mind.

After a little walk with Marcus she went up to her room to rest, for she wanted to give Marcus time in which he did not feel obligated to keep an eye on her or keep her entertained. So as to free him to do what he needed to do regarding his business on the northern coast, she pretended to be tired. Before Marcus left her at the door of her room he suggested he could drive her to Barcelona the next day, but she declined, saying that the bus would do and that he should look after the jobsite that also gave him headaches as well. He was not happy letting her go alone, but she seemed to be determined and so he left it at that.

On the yacht the phone rang and Mel went to answer it, and shortly after she came back to the two men waiting for her with lunch. "That was Frederico, he would like to meet with us as soon as we can in Sarriera, which is up the coast past Barcelona. He said that Kate was staying there in a little hotel. He and Marcus had checked into it as well to keep an eye on her, until we get there."

Sam looked at Mike, who just held his hands up. "I know what you are thinking son, but this is a sail boat not a speed boat. We will be there sooner than later though."

In the far north another phone rang. "Yes, what's new?" a deep impatient voice answered. "How do you know this, and how reliable is the information?" and there was silence again. "She said that herself?" he said and then after listening to the other person on the phone he concluded, "No, I will come to Barcelona myself. You said 11 a.m. at the train station? Then she should be easy to spot ..."

In the late evening Kate had a little bite with Marcus and turned in earlier than usual. She wanted to pack a little to get ready for the next day. The next day came faster than expected. She got to her bus right on time. Even though the bus was full and hot, the scenery made up for it. It was simply breathtaking. They drove through wineries and along a beautiful coastline that reminded her of the Oregon coast – apart from the vineyards of course.

She got to the train station early, so she looked around in the shops inside the station waiting to hear or see Tina, which did not take long.

"Kate," she heard from afar, which made several heads turn, "I was worried we would not find each other," Tina said as she reached Kate. She gave her a hug and pulled her towards the exit so they could go and explore the city.

"How was Madrid?" Kate wondered.

"Good, how was Sarriera while I was gone?"

"Oh, I robbed a few banks and set the hotel on fire, otherwise all is well. But seriously, I have met my extended family, can you believe it?"

"You did what?"

"Yeah I know, I had a hard time wrapping my head around it too, and get this, I am a Countess, can you believe it? My great great uncle is a duke here in Spain from somewhere up north and he is traveling with Marcus, who is also a Duke. Can you believe it? I spent all day yesterday with them. They are really nice, that is if you understand Spanish, for the older duke does not speak English, so Marcus had to translate. Poor guy, we must have exhausted him."

"You met a duke?" she said standing still and holding Kate's arm.

"Correction, I met two dukes, and you were nowhere near," Kate grinned, satisfied.

"Will you see them again?" Tina wondered as they finally started walking.

"I hope so. If not, Marcus will send the cavalry after us, I believe. He is as protective as my boys are and ... Sam ... well, was ..." she swallowed hard and needed to change the subject fast.

"Now tell me, how did the thing at the consulate go?"

"The what?"

"The consulate, you did go, did you not?"

"Oh yes, good, good. Two dukes, hard to get over that one," Tina said distractedly.

"So, what are we going to do?" Kate looked expectantly at Tina.

"First we get a coffee and then we start looking around the city, then the beach ... how is that for a plan?" Before she knew it, Kate was whisked off in the direction of the city center. Yup, Tina was in her element again.

They went to get a coffee. Starbucks seemed to be everywhere and even though she found their coffee just a bit too strong the Spanish made their coffee even stronger, unless one could find the version with milk. They were about to walk over to a statue at the nearest park, when a gentlemen stepped back and bumped Kate, so that she spilled her coffee all over her white shirt.

"I am so sorry, I hope you did not hurt yourself with the hot coffee," she heard in English with a strong but interesting accent, from the man who had bumped into her. He was dressed like a typical tourist in shorts and shirt, a hat and sun glasses, and appeared almost more distressed than she was, for she really needed the coffee right now but instead she was wearing it. He passed a few tissues to her, which he got from the hot dog stand next to them, and he introduced himself. Everything happened so fast that Kate could not even get his name, but noticed that he was nice looking and had an apologetic and winning smile, and a fair complexion.

"You are forgiven, but stop the apologies. It is nice to run into someone who speaks English. Where are you from?"

"Are you hurt? I mean the coffee was hot, was it not? Let me make it up to you. How about dinner at the beach down there?" he pointed down the street. "You have to allow me to make this up to you. So 7 p.m., would that suit you both?" Tina just watched the whole thing, amused, and looked at Kate. "Well?" she wondered.

"Yes, all right, see you at 7 p.m.," Kate laughed, still cleaning coffee off her shirt. The man took his leave, saying he would look forward to meeting them again and disappeared in the crowd.

"Good thing I brought a change of clothes with me," she whispered to Tina. "And he is handsome as well, that's good. There you go Tina, your chance has arrived ... maybe we have found one for you after all, but don't look at me, I am done with that stuff, never again ..." she said, grinning – but the male attention did feel good.

"We need to find a store, so that I can change and then let's make a start with your tour of the city," Kate went on enthusiastically. They had a fun time traveling through the city, looking at museums and churches, but the best was the fun they had in the store, where she changed into a shirt they sold there. She had fully intended to put on one that she had brought along, but the blouses did look rather beautiful and she did feel like treating herself to something new.

As the sun set they went swimming on the beach and then changed into something more dressy to meet the coffee spill guy, as they called him throughout the day, whenever the subject came back to him.

They did not have to wait long before he showed up with a friend. "Hello again," he said with an attractive smile, "You did not get any more coffee that I could possibly spill over you again, did you?"

Kate had to laugh. "Nope, I am spill proof right now."

"Well, this is my best friend Pete, Pete these are the lovely ladies I told you about from the park this morning."

"You never mentioned that they are so stunning, 'beautiful' was an understatement," he said, smiling back at them.

"And he paid you how much to say that?" Kate wondered, laughing back at him.

"Lady, you need a mirror, for you are beautiful without parallel," he said seriously.

"Well then, that Spanish tan is doing me good, Tina what do you think?"

"When he is right, he is right," Tina smiled back, but Kate could sense a note of caution in her, having known her for so long now. The men led the way to the table they had reserved and Kate hung back with Tina.

"Everything all right?" she wondered, leaning towards Tina. "I hope so," Tina whispered. "This all looks so fun and innocent, but I have a funny feeling about it all … don't know why …"

"Ah Tina, relax, enjoy and maybe the other guy, Pete, will take a liking to you, as well. There is something to be said about choice …" she said and Tina could not reply for they had arrived at the table where the men were waiting for them.

"Dinner is on me, of course, to make up for this morning," he said and Pete offered the chair on the right side beside him to Tina, so that Kate sat on the other side.

"Don't worry about it anymore, and I can pay for my own meal," Kate said, laughing at him.

"Not at this table you don't! So what you do fancy tonight?" Kate looked at Tina and they both said "steak," for Kate knew Tina well and that was her favorite.

"Women after my heart," he said and called the waiter over. He ordered wine with their meal and afterwards they talked for a long time over a glass of wine about Spain and coffee and food.

There was beautiful music in the background, which was conducive to a very relaxing atmosphere. Shortly however Pete had to excuse himself for he needed to leave to make a phone call, and the three of them went to walk on the beach. The sky was clear and the stars were easy to see, so Kate looked up and wondered what could be read in her stars. "Do you know the constellations?" he asked her.

"Nope," Kate said, "Not well enough to speak about. I know the big dipper and the small one over there. There is the W over there and the North star over there, and that's about it for my understanding of the stars," Kate said, getting dizzy from looking up, or from the wine she seemed to have drunk too much of.

"Well then ladies, let me take you on to a trip to the stars," he said and got a blanket from one of the hotel beach chairs and laid down on it, tapping beside him on the blanket.

"If we keep on standing I will get a stiff neck, so let's do this lying down. I will be good, I promise," he said laughing.

Kate looked skeptical at first, but then decided to humor him. "Just to let you know I have a cousin who would be willing to tar and feather you, if you try anything funny," she said laughing but also warning. Tina just sat on the sand beside her. She said that she did not feel so good looking up, so she would just listen.

So he began with his story of the stars. He began with the North star and then continued on with the different star constellations that make up birthdays. Soon Tina joined them and lay intrigued beside Kate to follow the interesting conversation. Somehow Matheson, as it turned out his name was, got tired and fell asleep while Kate was explaining how the North star was the only one that did not move. Tina and Kate were still discussing how it was possible that the star was not moving, when they heard snoring beside them.

Giggling, they kept looking at the stars, making up their own constellations and soon fell asleep as well. It was Tina who woke first, feeling cold and she bumped Kate, waving at her to come. They covered Matheson up with the blanket they had laid on and left him sleeping on the beach.

"I wonder what happened to Pete," Kate wondered out loud, still feeling rather tipsy, when they were far enough away not to wake Matheson.

"Well if you think I can handle another round of constellations, then you are wrong," Tina said yawning. "I need to sleep and then we have to head off to the hotel in Sarriera."

They got their bags from the restaurant staff and were walking down the main road when a dark limousine stopped beside them. Out stepped Marcus with a worried face.

"I got worried, since you did not come home, so I took the liberty of looking for you. Are you all right?" he looked at them both.

"Oh Tina, this is Marcus, my knight in shining amour, also my distant cousin, AND one of the dukes I told you about," Kate said chuckling, and then she stepped to his side and tucked her arm into his. "Tina, Marcus. Marcus, Tina."

Marcus nodded at Tina, but looked with concern at Kate. "Are you all right?"

"Yes I think so, I may have had a bit too much wine, even though I can usually handle two glasses, I am afraid this stuff down here seems to be stronger than I am used to."

"Well, let's get you ladies back to the hotel and after a good night's rest, you can tell me all about your day." He pointed to the open door and Kate and Tina found a seat in the roomy vehicle.

"You came to search for me in a limousine?" Kate said, looking around for it was rather impressive.

"It is my uncle's, and he would not hear of picking you up any other way, Kate," he said apologetically, and then said something in Spanish to the driver and they drove off.

Kate was so tired that she fell asleep leaning against Tina, who surprisingly was wide awake.

"What's made her so sleepy? I've never seen anyone behaving like this after only two glasses of wine. Perhaps I should ask how big the glasses were," Marcus said, smiling at Tina.

"No, this is unusual for Kate. I cannot be sure, but I thought that there was something fishy going on, which is why I did not drink anything. I gave all my wine to the plant beside me. When it comes to Kate, I am very careful."

"Thank you for that," Marcus looked at her in a questioning way.

"Yes," said Tina, and Marcus just sighed in relief and said, "I thought so. Good thinking on his part."

"Nope, you got that wrong. Selected by the unseen," she said, not expecting Marcus to understand, while looking out of the window.

"It was one or the other," Marcus said and Tina looked at him in surprise. He pointed to his neck to indicate he did understand, and Tina put her finger to her lips to make him understand he needed to be silent about it, but Marcus just grinned and continued reading his messages on his phone.

"Some odd activities are going down, and we are not pleased that they are happening on our land. I have received word from one of the Dons that there were several suspicious ..." He stopped, not wanting to be heard by Kate. One never knows how much people actually hear even when they are sleeping. "She must be kept safe here at any cost, we owe her that," he said very softly to Tina.

"We all are working hard on it, but somehow someone is always a step ahead of us," Tina said quietly.

"Yes, that has us worried as well, even though we now have eyes and ears everywhere, thanks to the Dons who came to the meeting with Sam. He impressed them all," whispered Marcus, but when Kate started moving they both fell silent.

Back at the beach Matheson was woken by Pete. "Wow, I totally passed out here, where did the ladies go?"

" Don't know, they left around the corner and when I tried to catch up with them, there were only cars but no sight of them."

"Did you get it?" he asked Pete.

"Of course, I took a few pictures. You guys looked rather cozy."

"That was the idea," Matheson got up with the help of Pete and they both went back to their waiting car.

"These will have to do. I was hoping to get more, but I think they will do the trick, with a bit of cut and paste and Photoshop."

"Marcus," Kate had woken briefly.

"Yes Kate," he looked at her, hoping she had not overheard Tina and him speaking earlier.

"Marcus, I would like to go dancing tomorrow, where is a good place to go dancing?" she said looking at him, tired and still feeling fuzzy in her head.

"There is a great place here in Barcelona. I will take you tomorrow, but now sleep," he said smiling. He thought she must be feeling better if she was making plans.

"Tomorrow?" Tina said looking at him.

"I guess so," he said shrugging his shoulders and opened his laptop to write a message.

The ride was long. The tinted glass of the limousine made even the cars beside them fade, so only the shining of the screen of Marcus's computer lit the inside. Outside there were few lights as they drove back the way they had come, through the vine yards.

At the hotel Marcus woke Kate, who made it up the stairs and into bed, with some help from Tina.

"You think they spiked the wine they gave us?" Kate said to Tina.

"Yes, I think so," Tina replied while tucking Kate into bed.

"You can't trust men, Tina. I think this has finally sunk in, even for an optimist like myself," and she turned around and fell asleep.

"Key is, you need to be selective, Kate, but our men can be trusted, you will see." And Tina turned off the light and left the room to make a call herself.

"You are OK?" was the first thing she heard on the phone.

"Yes of course. But I think Kate got a bit too much of whatever it was they gave us," Tina said.

"How did you get away with it?" Micha wanted to know.

"I fed the plant. Something just did not smell right, and you know my nose," she said smiling.

"Good girl. But I am worried. This is getting too close. What are we missing?" he wondered.

"I do not know, but keep it between us two, I do not want to worry Sam more than he already is," she said forcefully.

"Agreed, but you need to keep in touch more often, can you do that?" he wondered.

"I will try. Stay safe, love."

"You too. Love you. Bye." This was a hard time for them all, but it needed to be seen through to the end, and failure was not an option.

"Everything all right?"

Tina swung around for she had not known that there was anybody in the lobby with her. Marcus put his hands up to defuse her shock.

"I thought you had left!" she said sharply.

"I have a room here as well, remember?" he said, smiling at her.

"No, Kate forgot to mention that. So sorry," she said, now feeling how tired she was as well.

"Never mind. Is everything all right?" Marcus wanted to know.

"I guess so, just communication stuff," she said looking back at the phone.

"Miss him a lot?" he wondered, looking probingly at her and then continued, "I miss my wife and daughters as well. Right now they are all asleep. When I am not at home, the girls sneak into our bed and sleep with their Mama. I do miss my family as well, you see, so I hope we solve this soon. They have been asking when I was coming home and what I will bring them, when I come," he said grinning. "And my wife threatens me with the worst things if I forget to bring Kate along, for her family would all like to meet her. I still do not know how to pull this one off, but for the sake of my peace, I will have to find a way," he said thoughtfully. Tina grinned at him.

"If I just could figure out who is after Kate, I would sleep so much better," Tina said tiredly, "But now I had better turn in as well. Tomorrow could be another long day. Dancing again. Oh well." She smiled at Marcus and walked back up the stairs and climbed into the other queen bed.

"I will find out, if it is the last thing I do, starting with that guy Matheson and his friend Pete," she said sleepily, and then fell asleep.

Swimming at the Bay

O F COURSE TINA WAS ANGRY, as Kate had expected. She was not happy that Kate had gone to the beach, on the bus and worst of all, to the coral reef, without her.

"You promised to stay at the hotel, you promised!" Tina whined at Kate.

"Oh stop it. I will make it up to you. Come on, let's go to the beach and start with what bugs you the most, check out the reef, happy?" Kate wanted to know but Tina gave her a pouting look, so Kate smacked her playfully on her behind.

"Snap out of it, put on that smile of yours and let's go have fun!" Kate said while racing down the stairs to the beach.

Tina was vigilant to see if anything was out of place, but she could not see any possible danger, so they raced along the shore to the totally sandy part of the beach, but not before Tina discreetly texted their plans to Micha.

The beach was not more than two kilometers long, but it had beautiful white sand and warm, blue water. They warmed up a little in the sun and then splashed into the water, to check out the coral reef with their snorkel gear. Never had Kate seen the water so clear. It was even clearer than the day before. The fish were swimming around them as before, except that Tina had the same reaction to it as she did yesterday. She signed Kate to come up a few times just to say, "Did you see those?" or "Did you see that?" only to go right back down again. Once a school of very small fish swam toward Kate, split right in front of her and then united again behind her. What a rush! There were now more blue and yellow fish and less orange than the day before, but as before the coral was buzzing with life. Star fish and anemones moved with the algae, all in such harmony that one would think that time stood still here above the ocean floor. Tina seemed to be enjoying herself, but she seemed to be a bit jittery this morning. Kate assumed it had to do with a lack of caffeine, so she left it for now. Then they swam back to shore, dried off and fell asleep in the sun, only to wake with sunburn an hour later.

Laughing, they applied more lotion and relaxed, listening to the waves washing in and out, the seagulls singing over their heads and the wind in the hills. There was so much peace here, that Kate could have stayed forever, but soon it became obvious that something was bothering Tina.

"All right now, what is wrong with you today?"

"Let's go back, I think I have had too much sun," Tina said and sat up on her towel, just as her phone buzzed to indicate that a text message had arrived.

"Do you ever leave home without that phone?"

"No, I need to stay in touch with my parents, you know, overly protective," she said looking apologetic.

"Oh yeah, I forgot, better not keep them waiting," Kate said and turned on her stomach to bake the other side as well.

DON'T MOVE. STAY PUT! MICHA.

Oh no, she thought, they have been found, and now it was up to her to keep Kate safe, but knowing that Micha was not far gave her some sense of security. They were in danger no doubt, here out in the open. There was nothing in sight under which they could take cover.

Along the beach she saw a man approaching, he seemed to be collecting shells, in the other direction the older couple from the dining room were trying to get comfortable in their beach chairs, behind them some fishermen were mending their nets, and out to sea was a far-off sail boat, too far to be a threat. So where would someone come from if they wanted to ambush them? The phone buzzed again.

LOST CONTACT. GET TO SAFETY!

"Kate lets go to the room, quickly, please."

Kate was startled and looked up. "Where's the fire?"

"I need to go. I don't feel so good, will you come with me?"

"Of course, let's go." Kate got up in a hurry, wrapped her towel around her waist, helped to put everything they had brought along in the bag, and both rushed back to the hotel.

Just as they came up the stairs that led up to the hotel Tina had the kind of bad feeling that she always listened to.

"We can't go that way. I need to find a toilet. Faster!" she said to Kate, pretending to have the runs.

"How about the store down there? They should have a bathroom, what do you think?"

"Let's go," but before they could get far a hand came up out of nowhere over Kate's mouth, swinging her around and under a boat that was upside-down for repair on the shore.

Kate heard Tina jumping under another boat and then Kate heard the fizzing sounds of bullets flying through the air and one would have hit her, if it had not been for the person who was holding her firmly in place. She heard a familiar groan and after a few more minutes all was silent. Her heart almost stood still, not from fear of the bullets flying, but because of the sound she recognized.

'Sam, is that you?'

'Shhhh.'

'Are you hurt?'

'Shhhh.'

"All clear!" she heard Micha calling out loud. "Sound off!"

Kate could hear different people giving an OK, and then Micha came over to where she was under the boat.

"Sam, Kate, are you guys OK?"

"Well, thanks to this bullet proof vest I am, but it's so bulky we almost didn't fit under here," Sam said to Micha, then he held up his hand and Micha walked off, securing the area and giving them space.

Sam turned Kate around so that she was below him. He checked her for she could barely talk.

'All well, honey?' he asked her, without moving his mouth.

'You took a bullet for me, how can I be well with that?' she replied in her thoughts.

'Yeah,' he grinned, 'Am I your hero now?'

'I don't need a hero, but thank you.'

'I almost died up there, watching the whole thing unfold. These guys mean business, but I think that apart from the ones at home, we have them all now. There was no way I was going to let anybody touch you, so regardless of Micha's opinion, I was part of the plan to get you out of the line of fire, and it worked,' he told her in his thoughts. 'I still have some moves left,' he smiled, pleased with himself.

She looked at him for a long time and he grew sober. 'You want to run away again?' He put his weight on his side and before he could shield his feelings fully from her, she could feel how much the thought hurt him.

'So, you have been cheating.'

'Sorry?'

'You can block off your thoughts, the ones you don't want me to see, hear or feel?'

"What's the difference? I will not restrain you, but I will follow you wherever you go, for you and I are a package deal. But to be honest, I would prefer to come to some rest. Chasing after you might have been fun in the beginning, but after a while it becomes exhausting and heartbreaking," he said out loud to her.

'To the end of the earth?' she thought.

'If I have to ...' he smiled, tired.

'Hmmm ...'

She could feel the temptation rising in him and was wondering if he would respond to it and he did. He bent over her face and carefully, as if she was breakable, he kissed her, and to his relief she returned his kiss.

'Thanks the Lord on hands and feet,' was his thought.

'Amen.'

'I forgot for a moment that you can hear my thoughts.'

She smiled. 'Peace?'

'Peace.'

"Sam, all is clear, there is no threat in sight, so you guys can come out. Now, I need to see you guys, want to see how well the vest held up, could you guys come out from underneath, please?" Micha was standing impatiently beside the boat.

Kate was the first to roll out from underneath the boat and then Sam followed.

Micha took the vest off Sam and inspected it. The bullet was stuck in the middle of the chest, if Sam had not been on top of her, she would not be standing beside him right now.

"This is a special vest and these," he pulled the bullet out of the vest material, "and these bullets are not ordinary bullets either."

Standing beside Sam and listening to Micha, she could feel that Sam had found her hand and held it, while stroking his thumb over the top of her hand. It was so calming in the midst of the furor, and even though she fought it hard, she started to shiver.

He looked down at her, concerned. 'You all right?' he wondered and his eyes probed her.

'That was scary,' she thought.

'The thought of losing you, yes, very scary, but that just now ... I am sorry for frightening you, but we saw this coming,' he thought. Then he gave her hand a squeeze to confirm she would be all right now, and held out his hand, after which everybody excused themselves and left to secure the area and the hotel for their return. Only Micha and Tina remained.

"How did you do that?" she whispered to him, shivering.

"What?" he whispered, amused.

"You did not utter a word, yet they knew you were ordering them to leave?"

"Ah, that is a perk reserved for me alone, sorry sweetie." And he kissed her on her forehead and nodded to Micha, who had given the vest to one of the men. With his arm around Tina's shoulder, Micha came to stand next to Sam. Kate looked at Tina and then at Micha.

"So that's why you were not interested in anyone, you had found someone already," Kate said when she saw how Micha held Tina. There was an intimacy in the embrace.

"Kinda my husband, Kate," Tina said a bit sheepishly.

"Oh, married on top of it all, anything else? Wait, you are married to Micha, and Micha works for Sam, so you knew Sam?" Kate looked at Tina, clearly shocked.

"Honey," she heard Sam say, "She was your security detail and my way to know where you were. She reported to Micha, but sadly, not too often, and he reported back to me even more rarely, only when it was deemed to be safe."

"Can we trust Micha?" she said with humor, so that everybody started to laugh.

"Everything is arranged," said one of the men behind Sam.

"Oh good … I have been looking forward to this for years. Micha, you are back with your wife, for me that means no more snoring Micha, and instead I get you, Kate. What a sweet treat after all this."

"Say what?" she said shocked.

"We are swapping rooms at the hotel, if you do not mind," he said, now more careful and cautious. He could feel her resistance rise and had to think of something fast before she had time to build up a defense.

He heard her speaking lightly to try to cover up her thoughts: "Naturally, Tina needs to be back with her husband, and of course we will find you someone to keep you warm," she said teasingly.

"Grrrrrr," was the only thing she could hear and then he picked her up, threw her over his shoulder like he used to do in the old days, and walked back towards the sea, kicking off his shoes and walking straight into the water, fully clothed.

"Sam, you are still dressed!" she started laughing between trying to catch her breath.

'Let's swim.'

'Where to?'

'Around the bend there is a little cove we discovered while finding the best vantage point to keep an eye on you two.'

'Can you swim with clothes on? It isn't as easy as it looks …'

'Swim ahead …' he thought in a teasing way.

So she took a few strokes and when she looked to see his progress he was gone.

"Sam!" she said out loud.

'Shhh, you will alarm the guards, I want privacy. Talk with your thoughts.'

'Where are you?'

'Below you, silly.'

She looked below her and saw he was diving, trying to shed most of his clothes, and by the time he came up beside her he was undressed.

"What will you wear on the way out of the water?" she said, laughing.

"I already told Micha to have some clothes for me on some rocks, so no worries, now where were we?" he spoke out loud.

"We?"

He tugged on her legs and pulled her deep underwater. Before she could get back up to get air, she was wearing only her bathing suit, her wrap and towel were gone.

"Hello there," he said, when he came up right beside her to pull her closer. The playful teasing way Sam was having fun with her was exactly what Kate needed in order to mend.

"Where is that cove?"

"Tired already?" he said laughing, but not letting go of her.

"Well, sort of, not really," she said carefully.

He kissed her and his hands glided down her body and then he sighed, "Let's go." Sam was a good swimmer, but so was Kate, and they raced in the direction he pointed.

There where little pools everywhere in which the low tide had trapped the water between rocks. In those pools the sun had warmed the water up even more. They headed straight for one of those warm pools.

"Man, this is like the tub at home, come and check it out Kate." Kate climbed out of the water, swung her feet into the pool and let herself glide into it.

"This is unbelievably warm," she said, and Sam pulled her onto his lap and looked down at her.

"I missed you. I miss us, Kate," he said soberly.

"I know. I miss us as well."

He stroked the hair out of her face and traced his finger along her eyes, nose and mouth.

"How do we get it back?"

"Time, patience, courting," she said quietly.

"Courting?" he said, puzzled.

"Good old fashioned courting ... maybe ... You know, rebuilding trust and comfort."

"All right, but you will not run anymore, OK? I am allowed to make mistakes and so are you. Play fair, give this a real chance, can you do that? Can we agree on those terms?" Sam wanted to know and Kate thought for a moment and then nodded, "That sounds fair to me as well."

He turned, lifting her off him and to the edge. Having her so close with so much skin contact sent his body into a frenzy and he did not want to jeopardize the headway they had made up to this point. They both had their upper bodies leaning on the edge of the pool, looking out to the sea while enjoying the warm water and chatting. First they talked about everyday things, and then they discussed their experiences when they had been apart. There was so much to catch up on after such a long time apart, and they intended to make every moment count.

When the sun sank, Kate and Sam swam back to the beach. Micha and Tina were waiting for them with towels and fresh clothing, and they took the housecoats and walked back chatting with them. Sam wanted to know what Micha had found out from interrogating the men they had caught, and Tina and Kate were discussing the agenda for tomorrow.

"So how much was sincere interest and how much was I your job, Tina?" Kate wondered as they walked up the steps to the hotel.

"Ninety-five percent interest and fun, five percent job. I had so much fun with you; you are an awesome lady, Kate. So Kate, no more screaming at nights now?"

Kate laughed, "I think not, I hope not, and if I do, you will not hear it."

"Lucky me," Tina said, grinning at her. "See you tomorrow morning, Kate, sweet dreams."

Sam was behind her and took the key from her and opened the door. He could feel the anxiety rise in Kate, so he just looked down at her and whispered, "One step at a time," and opened the door and closed it behind them.

"I am not sure ... I am ready for this yet ..." Kate whispered, leaning against the door.

"Time for a shower, would you say?" Sam walked into the bathroom and turned on the shower and went to get her. "Come on, let's enjoy the shower shall we?"

He took off her housecoat and pulled her into the shower. There he started by washing her hair and then her body with such gentleness that Kate started to melt. He carefully pulled her bathing suit down to her waist and bent down and kissed her gently while washing her back.

"My turn," she said bravely and took the soap out of his hands and started to wash his chest, tracing his scars with her fingers. He quickly turned and showered himself off and then passed the towel to her so she could dry herself and take off the rest of her swimsuit.

When she arrived back in the room she had her T-shirt and shorts on, and he was sitting reading something in the paper, with his shorts on as well.

Kate had some time to look at Sam's scarred body. He was not very comfortable at first, but when she took some almond oil out to massage his skin, he relaxed. Her healing hands on his deprived body relaxed him, but they also heightened senses that he was trying so carefully to control. He wanted nothing she was not willing to give, so he had to wait, and he would. She began with his back that had not healed very evenly, so she applied oil to her hands, rubbed them and then released her shining hands with the oil on his back. It was amazing to watch how the skin below her hands responded. The bumps of the individual skin grafts smoothed out so that when she was finished only lines from the scars were visible. She continued with his arms and legs and he watched in amazement as she meticulously and precisely worked over every inch on his body.

"So now how does that feel?" she said after a long silence.

"Amazing."

'Time to sleep.' She leaned over to turn off the light but before she could reach it, his arm came up to stop her.

"Wait," he said out loud.

"What's wrong?" she responded.

'Leave the light on,' he thought.

'Are you afraid of the dark now?'

'No, I want to see you. I am afraid that if I fall asleep you will disappear,' he admitted sheepishly. 'Besides, it is my turn.'

He took her T-shirt off and then he took the same oil she had used on him and massaged her shoulders and then motioned for her to lie down and continued with her back. He could feel the tension flow right out of her. She started to relax to a point at which she almost fell asleep. He could not sense any anxiety and fear and she was starting to get accustomed to his touch again, which was progress. Her skin felt so soft and he closed his eyes so he would remember every inch of her.

'Sleepy time,' Kate said, misreading his closed eyes when she opened hers.

"Yeah, let's ..."

Sam pulled her to his side like he always had, and they fell asleep quickly. Their bodies well remembered the comfort they felt with each other. It was the first night in a very, very long time in which Sam slept restfully and deeply and Kate had no nightmares. Their bodies finally got some well-needed rest, and they slept until very late, so that by the time they joined Tina and Micha for a coffee in the lobby it was already well into the afternoon.

"Told you they are alive," Tina said to Micha, who looked sheepishly at her.

"By any chance is there a time when you could try to be wrong? Just for decency's sake or out of pity for me?" he smiled at her.

"When are we going back?" Micha wanted to know from Sam, who was making himself comfortable in a seat beside Kate.

"Let's have a holiday here. The kids are doing great, nobody knows anything so nobody is missing us, and the people that were causing trouble have almost all been captured. Do you like to go fishing, Micha?"

"I was born into the service of protection not of fishing, Sam." Micha looked annoyed, but Sam just gave him an amused look.

"Is that so? Now is that a yes or a no? The ladies want to go shopping, and you and I will go fishing. What do you say?"

"Like I have a choice."

"All right, what would you prefer to do?"

"I'd like to see the market myself, how about we join the ladies?"

"All right, let's keep on protecting the unprotected ... now from what I hear about Tina, that would be the merchants, right? Those poor suckers will not make a cent today, not if Tina has anything to say about it."

They all went to the market and watched Tina in action, haggling over prices and getting good deals.

"At times I feel sorry for the retailers," Micha whispered to Kate.

"I know what you mean, I feel sorry for them as well."

Family United

A S THEY CAME BACK from the market they laughed themselves silly, remembering how Micha had tried to imitate Tina's haggling and had failed miserably.

"Micha, there are things you should leave to the pros," Sam said, laughing so hard he had to hold his sides, and then slapping Micha on the back, "You will never be like Tina, not even if you try."

"Well, I can't be good at everything, but I have kept you safe this far, have I not? ... And that is all that counts, from my point of view."

"Yes you have, now let's eat; all that protection would be in vain if we starve to death." Sam's arm went around Kate's waist and he pulled her closer to kiss her on the forehead. "Hungry?"

"Starving," she said, grinning up at him. "Say, how long can we stay here?"

"Well yeah boss, how long can you stand staying here in the warmth of Spain's sun?" Sam said, grinning at Micha.

"Well that is hardly up to me, I am not the BOSS, so you let me know when I should make arrangements to get back."

"Well Kate, how long would you like to stay?"

'There is still some catching up to do ...' she thought and looked at him.

'There most certainly is, but we have to give them an idea, how about three weeks, too long, too short?'

'Good for starters, I think.'

'Me too.'

"Well let's say three weeks, all the guys deserve a break as well, wouldn't you say?"

Tina bumped her elbow hard into his side.

"Ouch, Tina, I get it. Yeah, I think we could use some down time as well. I will make arrangements."

Tina just rolled her eyes.

"I need to use the ladies, if you want to go ahead?" Tina suggested, but Kate wanted to have a moment with Tina, so she went into the bathroom with her.

"Tina, how are the boys? Have you heard anything? Are they safe? Are you in touch with them at all?" Tina looked at her, surprised.

"Kate, we doubled security as soon as Sam found out about the shooting up there. If something is going to happen it would be more likely to happen down here, because we have less people here, but I think our worries are over."

"Are they well?"

"They are both well, Kate. And we have not flushed out who it is up there yet, but we are close. What is worse for the boys is not hearing from you, Kate, a worry on top of everything else, it isn't fair to them."

"I can't lie to them, Tina, they do not know about Sam, and they would misunderstand if I was happy on the phone."

"Let me ponder that dilemma, for now you concentrate on Sam and mend what needs to be mended. We will do everything we can do to keep you safe and still make the time here as pleasant for you as possible, deal? After all, we are more than just security. We are also friends, are we not?"

"Yes we are, but let me know more details the next time you speak with someone from home, OK?"

"Promise, cross my heart," Tina said and then she started to get restless. "Now could I use the toilet, for I was not coming in on pretense ..."

"Oops," Kate started to chuckle and stepped aside.

The men were laughing at something outside when Kate joined them again. It was good to hear Sam laugh like that again, there was much they had to catch up on and a holiday together was just what they needed.

They went for a nice dinner together, but soon said good night because Kate wanted to go for a late night stroll on the beach, and Micha and Tina wanted to turn in early.

'There will be no flying bullets, only seagulls tonight, will there Micha?" Kate said lightly as they parted ways.

"Do not worry Kate, we have people here around the clock, but tonight is my night off, so Tina, let's go, before Kate changes her mind and wants us to join them for a night cap ..." he said to Tina and pulled her along in the direction of the hotel.

Tina looked apologetically at Kate and Sam, but played along, "Yes Master ..." and then in the dark they heard Tina laugh and Micha say, "Bad girl ..."

"Well, where would you like to go? Should we get the towels as well?"

"No, I have changed my mind. Follow me," she whispered to him and guided him back to where they had come from. Only at the restaurant they turned left and went up the street where the market used to be.

"Where are we going Kate?" Sam said, intrigued.

"At night they have street parties here with live music. And ... there is dancing," she said excitedly.

He just chuckled, "Of course, dancing. How could I forget?"

Just like the night when she had been there with Tina, so also tonight there was lovely local music and dancing in the street. There was nothing Kate enjoyed more than dancing with Sam, listening to music and drinking in fresh sea air. Yes, life was on the mend again.

They found a table and from there they watched the locals interact with each other, observing the family dynamics of the people of the village. Sam went to get them margaritas. While he was gone Kate observed a young girl, not older than seven or eight, dancing with a boy of the same age who was imitating being an adult. It was such a funny sight. Sam took the opportunity to check in with Micha. Even though he could have done the hand thing, he decided to call on his phone, just in case he was interrupting something he should not have.

"Sorry to interrupt Micha, but I think I will take Kate to do some snorkeling tomorrow, because she talks about nothing else. Then we will hang out at the cove, is there a chance you guys could leave a picnic basket for us, so I could surprise her with that there? That's all, sorry for the disturbance while you are off."

"Nah, we are still checking in with each other, so we are all on the same page, you know. The cove, all right, I will have a basket of food taken over there. Have a fun time, but I have to go, got a call coming in."

"OK. Let me know how things are at home and how the kids are doing, OK?"

"Yes. Bye."

Tina looked up at Micha with a questioning look.

"That was Sam. He is worried about the boys," he said, before answering the ringing phone.

"Yeah, Kate is too. So I did something you will not like, Micha..."

"Hang on," he said to the person on the phone, and looked at her with concern, while covering up the phone so he would not be heard, "How MUCH won't I like it?"

"I think it is brilliant and besides, it's kind of too late to object," Tina looked pleadingly at him.

"My night off will not be off, will it?" Micha said, groaning.

"I'm afraid not, but I will make up for it, promise ..."

"How much will you make up for it?"

"I will make it worth your while, how is that for starters?"

"Bring it on then ... I can't wait, but right now I need to take this call ..."

"Go ahead, but we need to leave in thirty minutes," she said as she got herself ready.

"Leave? Where to?" But Tina did not respond so Micha went back to the phone, and just grunted, "Women," when he was asked something, and then he heard a laugh on the other end.

When Sam came back to their table he saw Kate watching something on the street corner with amusement. Sam noticed that the kids danced very well, and it was just like Kate to be drawn to such a scene. Sarah, their daughter who had died as a premature infant, would have been around that age, maybe a bit younger, but the memories hurt so he pushed them away. For now he had to court his own wife again. There was much damage between them that had never been there before, he noticed that when they blended. There was an incredible amount of hurt, loss of trust and confidence. All that needed to be rebuilt, so he would have to start to win it all back again, starting tonight. At least she was open to it.

"Well, here is your margarita, Senora," he said with a smile as he approached the table where she was sitting.

"Well thank you, Senor," she said giddily back, still watching the people. Everything was decorated and people were dressed so colorfully, in a way that would have looked good nowhere else but here. The musicians played well and occasionally one or the other person sang with them. After they had finished their drinks and were walking back to the hotel, Sam took her hand and swirled her around as he had seen the people in the streets do when they were dancing.

"Well, I have been thinking, Kate, how about you show me the coral tomorrow?"

"Uhh, how fun, yes, we have to do that first thing," she looked at him with excitement.

"Kate," he pulled her closer to him, "Are we OK again?"

"For starters ... Don't you ever, ever, ever, EVER, shut me out again ... under any circumstances, whatever they may be. Never ever, ever, ever do that again!" she said, going quickly from giddy to sober.

"All right, but you have to admit it kept you safe."

"No, you are wrong. Safety is not only to keep someone from being harmed, but also to give them a feeling of being safe within. Others might not have been able to hurt me thanks to your actions, but as you know, we don't do so well separately. I am surprised you have forgotten how it felt when I was in Vancouver and you were at home thinking I would not return. How well did you do?"

"Don't go there right now. You are right, I did forget. And I will promise."

"Sam, even before that glowing thing and all the other weird stuff, we always were stronger together, we are too vulnerable separately, how much more proof do you need?"

"Yes, yes – Now ... Are we OK again?" he said, pushing his luck, but she remained thoughtful, wanting to be honest from the get go.

"We are, I think, in the process of ... mending," she said, searching the depths of her being, examining her feelings as she spoke. Honesty was really important now, she thought, and her words rang true to her and her feelings.

"In that case," he picked her up and put her over his shoulder again, and walked into the hotel lobby and up to their room.

"Not the Tarzan thing again!" she complained, barely able to get her breath between the laughing and puffing.

All night Sam just held her close to him. Building up the trust, as Micha had suggested, and it seemed to be the right approach. He had to be content with the baby steps of progress they were making. Still, he could feel her tensing around him, something she had never done before. For Kate having him so close was something she had to get used to again and for some reason somewhat unsettling. When he woke her with kisses she grinned and said dreamily, "I would like to be wakened like this every morning,from now on," but then she yawned and asked, "What's up?"

"I promise that I will never, ever, ever, ever, shut you out under any circumstances whatever they may be," he kissed her for every word, "But you have to promise me, that you will never, ever, ever, ever take that ring off your finger," he looked down at her hand and put back the wedding band that she had given to Micha some time back. She looked surprised, but then said, "All right, I promise."

She looked at her hand again, which now looked more complete again and reached for Sam, when there was a knock on the door.

"Unless there is fire or broken bones, do not enter!!" Sam growled, for he hoped Kate would not stop what she had started. This was what he had hoped for all night, and now the knocking at the door threatened to mess it all up. He bent down to her and kissed her, but then there was another knock at the door. Resigned, he gave her a look that said that this had to keep, but that he was not finished.

"Sam, I need you, could you please join me in the lobby in ten minutes?" Micha said through the door.

"Why?" was Sam's angry reply. His lack of politeness earned him a warning look from Kate.

"You'll see, see you in ten ..."

"Ten minutes is not enough time for anything," he said disappointedly to Kate, "So we will continue this later ... yes?"

"Go tend to the fire or the broken bones ... but keep your promise in mind!" she looked at him warningly, and then she rolled out from underneath him, walked seductively over to the bathroom and looked provocatively over her shoulder, "Just think what you are missing out on right now ... oh well ..." she added teasingly, as if her body language and the cute teddy she had on was not enough to drive him crazy.

"Postponed is not missed!" he said, rushing through to the shower and grabbing the toothbrush she handed to him to get it all done at the same time. He quickly slipped into his khakis and the short-sleeved shirt he had left casually hanging over the chair, pulled on his tennis shoes and walked out of the door.

"Postponed ...!" he said warningly to Kate before he closed the door.

"Are we still going to the coral?" she quickly looked out of the bathroom door, which made him open the door again.

"Absolutely! See you shortly for breakfast," and then he shut the door.

Micha was waiting for him in the lobby. He took Sam to the side when he saw him approach.

"Micha, this better be good, I mean really good," Sam looked at him warningly.

"Oh, this is more than good, and keep in mind this was Tina's doing, I had nothing to do with it."

Around the corner came Tina, now not so sure of herself, looking at the strained faces of the two men.

"All right, here is the evil thing I did, considering that you and Kate have been worrying about the boys, I figured, let's bring them here. They can get used to the thought of having you back again and be united with their mother. Now was that such a bad idea?"

"Is she saying what I think she's saying?" Sam looked at Micha.

"Tina brought the boys down here, they are waiting to see their mother not you, but I think first they should have a talk with you. Secondly, they do not know about the danger they were in, they do not know about the security they had, and they don't know about the security down here either. They are not aware that that bystander most likely saved their lives."

"The kids are here! Well, I think you need to do some explaining first, before I can go in to see them. Where did you say they were?"

"Next door, at a café that also serves as a meeting place for the locals. They have agreed to give us the room this morning, for they had nothing booked there yet."

"Good luck to the both of you, Micha. I will be waiting outside and listen to hear when is the right time to join in. Be kind and gentle, as this will be hard for them to take."

"I will be as kind and gentle as you have been with Kate," Tina said shortly.

"Ouch." Sam looked angrily at Tina for now she really was overstepping her boundaries.

"Tina!" Micha looked at her in shock and then looked at Sam.

"Sorry Sam, I know it was not my place to say that, but I was right." But Sam did not say anything, he just waved her away.

He followed them from a distance and then leaned close to the door of the room where Micha and Tina were meeting with Michael and Daniel.

"Well, this is a really nice spot for Mom to relax. But tell me Micha, what's with all the secrecy and fuss?" said Michael, relaxing in a wicker chair next to Daniel. Both looked tired from the journey and the little sleep they had had on their way from the airport to the coast, but they had changed into shorts and T-shirts as well, and were starting to blend right in.

"All I want to know is … has she gained some weight, is she doing well?" Daniel asked anxiously.

"Gentlemen, please, there is something you both need to know and catch up with. This is many months overdue, and it will be hard for you to handle," Tina said.

"First you need to know what our function is," Micha began formally. "Just as Daniel, and now also you Michael, were born into a position of leadership, Tina and I were born into the role of security, protecting the seat and family of Von de Vorg, so to speak; we are part of the security detail."

Michael leaned back further into his chair, looked at Micha and then said: "Look, no offence, but whatever you are is all fine and well, but we would like to see our mom pronto, if you get my drift – I can't see where this is going or why it's relevant to us."

Sam heard him from behind the door and liked how Michael approached the situation. He was not intimidated one bit, he seemed to have a strong head on his shoulders and he had grown up a lot, he could tell. Sam also realized that he had missed out on a lot and he fully intended to catch up, he promised that to himself.

"Michael, please let me finish, you will see right away where I am going with this," Micha had become more tense, Sam could hear it in his tone.

"Sam's accident was not an accident; Michael, does that get your attention?"

"What?!" Both boys jumped up from their seats.

"What the hell are you talking about?" Michael was obviously furious, but Daniel must have held him back. "Speak up, what are you talking about?!"

Sam wondered why Micha was so intimidated by Michael, who he remembered as being only a bit taller than Kate.

"Hang on Michael," Daniel said urgently, "You guys are the security detail, so why are you here with Mom? Is she in danger?"

"Shit yeah, now man, would you please answer our questions?" Michael was hardly able to contain himself.

"Yes she is," said Tina in a matter-of-fact voice, as if she was not fazed one bit by Michael's anger. "Well to be precise, she was, we had some flying bullets the other night, but that's in the past now. The same is true for you guys; if you think that the shooting a couple weeks or so ago was an accident, then you are sadly mistaken," she added quietly. One had to give it to Tina, she could keep her cool and most certainly could deliver a punch line well.

"Daniel, slap me hard, this is so far out there, I MUST be dreaming," Michael said, but Daniel just whispered quietly, "Someone killed Dad?"

"Who would do such a thing? Who would dare to do that?" Michael's voice was shocked.

"What do you think? You are invincible? Or that the crest you have on your back is worthless? Maybe you will reconsider now ..." Tina said.

"All right, sorry Tina, let's back up for a moment, all right?"

"Daniel, are you OK, should we take a break?" Michael was next to his brother and had his hand on his shoulder.

So Kate was right, Michael had taken his place beside Daniel and was protective of him; Sam was impressed and his heart started to swell with pride. He could not wait to be near them and hold them. Together they created a force worth fearing, a united team.

"Nah, I get a sinking feeling they are not done yet, is that right Micha?" Daniel looked at Micha.

"Nope, the best is yet to come."

"The best you say? What the hell? Dad got killed and you call that the best? Daniel, so help me I will beat this guy to a pulp, if I stay here one more minute. Where is Mom?"

"Michael, sit, calm yourself, stay right there, we will go in a minute," Daniel said quietly, and Michael, to Sam's complete amazement, followed his request without an argument.

"Just so you know, I am doing this only for him," Michael growled.

"Now we would not be doing our job well if we let one of you die, would we?" Micha continued.

"Well, you failed to save the monarch, so ... ?" Michael sounded worn down. This had to be over soon, Sam could tell, for he knew Michael well. Michael was usually the cool headed guy, so either he was very tired from the flight or he was maxed out. Knowing him, the latter was more likely the case. Again Kate was right, the load the kids were carrying had been too hard for too long. It had to come to an end, and he could make that change for them.

"We did not, that is what I meant with the best is yet to come."

"What?" the boys said in stereo.

Micha was about to open his mouth when he stopped, frozen. The boys looked at each other, wondering what was wrong with the man.

Sam had his hand on the door and demanded that Micha stop. 'Enough of this! My turn.' He came in from the back of the room, so that the boys did not see him approaching.

"You are saying he is alive?" Daniel said shocked.

"That is exactly what he is saying, Daniel," Sam put his hand on Daniel's shoulders then he looked at Michael and grinned, "Hello Michael, good to see you both."

"Holy Moses. Dad!" Michael jumped up as if he had been stung by a bee and Daniel leapt up and hugged his father.

"How is this possible?" Daniel whispered into his Dad's shirt collar, and his tears ran down his cheeks.

"Next time you are doing skin grafts, have a lot of compassion for your patients; it is hell. First half year in a coma, and the next half in an induced coma ... and then the agony of skin grafts. Not a lot of fun."

Sam looked at Michael, who still stood there as if he had been struck by lightning. Sam waved him over and hugged him with his other arm.

"Darn Dad, don't pull a number like that on us, the last two years we've been to hell and back again."

"Michael, watch your language!" Sam said, grinning at him as they broke the hug. "And secondly ... you have grown at least a foot, no wonder Micha was intimidated by you," he said to Michael and slapped him on his shoulders.

"Was not!" Micha protested, but he was ignored.

"I have heard so many good things about the both of you and I am so impressed and proud of you both, it is beyond words."

"Does Mom know?"

"At first she was suspicious and then she found out herself. For you to know would have put you both in danger as well, so she could not tell you and since she can't lie well, as we all know, she did not trust herself and could not call you guys. It was my fault she was cut off from you, the only support that was important to her. But we worked on that. We just started putting things back together two days ago. That's when bullets flew ..."

"But why would anybody want to kill us?" Daniel wanted to know, looking at Michael.

"Well, it appears there is much we need to figure out, but due to Kate's background she has activated an ability in us, which we still need to figure out. So far I can tell you, that when we are connected, we are telepathic with each other, pretty cool ehh? Oh yeah, and I can call my security detail telepathically as well."

"Ah, you found a way to make this guy stop talking, did you?" Michael grinned.

"All right now Michael, Micha is head of our security, so show him a little respect, would you? And it is thanks to his wife Tina that your Mom is safe, and thanks to her that you are here. I was too busy trying to save my marriage; I was not ready to think about how to break the news to you guys."

"How did Mom take it?"

"She was very angry at first, and then she sent Dad to hell for what he put her through, but now he is sort of forgiven ..." came from the door as Kate walked in. She looked at Tina, "Uh, I love this telepathic thing."

"Mom!" Daniel ran over to her and scooped her off her feet, and then Michael hugged her so hard she thought she would pass out.

"How did you know?"

"Well, when your father's guard is down, I can hear what he thinks. And he was so into what you said, that when I reached out just to ask how much longer he would be, I heard what was going on here. Mind you, I almost had a heart attack first ... So I thought, I just had to come here for ... the doctor is in!" she started to laugh. "Oh boys, it is so good to have you here with us, I am so happy!" she said almost in tears, but then she looked at Michael with a raised finger. "You! You stop growing, you hear me. I am now the official dwarf in the family! Traitor!" she said, and then started to laugh.

"Yeah, kind of a dwarf, but also the prettiest," Sam had come to her side.

"Well after all that excitement, how about breakfast, everybody?" Sam suggested and put his arms around Daniel's and Michael's shoulders and walked out, back to the hotel. Kate watched her three men walk out together and she thought that it was the most beautiful thing, fathers with their sons. Then she turned to Tina, who was crying because she was so moved by the reunion.

"I cannot imagine what you had to do to get the guys here, but I will be eternally grateful to you both," then she hugged Tina and they linked arms and followed the rulers of Von de Vorg.

"With people like you two, the function and survival of this family might just be possible," Kate said seriously, but also with a hint of humor.

"Micha, when is your day off?" she looked at Micha with both humor and pity.

"You know, I would not have missed this for anything. This was worth working through the night," he said, grinning.

After a lot of exciting chatter at the breakfast table, Michael and Daniel set out to check the water skis and the hang gliders, deciding to give their parents some space. They would be back in the very late afternoon to check in with them, so Sam took Kate snorkeling as promised.

Before they went to the beach they rubbed each other with lotion, talking about the boys and how they had changed and matured. Kate was busy with his back when she stopped.

"Sam, what is amazing to me, is that despite the skin grafts your crest never changed," she said as she rubbed lotion over the scars, but his skin was now less bumpy, thanks to Kate's caring hands.

"Well, because it is not a tattoo, it comes from the inside somehow."

"Have you seen Michael's yet?"

"Nope, we will check it later, let's go ..."

They went swimming at the same spot where she had been with Tina. Like Tina, Sam marveled at the brilliance of the colors, while Kate just watched him. He was still so much the same. With his back to her, the broad shoulders with the large crest on it that looked so threatening, well maybe she also saw it that way for she felt that way. Yes they had been to hell and back again, but they had survived as a family, not only that, but the boys had grown stronger in their relationship with each other. Sam was wiser she believed, and she herself now appreciated what they had much more than she ever had before. She stopped, held on to a part of the coral, closed her eyes and touched the crest with her other hand.

'Thank you for keeping the bond of our family intact and Lord thank you for bringing us together again and for keeping us all safe,' she prayed.

Sam froze, and his crest responded as he heard her thoughts loud and clear. When she opened her eyes to continue swimming in his direction she almost bumped into him, for he was right in front of her, and she found herself looking right into his face. He took off his mask and hers and kissed her, and pushed them upwards to the surface.

"Don't ever leave me again," she said wrapping her arms and legs around him like a monkey. He held her for a moment, and then with his head he motioned to her to follow him. He swam to the cove and on the small patch of sandy beach he caught her and rolled her below him.

"I never left you Kate, I could not tell you in order to protect you, just like you could not tell the boys in order to protect them. You and I cannot be separated, there is more to it than just you and me. That's why we need to find out exactly what is going on, and why others are after us."

She pulled up one leg and pushed against it, rolling him over so she was on top of him. Although she was so much smaller than him he just let it happen, and even helped a little to see what she was up to.

"Don't ever leave me again, Sam, emotionally. Turning away from me like that has given me nightmares ever since then, every night," she said soberly.

"Would you have kept your distance otherwise?"

"No, most likely not, but you should have known that we are not meant to live separately, Sam," she interjected. Then something caught her interest in her peripheral vision.

"What…?" he wanted to know.

"A tent. Where did the tent come from?" she looked towards the beach.

"A what…?" He turned and looked up as well. It was not the kind of tent in which one would camp, but more a square gazebo type of tent with mosquito nets as walls and solid canvas on top. The posts had canvas material bound to them, so that the walls could be closed. Inside was a large air mattress covered with a blanket with a nice cover and lots of brown, white and burgundy pillows. There was a tray on the blanket with dishes and glasses, and in the corner was a large cooler.

"Wow, Micha went all out," Sam said grinning, and helped her up and climbed over the rocks to the tent with her.

"Uhh, this is nice." Kate looked around in the tent and grabbed towels for both of them from the top of the cooler.

"Hungry?" she asked him.

"Yeah, come here." His eagerness to have her close was constantly on his mind.

"No, I mean food!"

Her anxiety grew and she could feel her heart pounding as she tasted his desire and need. It was two years since they had last been together; that was a very long time and what were his expectations now? She almost recoiled from the intensity of his emotions.

Sam tuned in to her as well and felt her anxiety grow, so he sat down, with his back to her. This was worse than he thought. She feared him, even if she would never tell him, he could feel it in her when he listened into her. He had to get out of here, cool down, back off, even if this meant physically and mentally hurting, even if this meant dying all over again in a different way.

"I will let you get comfortable, I will be right back," he said quietly and climbed over the rocks and dashed head first into the water.

What was that all about, she wondered? What did she do wrong? What did she say? Was it too harsh to tell him she wanted something to eat first?

She sat on the blanket and waited and after a while she decided to look for him, for he had been away longer than she had expected. She swam around but could not find him, so she went back to the tent and got out of her swimsuit and wrapped herself in a dry blanket and sat on the rocks waiting for him to return. Another half an hour later she saw him swimming back. He walked out of the water when he noticed her sitting on the rocks.

"Where were you?" she wondered, a bit hurt.

"All the way back to the coral, and then I realized I had to make it back here, I almost ran out of energy. Did I miss something?" when he noticed her wet hair.

"When you did not come back I went to find you, but it never occurred to me you would go all the way back to the coral," she said and then she followed him back to the tent.

Her heart began to race again when they were back in the close confinement and intimacy of the tent. Whether it was excitement or anxiety, it was not easy for her.

Sam took a towel and dried himself off.

"Why did you leave?"

"To cool off," he said casually. "What did Micha put into the cooler?" But then he picked up her mood again and sat back down on the blanket, groaning.

She sat beside him, wondering what was going on.

"Well?" she said looking at him.

"Well what?" he said, hoping to hide as much as he could.

"What is going on?"

"You tell me ..."

"What?" she was baffled.

He took a deep breath. "Since when are you afraid of me, Kate?"

"What?"

"Since when do you fear me so?"

"Fear you?"

He took another deep breath and looked down at his hands that were folded on his towel that was wrapped around his waist.

Kate kneeled in front of him and took his hands into hers. "Honey, I do not fear you, but I am also not a microwave. I am so happy to have you back, but ..." How could she explain this one to him, if she herself could not quite understand why she felt such anxiety when they were trying to be intimate? That had never been the case before. All of a sudden she could feel the weight of the day, the tiredness from the long swim.

"Sam ... just hold me for now all right? Wait for me, could you?" she said and with that he hugged her and they laid back on the flat puffy surface that was set out as a bed.

"I am beat too ... that was a long swim ... the later one." He did not want to get impatient with her, but a man had needs, yet if he played it well, they would find each other again and they would ... he was determined they would.

They lay side by side on their stomachs, talking while picking at the grapes that they found in the cooler, and then rested, snuggled up against each other. Later they woke, famished, and went through the cooler, looking to see what else Micha had packed for them. It was almost like Christmas, searching for gifts, only they were all high end foods. After their hunger was satisfied, they swam a little more, and then went back to the coziness of the tent.

Sam had a hard time keeping his hands off Kate and she seemed to enjoy his exploring as well. "I seem to be unable to get enough of you," he said, lazily grinning beside her. Then he rolled on top of her again, leaning on his elbows to keep his weight off her.

"I love you, Mrs. Von de Vorg, now more than ever, you know that? And if I have to wait a hundred years for you, it will be worth it," he said smiling down at her, but then he heard a noise not too far away from them.

"A hundred years? That is way too long for me," she suggested enticingly. Her hand glided up over his chest and around his neck, pulled him down to her, to kiss him, but he froze and looked at her seriously.

"You've got to be kidding me," he said in frustration, and dropped his head on her chest. "Whenever it becomes interesting ..." he groaned, and then realizing the seriousness of the situation he reached for her in his thoughts with urgency.

'Kate roll me to the side playfully as if we ... you know ... but remain on the side with me ... will you?' Kate looked at him in alarm, and he responded by trying to smile reassuringly, but without success.

'Not again, please Lord,' she begged inside, worried and loud enough for Sam to hear.

'Kate – please,' he said and with that he turned them, so that his back was covering her securely, away from where he had heard the noise. He stretched the hand on which she laid and pointed it towards the village.

'Micha! Where the hell is our security?'

'Why? What's wrong?'

'Why am I staring down a gun barrel?'

'Honey, tell him about the red point in the tent,' she looked meaningfully in a specific direction.

'Oh great,' he thought back, 'our chances have just been dramatically reduced.'

'What is going on, Sam?'

'Kate just noticed a wandering red point in the tent, you know what that means? ...'

'Are you still at the cove? Can you get to safety somehow?'

'No. How? We are fully exposed in the tent!'

"We will be there ASAP. There were two people posted at your location. I do not understand what happened and how security was breached, and where the guy came from.'

'Did he follow the boys?'

'Oh no, that is possible. Hang tight.'

"Whenever you get brave enough, someone interrupts us. Can you tell me later what you had in mind?" he whispered into her hair and stroked her back, since she had started to shiver again.

"If we live and are able to tell this tale ..." she said, worried and when she heard her own voice sounding so fearful, she decided to be braver than that, so she added enticingly "Maybe ..." with a sexual undertone that would have driven him crazy under normal circumstances.

"Maybe? No way ... Postponed ... OK?" he said kissing her gently, while he wondered if this would be the last time he would be able to hold and kiss her like this. The red dot was still searching for a target in the tent. The mesh must have been concealing them somewhat, so as long as they did not move and as long as the dot kept on searching they were safe.

Michael and Daniel were walking through the bushes a couple of hundred meters from the beach. Michael had lost a part of some equipment they had borrowed, and without it they would only get half of their damage deposit back. Suddenly he felt panic rising within him. He looked back to where he had left Daniel, who came running towards him.

"You OK?" they said in stereo.

"Something's wrong. You can feel it too, can't you?" Daniel said to Michael.

"Daniel I am not a healer, I work with the navy and we kind of do things a bit ... differently. Could you follow my lead in this, this time?"

"What do you have in mind?" said Daniel urgently.

"Mom and Dad went snorkeling and from here I cannot see anyone swimming in the coral, can you?" Daniel shook his head. "Plug into your senses, doc, let it guide you to where they are and then do as I say, can you do that?"

"Sure thing, Rambo," and they went quietly on. Daniel tuned into his senses and they were suggesting ahead and then toward the coast. He pointed in the direction he was sure they would find their parents.

"All right now it's my turn," and Michael went into a crouch position like he did when he tried to sneak up on the sea lions he was studying, and walked through the bushes almost without sound, so that Daniel had a hard time catching up with him.

First they stumbled over the body of a man who had been knocked out cold. Daniel checked that the man was alive, as Michael vanished through the bushes. He had locked in on a target and he did not want to stop for anything. He picked up a larger stick and pressed on, zeroing in on his target. Just when the man tried to cock his gun to aim towards the tent, Michael swung his stick and slammed it over the man's head, knocking him unconscious.

"No more of that shit!" Michael screamed at the guy. Daniel was at Michael's side within seconds. He checked on the man and then looked up at Michael.

"I am glad you are on my side. Having you as an enemy does not look too healthy."

Sam was relieved when he heard Michael.

"We have to talk to him about his foul language, Kate," he said to her, helping her up and walking over to where he heard the boys, to find them standing over a man who had a bleeding wound on the side of his head.

"I think this guy will need more medical attention than the others did," Daniel said, while looking respectfully up at his brother.

"What?! Did you want me to first ask him how hard he wanted to be hit, or should I have been more polite and said, excuse me Sir, would you mind if I bash you unconscious so you cannot shoot my parents?" Michael said, looking questioningly into his brother's face, which got them all to laughing.

"Thanks boys. That was a close one."

"What is this? Is it hunting season and we are the targets?" Michael said, frustrated. "I thought this was a place where people come to have fun and take holidays ... not to shoot people and crap like that!"

"Michael!" Kate warned him.

"Oh hell Mom, this is just a bit too frustrating to keep my language in check."

"Michael?!" she looked at him warningly.

"Fine. Sorry."

Sam held out his hand and let Micha know that they were all at the tent and that Michael had taken out the would-be shooter.

"What is he doing, Mom?" Michael whispered to his mother, and Daniel wanted to know as well.

"He is talking to Micha, pretty cool, ehh? How did you know that we needed help?" she asked.

"We both felt really uneasy and Daniel could tell where you guys were by using his connection and I did the 'Rambo' thing, as Daniel calls it," Michael said, looking down at the man lying in the dirt. "Who the heck are these guys?"

"I don't know much about it myself, sorry boys ..." Kate had no idea.

"Um Dad, sorry to interrupt, but tell Micha that his men are knocked out up on the hill. They could use help as well."

"You guys hungry?" was Kate's next thought.

"Starving – you have anything to eat in that love shack?"

"Michael!"

"I think they need to get at it," Daniel said, laughing.

"Daniel!" his father warned him.

"Oh come on you guys. We are grown men here, not children," Daniel complained.

"Then why are you disrespecting your mother with that kind of language?" Sam scowled at both of them, but then he thought differently.

"But enough of all the heavy. Turn around so I can see your back, Michael," he said grinning. "Yup son, you are now most definitely stuck with us," he clapped him on the shoulders and then took the lead back to the tent. Michael's crest was like Daniel's but with one less dragon, and it also had something that Kate had seen in the Duke's book. It had something from the Spanish crest and combining both crests of both families, obviously different but also just as powerful in its own right. Watching the three broad-shouldered men, each marked handsomely with a large crest on their back, she felt almost like an outsider.

'Thank you for my family,' she thought.

"Amen," she heard Sam call out loud to her.

"Amen what?" Michael wanted to know.

"Tell you later," she said while picking up her pace to catch up with them.

They ate everything that was left in the cooler and then Sam looked at Kate. 'Together finally,' he thought and she just smiled, 'Yes finally.'

In the evening when they all had turned in, Kate shivered most of the night from the experience. No amount of massage or soft speaking helped. She was afraid of losing her reconnected family again. Fear and tension broke loose and she cried as Sam rocked her to sleep.

This was exactly what he wanted to protect her from, but she was right. He was much sharper and his senses were much more heightened when she was around him, otherwise he would never have heard the noise so far away from their tent. Eventually she fell asleep, clinging tightly to him. In the morning she put on her brave face and by the time the boys joined them for breakfast in their room everything seemed to be back to normal; only Sam knew better.

Shortly, Micha and Tina arrived for a debriefing. They wanted to discuss the events and consider where the threats came from. They made little progress, and then there was a knock at the door and someone delivered a large manilla envelope. Micha was about to get up to take it, for he always checked everything first, but Sam just reached out absentmindedly and took it from the man who brought it over, while still speaking with Michael.

"How many people know about this thing Micha is talking about, you know that light thing?" Michael wanted to know.

Kate playfully lifted her hand and snapped it open so the light would show, which made Michael jump to his feet. "Yeeh, Mom, that is freaky! If you would please ... don't do it again. What will my friends think?" and everybody started to laugh.

"Well anybody who knows our history may have read about it. It is known to give the carrier a massive advantage over his opponents, so it has been silenced for many generations, to have fair battle fields."

"What do you mean silenced?" Daniel wanted to know.

"Well the crossing of the lines was avoided and it was not spoken about again," said Sam matter-of-factly. "When our ancestors – your mother's and mine – crossed the lines it was to some extent on purpose. The Nordic clans had been at war with each other for far too long and they all decided they wanted to have a leader over them, to calm the battle grounds, so they could come together. It worked, but when the Spanish bride left, the alliance was broken and the battle began over the throne. One tribe especially was interested in the power it held and was more than happy when she left so they had an advantage, which they used well. If I remember correctly, they were still beaten by the ruler's army, which was still strong and loyal at the time, but the power of the throne never fully recovered, and nobody knows why. Bottom line was, that it takes two to be that powerful. To have this occur again now, even though accidentally, would mean a double defeat for those who fought against the ruler at the time. If they still have pride and honor regarding their history, they could possibly be prime suspects in this whole thing."

"This is about the power of a forgotten history?" Michael sat down with his mouth open.

"No, I think, as I said, that it is about pride and honor," Sam said, "for some, still a powerful thing, believe it or not."

"So if I get this right," said Daniel, "then to kill either Mom OR you would do the trick, but why go after all of us as well? There must be more to this."

"My guess would be that you carry the gene that has the potential to carry the crown and that makes you a potential threat to the elusive leader of the free region in the north," Kate said quietly. "You know too much already about the possibility and if all of us were gone and had no descendants to pass down the gene of the crown, the threat of the rise of a leader who they would all have to acknowledge would be permanently erased."

"Why would someone go to so much trouble? I mean, today this means so little, doesn't it?" Michael wondered.

"If we have the fabulous crown gene, why did our ancestors leave the land and settle on the western continent, all the way at the other end of the globe?" Daniel wanted to know.

"Well, I do not have all the answers either, this is what we need Mary for, but ..." Sam stopped in mid-sentence and looked intensely at what he had pulled out of the envelope.

"As for me, I am glad we are all safe and I hope that one day we will find a way to keep the peace with whoever means us harm," Kate said and then got up to get herself some more coffee.

Micha's eyes were intently fixed on Sam. What was in that envelope, he wondered.

Sam looked up angrily at Kate who just turned around and looked at him, confused.

'Are there other reasons, why you would not want me to touch you?' He fired his thoughts at her.

'What makes you think I have reasons? And what makes you think I do not want to be touched by you? I never said anything of the sort,' she responded, still confused.

'Your anxiety when I touch you ... is it because you have moved on?' his eyes became hard and furious.

"WHAT?" she said out loud, shocked and angry. "What on earth are you talking about?! Where is this conversation going!"

Everybody stopped in mid-sentence and looked up.

"Conversation ...? Which conversation? Ours or yours?" Daniel wanted to know. "Mom, we do not do that telepathic thing, what is going on?" Daniel looked at his parents.

"Forget it! I need fresh air," Sam said and got up, smacked the envelope on the table, holding onto one piece of paper and left the room, slamming the door shut.

History Revealed

S AM STORMED OFF, furious and frustrated. His walk told everyone to stay away from him. He had had enough. The picture he held in his hand confirmed everything he had feared the most. In his anger he crumpled it up into a ball and threw it as far as he could. A battle was only worth fighting if one had a remote chance of winning, but this fight seemed to be unwinnable; it was not even worth trying anymore.

Micha called him a few times and tried to reason with him and get him to return, but Sam was not willing to listen anymore. Down at the beach he pulled off his shirt and dove into the water. Soon his hurting lungs forced him to come up for air. He swam along the shoreline and passed the little cove where he had been with Kate the day before, but looking at it hurt, so he took another deep breath and went below the surface. Here under water it seemed as if he could escape the worries and the hurts of the world. His surroundings enticed him to search and discover more, and he was pleasantly distracted, if only for moments.

Beautiful, colorful fish swam around him as he explored the shoreline and then he remembered the underground cave he had found and showed Kate the other day and decided to take refuge there. He came up for air once more and then went deeper to find the entrance to the cave. After a short swim through the passage he came up to discover the cave was as they had left it. Light shone through the open gap at the ceiling to the flat rock below, which was arranged like very wide steps towards the back of the cave. As he pulled himself up he marveled at the warm temperature in the cave, considering that there was little exposure to the sun. This was a perfect place to relax and reflect. So he laid himself on the flat rock half way up to ponder over the events of the last past few days and hopefully come up with a plan of how to proceed without Kate. Even though he was resolved about it, it still hurt, but he had to respect it for what it was.

Not realizing how taxing those thoughts were and also due to the long swim and his many sleepless nights, he fell asleep before he knew it.

Back at the hotel, Kate was totally confused and stood stock still with her mouth open.

"Mom, what was that all about?"

"I have no idea boys," she said, confused.

Micha got up and ran after Sam, leaving the door open, and Tina took the envelope from the table. Almost at the same time Marcus and the Duke arrived at the open door.

"May we enter?" Marcus wanted to know, looking at everybody in confusion. "We just passed Sam who was running down to the beach, and now Micha in the hall ... what is going on?"

"Marcus, please allow me to introduce your uncle to my sons, Michael and Daniel," Kate said. "Michael, this is your great uncle Duke Marcus and your even greater uncle, whatever that makes him, Duke Frederico de la Rosa de Maya." Marcus immediately translated.

"Hola? bienvenido a España," the Duke said with a warm smile to both boys, shaking their hands.

"This is getting cooler by the minute, but can we get back to why Dad stormed out?"

"Oh no," said Tina, drawing everyone's attention to her. "Kate, do you remember when we went to the beach with that Matheson character?" she wondered.

"With whom?" Michael wanted to know.

"Oh, your Mom has a wild streak, didn't you know?" Kate said smiling, but then thought better and changed her tone considering the situation.

Marcus came over and took some of the pictures out of her hands and looked at them. Then he explained to the Duke in Spanish what he thought about what was happening. Then he turned to Tina. "These are well done," he said, so Kate came over to look at them too and gasped. In the pictures one could see her beside Matheson on a blanket on the beach, looking somewhat cozy. The next one showed it from another angle.

Michael also got up and looked at some of them.

"Well Mom, who is that guy?"

"I really do not know. I just ran into him, he spilled coffee all over my shirt and made it up by inviting us for dinner, and then for star gazing," she said still stunned.

"He fell asleep beside us," Tina added. "Told you there was something fishy going on," said Tina to Marcus who was translating to the Duke.

"You said I was drugged. You were not joking, were you?" Kate said, looking at Tina who just shook her head.

"I did not want to worry you Kate, so I did not press the point. But Marcus and I had a strong suspicion. Only we both thought he was out for an easy good time, not more," she said, still looking from one picture to the next.

"Well, it seems there was a larger agenda here," Marcus suggested.

Then Kate looked at the door through which Sam disappeared. He had walked off thinking ... what? That she had been unfaithful? The thought hurt. – Fine! – If he thought that little of her, then she was done too. She had never given him any reason to believe that she was unfaithful, never ever. He had not even asked to hear her side of the story, well then go to ...

Still, this all just did not feel right, regardless of how in the right she was. Even her sons had looked at her in confusion, not knowing what to think and how she could fix it, and deep down she had no idea either.

"Countess!" the old man said expectantly, looking at Kate with entreating eyes and shaking his head.

"Countess? Mom? What is he saying? You are now also a Countess?" Michael was so surprised he could barely get the words out.

"What!? ..." Kate looked annoyed.

The Duke rattled on in Spanish and Kate listened and then looked at Marcus.

"He said ... Do not leave things unspoken. This is beneath you, we all know you better. Sam is insecure about the bond that ties you together. If nothing else ... But please let him know, who he is letting go, as well," Marcus translated, "We have hinted it to him but he seems not to get it."

"That was not all he said, was it?" she said looking at Marcus, which made him look sheepish so she only could grin, realizing that the Duke was infuriated and that Marcus did not want to translate everything he had said.

"All right, all right, I will swallow my pride and admit when I should give in. Which direction did he stomp off in?" she wanted to know. She heard Marcus translate something to the old Duke, who lightened up at the news and again said something in Spanish.

"Spoken like a queen," Marcus translated back to her, grinning.

"A little help?" Kate looked around her, when Micha came back into the room having heard the last bit of their conversation.

"He dove off into the water. I can't swim as fast as he can, neither can I dive for that long, and he knows it, so there was no point in me following him. Kate, there is more." He gave her pained looks, looking at the empty envelope on the table and the pictures that everybody held and inspected.

"Sometimes it is good to stop and verify before jumping to conclusions, and I would have if I had received the pictures first. Jerry received this envelope and it was addressed to Sam. Instead of checking with me he let Sam have it first," and with that he looked accusingly at Jerry, who looked guilty and protested, "Sam just took it from me."

Micha pulled a crumpled-up picture out of his pocket, the one that Sam had thrown away, and gave it to her. Kate unfolded the paper and looked at it, horrified. It showed her lying with Matheson on the blanket on the beach, cozily sleeping. Tina was cut off, so it appeared Kate was alone with Matheson. "Who brought this here?" she demanded.

"As I said, it was an anonymous drop off, Kate. By now I know you better than to jump to any kind of conclusions, but I do understand Sam. With emotions running hot like they have been lately ... he has come a long way and now he feels outrun, so he reacts with anger and feels defeated ... If I saw Tina next to that guy, I would have freaked out as well, and we have been married a long time. Sam loves you and I think that he believes he has lost you, can you blame him?"

"There ... darn ... nothing went on. We star gazed and fell asleep, that is all!"

Micha looked at Tina who confirmed the statement with an emphatic nodding of her head.

"The guys told me that they could see Sam from above the cliff, but he disappeared shortly past the tip of the rocky point south from here. That fool makes my life a living hell, running off all the time. Mary will have my head, one of these days." With that he flung himself defeated onto one of the chairs beside Tina, who just looked at Kate expectantly.

"Well love," Tina said to Micha and then to Kate, "He can outrun you guys, but he can't outrun Kate, just as Kate can't outrun him. Isn't that so, Kate?" she said, looking at Kate with her eyebrows raised, hinting at something that the men did not understand.

"Good to have at least one person here who has some faith in me," said Kate, grinning back at her, which made the men look at her in frustration.

"All right, you are all on board," she said with a laugh. "Fine, I am going. I guess someone has to do the dirty work." And with that she grabbed something from the cabinet, and left the room with Tina at her side.

"You know where he is, do you?" she said, following her up the stairs to Tina's room, where Kate changed into the new two-piece bathing suit she had bought recently at the market. The top part looked a bit like the style of her wedding dress. Maybe that is why she liked it so much. It was a beautiful periwinkle blue top, with material that looked like it was wrapping itself around her body. The separate navy blue bottom had a short skirt attached. It made her look cute, elegant and sexy: a combination she had sought for a long time in a bathing suit. She had finally found it at a small market in this little fishing village.

"Yup," she said, grinning back.

"Are you going to tell me?"

"Nope," she said as she pulled up the swimsuit bottom.

"It's a secret, but you can think of me and hope for the best," Kate said as she left the room and headed off to the beach.

"You know you can count on me anytime and you also know how you can reach me," Tina said, before Kate walked into the water and swam off. "Of course I do, so now stop worrying and take care of the boys so that they stay out of my way," Kate hollered back, turning and smiled encouragingly at her before she took a deep breath and dove under the water.

Around the first tip of the rocky shoreline she came up and swam in a relaxed way past their cove. Yes she thought, they had a long road of obstacles behind them, but it was also really high time to have it come to an end. She could taste in Sam that he had been running on empty for some time now; it was a surprise to her, that he had lasted as long as he had. She also knew that when he sought solitude as a refuge instead of her, that he was at the end of his rope, regardless of what he said or did to convince her otherwise.

She had to dive a few times until she found the opening to the cave he had shown her the day before. To have enough energy to make it that deep and through the passage, she took a break on shore and when she felt rested enough she dove and swam as fast as she could down to the entrance and through it, and just made it to the inside before she ran completely out of air. Even though her lungs were screaming for oxygen, she came to the surface as quietly as she could, unsure what to expect inside. First she could not make out where he was, but then she saw Sam sleeping on one of the flat steps half way up the back of the cave. Quietly she pulled herself out of the water onto the rock. She tried to control her breathing and when it had returned to normal she pulled her feet out of the water, stood up and walked carefully to where he was, and laid beside him. Her plan was to wait until he woke and then talk out what needed to be said.

She had almost fallen asleep herself, when he stirred and opened his eyes to see her lying beside him. He looked around to see if there was anybody else there, so she said quietly, almost hurt: "No, I did not tell anybody about this secret hiding spot of yours, and yes, I came alone. Is there anything else you would like to know?" she said bitterly.

"What else is there to say?"

Sam believed the picture was true, Kate could see that in his eyes. She lifted her body off the rock.

"You think that little of me?" she said hurt.

"It is enough, Kate no more of this, please." Before she could say any more he looked miserably at her and jumped from up high into the water below. Wanting to say more yet not knowing where to start he needed time and distance to think this over, so he left everything unspoken. Kate watched his shadow glide through the water, but instead of turning to the passage way to the right as she assumed he would go, which led to the sea, he turned sharply to the left.

"Fine, go. Be miserable, you deserve no better right now. I don't care!" she said, hurt, with tears welling up. Even though she was trying to be strong, the tears were running down her cheeks. How could he doubt her that much, how could he?

'Remember your standing here. Tell him who you are and who he is letting go,' was the thought that was nagging at her. Well she had promised to do so, but he was not willing to listen, so what was the point? She would make it easy for them all, just simply get on a bus and this time she would make sure that nobody could ever find her, leaving Tina behind as well, a not so pleasant thought, for she had grown fond of her. She would explain to the boys that she needed time to find herself. That should satisfy their curiosity. Marcus would have to wait for the family reunion, but he would survive. Then Kate began to realize how utterly juvenile her thoughts were, and tried to pull herself together.

Well fine then, she would go after him and save the day, but this time she would tell him off as well. With a deep breath she jumped to get a head start in the air and dove to the left after Sam. Under the water she could make out another passageway, one that was narrower than the other before and windier. She kicked hard not knowing how far it was until she could get more air, following the rigid walls. Her lungs were beginning to complain and she started to panick as she realized that she was out of air and there was no end in sight yet.

'Faster', she thought, but she knew that the odds of her making it were slim to none. She went to the roof of the passageway trying to find a pocket of air but could find none. 'Oh Lord, no ...' her heart pleaded. Her thoughts screamed for him. As she felt her consciousness fading and drifting into a black nothing, her mind started to flush thoughts and memories before her. But there was also something new ... she saw a beautiful young woman looking sadly at her. Her heart was broken just like Kate's, she could see that in her eyes. She seemed to smile and reach out to Kate and then she whispered, "Contessa live. You know how it felt. Set the truth free, for me and for you. Let the world know the truth of it all. Justify our name, our history. For me ... and for you. Then she faded away again, leaving Kate wanting to fight once more with all she had. With the last bit of her strength she reached out to him: 'Help! – SAM!!'

Sam had arrived at the other end of the passageway. It was a long swim even for him but it was worth it. When he came to the surface out of breath he realized that he was in an even larger cave with several other pools in the back. The temperature was warmer in here and so was the water. He could see the water steaming in the far pool. This must be a cave with hot springs. Well maybe if he soaked in one of those he could get his head to clear a bit. He climbed out of the water to check out the cave, and sat on one of the warm stones checking the temperature in one of the pools. It reminded him of those hot tubs at the swimming pools at home, almost the same temperature, if not a bit higher, but very comfortable. He was about to swing his feet over the edge to get into the warm water when he felt an intense feeling of panic and anxiety flooding him.

He looked back into the water from where he had come, walked over and put his hand into it, puzzled. The panic grew stronger, magnified in the water. His mind could hear Kate screaming for him loud and clear.

"Kate?" he said out loud as if he expected an answer, even though he knew perfectly well he was alone.

Beginning to panic himself, he pushed off the edge with a forceful jump and dove back into the water through the passageway he had just come through. Around a few more bends he could make out Kate searching for air pockets on the roof of the cave passage and slowly losing the battle. He grabbed her wrist and pulled her forcefully down to him, grabbed her head and pressed his mouth on hers to breathe air into her mouth, but she did not receive it. Desperately he turned and pulled her along with him back to where he was moments before. As she was so light and small he could pull her effortlessly and quickly to the surface, up to the edge and lay her on the sand. He massaged her lungs, frantically searching for any signs of life. Relieved, he fell back to his knees when she started to cough and rolled on her side grasping for air, slowly recovering. He waited for a little while for her to get her breath back, then he lifted her onto the flat rock, but she was like a rag doll, barely able to hold her head up from exertion. Finally when the shock was over, she started to cry so he held her in his arms a bit longer. After she stopped, he placed her on a higher rock, bringing her eyes to his eye level and looking at her puzzled and shaking his head. Kate could barely move, nor was she able to put up a fight. The lack of oxygen and then the crying and the shock had incapacitated her. Her legs and arms felt like rubber. Sam had to steady her so she would not fall off the rock again, giving her time to orient herself to where she was.

"You never give up, do you?" Sam shook his head in disbelief.

"It was further than I thought it would be, and no, I am not a quitter if that is what you mean." He could not help but grin for a moment, for that is something her father always said. They did not say anything for some time, but Kate could sense that Sam was miserable even though he said nothing. Her breathing became more regular and calmer, until at last she could get up and stand before him, but not without holding onto the rock to steady her, for she still could not rely on her feet to keep her standing firmly.

"Oh ye of so little faith," she mumbled more to herself, but loud enough for him to hear as well. He just got up and stood in front of her. Remembering what had occurred before all this brought his thoughts back to grave feelings. His face fell and hurt was written all over it.

"Sam ..." she reached out her hand to touch his face.

"Who was ... is he?" he whispered.

"A nobody ... but that is completely beside the point!"

"It is my point. But I hope you are happy and we will leave it at that," he said as he stepped back from her, ready to retreat to safety, for he did not want to think about having lost it all. This would be the last straw. Emotionally, he would not survive this blow, he was sure of it. Before he could turn his back on her she raised her voice in a sharp authoritarian tone that would have made even the wind stop blowing.

"Stop right there!" she snapped loudly.

Sam froze. This was a new tone he had not heard from her before, and he turned, questioning and confused. Somewhere inside of him his pride was stirred. How inappropriate for her to address him like this. After all, he was ... Was he really? What was the point of it all? Without her, he did not want any of it anymore, he was seeing the value fade right before his eyes. But his rational side cautioned him, for it told him that this was the side a man should fear from his woman, the sharp edge of the sword that could be highly potent and frightfully dangerous. On the other hand it filled him with wonder: Where did she find the strength at this moment to stand up to him in her weakened condition? What gave her so much energy and what was it that she could possibly say, that she thought could change his mind? Out of curiosity he gave her the benefit of the doubt, so he turned fully and listened.

"I have had it now too. You WILL listen until I am finished and then you may do as you will." She said walking over to him but remaining out of arm's length, letting him know that she was addressing him in a formal way and that she was considering his safety more than hers.

"I have something to say about all this as well. I have been talking with some people around here, and I have had their information confirmed in a book that looks just as old as the book about the Von de Vorg monarchy." She took a deep breath and continued fiercely. "It has been brought to my attention that I am not as powerless as I thought I was, nor as powerless as you assumed I was. Apparently you are not talking to someone who you can easily dismiss, a right you seem to enjoy exercising these days!" she said forcefully and sharply, but her eyes were welling up. As angry as she was, she was very hurt as well. "If I get the sequence right then I am apparently Countess Katerina Delante de la Rosa de ... Katerina de la Rosa de Maya de Von de Vorg. The last bit is thanks to you, of course."

She shook her head in disbelief that she was even able to get it over her tongue and to his astonishment as she proclaimed her status her mark changed right before his eyes. She could feel the change as well, the stabbing, burning sensation on her neckline. She started rubbing it in annoyance, to ease the burning sensation, and after she lifted her hand off, the pain seemed to have eased. He noticed that her mark changed to the same as his, acknowledging her place under his people; only the ribbon of the crown that went through the crest was thinner and daintier than his crown, and some Spanish icons had now added themselves very noticeably around the crown peaks. "Ouch," was all she could say, rubbing her neckline some more, but still addressing him. Sam stood mesmerized, watching her crest rearrange itself. He was still watching her mark as she spoke and came closer and stopped short on one of the rocks above him, bringing her height close to his again, so that she was a little closer to his eye level. She took a deep breath and continued.

"AND, if I get this right from what I am reading about your history, then I know, that you have been playing a bluff – and that you played it for way, way ... WAY too long! You see..." she said and took another big breath, releasing a flood of tears that began to run freely down her cheeks, "... according to the traditions of your Viking ancestors, it is not the man who releases the wife, it is THE WIFE WHO RELEASES THE HUSBAND!" The last part came out almost shrilly, for her voice was choking on her anger and tears. After a moment she added quietly, trying to regain control again: "Even though these days there is no difference, yet we both know, that we have no choice but to abide by the traditional ways of our past, for we are closely connected and directed by it." With a resigned tone she finished by stating quietly, "Now you might outrank me many times over," she took a deep breath fully intending to finish this proudly, and added, "But you are on Spanish soil right now, the soil of MY ancestors, which leaves you with little authority here! As your wife I have not released you, neither will I, but rather I am staking my claim. The treaty between our families, made many generations before, will be fulfilled in me. The debt will be paid and if you would like to release me after the 15-year treaty, then you may do so with my permission."

She took another big breath and exhaled, and then finished a thought that had just come to her. In a quite voice she spoke almost more to herself, as if she was thinking out loud. "You think this could have happened to the pure girl of that old story? It would make much more sense ... Her husband did not believe in her devotion and she returned, because she was heartbroken, not because she did not like living there ... That would explain why your ancestor did not return to reclaim her, for he knew he was wrong. Knowing what I know so far of you and your history, this is a more reasonable explanation of why an aggressive breed like the Vikings did not retaliate and return to get what was theirs by treaty, or beat the crap out of Spain, now isn't it? So come to think of it, there is no need for any type of claim." She was a bit surprised at herself, for logically deducing it all, but she was not done yet.

"You made your point very clearly, message received ... but now I would like to tell you, like it or not, that this time ... I ... will have the last word." She smoothed her hand over her crest and then before running out of steam she added, "As for that God forsaken long title of Countess Katerina blah blah blah," she took a deep breath and continued, "I demand a kiss of apology this instant, my Lord," she said, weak but firm, trying to keep her voice even.

Being speechless was not a common thing for Sam, but it took him a moment to take in the information. That was the missing piece. She had found it, and that was why she was wearing a crown. If she was right, she had purified the royal bloodlines by joining his. It was stunning and shocking at the same time, and now looking at her it was also amusing. It still puzzled him that he always found her so attractive when she was angry, but he humored her and said as soberly as he possibly could , "As you wish," while he took a big step up the rock and kissed her on her forehead.

"Don't play with me, Sam!" she growled, her eyes spitting fire. With a suppressed smile he lowered his head and pecked a kiss on her mouth.

"You want to be flogged?" she wondered.

"They still do that?" he said, grinning. His heart beat faster and his mind was almost afraid to hope, but they were talking just like they used to in a time he longed to have back so badly, and they were really connecting.

"With all the weird stuff going on, I would not dismiss it," she said warningly.

"Kate, kissing you is not a duty but a pleasure, and you don't seem to mind it either. But I need to know, for you cannot say you do not, since I can feel what you feel without you telling me, why do you fear me when I touch you? I did not do anything to make you fear me, or did I?" he said quietly.

"Fear? No, not fear. I felt anxious, for I could feel your intense feelings towards me and I was worried about what your expectations would be, and if I ... it has been a long time ..." she said swallowing hard, then looked at him with her eyebrows raised as if he was to guess what she wanted to say.

"You thought that I would act upon those feelings and just rush over and have my way with you? What I feel does not control what I do, my feelings are part of me, yes, they are undeniably there, but I am in control of them – and if I were not, we would be in great trouble."

"I see. Sam listen ... Let's make a rule here, OK? No tuning into each other when we are together in an intimate way, for men do not understand women and women do not understand men. The things that we feel are foreign and incomprehensible to each other. I think it is best if we do not know about each other's inner workings. What do you think?"

"So you do not fear me?"

"No, just the intensity you bring with you, and I am a little afraid that I won't be able to live up to your expectations," she added quietly. "So where were we?" she wanted to know.

"You were demanding to be kissed, without so much as a please!" he said accusingly.

"Well?"

So he kissed her carefully on her lips, considering what she had said. It was interesting to learn that women had the same performance anxiety as men. When she softened up to him he lost the train of his thoughts and deepened and intensified the kiss. Her hand came up and touched his chest, and his body reacted instantly and strongly to her touch. The deep longing to be united with her again flooded his mind and body, almost to the point of pain.

Then she withdrew, ducked under his arms and he heard a splash behind him.

'You have to be kidding me!' he thought, holding onto the high rock she had sat on earlier, 'Are we back to the running thing again?' Only this time he was fully immobilized. His arousal was so intense that it was at a painful level, flooding his body in waves. Her touch had been enough to send his body over the edge, so that he was in so much pain that he could not move.

'Think of something bad, something disgusting, that should work as a downer', he thought. Something that would relax him sufficiently, so he could get into the cold water which should work like a cold shower. 'All right think of ... grandmothers ... with knitting needles, dogs pooping on the lawn ...' But nothing was effective, so he almost doubled over from pain. How can a man need a woman that bad? It should be outlawed, for it was way too cruel.

At a loss as to what to do, he closed his eyes to try to relax, then he felt a wet, cool hand on his upper arm. With a sweeping motion his arm scooped her around her waist and pulled her in front of him.

'I was not running, I was full of sand', he heard her thoughts, so he answered without opening his eyes, fearing that if he opened them, she would disappear again.

'Kate, enough of the running thing, could we call it quits? If you run I would have to pursue, I have no choice, we are meant to be together. I was wrong in Vancouver and I have paid for that mistake for almost half a year now, is that not enough? Please, just remember your crest, it is .... besides.... oh Kate... I am exhausted and right now in dire need of you and your body. Please ... I raise my white flag for peace. I love you. Please love me back ... again.' He did not know what else to think and his heart seemed to convey and tell her more than he had wanted to ever admit. The most important thing for him was to change her mind and win her back, but he had to find a way, right now, to find release from this pressure and pain in his body and heart.

She stood there motionless, listening intently to what he thought and letting it heal her hurt. This is what she needed to hear. It was honey for her soul, but it came with an underlying pain that had nothing to do with what he said.

"Are you all right?" she whispered.

"No," he whispered back into her hair.

"What's wrong? Anything I can do?"

"You, you are the only one who can help right now, love," he said groaning.

"What do you mean?" she said quietly. He pulled her closer to him so she could feel what he meant.

"Oh," she said, her hands gliding down his body, which did not improve matters. "I see ... Nice to know I still have that effect on you ..." she said, smiling shyly.

He opened his eyes and looked straight into hers. "Are you kidding? You always have that effect on me, as I hope I have on you ..."

Kate opened the button of his Bermudas, which fell to the sand like a rock, due to their wetness. He lifted her up and sat her back up on the stone on which she had sat earlier, pulled her closer and kissed her. Their bodies did what came naturally to both of them, reaffirming the bond between them and releasing Sam from the painful pressure. His arms were around her and holding her tightly to him, never wanting to let go of her. She had her feet wrapped around his waist and even though they had both now relaxed, they remained intimately connected. His kisses intensified, telling her a lot more than words could say, and their bodies responded accordingly. Hours later they came up for air, side by side close to the warm pool, only this time tangled up in each other, gently stroking and kissing.

"Now do you think you could finally hear me out, Sam?"

"There's more?"

"The pictures ... We had too much wine. Tina thinks I was doped. We decided to star gaze and we fell asleep. Well, Matheson started to snore beside us and we fell asleep shortly after that as well. Oh, and Tina was right beside me, which was missing from that picture of 'Truth'," she said, making quotation marks in the air.

"So what's with the 15 years – you seem to like limits and numbers. First we overcame the three-year deal, but now we have a 15-year deal ... Also, you have to tell me more. By the looks of it, you have found your roots and learned a bit more about our history. Care to fill me in about what you've discovered so far?" he said, kissing the crest on her chest.

"It is rather interesting and if things keep going the way they are, I will turn into a history buff," she said, grinning back at him and putting her arms around his neck. "All right now: a long, long time ago, when the Vikings invaded Europe, one of the Viking clan leaders, your ancestor, was about to do the same as they did everywhere else in the northern region of Spain, as they did all over Europe. They came, invaded and conquered or destroyed, the same to them. To protect his people the Duke of the region, my grandfather's grandfather ... several generations before the Duke you might have met if you had not dashed out of the hotel so quickly, proposed a treaty between the Viking clan and the northern region of Spain, by offering his daughter to that Viking clan leader. Now the girl must have been some beauty, for Vikings did not do such things at the time with their enemies, only with other Viking tribes. I guess the daughter was very beautiful, or the clan leader was a bit of a progressive thinker, for he took the offer. The plan was to ship the girl and her servants north to join up with him. The treaty was permanent, providing that there would be no more invasions of Spain by the Vikings, and in return he could have her for 15 years. According to the treaty, should she choose to leave to be with her people after that, she was free to go, but she would have to leave any offspring behind."

Kate sat up and looked down at Sam, who folded his arms under his head to continue listening to her.

"Well, they kept their bargain and sent her up north, but she left him in the second year, the history book claimed that she found them too uncivilized and barbaric, and so she went down by ship to rejoin her family. They were not pleased about it, fearing retaliation, and apparently they still fear retaliation to this day. They are a rather superstitious bunch, believing in curses and the like. Well anyway, she was pregnant when she left, and she gave birth to a son in Spain. After that she joined a convent. The Viking servants who had escorted her home on the boat, abducted the infant at night when he was one year old and sailed back, returning him to his father up north. To this day the Spanish owe a debt to the Vikings, but through all these generations no one has been willing to stand in for her, to fulfill her duty. The Duke spoke of a fear of impending doom for his people, because they did not honor the pact they made. He said that when you and I met, not knowing about our history, it was predestined that we would marry. The crest was claiming what was promised in the treaty. There was little we could have said or done to change the path that was set out for us. Well, that is where I draw the line. I still believe we have a hand in our own destiny. Now this is as I said the duke's version, but you know I believe now that history really repeated itself here. What is not mentioned in the history books and on the walls at home is that the whole story was not recorded correctly. Something similar with the same intent, like what happened here with us, happened then. A deception making the Viking ruler believe his wife was unfaithful and having her leave due to heart break makes much more sense when you look at the larger picture. He knew that she would have never done anything like it, therefore he never retaliated to demand her back or even force the treaty or else .... What if like you Sam, he thought of having lost her to someone else, those people may have wanted to split the power of the ruler and succeeded in the end, simply via deception on their part not on the part of the Spanish lady. This makes much more sense. Besides ...," she added more like a whisper, "she told me so."

"Say what?"

"Now that is something I really cannot explain, but things happen when you are between ...." but she could not finish for he held his finger over her mouth.

"No more of death and dying, love, no more..." Then he looked at her, "Countess Katerina de la whatever it was, sounds good," he said, grinning.

"Are you mocking me?" she wondered.

"No, no, just stating facts. So here I was looking for help with my son and I landed someone important, eh?" he said grinning, repeating something she had said to him long ago, when they took that fateful walk up to the family chamber in the mountain side.

"Yeah, go figure," she said thoughtfully. He reached up and pulled her back down to him so that she was lying on top of him. "I am glad it is you," he said and kissed her.

Family Reunion

WHEN THEY ARRIVED back at the hotel everybody had left their room, so they had a chance to take a really long shower together, to remove all the sand and salt, but it was not long before the phone rang.

"So, Dad ...." Michael probed carefully, "Is everything cool again?"

"Don't tell me YOU have been worried," Sam said, grinning.

"Well, you know what they say, about how damaging it is to the children when the parents don't get along and all," Michael said, laughing.

"Children ... yeah right ... well, anything else? MICHAEL," Sam wanted to know, watching Kate, who was looking around the doorframe, wondering who was on the phone, and then when she heard Sam pronounce his name, she smiled and went back to drying her hair. The kids had been worried, and rightfully so, but now the problems were behind them. They had made a good start and were on the right track to get back to where they used to be. It could so easily have gone wrong, she thought, running her fingers through her hair to make it dry faster. She remembered that evening with Matheson and

241

that guy ... What was his name? Right, Pete or something like that, how low to do what they did, and why, she wondered, why?

Sam looked at her in the mirror, wondering where she was in her thoughts.

'Hey, what are you thinking of right now?' he looked at her smiling, but she was still serious.

"Now what?" he groaned, worried. She turned off the blow dryer and looked at him in the mirror for a long time.

"Sam what would have happened, if you had not believed me?"

"Believed what?" he whispered into her ear, putting his arms around her from the back.

She thought about that night and he saw the thought in her head, like a snap shot of the beach.

"Who ... Where ...What was that?" Sam said, stunned, and turning her around to look into her face.

"What?" she wondered.

"I saw something I had not seen before. A beach lit by lamps from the restaurants and board walks."

"That is almost unbelievable. I was thinking of the night those pictures were taken. Thinking what would have happened if you had not believed me. You saw that?" she said stunned.

"Let's try that again."

She concentrated, took a deep breath and leaned her head against his chest and went back there.

Sam could see flashes of different images and then it was like watching a movie. She showed him the beach, the beauty she had enjoyed and ... then it stopped. He lifted her chin with his hand and looked into her face.

"Don't give up yet," he said while kissing her nose. "Try again. Please?" he said and imitated her puppy eyes so that she had to laugh.

"It is not as easy as you might think, but with those eyes ... who could say no?" she said smiling.

He put his hands around her neck with this thumbs on her cheek and put his forehead against hers and closed his eyes. She closed hers as well and concentrated. 'Who could ever say no to him?' she thought. He grinned but waited.

She concentrated and then showed him the beach again, the moon, the lights. Then she was at the table sitting across from Tina with a man on her right and on her left. Sam tensed when he saw what she saw but remained focused. She showed him Matheson and then she looked at Pete, who excused himself and left the table. They had a steak dinner and wine, and Matheson talked with an accent that Sam somehow recognized having heard before, but where?

Then she was on the beach, dancing to the music and waving her hands, and he had to smile. But all of a sudden the pictures became all mixed up, and then stopped.

"What happened?" he opened his eyes looking at her.

"Stop what you are doing, honey," she whispered.

Yes, he liked hearing her calling him that again, he had missed that, but still he did not know what she meant and looked down at her, puzzled. She put her hands over his and then curled her fingers over his thumbs, which were caressing her cheeks.

"Oops," he said smiling and stopped. "I did not think I had such an effect on you," repeating what she had said when his body responded to her touch in the cave. He kissed her forehead and then put his head against hers and closed his eyes again.

"Let's get back to the movie, sweetie," he said, smiling.

"You are not helping," she smiled, but then she closed her eyes and went back to that evening, the dancing, and then Matheson speaking to her ... and then she opened her eyes again.

"Sam, I can feel you tensing. He is no threat to you, you know that, don't you?" she whispered.

"Let get back to the movie, but I hate to think what I will do with him, when I get a hold of him ..." he said, growling.

"Don't you think you're over-reacting a bit?" she said, caressing his hands in an attempt to relax his mood a little.

"Kate, this is not only a matter of you being my wife. He dared to pull this one off against the house of Von de Vorg. In olden days he could have been killed just for looking at you. Does that put it into the right perspective?"

"He did not know who I was, honey," she said, but he just shook his head.

"Yes he did, how else would I have received the photos?"

She wanted to say something but then her mouth hung open in shock.

"Show me more love," he said, smiling at her stunned face. He closed his eyes and put his forehead against hers again. 'Fear not my Lady; you are in safe hands ... now ...'

'I love you, Sam.'

'As do I.'

She looked up at his face and then closed her eyes again.

'Go back to the last thought,' and he kissed her on her forehead again and then rested his head against hers.

"As you wish, my Lord," she said teasing.

Before he could respond images flashed wildly and then slowed down to show her lying on the blanket, with Tina on one side of her, and Matheson on the other side, explaining the constellations.

"Wait," Sam opened his eyes, "Please go back and look at his arm for me."

"What?"

"Please look at his arm for me, I need to see it more clearly, could you?"

"I only saw it very briefly, why do you want to see it?"

"Hold the moment would you, I need to see something," he said, sounding excited.

He quickly closed his eyes again so they would not give away what he thought, and she showed him what he asked, realizing that Matheson had a round tattoo on his arm.

"Thank you honey, that is all I needed to see," he said and kissed her, then left the bathroom and shortly after she heard the door of their room shut and he was gone.

What was that all about? She hurried to dry her hair, got dressed quickly and then went to find him.

There was a lot of commotion in the lobby and Tina quickly joined her.

"What is going on, Tina?" Kate wanted to know.

"We have a lead and Marcus is giving us the Intel we need, for it seems he has people everywhere since that thing happened with Matheson. He underestimated him and that is why they got to your tent too late. It was a miracle you had Michael there; although I am glad that neither Marcus's people nor Micha's were there, because it would have been a bloodbath."

"A blood bath?" Kate said faintly.

"Well, all went well Kate, so no worries, but now they have

something that could bring this all to an end," Tina said excitedly.

"And you would rather be with them than babysitting me, right?" Kate said, smiling at her. "Go, I need to catch up with Michael and Daniel, and they can keep an eye on me," Kate said with a laugh, and Tina went off after them.

"Mom?" Michael said, standing beside her, looking a bit confused and overwhelmed.

"Ah, games big boys play, let's leave it to them. I'd love to talk to you both up in the room. Let's grab a coffee and catch up, shall we?"

While Kate was safe with her sons discussing matters about home, Sam, Micha and Marcus pursued their own issues and it took until late into the night before all was sorted out.

Sam spoke to a clan leader who had fierce feelings regarding the development and rebirth of the crown, but after Sam had spoken with him for several hours, the atmosphere changed. Sam had to first threaten him that he would make it known to all tribes that he had risen against the crown; also, he would make it know that he had been defeated, just as his ancestors had been in the past. That got his attention quickly. By the time he had hung up, Sam had not only made the impossible possible by making a friend of an enemy, but he was also invited to visit some royal seats in Sweden, Norway and Iceland.

Marcus told Kate later, that he had never heard anyone handle political affairs as smoothly as Sam. He told her that Sam had dealt with a resentful foe, who needed to be threatened with severe repercussions, and had then used reason and gentleness to achieve compliance and understanding. Not only that, but Sam had even been invited to visit his estate and meet his family. "Just unheard of," mumbled Marcus and excused himself, shaking his head as he left. He said he needed to debrief with the Duke, who was anxiously waiting to hear about the new developments.

All of the men were called in from the field, and sent home on a plane. Mike dropped anchor in the bay, and they all enjoyed the Spanish hospitality. Marcus's wife had been demanding to meet Kate for so long, and Marcus was finally able to bring his family to meet Kate and the rest of her family.

When it was time to go home, Kate found it hard to say goodbye to the wonderful, peaceful town. To prolong the return, they all went home on Mike's sailboat, giving Kate more time with her family, and especially with her father. The journey home was interrupted by a short stay in northern Spain to keep a promise made to the Duke to visit his estate. After a whirlwind of meeting so many relatives, Kate was more than happy to be at sea for weeks, hearing nothing more than the chatter of her little family and the sea.

Sitting with Sam's arms around her, watching the sunset, Kate thought that if she had her way, they would now be together forever.

Kate and Sam will return soon in
Von de Vorg: Soul Mate
Read a preview now!

Contentment

S AM SAT ON A ROCK AND THOUGHT OF THE TIMES OF TRIALS, when he thought he would lose everything and everybody. It was a time of incredible sadness, pain, valor, and survival, but also a time of joy and pride, a homecoming in the sweetest sense and a time of growth and discovery.

He closed his eyes and revisited that moment.

He went for a long walk to clear his head, the day when their journey started. Pondering and planning, knowing that he needed to make a major decision fast that would affect many, many people, even nations. He had all the facts he needed to make up his mind, which required action undeniably soon; still he hoped for another solution or another way out other than the obvious.

Just following the terrible news that was reported on the daily newscasts around the world, was a good indication that he needed to act now. Not to mention that the crest had made itself heard as well, giving him dreams now for several nights. Flashes of pictures became increasingly urgent and impatient. They were always the same images: beaches, waves, storms, crystal clear waters, as if he were one moment flying like a seagull above and the next swimming under the water like a fish. Those visions had been inviting at first, but now became faster and somehow more vivid, demanding to be heard and acknowledged. Yes, what needed to be done, started today. It would mean leaving behind all that he treasured, as well as the people he loved. He loved this place; the area his ancestors had chosen to settle. He loved the house that was home with Kate for so many years, the hill with its secrets and even the river all had a special place in his heart. He would miss visiting his son and daughter in-law. Now he had come to the hill to say goodbye to the chamber of his ancestors, as he saw it, his direct line to his grandfather. It was just another fifteen minute walk until he would be there, so he let his thoughts drift off.

Yes, what Daniel and his wife Tanja spoke of, had lobbied against so fiercely, and had lost now became a reality. He should have paid more attention when Tanja spoke of the dangers; maybe he would know a bit more now to help him see more clearly. They had both been right from the start and now thankfully did not have to witness seeing it come true. The explosion in one of the testing institutes, which Tanja opposed so diligently, had taken out the facility and the whole area. It had wiped out all who knew anything about the research and the contagion or compound that had been released into the air had affected people in the worst way. It changed their DNA and brain structure, removing the part that differentiated men from animals, turning humans into vicious animals, pitted against each other.

Tanja had worked on the research as well, but she wanted to identify the defective DNA strands that people had that passed genetic diseases and cancers on to the next generation. She lobbied against using it as a weapon, like the military had in mind.

Now even to attempt to stop it from spreading required knowledge. Not that there was time, since the spread was so quick and all the laboratories were overwhelmed with the fast development of the contagion. If there had been people who did know anything about the research other than the fact that it existed, they had all died, leaving only devastation behind for the survivors and humanity as a whole.

The changes in people were different. The incubation time was not clear and seemed to be different depending on the age and health of the person. How it was transmitted, nobody knew, but in a world where one could reach anybody in 48 hours, it quickly became a global matter. Savage attacks were the definite signs that a person had been affected and it was spreading around the world like a brush fire. Soon, it also reached Vancouver. It would be only a matter of time until it would create a problem in Sam's area. He knew that he had to move his people to safety, right after he had sent word to the clans of the north to get to safety as well.

Matheson thought at first that Sam was kidding, but considering the world situation, high danger level, and the inconclusive data, one decision seemed as good as any other. So, he passed the message on to all the other tribes and old clans with Sam's warmest and best wishes. The surprised reaction had been echoed by all the clan leaders who had received Sam's message, but they followed his instructions.

When he thought back, he still treasured how wonderful it had been. They remained in touch with him after so many years. Through many visits friendships had been forged, and alliances were created, something he had never dreamed possible. But to be the ruler of all tribes, came with an enormous responsibility, price and weight he would have to shoulder to the end of his days. He hoped they took what he said seriously. As Matheson always said when Sam made a decision or ruling 'it is said, therefore it is so' – he hoped they took it literally now. If not, they would have no chance of survival, that is if all he was thinking, hoping, and planning was correct. The danger had been spreading at an alarming speed and would be on their doorsteps soon.

"Sam!"

Startled, Sam turned around, and saw Kate trying to catch up to him. Looking at her he had to wonder how she managed to age with such grace, but one could see time was eating away at her. Still for him, she was the most beautiful woman on earth, his queen, mother to his children, anchor and resting place for himself. She was the glue that kept them together, grounded and sane whether she knew it or not. Now she had a red face from exertion. She leaned against the side of the hill to rest and looked at him, shaking her head.

"I have been calling and calling you, but you didn't hear me," she said.

"Sorry Hon, I was deep in thought," he said, smiling, and walked back to her.

"I know, I have been listening … it was so much and so fast, that I could not get a word in … well, I also did not want to interrupt your … reminiscing." She took a deep breath and by the time he was at her side she had her breath back. "Honey, you are not alone in this you know, right? I think your plan is sound and I am not one bit happy about it either, believe me, but there is no other way that I can see either … I looked," she said, smiling.

"I came to say goodbye," he said sadly and looked up to the path that led to the chamber.

"I know, that is why I came as well. We started this together, we will finish the race together, yes?" she said, smiling at him as he reached for her and pulled her alongside him.

"As it has been from the start, so it will be to the end, a pleasure and necessity to have you along, my Lady," he said, smiling.

They walked and entered the chamber that almost seemed to be expecting them. As soon as Sam and Kate entered, the chamber lit up softly. The writing was visible on the walls without them even touching anything. Puzzled, Sam looked at Kate and they just watched as the writing seemed to erase itself and the light went into the center stone, where it remained glowing on the crest.

"You think …?" Sam looked at Kate.

"Yes, I think so too …" she said, took his hand timidly and both walked over to the center stone and looked at the glowing crest.

"You think we can take it with us?" Kate wondered out loud.

"Not sure, but I would not want to leave it behind, would you?" he said, grinning.

"All right, here goes nothing…" said Kate and together they raised their hands and they touched the crest as they had many years before when they received their calling to accept the crown. Just like before, as both touched the crest on the center stone, the chamber lit up brightly, but instead of lighting the walls the light went into both of them, marking their palms. Then they were in the dim light again.

Same took her hand and they hurriedly left the chamber. "What's the sudden rush, Sam?"

"I'll show you in a minute", he said and pulled her along through the narrow hallway outside of the chamber. As soon as they left, the hillside closed and the only visible mark that remained was Sam's family headstone. The gate was gone there was grass everywhere as if they had never before entered the hillside.

"Freaky…" Kate said, imitating David. This was his favorite word, when it came to the mystics of their family. Then she let go of Sam's hand, stared into his hand and looked into her palms which she raised to him so he could see the inside of her hands as well. "Now what?"

He looked from her hands into his for a while and then smiled. "It looks like we've got what we need. All right Hon, this is something that I can explain. No need for a book or grandfather," he said and showed her on one of his palms, while pointing to each part of the markings. "The big one that looks like a complicated circle is a Shield Knot, a symbol of protection and warning into the four corners of the earth. It would mean for those who oppose it, that it means business and for us who carry it, protection. Inside are the four corners that the Shield Knot is compartmentalized into. As I said referring to all four corners of the earth, but it has a message for us as well. In one of the corners it shows the marking of the sign of the Valknut, found on grave sites, it is the sign of the dead. My grandfather always said the three triangles represent the slain warriors, the rulers of today, and the future kings. Three triangles put in one and you have our chamber."

"And that one … It does not seem to belong to the shield either." She pointed to three parts overlapping flower-petal like design.

"That is a Triqueta, Trinity Knot, standing for earth, sea, and sky, now also for the body, mind, and spirit or the trinity of God. I think it wants to remind us that we need to consider all three elements."

"So … that explains what it means, but why do we have it on our hands?"

"Logically, we are its carriers, until we have found a new home for it again."

"Logically … yeah … when will the weird end for us?"

"If I have a say in it … never …" he started to laugh.

"You are still just a little boy in there, aren't you?"

"You mind?"

"Nah, wouldn't want it any different," she said, smiling, linking her arm into his and looking back at the hillside, that once held the gateway.

"I am going to miss our hiding spot," she said and then she looked up at him, noticing that he looked confused.

"What do you mean miss? You've got it with you, isn't that better?"

"Let me think about it," was all she said and then they walked back home.

As soon as they arrived Sam called everybody together at Mary's house and told them of his decision to organize the evacuation in a reasonable fashion, without too much panic. At first, there was resistance from the council, they did not say so but he could feel it. Yet when Mary gasped as Sam took a tea cup from her, they all started to listen to what got her so excited. Her eyes grew big and she dropped her cup and took Sam's hand, almost spilling his tea as well.

"Sam you are the carrier, the carrier of the chamber and its knowledge? Since when?!" she said breathlessly, and looked to Nicolas, the judge, who came to her side and the mayor. Both men were stunned and wanted to see his hands.

"Kate is too," he said and asked her to show her hands so all could see.

"That has not happened since we came across the plains, hundreds and hundreds of years ago! You are asked to move us from this place, Sam, otherwise it would not want you to carry it with you."

Hearing Mary, brought calm to everybody who was present. Now there was a general consensus that they would follow Sam to wherever he chose to lead them. Mary on the other hand almost had a heart attack in front of them, so Sam tried to calm her down by putting his hand on her shoulder; his light shining into her made her feel better.

"Mary, don't you worry me now," he quietly said, smiling down at her.

"Sam, bring our clan to safety," she whispered. "You have more than enough to keep everyone safe. Take the crest along with you. It is important for many things, for one, the people need it now as a symbol of power." He just nodded to assure her he would do his best. Mary had been very pale, especially tonight.

Mary had supported him with all the preparations, but that night she had died peacefully in sleep. The following day they held a short memorial service and buried her beside the rose bushes she loved so much.

A day later the whole town was on the move, leaving their homes and most of their belongings. Leaving the house had been most difficult for Kate. She had to leave all the good memories behind and when she closed the door for the very last time Sam had to hold her. They had hoped to live out their days here in this house, watching their grandchildren grow up, but all had gone very differently from what they had planned. Instead of peace and quiet in their retirement days, they were moving across a land that had become hostile to them all.

For Sam, it was the greatest test of trust and leadership skills he ever had to face. Trust, since he needed to believe in what the crest told him, even though it sounded surreal. He had tested the trust of his own clan around him and that of his people in the north to follow him to safety. Long before the explosion happened, he had felt that one day he would have to make that call. Sam told them that they needed to trust him in what he would tell them and to follow his lead. He still gave them the choice, but deep within he hoped they would follow his instructions.

After he had ensured once more that Matheson had passed on the message to all leaders, their convoy left. They moved down south, avoiding any cities, town, or settlements, so as not to come in contact with anyone who might be carrying the contagion. Eventually, they crossed the border that was no longer guarded. They travelled undetected inland but not too far from the coast. The worst was that resources became sparse. They soon ran out of gas and so had to continue on foot using the remaining fuel for other purposes.

Sam had hoped that his call to Matheson and the other clan leaders had been placed soon enough for them to make their way to safety, but he had no way of contacting them again. He remembered looking around himself. Many men were carrying luggage, as well as exhausted children. Detlaf's beautiful race horses now served to pull trailers with the belongings that had been shifted from trucks and cars into trailers that had been remodeled to suit their needs. He smiled encouragingly at the tired and worried faces of the children, hoping to ease their fears and concerns. His family had tried to keep the people safe, but he had no way of knowing how long they would be able to do so. He remembered having felt so old himself at that time and Kate, who had been walking with a slight bend, not wanting to complain of the pain in her back, which traveling had not improved. Yes, anything but that was what he would have wished for his family and his people. He would have wished to see them happy, content, relaxed, enjoying the sun and life.

www.ingramcontent.com/pod-product-compliance
Lightning Source LLC
Chambersburg PA
CBHW031942240626
47153CB00003B/826